THE APARA CHRONICLES (BOOK 1):
HIDDEN IN
BROAD DAYLIGHT

BY JEANNE RHODES-MOEN

DISCLAIMER:

An event takes place in this book in another country. It was based on where such an event might happen when I wrote this, and is NOT intended as a political statement.

In addition, any similarities to actual persons living, dead, or otherwise is unintentional. I have used some actual place names from Asheville for realism.

Some characters occasionally utter words in other languages. See the last page of the book: Foreign Word List for definitions.

Published By:
Jeannius Designs
Asheville, NC 28805
www.Jeannius.com

Visit www.aparachronicles.com

Dedication and Thanks

I wish to extend thanks to my daughters, Kaja and Thea, and friends who put up with me while I wrote this book and the sequels.

A special thank you to Nicky Rea, who worked as my editor, proofreader, mentor, and helped me take my writing to the next level.

Thanks to my writing buddy, Rea Marie. We helped each other maintain our sanity during our mutual writing endeavors.

Last, but not least, a special thanks to my dearest friend of over 20 years, Gillan, for continuing to make a difference in my life, even at a distance.

Books in Series

HIDDEN IN BROAD DAYLIGHT (MARCH 2024)

IN YOUR DREAMS (MAY 2024)

PERSISTENCE OF VISION (AUGUST 2024)

GOING VIRAL (NOVEMBER 2024)

PHOENIX RISING (2025)

WORLDS COLLIDE (2025)

All books will be released during 2024-2025

ABOUT THE AUTHOR

Jeanne Rhodes-Moen was born in Washington D.C. in 1966. She grew up in Maryland, and attended Hood College, where she received a B.A. Psychology and a second B.A. in Math, Secondary Education.

In 1991, she married a Norwegian and moved to Norway, where she made jewelry based in their traditional filigree fused with her own imaginative style. Her first book, Silver Threads: Making Wire Filigree Jewelry, was published in 2006 by Kalmbach Books, and is currently available as Print-on-Demand and eBook on Amazon.

She and her two daughters moved to Asheville, NC in 2005 after her husband passed from diabetic complications. Since then, she has done a combination of jewelry, lapidary, and jewelry photography.

More recently, she has been using her creative skills toward this series: The Apara Chronicles. A science fantasy book series; of which Hidden in Broad Daylight is the first installment.

Jeanne and her daughters all deal with ADHD, but she finds that it has a positive effect on her creative abilities.

TABLE OF CONTENTS

PORTENT

She stands atop a mountain, face turned toward the rising wind as heavy dark clouds roil and thrash across the sky. Gloom envelops her. She searches the lowering skies for their source and tries to stop them, but they roll in like billowing tanks, crushing everything in their paths. The nearer they come, the darker they grow. Jagged lightning strikes the mountains surrounding a valley below, sending cracked, jigsaw-shaped stones crashing down the mountain, setting forests alight with fire. The wind fuels the flames, engulfing every-thing at unimaginable speeds until the valley resembles the charred remains of an impact crater. Lissa screams in anguish and guilt, be-cause it was *her* job to prevent this, and she failed.

Distraught and drenched with sweat, Lissa sits bolt-upright in bed. Her heart pounds like a bass drum and she reaches over and shakes her partner out of a deep slumber. "Kari, *KARI!* Wake up!"

Kari groans and looks at her clock, blinking the sand from her eyes. It's only about 4 a.m., even though there are hints of daylight glimmering be-tween a set of blackout curtains. "What is it?" She yawns, still half asleep.

"Something *is coming!* Something *catastrophic*, but I can't get a handle on what!" she exclaims. Lissa's out of breath, her heart's racing, and her skin stings as if scorched by flame.

Kari props her head up with her arm and puts her other hand on Lissa's leg. "Are you *certain* it's a *precog*?" she asks as she senses dread oozing from Lissa's soul.

"Yes, and I'm not the only one. This is the third nightmare I've had. Marc has had two similar events, and others are reporting them as well. None of us can see what's coming, we know it's major and disastrous, and many will die. I fear we may not prevent this one."

Kari crawls from the bed and throws on her robe, "I'll get the alert out to all the precogs," she assures Lissa. "Do you want me to cancel the interviews for new hires?"

Lissa shakes her head, smiling grimly, "We can't. I heard from Sara this morning that we need to be on the watch for some new potentials with powerful abilities. She, too, has a sense of foreboding."

"All right. I'll coordinate the interviews, and you and Marc deal with whatever's coming. I'm *sure* you can do it, *elskling*." Kari says, cutting through Lissa's anxiety like a knife in butter.

"What would I do without you, *kjæreste min*?" Lissa replies, though she shudders at the taste of ashes in her mouth.

THE AD

It's July, 2033, Tessa Waterford sits in an older, 1960s townhouse apartment in East Asheville. Her hair is uneven and unbrushed, hanging down about three inches below her shoulders, with long strands hanging in front of her face as she stares at her laptop through them. She's sitting on her living room sofa, eating cold pizza for breakfast, and sipping from a mug of instant coffee with the saying "If I were organized, I'd be dangerous" on the front. A laptop covered in various stickers sits amidst newspapers in front of her on a worn, wooden coffee table. Her clothes are mismatched, worn, and wrinkled, and she's a little on the heavy side, like she'd been inactive far too long. Her eyes look tired and sad, giving the impression of long-term stress and a losing battle to stave off depression.

This has become a daily routine for her. She gets up, grabs something quick and easy for breakfast, and sits with both paper and digital help wanted ads. Today, she has three local print listings, Asheville Craigslist, as well as two other job sites for the area in tabs in her browser. Mostly, it's the same old ads: retail jobs, nursing, work from home schemes, telemarketing, a few teaching jobs, Uber drivers wanted, and so on. She's on her third cup of strong coffee and about to give up for the day when a logo in the bottom corner of the local paper's help wanted ads catches her eye. The ad is for web designers to do work with charity organizations.

"Oh, my God! Just what I've been looking for!" She says out loud. "Almost missed it..." She trails off, her eyes once again drawn to the logo. She reaches out and rubs the tips of her fingers over the logo, halfway expecting to feel more than just the paper it's printed on, like it should be three dimensional, and more than a regular, printed logo. She shakes her head, like she's shaking off a fugue. *Let's see, phone number.... Contact Ms. Kari Andersen for application and information.* She reads, picking up her cell phone and dialing the number from the ad. The phone rings several times, and a pleasant-sounding woman answers.

"Inspiration Inc., Kari speaking. How may I help you today?" She asks in a well-practiced, singsong tone.

She pauses for a second and then jumps right in: "Hi, Kari, my name's Tessa Waterford. I saw your ad in the Citizen-Times today. I'm interested in an application for the web position." She tries to sound as confident as she can. She hears Kari typing away in the background.

"The Citizen-Times ad? Certainly, give me your email and I'll send you an editable PDF to fill out and email back. May I ask what drew you to the ad?" She asks casually.

She gives Kari her email and says: "Oh, the logo, but it's exactly the type of job I've been looking for. I've got experience with web design and maintenance, and I'm not really cut out for retail or nursing, and if I tried to do something like driving for Uber, my car would scare most people away." She babbles and laughs nervously.

Kari, sensing her anxiety, says, "Nothing to worry about, Tessa, we're only asking for marketing effectiveness. We recently redesigned our logo and we're wondering if it's eye catching."

"I'll say it is!" Tessa mutters under her breath.

On the other side of the line, Kari grins, hearing the quiet comment as though Tessa shouted it. She continues typing on her keyboard, getting a confused expression as she's unable to find what she's looking for. After a minute, she says, "I've sent the application. Please include a recent copy of your resume. I've got a slot for an interview tomorrow at 2 p.m. Does that work for you?"

"An interview already? But I haven't filled out my application yet? Don't you want to review it first?" She asks, surprised.

"Oh, *no.* Company policy. We interview all serious applicants. There's *so* much more to people than what they fill out on paper, so we prefer to interview everyone to get a firsthand impression.

Will we be seeing you tomorrow?" She asks.

"*Yes*! I'll get my application filled out *right* away and email it and my resume back to you. Do you need references?" She asks, a little uneasily.

"We'll get to that after the interview, *if* necessary." Kari reassures her.

"Alright, well, thank you." She's relieved, like this is a step in the right direction after having stood, mired in mud for ages.

Tessa fills out the application, attaches it and her resume, and the best photo of herself she can find to the email and sends it back to Kari. She gets up, grabs her purse, and runs out to get a haircut, so she'll look her best for her interview. She washes and irons her best outfit and gets a good night's sleep. Something feels right.

As she falls asleep, she thinks *I hope they can overlook the mess at my last job. After all, I had nothing to do with it. But so far, it's been all guilt by association. Maybe, this time, I should get Digital Danger out of the way. I'll tell them what happened, rather than just saying I worked there but wasn't involved. I don't think the others believed me when I said I wasn't part of it....* She drifts off to sleep, having odd dreams of being interviewed, and being asked many questions she can't answer, but eventually, she falls into a deeper sleep, vaguely remembering dreaming about walking with someone who asks her if she's willing to help people to the best of her ability.

INSPIRATION INC.

The offices of Inspiration Inc. are bright and friendly, with signs of personalization on the various desks and cubicles. In a large office off to the side of the main lobby, a door with the name Lissa Pedersen on a brass plate stands ajar. A tall, slender woman with blue eyes, short blonde hair, high cheekbones, and an almost ageless quality about her sits at a desk. She's watching several feeds on her computer monitor and making notes. There's a light rap on the frame of her open door. She looks up and smiles as she sees Kari, her partner, standing there. However, her expression slowly shifts to a more serious one.

"Am I sensing a problem?" She gets up and walks over to the sofa in her office, motioning Kari to come sit with her.

"Not exactly a problem, but more of a mystery. It's probably nothing." She says, handing her tablet to the woman. "Liz, she specifically responded to the logo, yet I can't find her in our database!" Kari says, sounding exasperated.

"Hm, that *is* odd. You did a full background check?" She asks.

"Yes, her name and social security number check out. No criminal history, and school records don't show any issues. In fact, her grades and school evaluations suggest quite a brilliant mind. The only potential issue I could dig up is she *did* work for Digital Danger when they closed down, but as far as I can tell, she wasn't involved with the criminal goings on." Kari says.

"Well, that's good. Did you set up an interview for her?" Liz asks.

"I thought it best. I have an odd feeling about her. It's hard to know what's going on without checking her out. She's coming in at 2 p.m. tomorrow." Kari says.

"Okay, good, see who's available. I want a full screening team

to check her out. Could she be one of the Lost Mission potentials?" She sits up straighter in her chair.

"Not likely, she's a little too old. If she is, she would have been unusually old when they found, prepped, and tagged her. Of course, They didn't
fully prepare any of that batch before their accident." Kari explains.

"Well, it's a mystery. Kind of a nice change. What about the
other respondents?" She asks, in a back-to-business manner.

"Mostly nothing spectacular. Mostly lower to mid-level potentials.
Nice to know where they are types. We'll do an interview, and a psi-
scan, and make a note in their files in case we need them. There is one
who is high on the psi scale, and was considered promising, but he
hasn't been followed up in about 18 years for some reason, but things
were so chaotic back then. We'll have to do some retesting on both
levels. He's your 11 a.m. interview." She explains.

"Use the same team for him," Liz replies, "Get a cursory scan
and if he still looks promising, then we'll find a place for him and
follow up with observation and eventual subconscious testing."
She gets up and goes back to her desk.

"Liz, are you still dwelling on the precog?" She comes over and
stands behind her partner, massaging her shoulders.

"It isn't just me, elskling. There's been a major increase in un-
easiness in our precogs lately; something's on the horizon. Something big, but no one can get a handle on it. It's like, whatever it
is, is so big, they're blinded by it, if that makes sense?" Liz says,
concerned, as she leans into Kari's ministrations.

"Well, I expect you to let me help you forget about it tonight.
You need to take a break; get a fresh perspective." Kari gives her a
firm grip to her shoulders forcing her to relax her muscles.

"You're too good to me, love! After all these centuries, I'd have
thought you'd have grown tired of my moodiness." She reaches up
and caresses Kari's hand.

"I'm *so* used to you by now." She sits on the desk to look Liz in
the eye. "Lissa Pedersen, we've been together for over 600 years

now! I'm so used to your 'moods' I'd miss even the bad ones if you weren't in my life." She says, pausing. "Now, I'm going to go get your team together for tomorrow. Peder and Jayla may be available. Marc will be there since it's his department. All three are strong telepaths, and you and Peder can team up as usual."

"Ya! It helps being twins!" She jokes. "Thanks. Pick up something good for dinner? I'm in the mood for some comfort food. Maybe something from home?" Liz suggests, smiling.

"Hm... There's an all-night place open in Oslo, I'll put in an order and pop over there to grab it before going home." Kari says, smiling.

"What would we do without our porting abilities?" She asks. "Please skip the *lutefisk* this time. Even I have a hard time stomaching that!" She laughs.

THE INTERVIEW

Tessa pulls into the parking lot of Inspiration Inc. about 1:45 p.m., in good time to appear professional, but not over-eager for her interview. It's a three-story tall, nondescript building a little off Sweeten Creek Road in South Asheville, near the Blue Ridge Parkway. It's the type of building you might not even notice unless you were looking specifically for it; otherwise, it fades into the background, or more specifically, the trees surrounding it, and goes unnoticed by most people. She gets out of her car, locks it, and goes inside. The main lobby is inside a secondary, glass door. She peers through the glass before going in. The walls are bright and colorful, the furniture, including the chairs in the lobby, look comfortable and welcoming, not sterile, and impersonal like in some offices. She thinks, *Here goes everything! Positive thoughts! Positive thoughts!* She takes several deep breaths and works on her focus, projecting confidence before opening the door into the lobby, smiling. There's a woman at the front desk with strawberry-blonde hair and blue eyes, who looks up and smiles engagingly at Tessa.

"Let me guess, Tessa? Welcome!" She stands to shake Tessa's hand.

"Yes, thank you. Call me Tess. You must be Kari. Nice to meet you." Tess extends her hand and gives a firm handshake. "Thank you so much for setting up this interview."

"My pleasure, I hope it proves *rewarding* for all of us." She replies, "The interview team will be with you shortly."

"Interview team?" Tess asks, anxiously.

"Yes, there are multiple staff members in the interview. It lets some observe while others ask questions. It also compensates if there are any personality conflicts or biases between interviewer

11

and interviewee." She explains nonchalantly. "Have a seat, they'll call for you when they're ready. *Oh!* There's coffee and cookies on the table over there, help yourself."

"Thanks." She says, heading over and filling a small paper plate with homemade chocolate chip cookies, and thin, rolled cookies with a pattern on them, along with a paper cup of hot coffee, and takes a seat behind where Kari's sitting. She eats a couple of cookies and sips some coffee, then puts them down on a table next to her chair, and closes her eyes, willing herself to relax. She uses a deep-breathing relaxation technique she'd learned years ago in college to control her anxiety levels before exams.

She thinks, *Breathe deeply and slowly.* She takes a deep breath between every thought. *Picture the warm, flowing water all around me, flowing, caressing, soothing...* she trails off. *What the...? Focus... focus...* She tries but can't stay focused. She has an odd sensation, like a tingling or hair standing on end feeling on her scalp. She shakes her head and opens her eyes. Kari is looking at her, head cocked to one side with a bemused look.

"I wasn't sure if you'd dozed off, so I hesitated to disturb you, but they're ready to see you now." Kari grins.

"No, not dozing, composing myself for the interview." She explains, standing up and following Kari to a well-lit office with the name Lissa Pedersen on the door. There are four people in it, two men, and two women. The short-haired, blonde woman closest to the door stands to greet her, extending her hand and smiling reassuringly.

"Hi, Tessa, welcome. I'm Lissa Pedersen, and my coworkers here are Peder, Marc, and Jayla. We'll be interviewing you today. Please have a seat." Liz says, motioning her toward the comfortable chair facing everyone in a circle. She looks around the room and it's far from a spartan, impersonal office. There are paintings of sea and mountain scapes on her walls, a large photo showing a river, or perhaps a fjord and high mountains on either side. There are some unusual, decorative wood carvings hanging on the wall.

Some look almost Celtic, or perhaps Viking? Besides books on a bookshelf, there are a few decorative bowls and other wooden items with stylized flowers painted on them in bright colors. She saw something similar when she'd gone to Epcot Center as a teen. *Rosemaling,* is the term that comes to her mind.

She takes inventory of the other interviewers, noticing a likeness between Lissa and Peder. She thinks, *they could be related. They look quite similar, but there's something more, a similar feeling to them.* The other woman in the room, Jayla, a young, black woman, has long, tightly braided hair, medium brown skin, and deep brown doe-eyes. Tess gets the impression she's younger than the others, even though everyone looks about the same age, mid 20s to early 30s, but something about Jayla's mannerisms shows a novice nervousness about her. Lastly, the man named Marc. He looks like he could be from somewhere else, maybe Europe. He has dark, slightly wavy hair, brushed back from his face, intense, sparkling, dark blue eyes that dance with intelligence and personality, in an olive-skinned face. There's something about the muscles around his mouth that suggests he probably grew up speaking another language. She's noticed people from elsewhere, even from the UK, show differences in how the muscles around their mouths have formed from differentiation in ways they speak. Americans have more relaxed mouth muscles, as their English is relaxed and sloppy, but Marc doesn't have that, even if he speaks flawless English. *Hell, I could say that about all of them except Jayla. If I had to guess from their features and names, Lissa and Peder are probably from one of the Scandinavian countries. That explains the office décor. Marc's harder to pin down, but I'm guessing more Southern Europe, maybe Italy, Spain, or France?*

She shakes Lissa's hand, feeling a slight tingling, reminiscent of a continuous static electricity going between their hands, but she refrains from flinching. "Thank you, Lissa." She sits in the empty seat.

Lissa goes to shut the door, and Kari reaches out and touches her hand. A flash of information from Kari to Lissa; a rapid mental exchange they refer to as 'pathing' tells her Kari tried to read Tess telepathically in the lobby and couldn't get much, but she could have sworn Tess noticed the incursion.

She turns back toward the circle and sits across from Tess. "Everyone calls me Liz around here. My family's Norwegian, and most people aren't quite sure what to do with my real name. We're very informal, more like a family than a group of co-workers. Could you work in such an environment, or do you need a stronger hierarchical structure?" Liz asks.

BINGO! Norwegian. She makes a mental note she was right about Liz's heritage. "Well, if you prefer informal, please call me Tess, and I'd be fine with an informal environment. I'm 'outside the box' as it is, so I'd actually prefer it." She admits, starting to feel a little more at ease between the more organic, friendly atmosphere and Liz's friendly words.

"Well, maybe we'll be a good fit for you and you for us." Liz smiles.

"That would be wonderful!" Tess feels encouraged but doesn't want to get her hopes up.

Marc turns to Tess, sensing an odd mélange of hope and caution, not wanting to get her hopes up. "You're applying for the web position, yes?"

"Yes, sir." She answers, mentally stumbling when she makes eye contact with him. It feels like he's peering into her soul, his blue eyes physically holding her, and piercing her façade to look deep inside.

"Hm, call me Marc." He says, smiling warmly at her. "I see you have about 5 years' experience in the field. What made you leave your prior web job?" He asks. He extends his mind to touch hers. She shivers unconsciously as his mind attempts to glean insight into the thoughts behind her words.

She starts to answer, then pauses. "Well, Marc, it's a complicated story, but I want to be up front about it. I was working at Digital Danger when the scandal came to light; you know, the one where the backend programming team was skimming money from every credit and PayPal transaction. So, I didn't so much leave my last position as it became non-existent." She rubs her left temple without thinking. That odd sensation she had in the lobby is back, and stronger than before. She thinks, *What the hell is that? Did they put some pot in those cookies or something?*

"So, you were not personally involved with the backend team?" He focuses on her to get a good sense of her ethical and psychological nature, encouraging her to continue honestly.

"No. I was not involved with the backend team's criminal acts; however, I was involved personally with one of the guys in that department. I wasn't aware of what was happening until it had been going on for months. He tried to drag me into it, and confided in me, and..." She sighs. "I was so horrified by the magnitude of their crimes, that... well, it was me that reported them to the police." She admits.

"If I remember correctly, the police claimed it was an anonymous tip?" He asks.

Tess closes her eyes, feeling the pressure in her head increasing. "It... it was the deal I struck with the police. I went to them personally. I told them I had information about the crime; gave them everything I knew, including some printouts of the coding I used my ex's password to access and print out. However, I told them I wanted my name kept out of it, and didn't want to testify in person, but would give a deposition if they could keep it anonymous somehow. I was already dealing with finding out the guy I cared about was involved in this mess, and even though he was pressured into it, I had to end it with him after that."

She continues, "I did tell the police he had been pushed into working with them, practically blackmailed into doing what they wanted him to do. But in the end, it really was his choice, and it was not a choice I could live with as his companion. So, I broke all ties with him; even moved across town. Unfortunately, it's been nearly impossible to find work, due to the very fact I worked for Digital Danger. It's tarnished my reputation, making me tainted goods in the field locally." She explains.

"Well, we don't make such assumptions here, and we appreciate your openness and honesty about it. Something we look for in our employees is an exemplary sense of ethics and willingness to do the right thing, as we work largely with charities in my department." He gives her a warm, reassuring smile that both puts her at ease on one level and unsettles her on another. He sends a telepathic message to Liz. *She's damn hard to read, but I can't sense any deception about this. Maybe you can get someone at APD* (Asheville Police Dept.) *to verify her story?*

Hmm... I can holler at Jim, he's over there these days. Mostly doing public relations, but he can check into it for me. Liz paths in reply.

Tess relaxes a notch, having gotten the whole thing out in the open for the first time. She thinks *I've always avoided talking about it openly in earlier interviews and it always came back to bite me in the end. Let's hope this time, being open counts in my favor.*

It all happened over two years earlier, and Tess received a sizable reward for tipping the authorities, as well as compensation paid by the company to all it's out of work employees who were not involved in the scandal, but the money is running out, and she's desperate to find work, as her bills have gotten harder to cover each month. She also spent some of the money on online courses to keep her skills up to date but is uncertain how she'll do when put to the test. Just as she starts to relax, that strange sensation on her scalp comes back, stronger than ever. Instinctively, she pushes it away.

Liz! Did you catch that? She pushed me out! Marc paths.

Kari told me she, too, had the impression Tess could 'feel' her probing, and you know how gentle she is. Liz paths in a lightning flash reply. *Peder and I will try.* Peder, hearing her mental reply, nods slightly toward her. All of this takes place in a couple of seconds.

Liz refocuses on Tess. "Do you have any issues with working odd hours or even working from home when deadlines require it?" She asks while Peder slips into Tess's mind while her focus is on his sister.

She pauses for a second, annoyed by the tingling, which has practically become a vibration in her skull. She thinks, *Damn it! I can't focus with this shit going on!* She takes a deep breath, willing it to go away, imagining a bright, white light bursting out like a supernova from the center of her mind and washing the feeling away; another technique she'd learned for washing 'anxiety' away before exams. She's facing Liz, so can't see the expression on Peder's face is one bordering on painful shock. "That shouldn't be a problem. I'm a night owl, anyway. As long as it's only occasionally, and doesn't take over all my free time, it shouldn't be an issue," she says, smiling now that the feeling has finally been vanquished.

The interview goes on for another 17 minutes, but no more attempts are made to scan Tess or read her mind.

"Thank you for the lovely interview, Tess. We have to discuss things, but I promise, we won't keep you waiting too long. Please make sure Kari has all your contact information in her system, and we'll be in touch quite soon to give you our answer." Liz says, as business-like as possible.

"Thank you, all of you, for considering me. I hope you can find a place for me. I'd really appreciate a chance to prove myself useful." She says, smiling, as she leaves the room and closes the door behind her.

She stops and confirms her information with Kari, including two alternate email addresses and her Facebook page. She has a slight sensation of that same vibration while she's finishing up with Kari, but not so bad she has to try to vanquish it again. She opens the door to leave, and goes out to the car. The sensation slowly dissipates the further she gets away from the office and the people within.

She gets in her car, thinking about her interview; she goes over what was said and their reactions. *I think it went well, but I've often been disappointed before. It's crazy, though. I feel like I belong there, even with that weird head stuff.* She thinks. *I sure hope it's not the start of migraines again. I really don't need that with the stress of potentially starting a new job.*

After about ten minutes of rehashing the interview in her mind, Tess starts her engine and takes the Blue Ridge Parkway home instead of the main road. She makes a quick stop at the store once she's off the parkway, and grabs some milk, eggs and several two-liter bottles of caffeinated soda. About an hour after her interview, she pulls into her parking spot in front of her apartment. A neighbor's cat is sitting outside her front door playing 'pawsies' with her own cat, Mabel, through the gap under the front door. "Shoo, Pooka! Go home! Mabel doesn't want to play with you." She chastises the fat, older, gray tabby. He rubs up against her legs as she unlocks the door, and then saunters off, his tail high in the air until he sees a bird and goes into stalking mode. Tess shakes her head, knowing the fat old tabby will never catch the blue jay he's set his sights on, and may even regret the hunt, considering how blue jays can be.

She unlocks her door and goes in, going through her mail as she stands just inside the door. *Bills! Bills! You've been pre-approved for 10 different, high interest credit cards! And naturally, we've been trying to reach you about your extended car warranty junk mail.* She thinks, snidely, and throws the pile of mail in a box by the front door. She kicks off her shoes, changes back into more comfortable clothes and then grabs a bag of chips and a Dr Pepper from the kitchen. She sits at her laptop and checks her email anxiously, reminding herself it's been only about an hour since the interview finished up, so she shouldn't be disappointed if there's nothing from them yet. She sits in her overstuffed recliner and turns on the TV. One of the cable stations is showing Buffy the Vampire Slayer reruns, and she figures it's better than putting on the news or some reality TV thing. She's hopelessly unfocused, like she's used up all her mental reserves and eventually dozes off.

CONUNDRUM

Shortly after Tess closes the office door behind her, discussion begins.

Marc is the first to speak up, incredulous. "You say she's *NOT* in the system? With a mind like that?"

"Nope. Kari's checked and rechecked. Her information, ID, and so on all checked out, but nothing about her in the database. Though, I dare say I've not seen many who were in the system who showed levels of potential like that. This is rather curious." Liz sits again, absentmindedly drumming her fingers on the screen of her tablet in contemplation.

"Peder, you looked like someone gave you a good swift kick. What exactly happened?" Marc asks.

Peder's face shows uncertainty as he searches for words to describe what he experienced. "Honestly, I'm not quite sure. I tried to slip in while Liz kept her occupied. I was making some headway when it was like an energy wave blasted out from her. I've never felt anything that strong from a human before, not even from a highly rated potential! Closest I've had to a headache since I was human!" Peder says, shaking his head slowly.

Liz leans back in her chair, her hands together with only her fingertips touching, looking thoughtful. "I'm really not sure what to do with her. By our own rules, we shouldn't even be considering her since she's not a potential. Yet, somehow, it feels like we need to understand what's going on. Kari feels the same way, which is why she scheduled an interview, and we all know how accurate her people reading skills are." There's an unsettled energy in the room everyone feels, like part of Tess, or a shadow of her psychic energy remains.

"I agree. From what I could sense from her, she's extremely intelligent, creative, and psychically gifted, albeit largely latent. From her answers about Digital Danger and what I could glean of her emotions about it, I'd say she would also score pretty high on our ethics scale." Marc pauses. "I'd be willing to have her in my department for observation. Maybe we can find a use for her eventually, even if she can't become one of us?"

Jayla, a relatively recent addition, has been quietly processing her observations. She clears her throat cautiously, and asks, "I read that earlier, people were not DNA tagged at a young age to make them compatible as they are now? Isn't there some way *They* could make her compatible?" Her voice is quiet, and a little wavering, like she's still getting used to speaking up and being taken seriously.

"When Liz and I were changed, they didn't make people compatible until they were older, usually shortly beforehand, but there was an unacceptably high rate of psychological issues. Some people couldn't deal with the change and the fact they were no longer like everyone else, especially in some of the more religious individuals. Remember, today, *They* not only put in the genetic key to make someone compatible with the virus, they also do subconscious preparations to reinforce strong ethics, psychological wellbeing, and adaptability, so people won't freak out when it happens. The first, and only, person I changed couldn't handle the responsibility of his new abilities and increased physical strength. He ended up killing several people because of that. In the end, he had to be killed as well, and dispersed to prevent him from coming back. He was a good friend of mine when we were human, but in the end, I was responsible for his death." Peder explains, a wave of remorse crossing his face, even after centuries.

"However, if she proves to be adaptable, perhaps we could convince them to make some sort of special exception for her? There really was something about her I've not felt with other potentials, like she's vibrating at the right 'frequency'." Jayla scrunches up her face, trying to explain what she sensed about Tess.

"It's quite risky, as Peder explained. The loss rate was, as high as twenty-five percent due to the psychological trauma of trans-forming an unprepped subject. Plus, there's the matter of choice. When we were changed, we didn't get a choice. They chose us, or we suggested people to them who could be trusted and useful."

Liz continues. "By the time you were transformed, they'd been using early pool selection for about three centuries. They chose children they deemed genetically, psychologically, and psychically suitable, and each of them was given a choice on a rudimentary level, not specifically to become Apara, but they were given the choice to help humanity over their own self-interests. This turned out to be key in the psychological scheme of things, for only those who had that innate instinct to put others first were likely to cope well with the changes and the power bestowed upon them. Once they instituted that program, then the complication rate dropped to less than two percent, and was usually manageable, such as mild depression and adjustment disorders." Liz explains. "In or-der to get that same element of choice for someone like Tess, we'd have to tell her everything, get a kind of informed consent, and then, who knows if we'd be able to bury those memories if she re-fuses. The only other alternative would be to directly involve our 'Benefactors', and get Them to give her the same spiel as they do children. Unfortunately, adults don't deal with such things as well as children. Adults have too many fear-based biases, and I dare say many humans would freak out if they had to deal with *Them*."

Marc continues where Liz left off. "Plus, they prepare far more candidates than we will ever need, because some, while they were suitable early in life, might not be suitable as adults due to upbring-ing or various life traumas, which could make them too unstable or risky. So even those who were willing, and DNA tagged as children are not certain to join us. In addition, the older a potential is, even with early prep, the more difficult the adjustments can be." Marc glances down at his tablet. "Tess is 28, which is also nearing the upper limits of the normal window for transformation. Never under 18 unless there is a rare medical exception where they will die before they turn 18, and rarely over 30 or 35 and never once they've settled down with a family. That's usually too traumatic for most. There are rare exceptions, but they are on a case-by-case basis and usually involve someone with a unique skill set." Marc explains. "Plus, there's the additional issue of 'de-aging'. If we transform someone who's in their 40s or 50s, even if they adapt psychologically, we must deal with their de-aging to where they appear like they're in their late 20s or early 30s. And that usually involves an identity change and relocation, which can be particularly hard if they have living relatives or a strong network of friends."

Liz sits back in her high-backed desk-chair with a thud, making it bounce. "So, we're back to where we started. What do we do about her?" Liz asks. "If you're willing to supervise and observe her, Marc, then she'll be your responsibility if anything happens with her such as her finding out things she shouldn't know. All the other humans here are compatible, so can be changed if they find out what we are, but her? You're going to have a tough time if things take an unexpected turn; I suspect if we can't read her easily, it's going to be *damn* hard to redact her memory as well!"

"I'm willing to give her a chance. As Jayla suggested, they *could* make an exception for her..." He holds up a hand to stop Liz's objection, "though I completely understand it's highly unlikely. My gut feeling is she belongs here, and oddly enough, I sensed she feels the same way, at least on the surface." Marc pauses to gather his thoughts before continuing. "With your permission, I'd like to port over to her place when she's asleep and try to read her. Perhaps her natural shields will be down?" Marc suggests.

Liz sits back up straight, looking Marc in the eye and nods curtly. "Alright but take every precaution. Subtlety may be your best option. Instead of pushing her into sleep psychically, take one of the wave generators from Medical. Ask Sara to set it to the right frequency for humans. Port it into her place somewhere unseen and let it take effect, then try reading her. I'm afraid if you try to mentally push her into sleep, you'll only trigger her natural shields again." Liz suggests.

"I'll do that. Is Sara around today? I thought she was making the rounds of the West Coast centers?" Marc grins subtly now that Liz has given him the go ahead. He doesn't understand why, but something about this young woman has touched him, and he has an urgency to understand her, and even help her. He stands to leave but waits for her answer.

"She should be at the Med center in Sanctuary. Some of our newer members tripped a series of landmines in Gaza last week. She had to postpone her rounds until she got them. She's pulling a 'Humpty Dumpty', you could say." Liz says.

Marc grimaces, imagining the gruesome job involved in physically reconstructing someone after a land mine, so their bodies could regenerate and heal faster. The more they could re-assemble of their original bodies, the less had to 'grow back'. *Ugh! Glad I've never been in such bad a shape! I've had my share of stasis events, but not where I had to have the puzzle pieces put back together.* Marc thinks, and leaves Liz's office and stops to talk to Kari briefly. "So, did our little conundrum head home, or did she hang around a while?"

"She was here for a couple of minutes, doing exactly as Liz apparently told her to. She made sure my info on her was up to date and accurate, and then she left. Don't know if she went home or not, I couldn't get a read on her except she's hoping to get a job offer from us." She says as a half question, also quite curious about their little mystery woman.

"Been listening in again through Liz?" He chuckles.

"When two people have been together as long as she and I have, it's hard not to pick up on the other." She smirks.

"Well, I wouldn't know." He gives Kari a wink and a wry smile.

"You're just a perpetual bachelor, aren't you? Someday you'll find someone to partner with on a long-term basis." Kari jokes.

"After several centuries avoiding that fate, she'd have to be pretty special for me to give up my independence!" He elaborates. "Until then,

I'll stick to more casual liaisons with our own." He winks at her, knowing she and Liz are together, but he enjoys her unsettled look.

"You Frenchmen are *impossible!*" She says, laughing, but then turns serious, a look of sympathy in her eyes. "But seriously, don't you *ever* get lonely?"

Marc gets a sad, wistful expression for a split-second. "There are far worse things than being lonely, and I've been there, and don't want to live through that ever again!" He knows she's aware of his history; after all, she was around when Liz changed him into an Apara centuries ago, and knows what he lost in the process.

Marc walks to his office instead of taking the quick way and porting. He puts his tablet in a carrying case so he can make notes while he observes Tess in her home, and then vanishes from his office. He reappears outside a large building with aspects of age-old architecture mixed with futuristic features. The building is surrounded by forest on all sides, and while there is a 'parking lot', there are no cars, only various equipment. The atmosphere is almost too still, as though beyond this little cluster of buildings and pavement, there isn't any sense of civilization nearby. Marc hears a river a few hundred meters away, as well as birds and other animals in the forest. He can smell the sweet smell of pinesap alongside the damp smells from the river and a nearby waterfall as he walks into the building. The Atrium where he enters has a towering ceiling with floor to ceiling glass, tinted slightly gray to reduce the glare. There are decorative plants around the room, including a flowering vine wrapped floor to ceiling around a support pillar. He walks up to the front desk and is greeted by a young, black man.

"Liz sent word ahead. Sara just went off to her office to get what you need ready."

"Thanks, Femi. I know the way all too well!" Marc heads up the stairs to the third floor and knocks on the open door of an office cluttered with knickknacks lining the shelves and all over the desk. A small woman with angular features, dark eyes, creamy, light brown skin and straight, jaw length, black hair looks up and waves him in impatiently.

Marc shakes his head, snickering under his breath. "Sara, one of these days, they're going to have to build you a separate office for your Star Wars collection."

"Hey, can I help it if I'm obsessed? You know I was an extra in *every* single live-action Star Wars production, including the Christmas special, the TV Ewok movies, and the various modern series!" She says seriously at first, but that changes to an ear-to-ear grin at Marc's expression. "What can I do for you today, besides make you gape in horror at my bad habits?" She jokes, putting a baby Yoda model back on the shelf.

"Sara, if I didn't know you are older than many of us put together...." Marc says in exasperation. "Anyway, is the wave generator Liz ordered for me ready? It doesn't need to be too strong, just enough to make a human doze off." Marc says.

"Hm? Losing your touch? I thought you were good at putting people to sleep?" She says sarcastically. Then, seeing his impatient expression, says, "I'm kidding! Sometimes you're as serious as a Sith!" She jokes, unable to resist using one last Star Wars reference to torment him. "Here you go. One class-3 wave generator set to sleep for humans. Make sure you turn it off and take it with you or whoever you're lulling into dreamland will have a hell of a time getting up and staying awake until you do. The power source lasts about a month on one charge." She says, handing him the small silvery green sphere with a small button on one side.

"Thanks, Sara, or should I start calling you Mistress Yoda?" He jokes.

"Hm, only if that is a reference to my wisdom and not my complexion!" She laughs and wanders off to make her rounds.

Marc stands there for a second, the wave generator in hand, shaking his head. *Sometimes, I'm not sure if she's crazy or the sanest one of us all.* He thinks.

He vanishes once again, this time not reappearing but 'lingering' in the zone just outside physical reality they refer to as Limbo. He's in front of Tess's townhome apartment. He can easily sense her, as her mind is unique. Even though he hasn't been able to read her, he'd recognize her 'feel' anywhere. He focuses on her mental signature and relocates to her living room, still beyond human perception, where he can observe without her knowing he's there. She's sitting at her computer, checking her email. She's disappointed, and gets up, grabbing a bag of chips and a soda from the kitchen, and climbs into a beat-up recliner in front of the TV. Marc drifts toward her chair and rolls the activated wave generator from his hand and into physical reality under her chair. He lingers and waits for the wave generator to take effect. She turns on the TV and flips through the channels, settling on one showing a lot of older, syndicated shows. He glances over to the TV and recognizes the show and rolls his eyes. *Buffy the Vampire Slayer? Oh, please!* He thinks. She nibbles on her chips for a few minutes, nearly dumping the bag in her lap as she starts nodding off. She starts awake enough to put the bag on the table next to the recliner where her soda is, leans back in the chair, and falls asleep.

Marc gives her a few minutes to settle into a deeper sleep state. When he notices she's entered REM sleep, he phases into physical reality and silently settles in a nearby chair. Closing his eyes, he pictures himself sliding into Tess's mind, reviewing random memories and images from her dreams. He gets a feel for who she is. Her mind is like a sparkling gem in sunlight; complex, full of intelligence and creative energy, but with splashes of frustration and depression at not being able to find work, or move on with her life, or do anything meaningful. He also senses an abundance of guilt for wrecking her last relationship. Even though she knows it was the right thing to do; she feels guilty for betraying her ex, *Colton? Or was it Ox?* Part of Marc wishes he could do something for her. She's having trouble seeing herself clearly. He stands, watching her sleep, then holds out his hand and the wave generator rolls out from under her chair and floats up to his palm. He closes his hand around it, shutting it off, and dematerializes at the first sign of her stirring to wakefulness.

He returns to his office and sits on the edge of his desk for a few minutes, gathering his thoughts. *I've got to make this work, if not for us, for*

26

her. She's got so much going for her, but she's like a gem under a pile of dirt. Her brilliance and inner beauty are there, but no one can see it, including herself.

He heads down to the main lobby and crosses it to get to Liz's office. He knocks softly on the frame of Liz's open office door. She looks up and sees Marc's face, and something she's not seen often from him: deep, undisguised compassion. Marc has spent years pretending not to be lonely or miss his humanity, though Liz knows the truth. He'd been one of them for several centuries, and he still hadn't let go of the pain he felt when his fiancée left him for another shortly before Liz changed him and his life forever. What Marc never knew was Liz didn't turn him because she felt sorry for his loss. She'd been told to create the loss so he would be unencumbered by a relationship when she recruited him. She didn't change him because she wanted him, as she already had Kari, but because she was told to, as They had chosen him to be one of them. After all these years, she's never told him about her part in his loss, but she's seen him go from a man in love, to a shattered one, to someone who's sworn off getting closer than necessary to anyone. He spent years watching his fiancée from afar, with her family. He grieved when she died, placing flowers on her grave every birthday for the first 50 years after her death.

Now, what she sees is a spark of something she's not seen since he was human; unadulterated compassion for another radiates from him, his emotional barriers disarmed by something about this unusual woman. He's always been friendly and never cruel, but always kept his emotional distance, until now. *Ironic for an empath.* She thinks. Something about Tess has touched something long dormant in him. She wonders if Tess could be a healing influence, or if her presence might wound him even deeper since she's not compatible. *Maybe it's worth taking this chance if it means healing that age-old, deep wound I inflicted on him.*

"So, how'd it go? Find out anything useful?" She asks softly.

Marc comes in and sits on the sofa in her office, silent at first as he gathers his thoughts, then speaks. "Liz, she needs this job. Whether or not we can change her or use her doesn't matter. If she gets another rejection, especially one where she oddly feels she belongs and could thrive,

I'm afraid it will send her into a downward spiral psychologically. I'll find something for her to work on. And we'll observe. If need be, I have some human friends in the web industry. I'm sure I could implant some suggestions they hire her away from us if things get too complicated here."

Liz sits there listening, tapping her stylus against the edge of her tablet. "Okay, she's all yours for now. Do as you see fit. Just don't let her in on any company secrets!" She says. "I assume you'll let her know?" She asks.

"Yes, I'll call her shortly. Thanks! I'm not sure what it is about her, but I need to help her." He says and walks away to his office to call Tess and give her the news.

After he leaves Liz's office, she quietly comments, "And if helping her can help you finally heal, then the risk is worth it." Liz puts her tablet down, packs up her laptop and other items, including the tablet. She reaches out to Kari. *I'm heading home. Don't forget our dinner plans.* She paths with a mental smile and feelings of hunger.

Already put in an order. I'll pop over as soon as I finish my summaries from today's interviews. Speaking of which, any decisions on our little mystery? Kari paths, while opening the file for Tess. She halfway expects Liz to tell her to close the file since she isn't in the compatible database.

Marc wants her... she trails off, thinking about the potential dual meaning of the expression. *He senses she really NEEDS the job and will supervise and observe her. It's in his hands now.* Liz explains.

Well, well! That's a surprise! You still have a soft spot for Marc, I see. Kari replies telepathically.

As always; he knows the risks, and she's a mystery begging to be solved. Liz quips, knowing it's now out of her hands.

Kari shakes her head subtly, knowing how hard it is for Liz to hand over control, as she feels particularly responsible for Marc, one of her many transformees. *Ya! See you when I get home from Oslo. Ha det!* (Nor: bye)

FINALLY

Marc sits in his office chair, stretching, feeling like his body has been in one giant knot until Liz gave the go ahead, and now the knots are relaxing because things feel right. He pulls up Tess's cell number on his tablet, pushes a button, and calls her.

"Hello?" Tess says, groggily, still only half awake. She looks around the room, a little disoriented. A different episode of Buffy is on, and she picks up the remote to mute the TV so she can hear whoever's calling.

"Hi, Tess. This is Marc Girard from Inspiration Inc. Have I caught you at a bad time? Sounds like you were sleeping," he says, grinning to himself, remembering her completely passed out in her ragged, old recliner.

"No, it's fine, I was... I must have dozed off in front of the TV. I guess that interview took a lot more focus and energy than I expected." She yawns.

"They can do that." Marc says. "The reason I'm calling, however, is to let you know I've got a position for you in my department if you want it. It's entry-level web design and graphics work. Some client interaction, but limited until you get your feet wet."

"Really? *Oh my God*! Thank you so much! That's *amazing*! When can I start?" She's now fully awake and sits up in her chair.

"We're doing a new-employee orientation tomorrow morning for a couple of others we've hired. Since you're currently unemployed, would tomorrow be too soon for you to start?"

"No! That's *fantastic*! I can absolutely start tomorrow!" She sits up straight and leans forward. The recliner snaps back into the vertical position, nearly throwing her out of it in the process.

"Okay. Come in about 11 a.m. I need to get some things in order first. We'll do a run-through of our system and get you settled in. There are two other new people as well, so you won't be the only one learning the ropes." He says.

"This is *awesome*! Thank you *so* much for giving me a chance! I really appreciate it!" She's so excited and relieved she's finally gotten a 'yes' after an interview.

He feels good inside when he hears the joy and enthusiasm in her voice, like he's already made a difference in her life. "Aren't you curious about the pay, benefits or hours?" He's amused by her unconditional, positive reaction to the job offer.

"*Honestly*, it's a job, and, well, something just feels right, even though I really wasn't at my best earlier today." She admits. She reaches over and takes a sip of her soda to relieve the dryness in her mouth after napping. *Must have been snoring again, I guess.* She thinks, taking one more sip.

"Oh? You certainly were doing quite well from *my* perspective. I'm looking forward to seeing what your *best* is." He smiles on his end of the conversation. He thinks, *I suspect we'll get some interesting surprises from this one.*

"I'm not sure what was going on, but it may have been some kind of silent migraine or something. No pain, but I felt odd, like there was pressure in my head. I wrote it off to stress and used some relaxation and visualization techniques to get rid of it, but it made it hard to focus a couple of times." She admits.

"It was probably the stress of being interviewed, but you did fine. I'll see you tomorrow. Bring the usual documents you would bring to any new job. We may need you to take some aptitude tests in the next couple of weeks. Nothing to worry about, okay?" He reassures her but thinks: *I bet those aptitude tests will show her off the scale. From what she described, she obviously felt us reading her. I need to make a note to remind everyone to limit any attempts to read her, even casually, or we might get more than we bargain for.*

"Sounds fine. See you tomorrow! And again, thank you *so* much!" She hangs up, leaps out of her chair, and jumps up and down in celebration, nearly stomping on Mable, sending the cat scurrying off away from her, nearly sliding into a 3D puzzle on the floor Tess spent days on. The spooked cat turns sharply, making a skittering sound with her back claws on the wooden floor, and zips up her wobbly, floor-to-ceiling cat tree where she stares down at Tess from the top tier, agitatedly twitching her tail, eyes wide and pupils dilated.

"Silly girl!" Tess walks over and reaches up to Mabel to calm her, but Mabel swats at her hand and hisses a couple of times before settling down on the top tier and rolling over on her back. looking at Tess while upside down.

"Mabel, I swear you got brain damage from back when you fell off that thing!" She reaches up again, this time letting Mabel sniff her fingers. Mabel relents and lets Tess scratch her neck, returning the affection by cuddling her hand and licking her furiously.

CUBICLE IN THE LION'S DEN

Even though she doesn't need to go in before 11 a.m., Tess sets her alarm for 7 a.m., showers, lays out her clothes on her bed, spritzing them with a little fabric refreshener for good measure. She goes to the kitchen to get some food while her hair dries. Opening her fridge, she reaches for the last two slices of cold pizza and stops herself. *NO! This is a new day, and hopefully a change for the better.* She thinks and puts it back in the zipper bag and takes out a box of eggs, checks the date. *Hm, only a month past the best by date.* She grimaces. She heats a skillet, and carefully cracks an egg. When it doesn't smell like a sulfur bomb, she thinks *I guess it's okay then.* And cracks another into the pan, adding salt, pepper, garlic powder, and paprika to the frying eggs. She wants to make toast, but when she looks at her loaf of Italian bread, it's got blue-green, fuzzy spots of mold on it as she'd not touched it in about a week. She picks it up carefully, by the edge of the bag and tosses it in her garbage. She fixes instant coffee and sits with her fried eggs at the dining room table with her laptop. She takes inventory of what's in front of her and realizes, *this is the first morning in a couple of years I don't have help wanted ads, newspapers and so on spread out here. Let this be a turning point in my life.* She takes a bite of eggs and a sip of coffee, opens her laptop, and checks her mail. There are some emails from Kari with forms to fill out for health insurance, tax-withholding, and other formalities. She saves them to her cloud drive and goes over to Facebook, posting in large, capital letters with a party themed background.

I GOT A JOB!!!!

She checks her notifications and interacts with the few friends who comment and congratulate her.

Time flies by, she gets dressed, does her makeup, and styles her hair. She looks down at her makeup and realizes it's about four years old. *Guess I know what I need to buy when I get my first paycheck.* She resists dumping it but promises herself she'll toss it all when she can afford new. She finishes and heads in a little early, stopping at a grocery store to buy a store-made sandwich for lunch, and a six-pack of small bottles of Dr Pepper. She thinks, *I want bottles! I don't know how many keyboards I killed at Digital Danger drinking canned soda instead of bottles. I'm surprised they didn't take it out of my paycheck.*

Tess arrives at Inspiration Inc. at 10:52 a.m. She goes in through both sets of glass doors, smiling, and hands Kari the various forms she's filled out, neatly laid out in a folder. "Here you go! All the forms you sent me, and a copy of my social security card."

"Welcome back! Thanks for being so prompt with these. Marc asked me to show you to his department. There are a couple of others there for orientation." Kari gets up to show her the way.

She leads Tess down a long hallway painted a nice pastel blue with framed photos from around Asheville hanging on the walls. The hallway turns a couple of times, passing various individual offices, some doors are open. She notices Peder working on his computer, and she notes his expression keeps changing, as though he's talking to someone. Finally, the hallway opens into a larger room, with white walls, but colored borders over each cubicle. Kari explains, "The different colored trims indicate distinct skill sets. Blue for those who work primarily on front-end design and content, red for those who work more on the back-end programming, and purple for Alan, who's our graphics guy."

Tess smirks. "Which one do I get? I've got experience in 'all of the above.'" She leans her head to one side, waiting for Kari to answer.

"I'll make a note of that, but most likely, you'll be in one of the blue cubicles, even if you end up doing some of your own

34

programming and graphics. This helps people who aren't in this department find the right person for the job."

"*Cool!*" Tess replies, looking around the room.

She looks at the other two new employees, the first is a short, muscular looking girl, with medium brown skin, short, curly dark hair and geeky glasses, wearing jeans and an AWOLNATION band tour t-shirt. Her first impression is she's African American, but her eyes look more Asian. The other person is an attractive guy with auburn hair and piercing green eyes that twitch noticeably when he focuses. He's wearing black designer jeans and a plain black t-shirt that's intentionally too tight to show he 'works out'. Tess takes an instant, instinctive dislike to him. She tells herself she should give him a chance, but there's something about the way he looks at her, how he watches her as she enters the room, like he's a lion watching potential prey. She shivers as she breaks her brief eye contact with him.

Marc looks up and smiles. "Welcome, Tess. Hope you slept well and are raring to go?" He asks.

"Yes, oddly enough, I slept unusually well, though I may have over-dressed." She grabs the empty chair farthest away from 'Mr. Black T-shirt egomaniac', as she thinks of him.

"We don't have a dress code, but do ask our employees to dress professionally if they're going to be meeting with clients that day. However, casual is fine for most days. Anyway, let me introduce you to the other two new team members. This is Amy Ledbetter; she's going to be doing some of the same work you do with web design, but also planning work directly with our clients. And this is Jason Templeton, who will be working more on the programming or back-end of things, PHP, ASP, JavaScript, custom SSL certificates, shopping carts, and donation integration and more. He's also apparently good at making custom WordPress templates if either of you need them. Amy, Jason, this is Tess Waterford, apparently, she does a bit of everything: design, programming, and graphics, but will be officially in the design department. You three are the only people to make it through the interviews out of about 24 applicants." Marc hopes to emphasize how 'special' they are.

Did Marc actually hear me tell Kari I do 'all of the above'? Maybe he inferred that from my resume? Tess glances back at Jason when she thinks he's not looking, pursing her lips, and wrinkling her face up. *Just what I don't need! Another asshole programmer with an ego in my life.*

Marc grabs a rolling office chair and sits facing the three of them. "I'll work individually with each of you shortly, so we can set up personal passwords and customize your machines. We do have both PC's and Mac's available, so if you have a preference, speak now."

Tess is the only one to speak up. "I can work on either, though at home, I've got an older iMac and a newer MacBook, so it may be easier for me to use the Mac to keep things consistent. I do have my laptop set up with the ability to run Windows and Windows programs if I need to."

"Alright, cubicle 8 has a Mac set up, as well as all the software you should need." Marc smiles, but notices odd emotions coming from Tess, like anxiety or aversion to something or someone. He keeps half a mental eye on her and goes on. "Amy, you're more a PC person, and you and Tess will be working on similar things. When you're not working with clients, you'll be at cubicle 7. Jason, why don't you take cubicle 2 down there? It's a PC, but it also has all the programming languages set up for use, including a Linux/Apache virtual environment for beta testing your programming." He thinks: *Interesting, she's happy to have Amy nearby and even more so Jason won't be. Wonder if she knows him from before?*

"You can all use the guest login on the post-it notes on your screens until I get around to each of you to help you set up your workstation." He goes over to Jason first, helping him, then Amy, saving Tess for last.

He brings the office chair he'd been sitting in earlier and sits next to Tess in her cubicle. "Alright, the first thing you need to do is set up your user profile with a user ID and password on your system. I don't need to know your password, but I need you to make sure it's a strong one. Anything personal, or notes you make, and so on, you can keep in your user folder on your computer, but any actual client work, you need to log into the main file server here and store those files on the server." He says, pointing to an icon for a server called Clients. "Each of you will have your own password protected section on that server, however, I and other supervisory level staff can arrange for others to access those files, if need be, for example, if you're sick and there's a deadline. All machines will be automatically backed up every Friday night, but if you have something critical you want to make sure gets backed up, save a copy to the server 'daily backup' and it will get backed up the same day. Got it?"

"Sounds reasonable." Tess smiles back at Marc.

"You'll also be able to access both your personal machine and the file server from home, but we'll go over those routines later. Use this program to log your hours for each project. This isn't to keep an eye on you so much as to know what to bill clients. While we have discounted rates for charities, we still have to pay our own bills." He grins. "Now, go ahead and set up your user account, and then let me know what username and password you'd like to use for the server and I'll set that up on the server end, okay?"

Tess says, "Sure, this isn't too different from the setup we had at Digital Danger, so I should be able to figure it out pretty quickly. By the way, you said there should be programs on here for web design, but are there also graphics and coding tools? Do you have Photoshop and any coding programs for the Mac? It's often quicker for me to fix something myself than to go to the programmers..." Marc senses that feeling of aversion again when she mentions programmers, and gets a flash of Jason's face, followed by what appears to be a blending of his face and someone else's, as though Tess was thinking of two people at once. "And unless it's something complex, I can do basic graphic work, so I prefer to do my own when possible."

"I'm not sure what all is on that particular machine, but why don't you take some time to look over it and make a list of any programs you want to add, and I'll have our tech people look into it." He suggests and stands, laying a hand on her shoulder in a platonic, reassuring manner. He notices she tenses up and flinches when he touches her shoulder, and makes a mental note of it. He walks away, sitting on a desk nearby to get a feel for the new employees, their emotions, thoughts, and who they are. *It's still not an easy task with Tess. Amy is easy to read. Hm, Jason is nearly as hard to read as Tess. Maybe he's just very focused, but the sooner we do those evaluations on him, the better.*

Marc lets them all explore for about half an hour and then announces: "Okay, everyone. It's 1 p.m., and there's lunch set up for you three in the conference room as a welcome. Why don't you take about 45 minutes to eat and get to know each other? I've got to go meet with Liz, but will be back to walk you through security procedures for our computer system, including remote access, as well as what we can and cannot do for our clients." He leads them to the conference room.

They enter the room, and there's a table set up with a tray with fresh breads, lunch meats, cheese, lettuce, cucumbers, tomatoes, fruit and some bowls of various salad spreads like seafood salad, egg salad, and ham salad. Tess picks up a couple of potato rolls, splits them and fixes herself a ham sandwich and an open face egg salad and one with seafood salad. She grabs a cup of coffee to keep herself awake and looks around the room. She sees Jason looking her way, so gravitates toward Amy instead, to avoid him. "Hi, Amy. Mind if I sit with you?"

Amy smiles and moves some stuff out of the way next to her on the table. "Sure thing. So, what do you think so far?"

"I like the place, and most of the people." Tess replies, taking a bite of her ham sandwich.

Amy grins. "Most? Let me guess, you're not big on enormous male egos either?" She laughs.

"Oh, God! I'm glad I'm not the only one who had that reaction. Marc is great, as are most of the others I've met, but, well, yeah, big egos and I don't mix. Especially in programmers." Tess shifts uneasily in her seat as she senses Jason watching her.

"Uh oh! I sense a story, girl! Do tell!" Amy pops a grape in her mouth.

"It's a long, complicated story, but let's just say my ex was one too, and I'd rather not be reminded of him, that's all." Tess sips her coffee, hoping the caffeine kicks in quickly.

"I *so* hear ya! Been there *so* many times! I was in the military for several years. Talk about walking egos! *Ugh!* So many of them thought they were better than me, including my current boy-friend, because I was a woman in the military. They soon learned, though." She smiles and takes a sip of her sweet tea.

"Oh? Please share! How did you enlighten the jerks?" Tess feels more relaxed now that she's making a friend among the other worker bees.

"My mom is from Japan and met my dad through a martial arts class she taught. Naturally, because of my mom, I began doing mar-tial arts when I was only five years old, and even did it competi-tively for a while, so when I joined the army, they soon had me teaching hand to hand using martial arts after I threw my instruc-tor the first day. Most men, when they saw all of 5-foot 1-inch little ol' me as their instructor, they all thought it was a joke. They learned the hard, and often painful way. Anyway, I got out of there a few months ago and moved here to be closer to my boyfriend. Worked fast food at first, but the brain-dead factor of many of my co-workers was making me nuts. I worked with web stuff while I was in the Army, running the intranet for the base, so when I saw the ad for this place, I figured what the hell! And called for an ap-plication." Amy grins, takes off her glasses, and wipes them with a napkin. "So, are you from here or new to Asheville, too?"

"Yeah, I've been here since I was about fifteen. My family moved out here because of work. They moved again, and I stayed. I was at a company that had some problems and closed down and it's taken me a while to find a new job, but something about this place really feels right." Tess finishes up her egg salad.

"*OH!* Are you the one who was working for Digital Danger?" Amy asks.

Tess gives her a frustrated look. "Yeah, that's me. How did you hear about that?"

Amy nods her head in Jason's direction. "Ugh! I think Mr. Ego has dossiers on you and me."

"Oh great, sounds like a stalker. Let's keep each other in the loop if he gives one of us any trouble, we can team up and keep each other safe." Tess suggests.

Tess and Amy continue talking and find out they are both science fiction nerds and are deep in conversation about the latest Marvel movie when Jason comes up and starts massaging Tess's shoulders. Tess flinches and pulls away, instinctively wrenching her shoulders free, swivels around and gives him a dirty look. "Hey! I don't like unwanted physical contact! Try *asking* first!" She says sternly to Jason.

Jason gives a snort of disbelief at her rejection, and spits out, "I've never had any complaints before...or *maybe* you prefer *other* company?" He says with a nasty tone, nodding toward Amy, assuming she's a lesbian because of her appearance.

Amy looks at him and rolls her eyes. "Shows what you know! I *have* a boyfriend." She says bluntly.

"Oh? Is she a *dyke* too?" He says, assuming *he knows* better.

"No, he's ex-Army and a cop. We met in the service where *I trained him* in martial-arts combat." She says, clearly implying a threat if he doesn't back off, she'll demonstrate her abilities on him.

He backs off from Amy with hands up in sarcastic surrender and turns back to Tess. "So, how 'bout it? Shall we pair up and take this place by storm?" He asks with a sleazy wink.

Tess turns to Amy, rolling her eyes and saying, "You know, I didn't need this luncheon to get to know Mr. Ego, I had him pretty much pegged from the moment I saw the look in his eyes." Acting as if he can't hear her insult him.

"Listen, you *little bitch*!" He says as Liz walks in.

"So, how's everyone doing? Getting to know each other?" Liz says, hoping to diffuse the tension and empathic sparks she felt coming from the room.

"Yeah, you could say that." Sneers Jason as he stomps back off to his seat with a huff.

"Tess and I have a lot in common, and I've promised to teach her self-defense, just in case she ever needs it." Amy says loudly, so Jason gets the message. She winks at Tess and gives her a knowing grin.

"Glad to hear it. Marc had to go deal with something urgent, so I'm going to be filling you all in on the rest of the orientation, after which, you can all head home and log in from there to familiarize yourself with the telecommute system, and we'll see you all in the morning around 8 a.m." Liz has them follow her back to the orientation room and shows them the ropes.

When the orientation's over, Tess gets up close to Amy and whispers to her: "Can you walk me out to the parking lot? I've got really bad vibes from Jason. He scares me."

"Sure! What are buds for?" Amy laughs. "By the way, I'm serious about teaching you some self-defense. He's a creep and I get the impression he wouldn't know the meaning of no."

"Thanks! I may take you up on that. Honestly, I was afraid I may have overreacted when he touched my shoulders. You see, I was in an accident as a kid, and I've got a ton of scars on my back and shoulders. They don't hurt now, but they used to really badly, so it's an unconscious reaction." Tess admits, questioning herself and her reaction.

"*Hell* no! You didn't overreact! That boy's got an ego the size of Texas, and he should know better than to do something like that. Some places, that would be enough to get him fired." Amy lets out a brief snort of laughter.

The two walk out together, and Tess drives home. When she gets in the door, she checks her mail and email, and gets a snack. As soon as she sits at her computer, her cell rings.

"Yeah-hello?" She answers.

"Hi, Tess. It's Marc. I wanted to check in on how you're doing. I got called away so wanted to check up with everyone after the orientation."

"Okay, I guess. The system's simple enough, though you may have a couple of security holes I recognize from when I worked at Digital Danger, but I can go over those later?" Tess declines to talk ill of Jason, as she doesn't want to come across as a whiner on the first day.

"I got the impression from Liz you and Amy hit it off, but the waters are rough where Jason's concerned?" He knows Jason hasn't been psychologically evaluated since he was a child, so is acutely aware there could be potential issues with him.

"I wasn't going to say anything, but since you asked, he's a walking ego, but nothing I can't handle, especially with Amy on my side." She acts like it's not a big deal. Inside, she still shivers at her first instinctual impression of Jason Templeton. *I am not gonna let my guard down with that asshole.* She thinks.

"Glad to hear it! I prefer to avoid office drama. However, you must tell me if there's an issue, okay?" He reinforces.

"I will. I had to deal with a bunch of walking egos at Digital Danger. I was one of only three women web programmers there, so I learned a few tricks to cope with testosterone overload." She quips.

Marc chuckles. "Anyway, I wanted to give you my cell number, in case you run into any problems as I may be in and out the next few days, and I've been working on who to give different clients to, so when you come in tomorrow, stop by my office and I'll brief you on yours. If you can't reach me by cell, call Liz."

"Sounds like a plan!" She says, "Hey, Marc?"

"Yes?" He replies, wondering what she's going to say. *Not being able to read her certainly makes things interesting.*

"I want to thank you and the others for giving me this chance to work at Inspiration Inc. You have *no* idea how much I needed to finally hear 'you're hired' rather than, 'I'm sorry, but the position has been filled' or the ever popular and vague 'you're just not what we're looking for.', when I always knew it was because I worked for Digital Danger and they didn't trust anyone associated with them. The few friends I've stayed in touch with from there had to drop it off their resumes and work in other areas, that's how toxic it got." Tess thinks, *I don't know why, but I feel like I can tell him this stuff. Got to be careful not to overstep, though. He is my boss after all.*

"I've got a pretty good idea. It's part of why we hired you. I could sense your need to be useful and to prove yourself again, that and your honesty about the situation, plus your experience got you the position. Tess, keep going the way you are, and I'm sure it'll all be fine."

Tess feels her eyes start to tear up, and Marc hears her quietly sniff in the moisture threatening to run from her nose. "Thanks. Hey, please don't tell Jason what I said. I don't trust the guy not to pull something, even if you rephrase what I said to be 'constructive criticism'."

"Don't worry, we're already keeping an eye out for any potential conflicts or problems. Just be open with us. You don't have to manage everything alone here." Marc reassures her. "Anyway, can you meet with me about 10 a.m. in my office tomorrow to go over your first assignments? I want to make sure you get off to a good start in case I need to go out of town for a few days."

"Will do!" Tess feels better after their conversation.

"Have a good evening and see you tomorrow!" He hangs up.

AND IT BEGINS

She arrives promptly at 8 a.m. the next morning at Inspiration Inc., greeted by Kari, who hands her a schedule for the day.

9 a.m.: Meet with Liz to finalize contract.

10 a.m.: Meet with Marc-client project assignments.

12-12:45 p.m.: Lunch

After Lunch: Work on projects.

Tess heads back to her desk in Marc's department. Amy is already there, headphones on and working on some sort of questionnaire on her screen. Tess taps her on her shoulder before she goes into her cubicle, and Amy takes off her headphones. "Hey, girl! Guess who's got first shift in with the boss this morning." Amy gives her a wide grin.

"Jason?" She raises one eyebrow and gives Amy a knowing look. She thinks, *I hope Marc took what I said to heart. I NEVER want to be on the receiving end of a grudge from Jason.*

"Yep! Marc called him in before he could even turn on his computer. Wonder if he'll say anything about yesterday? I'm sure Liz knew something was up." Amy gives Tess a look like 'that asshole's gonna get a whooping!'

"I hope it doesn't come back and bite me in the ass. I don't think Marc will say too much, at least not directly. He's probably just giving him his assignments." Tess purses her lips and has a subtle, worried look in her eyes. "What are you working on, anyway?"

"Some kind of psychological questionnaire. Gives you situations and you have to say whether you agree with the person's actions and why or why not. You know, HR type crap they get new employees so they can 'understand' us." She laughs. "Standard shit! Must have taken a dozen of these things while in the Army. I'm sure they'll be pulling out the good old Myers-Briggs test soon enough."

"Myers-Briggs?" Tess asks.

"Yep, a standard personality test. They often use it, so they know how we think and interact with others and so on. It breaks everyone down as Introvert or Extrovert, Sensing or iNtuition, Thinking or Feeling and Perceiving or Judging. It sorts people into one of 16 possible 'personality types' and from there, they think they can solve everyone's problems and conflicts." She laughs.

"Oh, yeah! I took it for a team-building thing in college. I was an Introvert, iNtuition, Feeling, and Perceiving, yeah, INFP?"

"Oooh! That's one of the rare ones. Last time I took it, I came out as an ENTJ, but the time before, my T was an F. I swing between the two. Unfortunately, the Intuition part doesn't go too well with the military. They don't like people being intuitive or impulsive unless you're higher up. They want you to follow orders. Which is one reason I finally left." Amy says with a huff.

"If you don't like following orders, why did you join in the first place?" Tess gives her an odd look.

"Because they paid for my computer education. But seriously, sometimes, I get a feeling when things are gonna happen; usually bad things, and they wanted us all to go to DC back when there were all the right-wing protests a couple of years ago? Something told me NOT to go. I tried to explain how sometimes I know stuff is going to happen, and maybe they should send us somewhere else. My C.O. told me he didn't believe in *female intuition*, but I could stay behind and do kitchen duty, you know, where a woman 'belongs' in their misogynistic little minds, if I didn't want to go on the mission." Amy says, her spunk turning to sadness, tinged with old anger.

Tess touches her lightly on her arm. "What happened? Something went wrong, didn't it?"

"Yeah, something went wrong, alright. Do you remember how a pipe-bomb went off at the Capitol during that crazy conspiracy-theorist protest where they thought pedophiles were hiding kids in tunnels under the Capitol?"

"Something about it. Weren't there like a dozen injuries and some deaths?" Tess asks, sitting in a spare chair in Amy's section.

"Yeah, the C.O. who put me on kitchen duty was one who died. Another was a civilian woman, and the final one was the bomber himself, who apparently realized he hadn't built it right and went back to fix it and it went off while he was holding it. Not the brightest bulb in the pack, that one. Ten others were injured, including my boyfriend, who got discharged early after that. He joined the police, and is a resource officer at one of the area schools. He recovered, but the whole mess left him with some PTSD, so that's why he's on school resource duty rather than active policing."

"Geez! Well, I'm glad you didn't go with them. Did they ever learn to listen to your gut instincts?" Tess asks.

"Are you kidding? We're talking about military mentality. I got fed up, and when my term was up, I *left*! Besides, Charlie, my boyfriend, was already out by then, which is what brought me here." Amy throws up her hands in a 'That's all, folks!' mannerism.

"Well, I should let you get back to your test-thingy. I've got an appointment with Liz to finalize my contract at 9 am and then another to go over assignments with Marc at 10, so I'm thinking it's gonna be a busy day." Tess looks up when she hears Marc's door opening, and sees Jason coming out, expression hard to read, but she can sense he's more than a little annoyed. "Make that a potentially, *long* day." She leans in and whispers to Amy. "Someone's pissed!" Then she gets up and goes to her cubicle and starts up her machine.

At 8:55 a.m., Tess heads down the hall to see Liz. She knocks on Liz's open door.

"Come in! I was just looking over what you gave Kari." She smiles. "Everything looks like it's in order, so we only need to finalize the contract. Did you have time to read it last night?"

"Yeah, it looked pretty standard, for the most part." Tess sits in a chair to the side of Liz's desk.

"For the most part? Anything you want to ask about?" Liz gives her a confused look.

"Not really, one section is worded a little oddly. Let me see if I can find it." She reaches out for the contract and skims it. "Here it is, under trial periods and promotions." It says:

> **Mandatory promotions: From time to time, we may find it necessary to promote an individual to a higher/new position without the employee's consent.**

Liz is surprised Tess noticed the clause, as it's preceded by a subliminal graphic that should hide it from anyone who was not subconsciously prepped. *Interesting, but then again, she did cite the logo. Maybe she's just sensitive to subliminal coding?* "You don't need to worry about that. It's only a technicality. From time to time, we adjust certain positions, changing the job descriptions and responsibilities. It merely means an employee can't use that, as an excuse to claim there's been a breach of contract and quit or sue. It's something our legal team insisted on putting in, no big deal." Liz smiles at her, sending subtle mental thoughts to Tess to forget about it and move on.

"Well, if you have a pen handy, I guess I should get this over with." Tess grins, but thinks, *Hell, the pay's good, the benefits are great! I shouldn't be worried about some odd wording.* Liz hands her a pen, she signs it, and hands it back to her. She has an odd feeling, like she's just committed herself to a long-term contract, but it feels good, like she belongs here, and like she can finally shut the door on the mess her life was before now.

"I'll leave a copy for your records with Kari. You can grab it on your way home today." Liz smiles, stands, and leads Tess to the door.

Tess heads back to her desk, and Amy isn't there. She thinks, *I guess it's her turn to talk to Marc.* She sits and goes through her computer, making notes of what programs she has, and what she would like. *Hmm, this one only has Photoshop Elements on it, not the full program, and no Illustrator. I'll ask him if I can install some Mac PHP tools I've been using at home, as well. The more I can avoid dealing with Jason, the happier I'll be.* She muses. After a few more minutes, she hears Marc's door open and Amy comes back. Tess can sense she's happy.

"Did it go well?" she asks, already knowing it did.

"Yeah, sure did! He's assigned me a couple of cool clients to start off with. There's a group giving low cost or free self-defense courses to vulnerable women, including assault victims to help them feel safe again. There's also a police group that sponsors a big brother/big sister type program that Charlie's involved in, so Marc figured that one would be good for me, too. You know, I think I'm gonna like it here." Amy smiles, slides into her chair, and researches.

"*Cool*! Wonder what he'll have for me?" Tess ponders.

She hears Marc's voice behind her. "Well, if you're ready, we can get started so you can find out."

Tess looks up, startled he snuck up on her. "*Oh*! Okay. I just finished going through the programs on my computer, so that's good timing." She stands and follows Marc into his office.

"Have a seat over there. I'm going to grab the project folders and my notes." He says, motioning her to a meeting area with several comfortable chairs and a sofa around a table. She wanders over and sits in the chair at the short end. Marc comes around with several folders, two tablets, and sits in a chair next to her. He kicks off their meeting by saying, "Okay, before we begin, I want to let you know you shouldn't have to worry about Jason bothering you again."

Tess is torn between relief and worry. "You spoke to him about yesterday?"

"Yes, but don't worry, I told him Liz mentioned it and we'd reviewed some security footage and noticed him being the instigator. I made sure he knows we don't tolerate unwanted contact, or sexual harassment in any form!" Marc smiles kindly at her. He's not sure why, but he is instinctively protective of Tess. He tries to read her reaction but gets hints of anxiety from her. "You don't seem totally pleased?"

"It's probably nothing. I saw him when he came out of here earlier, and while he didn't look angry, I could tell he was pissed off about something. I hope he doesn't take it out on me or Amy." Tess cringes at the thought.

"If he does, tell me or Liz immediately. We don't tolerate *any* harassment at Inspiration Inc." He reassures her.

She shifts in her seat, uneasy at Marc's protectiveness and her fear of Jason's reprisals. "Okay. I'll let you know. While we're on the subject, I went through my computer and was wondering if we could make some additions software-wise?" Tess asks quietly, hesitant to ask for anything.

"I'm not sure what that has to do with Jason, but never be afraid to ask for what you need." Marc smiles.

"Well, if I could install some Mac PHP tools, then I can do some of the backend stuff myself, so I don't have to deal with him every time I need some little back-end tweak done? I was also wondering if I can get a full version of Photoshop and Illustrator on there. I know they're expensive, so if you don't want to, I can bring my laptop and use my creative cloud account." Tess looks down at her notepad afraid he might say no.

"It's not a problem. We have site licenses for Photoshop and Illustrator, and if you have any preferred PHP or other tools, run them by Jayla in tech before installing them, so she knows what they are, in case there might be any conflicts or issues with them." His smile puts her at ease.

"I can do that. The tools I use are pretty mainstream, so there shouldn't be any issues with malware, if that's your concern. She makes eye contact, and gets an odd feeling, like getting feedback on a mic, only mentally or emotionally. She thinks, *That's weird. Like mental déjà vu.*

"I've got several projects to choose from. We've got a local Girl Scouts group, the Planned Parenthood on McDowell St, a homeless shelter in East Asheville, a women's shelter, and a food bank." He lays out folders for each of them. "I'd suggest starting with two projects. Do you have any preferences?"

"Actually, I do. I'd like to start with the Women's shelter and

PPH. I had a good friend who went through an abusive relationship, and PPH is always a good group to help. Too many people
think they're only about abortions, but they do so much more."
Tess picks up the two folders.

"They also go well together, both being women-centric organizations. I'd like you to look through the folders, and look at what
the client wants, and see if you can come up with any ideas for
features and layouts. This your tablet. Everyone here gets one,
and your daily schedules are sent through a common calendar on
here, as well as an internal messaging system. It also has contact
information for others here, as well as service providers you might
need, such as the companies we recommend for web hosting. You
should also use it to make notes in meetings because it will sync
to your desktop. Take it home with you and sync it there as well."
He hands her the tablet. "The passcode is inside the cover."

"Thanks. I've already got a few ideas to play with. I hope I can
come up with something you'll like." She takes the tablet and
stacks it on top of the two folders.

He nods and reaches across the table, lightly touching her
hand. An odd feeling, like non-painful, static electricity builds
where their skin touches. "Don't be afraid to be creative. The
worst I or our clients can say is 'no' to an idea, but if you never
take the chance and suggest it, there's no chance you'll get a yes."
He encourages her psychically, as well as verbally, knowing she
struggles with self-confidence issues.

Tess looks him in the eye after his kind words. "Thanks, I'll
keep that in mind. I'll get going on some mockups on paper and
make a list of ideas. When do you need them?"

"Let's see what you can come up with by tomorrow, and we can go over
that before you begin on any actual programming or graphics, okay?"

"Will do! And thanks again! You *won't* be disappointed, I
promise!" heads back out to her desk. She glances nervously over
at Jason before ducking down and getting to work.

She works the rest of the afternoon on her projects, logs in from home, and works more. She comes up with several useful ideas about how to make their sites interactive, including a 'what are my options' sections for unexpected pregnancies, an 'Am I a victim of abuse' quiz and a 'how to break the cycle' for the women's center.

Tess knows there are women who don't consider abusive behavior as wrong, but as normal treatment by a man because of low self-esteem and familial abuse their own families may have lived through. One of the fastest increasing sources of abuse has been some of the religious offshoots that emphasize a man's "God given right" to domination of women, and specifically, wives. This movement's been growing in strength in recent years with the Evangelical push toward Biblical literalism and "traditional religious values", especially between 2015-2028. It's lessened now, but is still a big problem in some areas where religion has a steel grip on communities.

This is one of Tess's pet peeves. One of her best friends from college had a relationship with a guy who acted normal until they'd been together a while. He would lecture her with scripture, and eventually beat her every time she spoke her mind or didn't listen to him, causing her to miscarry and go into a coma for two months because of brain trauma. Throughout his trial, he stuck to his story that she was his, in God's view, and if she left him and found someone else she would burn in Hell as the Devil's sexual plaything for all eternity.

When Tess goes over her ideas with Marc the next day, he's impressed and approves her approach, instructing her to go ahead and do a full site plan and begin basic html programming, and if she's up to it, some of the back-end programming for the quizzes and the panic button. He can sense she's relieved she won't have to seek Jason's help for every little thing.

Marc doesn't need to go away much in those first couple of weeks; he only leaves occasionally for an hour or two. She's happy about that, as she's anxious Jason may try something if he thinks he can get away with it with Marc gone for a longer period.

Marc makes extra time to work with Tess in those first weeks, getting to know her, and test her latent abilities without her knowledge. Several aptitude test sessions are set up with the new employees that also, surreptitiously test their skills and their sense of ethics, as well as psychological stability and adaptability, starting with the one Amy took that first full day, which is based on Kohlberg's stages of moral development, and naturally, the Myers-Briggs. There are various tests that may reveal personality disorders or leanings toward neurosis or even psychosis.

One day, Tess is working on the women's shelter site and thinking about her friend from college who inspired her to take on this project. Her mind wanders to her ex, Colton, whose nickname was "Ox", because he was big and stubborn, unless he was being pushed into getting involved with the wrong people. He turned to threats of violence in the end, serious enough she had to take out a restraining order. She's tried to put that behind her and not think about him, but knows he's coming up for parole soon, and she shivers thinking about it. *I hope he's not still holding a grudge, because if he is, I'm not sure he'll respect the restraining order. I need to make some emergency plans, just in case. At least I'm learning some self-defense from Amy, but maybe I should invest in some pepper spray or a taser? Who am I kidding? I'll probably end up macing or tasing myself. It's probably just as well, I swore off relationships after Colton. Sometimes, I think all the good ones must be taken or otherwise unavailable.* She thinks. Her mind wanders to Marc. *If only I could find someone like him. Intelligent, sensitive, a basic nice guy. STOP IT! DON'T EVEN GO THERE! He's my boss! Well, my supervisor. And even if there isn't a rule about fraternization here, after what happened with Colton, I'd be crazy to even consider it, and besides, a guy like him has to be taken...or gay. Still, if I could find someone like him out there, it would be nice to no longer be alone all the time.* Her mind wanders for about 15 minutes, then her computer beeps, asking her if she wants to log out of the file server due to inactivity. She snaps back to reality, hits 'no' to logging out, and continues with her work.

***

Tess has been working at Inspiration Inc. for about three weeks when Liz reaches out to Marc telepathically. *Marc? Could you come by for a second? I got Tess's evaluation back; I thought you'd like to see it.*

Be there in five minutes. I'm with her now, going over her projects. He paths back to her.

Turning his attention back to Tess, he says, "I'm so sorry! I just realized I was supposed to have a short meeting with Liz. I'll be back in a few minutes. I lost track of time. You're on the right track, though. Make it as easy and intuitive to use as possible and include that panic button you suggested, so women can quickly hide the site if their abuser comes in. You can wait here if you'd like; I won't be long."

She opts to wait in his office for him to come back, thinking, *At least I don't have to worry about Jason while I'm in here.*

He heads down the hall to Liz's office, goes in, closes the door and plops down on her sofa, as she's sitting in one of the chairs around the meeting table.

"So? Any news? Anything unusual?" He asks eagerly.

"Unusual, yes, news, no. Kari's tried various permutations of her name but no results. She also scanned her with no sign of a biotag, so even though she shares many traits with potentials, I don't see how she could be one of them. Her psychic skills, however, are higher than about any potential we've got on staff, or have seen in several decades, and her psychological tests are nearly ideal for a prime potential, except for the depressive tendencies." She says.

Marc sits and looks over the summary of Tess's evaluation.

Subject: Tessa Marie Waterford. **Age: 28**

Transformation priority: N/A

Estimated IQ: 155

Myers-Briggs: INFP, but borderline between thinking and feeling.

Kohlberg Scale: Level 3: Post Conventional Morality. The individual evaluates situations, societal rules, and laws to determine her actions, seeing the world more in shades of gray rather than absolute rights and wrongs. She focuses on fairness, what is right in a given situation, and the greater good. Upper stage 5, possibly 6.

General psychological evaluation: Intelligent, resourceful, and highly adaptable. Some issues with poor self-image and depression, but not insurmountable. Highly creative. Reasonably empathic. She shows some signs of ADHD, but that is typical with her overall evaluation, and not uncommon for potentials. No signs of neurotic or psychotic disorders. No signs of bi-polar disorders or instability beyond the aforementioned depression. Would likely adapt well to being transformed, *had she been compatible*.

Psychic evaluation: While her abilities are primarily latent, they have significant potential. She doesn't appear to be aware of her abilities but can use her mental shielding unconsciously, for example, when she 'pushed' Peder out of her mind using visualization that resulted in an energy surge. Her tablet sensor has detected multiple unconscious uses of said psychic abilities and energies, though no overt manifestations. Indications include energy signatures for possible telekinesis, some form of telempathic ability. Observations suggest she may be a people reader, but more observation and testing are necessary to confirm. While her abilities are largely latent, and therefore difficult to test, she has displayed signs that her overall potential may be one of the highest this center has seen in decades.

Conclusion: Had subject been compatible, she would have been highly prioritized for transformation.

Liz watches him read through the report. "I've forwarded the detailed results to your tablet, but the conclusion says it all."

Marc's frustrated that Tess would be an ideal potential, but isn't compatible. There's more to it than his feelings as an Apara finding potentials to recruit. It's becoming personal to him, even if he won't admit it to himself. "I don't suppose there's any chance our Benefactors would *make* her compatible?"

Liz shakes her head, frowning. "I really doubt it, though her psych tests show a high adaptability rating, they prefer to stick to tried and proven routines. I guess we can run it by them later, assuming she stays here." Liz wonders if Marc plans to keep her employed in his division now that her evaluation is complete.

He gives her a look of frustration. "She's doing excellent work on the charity projects and is thriving here. I'd hate to uproot her now. It'd be psychologically traumatizing for her to be fired, not to mention, I don't technically have a justifiable cause; not one I can *tell* her. I'd like to keep her on as long as possible. If she becomes problematic, I'll make some calls and get her headhunted for a good position elsewhere." He skims all her test results on his tablet; all of which would have meant a prioritized and definite transformation had she only been compatible.

Liz watches him as though she can see the wheels turning in his head. "Getting attached?" Liz asks after a few-second pause.

Marc looks up at Liz, annoyed. "Not in that way! More... *responsible* for her." He does his best to convince himself that's all it is.

Liz shakes her head and reaches out, grasping Marc by one shoulder, looking him in the eye. "I'd halfway hoped maybe those steel walls you've put up all these years were finally cracking. At least then, something positive could come from all of this." There's a hint of sadness in her eyes.

"Liz, after all that happened with Collette, I'm in no hurry to get close to anyone, let alone a woman I can't even transform if I wanted to." He admits.

"No hurry? That was over *four centuries* ago! I hate seeing you alone like this. Surely, there's someone among our own you...." She stops as he holds his hand up.

"Please, Liz, not another lecture. I know you brought me over and feel responsible for me, but this *is my* decision. It's simpler this way." He insists.

"You mean you won't get hurt because you won't let anyone get close enough to hurt you?" Liz laughs sarcastically. "The irony of a strong telempath hiding from his own, damn emotions! Okay, I've said my piece. You've been stubborn since I first found you. You'll figure it all out someday." She stands and grabs her tablet, and a stack of physical test papers. "Kari and I have plans this afternoon, and we've got to head out if we're going to make dinner in Stavanger. Time zones are hell for restauranting, even when one can pop across an ocean in the blink of an eye." She's frustrated as hell at her former charge, who's never let himself move on from the pain he felt at the end of his human life. She heads out to the lobby to get Kari, and the two leave, arm in arm, going into the elevator, and porting from there so no human eyes would witness them disappearing into thin air.

Marc can sense her frustration with him, but writes it off to *she'll never understand,* and heads back to Tess. Unfortunately, he's so unfocused after Liz's emotional reprimand he can't focus on work. After a few minutes of working with Tess, and needing to ask her about 4 times to repeat what she just told him, he gives up and says, "Listen, I've got some things on my mind, and it's Friday, why don't you cut out early and have a little extra weekend?"

"Thanks, but I wanted to get to a good stopping point with this so I can leave 'work at work' for the weekend." She smiles.

Marc looks at her, face softening into a soft grin. "Tess, has anyone told you you're too good to be true?" He's only half joking.

"Only you, lately. Wish it were true, but I'm just me; nothing that special." Her old insecurity rears its head once again.

Marc leans across the worktable toward her, gently putting a hand on her arm to get her to look at him. "Tess, look at me. *Never* forget, you're *very* special. You're smart, creative, and a good person. You're exactly the type of person we seek to hire, and those are rare. Do you *understand* me?"

She looks at him, shaken by the force of his words. Part of her finds it hard to accept, but says, "Yeah, I guess so. Sorry, I'm out of it today, too." Her thoughts shifting again to wondering if Colton has had his parole hearing yet.

Sensing there's more to it, he inquires, "Anything I can do to help?"

"I don't know, it's nothing work related, not really." She looks worried, creases forming around her eyes and in the corners of her mouth. Marc senses anxiety, fear, and regret emanating from her, as well as smell the associated epinephrine and other stress related chemicals oozing from her pores.

"Not everything has to be about work. If there's something you're upset about, please don't hold it in! I can tell something's got you worried." Marc reads her, but can only get a vague mix of concern, dread, and fear.

She really doesn't want to mix her personal dilemma with business, but she doesn't know whom else she can talk to. Reluctantly, she tells him what's bothering her. "Okay, there's probably nothing to worry about, but I was looking at Facebook at lunch; I checked my ex's brother's page, and it sounds like Colton may be getting out on probation any time now, if he hasn't gotten out already. There's a restraining order to keep him away from me, but I'm worried because he made some serious threats when he figured out I was the 'snitch'." She tenses up.

Marc is sympathetic, but also feels a protectiveness and anger that someone might hurt her welling up. "Look, you have my number. If he shows up or contacts you and makes any new threats or attempts to hurt you, call me! Anytime. I'm serious." In the back of his mind, he can picture Liz giving him a look and saying, *"Yeah, right, NOT protective at all!"*

"Thanks, Amy's been giving me martial arts lessons and general self-defense training." She gives him an awkward laugh. "I can kick her target dummy hard enough to set off its 'knockout' sensor. So, I should be okay. I doubt he'll follow through with it. He was too much of a wimp to say no to the others when he knew he'd be breaking the law; I doubt he'd risk breaking parole to take it out on me, but it brings back old feelings from when things went wrong." She speaks more confidently than she feels, something Marc notices.

He puts his hand lightly on her arm again and gives her a look of sympathy. "Tess, believe me, I know all about exes and 'old feelings' coming to the surface. Take a break, go home, and *get some rest.* You've been working late the last few nights and yes, I've noticed. I also notice you've continued to work after officially punching out. Take the files home if you must, but slow down, okay? You've more than proven you can do the job. Please make me a list of your off-the-clock hours. You deserve to get paid for your time." He puts a slight spin on it psychically, hoping she'll take the suggestion.

She looks at him; again, wishing more guys were like him, or the situation was different, and he wasn't her boss, or she could have met him somewhere besides work. "Okay! Let Liz know so she doesn't think I'm bailing." She stands, stretches, and gathers up her stuff. She yawns uncontrollably, feeling the long days hit her.

"You sure you're up to driving? I can get someone to take you home." He again sees a mental image of Liz chiding him for his protectiveness.

"I'll be fine. It's only about a 10-minute drive, but thanks, and have a good weekend." She says and heads out.

Marc watches her leave until she's out of sight, then closes his office door, and vanishes. He reappears in an old graveyard in southern France, where it's already dark. Many of the mausoleums and graves are in disrepair; ancient gravestones are everywhere where he materializes. Some headstones are broken, others so eroded you can no longer read the names on the headstones, and many are overgrown with ivy or askew, where ancient tree roots have grown under them and pushed up the stones from their graves. Some have no real headstones at all, only stone markers indicating there's a nameless grave below them. He walks around until he gets to a stone bench by one of the few well-maintained graves. This one is marked Collette Beauvais 1565-1598.

He sits silently for a while, thinking, *Maybe Liz's right. I should let Collette go and find a living companion. It's hard though. She was everything to me. It can't be Tess! That would put me right back in the proverbial fire. Even if I could do a few years, I'd have to leave before she can see I'm not aging, and knowing me, I'll still obsess and watch her go on with life, find someone, maybe have children, grow old and die, leaving me feeling even more alone than I already am. Not to mention, never being able to tell her what I am. Always having to hide things from her she can't be told.*

When he speaks aloud, he reverts to his native French, but speaks softly to his long dead fiancée, saying something along the lines of "I'm sorry I've not visited for so long. Even after all these years, it's still hard to let go. I've been trying, but now, I... I need someone to talk to, even if all that's here now are your dust and a headstone. I wish you could tell me what to do; tell me to move on, to 'get a life'" Marc flips briefly to the English idiom, and back to French again "but somehow, I still feel bound to you. Liz thinks I don't want to get hurt again, and that's part of it, but I also feel like I'd be betraying you if I move on, and I still wonder what I ever did to make you leave me." A tear rolls down his cheek, and he sits there for a while in silence. Knowing his long dead love can't give him the answers he seeks, he walks off behind a mausoleum and vanishes, taking some time to visit the town where he lived when he was made Apara. After hundreds of years, it's completely unrecognizable. *Maybe I should follow the example of this town. It has changed with time, perhaps it's time I do the same.* He wonders. He stops at an all-night café and has some coffee and a croissant before popping back to Asheville.

ALLEY, ALLEY OX IS FREE

Tess goes out to the parking lot, looks up and sees gathering storm clouds. Distant thunder rumbles, so she rushes for her car before it can pour. As she pulls out of the parking lot, she sees dramatic forks of lightning over the mountains, and the clouds release a deluge of heavy rain. She gets off at the exit near home, and grabs some fast food for dinner, as she's not up to making anything when she gets home. She drives the rest of the way home, but the rain is torrential, so she sits in her car and eats, checking Facebook and other social media on her smart phone while she waits. After a few minutes, she gives up on waiting out the rain, and sprints to the door, leaving her work stuff and tablet in the car. She gets in the door, closes and locks it and is absolutely drenched. She strips off her clothes and hangs them to dry in the bathroom. She uses a towel to pat some of the moisture out of her hair, and the remaining water from her skin. Feeling exhausted and rather miserable, she crawls straight into bed for a nap. Her cell wakes her at about 8:20 p.m. The ringtone is one she hasn't heard for a while, knows it's someone she knows, but can't remember who. She wakes groggily and answers.

"Hello?" She tries to sound more awake than she feels.

She's relieved to hear the voice of her old co-worker and friend from Digital Danger. He says, "Tess, it's Alex. Listen, I just ran in to Colton. He's out on parole, drunk off his ass, and ranting about getting you for ruining his life. I thought you might want to make yourself scarce until he sobers up."

Tess feels a sickening, wrenching, and dropping feeling; nausea hits her as her heart begins to pound, and her mouth goes dry as panic strikes. "*God!* Thanks! How long ago did you run into him?" Her voice quivers, though she hides her panic.

"About 40 minutes ago. Your number's changed, so it took me a while to track it down through our gang. Thalia had your new one." He explains.

She forces herself to breathe slowly, more regularly, despite the fear running through her. "I owe you one! I had a bad feeling when I heard 'Ox' might be freed." She says, now fully awake, thinking *I've got to stop using my nickname for him. My therapist told me after the trial to distance myself from him emotionally, so I should refer to him only by his real name, not my nickname for him.*

Alex chuckles lightly. "Yeah, forgot about that nickname. He sure could be a stubborn bastard! Just stay safe!"

She hangs up with Alex and gets dressed in record time, stuffing a few essentials in a duffle bag, including a wooden baseball bat she keeps under her bed for emergencies. She's dizzy, and realizes she's been hyperventilating since hanging up with Alex. She takes a minute and sits on the edge of her bed, finding some equilibrium, so she can deal with this mess. *I can't stay here. I'll go hide out at work. He may have figured out where I live, but work should be safe.* She reasons. She dumps some extra dry cat food in a bowl and turns the tap in the bathroom on a trickle for Mabel, just in case she can't get home for a day or two. She calls 911 to report a threat, but the police tell her they're so busy because of one of Asheville's street festivals, they can't spare any officers based on hearsay.

After being given the brush off by the police, she remembers Marc told her to call him. *I don't know if I should take him up on his offer, or if he was just trying to make me feel better. But what other option do I have?* She picks up her cell and calls. Instead of a ring, it goes straight to voicemail, so she leaves him a message asking him to call her back as soon as possible.

Frustrated, she goes outside to her car. The storms have ended and the sky's cleared. Steam still rises from the asphalt and is visible wafting up in front of her headlights as she drives down her street. She gets to the office 11 minutes later.

She uses her keycard to get in, goes into the lobby, closes the door, and makes certain it's locked tight. She jogs down the hall to her cubicle and logs in online. She goes to Facebook through the company account, as she can't view her ex's page through hers, as he blocked her account during the trial. She looks Colton's page up, and sure enough, the first new post in three years is a rant about 'that bitch that put me in jail and what he wants to do to her'. She thinks, *Damn! I guess he's still pretty pissed at me for everything.* She reports the post as a credible threat of violence to a friend, since she's on the company account, and hits submit.

The light goes on unexpectedly, and a woman's voice says, "Hello?"

"Liz? It's me, Tess." Her heart is in her throat at the thought it might be Colton.

"Tess? Is everything alright? I thought you'd be home by now?" She grows concerned as she picks up on Tess's growing emotional distress.

Not wanting to burden anyone else with her personal problems besides Marc, she says, "Oh, I came back. Do you have any idea where Marc might be? I need his help with something. I tried calling, but his phone went straight to voicemail."

Liz mentally locates Marc, and says, "You might try Pack's Tavern, downtown. He and some others from here hang out there on the weekends. Is there anything I can help you with?" Even with Tess's natural shields in place, she can sense all isn't well, even if she can't get the specifics from her mind. Her body language also screams of fear, and her sensitive nose picks up the acrid odor of epinephrine oozing from Tess's pores.

"No, he told me to call him if I ran into this problem and it's... it's really urgent." Tess tries not to sound completely freaked out.

"Well, try Pack's. You'll probably find him there. It's near the fire and police stations; between there and the Courthouse, downtown." She senses Tess's fear and hopes the police being nearby might put her at ease. *She's not afraid of Marc, but she's afraid of someone.* Liz notes.

"Ah! Yeah, good. Thanks!" She says and thinks, *like they're going to help.* She grabs her purse and keys, heads for her car and drives downtown. *Well, Ox would never go to Pack's; it's too close to the police station, so that's good. I can probably safely park and make it there without running into him. He'll probably go hang out at the biker place that opened on Tunnel Rd. That's really too close for comfort.* She thinks, as it's only minutes away from her apartment.

Liz debates giving Marc a mental shout. However, she's still annoyed at him for his frustratingly, stubborn insistence on remaining unemotional, and not wanting anyone else to develop feelings for him. *Let him deal with whatever's going on.* She thinks and vanishes, going back home to spend the evening with Kari.

Tess gets down near Pack's and searches for parking; with the street festival in town, it's crowded. The streets are full of parked cars, and people milling around; making it even harder to get through and find a spot. After about twenty minutes of driving around and around the streets near Pack's, she finally spots someone pulling out, and waits for that space, having to fight semi-drunk pedestrians as she backs into the parallel parking spot. Her frustration leads to impatience, and she honks her horn to get them to move. She gets out, locks it, and runs to Pack's. It's crowded, but after weaving through the crowd, she sees Amy and a few others from work. She waves at Amy to get her attention, and hurries over to them, nearly slipping in a small pool of spilled beer. A band is playing loud, classic rock covers, and she has to work her way through people dancing erratically to reach Amy's table.

"Amy, have you seen Marc anywhere? I need to find him; it's important!" She shouts over the band.

"Marc? Yeah, he was here. He left about 5 minutes ago. He was out of it and wasn't here long." She yells back.

"*Damn!* Do you know which way he went?" she asks desperately.

"Yeah, he walked past the windows and went down that way. He said something about that new club, Talisman?" She moves to the music as she speaks. "Are you okay? You look flustered."

She knows her friend would have her back, but she doesn't

want the petite ex-military gal to face-off with her crazed and drunk ex-boyfriend for her. She halfway hoped Amy might have brought her police-officer boyfriend with her, but he apparently feels awkward in crowds. Tess says, "Yeah, I just need to find Marc. I'll catch you online later!" She dashes out the door and continues on her quest to find Marc.

She heads in the direction of Talisman, down one of the less traveled streets in town. There are fewer people on this street, but she still has to dodge people on the sidewalk as she halfway runs, hoping to catch up with him. Her heart pounds in her ears. The post-storm humidity is high, and it makes running even more difficult. Out of breath, she pauses, and leans against a building, but looks up and sees him at a distance. She's sure it's him; he's got a special way of moving, unusually agile and controlled, which makes her think he's stronger than he looks.

She catches her breath, and runs to catch up, even though she's got a growing stitch in her left side, causing her major pain that makes her want to double over and cry. She tries to call out to him but is still so out of breath it won't come out; she can only wheeze and groan. She pauses, tries to calm down, and sees him turn off into an alley between some shops. She tries to run and catch up, but the stitch is still causing her pain.

She finally reaches the alley. It's long and turns a couple of times between the entrance on the back street and the main street, Biltmore Avenue, where several shops and Talisman are. She's hesitant about wandering down it in the dark, *you never know what if some crazy person could be lurking there*, but she convinces herself *Marc just went down there, so it should be okay. Besides, if I go around, I might lose him all together.*

She starts down the alley. The first part is darker than she likes as the lights along the walls are burnt out, and she must halfway feel her way through by touching the wall with her left hand. She reaches the first turn, which opens to a wider area with dim lighting. There's

65

a pile of old crates and pallets waiting to be taken to the dump along one wall. She starts to go around them, when she sees Marc, but he's not alone. Marc stands intimately close to a woman against an inner wall, near the source of the ambient light, a dim, flickering lamp. She thinks, *Oh shit! He's with someone! If I disturb him, he'll think I'm some kind of psycho stalker.* She ducks down behind the crates, not wanting to be seen or to disturb them. *Damn it! God! This is so fucking embarrassing! I can't let him see me. I can't lose my job because he thinks I'm following him like some obsessed puppy.* She thinks, looking behind her at the dark section of the alley, wishing there were some other way to get out that didn't mean going back through that darkness. She sneaks a look through holes in the crates, hoping maybe they'll move on so she can get out of there that way, but what she sees, once it registers, chills her to the bone, and makes her forget about Colton.

The woman he's nuzzling is completely unresponsive; her eyes open, body relaxed, and she's just standing there, though he isn't holding her up or forcing her. It's as if she's letting him kiss her neck but is completely ignoring it while leaning against the damp, grimy brick wall. Marc pauses, and stands up straight, like he's listening for something. It's then Tess notices the two marks on the woman's neck, and a smudge of red around each one. Marc looks around him, and Tess worries he may have heard her, so holds her breath and remains frozen. When he turns his head to the side, she gets a glimpse that makes her do a double take: he has two elongated, sharp teeth in his half open mouth. Her mind jumps headlong into panic, not believing what she's seeing. Her heart races and pounds, and the sound echoes in her ears like some creepy background music to this literal horror story she's watching unfold. Her mental shields instinctively slam into place, hiding her mind, and remaining silent, not realizing he's already heard her heartbeat from across the alley, and knows exactly who is watching him.

Some drunken partiers make a lot of noise at the other end of the alley; enough to distract Marc briefly, so Tess makes a break for it. She edges around the corner as quietly as possible, running blindly through the darker section of the alley, nearly tripping over unseen clutter twice, back out onto the street, running harder than she's ever run before, ignoring the humidity and the new stitch in her side, straight for her car back up by Pack's. She nearly knocks over an intoxicated couple making out near her car, yelling "*SORRY!*" as they stagger away, cursing at her in slurred speech. She fumbles with her keys but gets in, and almost floods the engine starting it. She pulls out, pushing her way through streams of half-drunken souls slewing out from downtown toward the parking decks on the East side of town.

She wants to blow her horn to make them move faster so she can put some distance between herself and what she witnessed but doesn't want to draw any attention to herself. She works her way through, deciding to run home. If there's no sign of Colton, she'll gather a few days' worth of clothes and necessities, put her cat in her carrier, and head out of town until she can clear her head, figure out what the hell is going on, and what she's witnessed. While driving, she thinks, *I couldn't have seen what I think I saw. It's not possible! Maybe they were role playing or doing fantasy sex or something?* She thinks, remembering the blank look on the woman's face, eyes open, and what was clearly a bite wound. "Vampires don't exist! *Period*! They can't! It's magical-mythological bullshit!" She says out loud to reassure herself, pounding on her steering wheel with one hand out of frustration, accidentally hitting the horn, startling herself, and amping up her anxiety.

A few minutes later, she pulls into her neighborhood and onto her street. She parks in a slot across from her townhouse instead of in front of it, and watches. There's no sign of anyone inside or movement in the bushes outside, so she takes a chance. She grabs her keys, sticks them individually between her fingers, like Amy taught her to, making sure she knows which is the house key. She rushes for the door, unlocks it, zips in, closes it quickly, locks it again, and leans against the door with her forehead resting against the cool wood. She's breathing heavily, her heart's pounding, body's shaking, and her mind is so stunned she needs a few seconds to force herself to calm down.

Her apartment's oddly silent aside from her breathing. Then she feels the warmth from a body behind her, arms planted around her on the door on either side. She swallows and says, "Ox?" figuring it must be him. *There's no way Marc could have gotten here ahead of me.* No response for a second, followed by a familiar voice, but not Colton's.

"Locking the door as soon as you get in is probably a good idea, except it won't keep someone out who's already inside..." Marc uses controlled, measured tones, "and it wouldn't keep me out even if you nailed the doors and windows shut," he says quietly, "but, it will keep you in."

Her stomach sinks and her heart rate flies through the roof as epinephrine surges into her system once again. She thinks in blind terror, *NO! Not Possible! How the hell did he get here ahead of me? Damn! Is he going to kill me? I've got to get out of here somehow!* She fidgets with the lock, trying to unlock it and escape, but it won't budge. Since she can't get it open, she tries another tactic, playing dumb. "*Marc!* What are you doing here?"

"I think you know. I'd recognize that brilliant mind of yours any day. Why were you following me?" He forces himself to remain calm, frustration and a touch of anger in his voice; anger not completely directed at her, but at himself for letting this happen. He keeps her hemmed in by the door. He tries to reach through to her, to paralyze her like the woman in the alley, but her shields are fully deployed from fear, and his attempts bounce off her mind like rain off an umbrella.

Terrified of what he might do to her, she answers his question, hoping it might diffuse the situation. "Ox, my ex, Colton..." She stammers out. "He's out of jail and..." She trails off, overwhelmed with tears of fear, though she's not sure who she fears most now.

He sighs, his mood shifting more to a mix of frustration and sympathy; he asks quietly, "He's coming for you, isn't he?"

"Y... ye... ss..." She squeezes out. She feels that odd tingling on her scalp again but can't think clearly enough to worry about it right now.

"You were coming to find me for help." He says, not so much a question, but reflecting what he senses from her public mind.

"P... please don't kill me! I won't tell *anyone* what I saw. I *promise*!" She pleads, a tear dripping onto one of his hands on the door, making him flinch.

He takes a deep breath and speaks as calmly as he can. "Tess, I'd never hurt you, but you witnessed something you never should've seen. It complicates matters. But I can fix that if you'll let me." He tries to reassure her. "Now, turn around and face me." He says, firmly, while gently nudging her shoulder to turn her around.

Fearing he'll rip her throat out despite his reassurances, she gambles and puts some of Amy's teachings to the test. She acts like she's going to comply, and then stomps on his foot with the heel of her shoe as hard as she can.

Taken by surprise, Marc drops his arms and steps back, losing his balance after the initial shock and pain of her attack. Tess, keys still in hand, slips past him, and runs for the kitchen, heads for the back door, and out that way. She kicks the swinging kitchen door open ahead of her, gets three feet in, and stops in her tracks as the door swings shut behind her. Marc's leaning against the back door, waiting for her, a look of sympathy, or perhaps pity, in his eyes.

"*How*?" She then tries to run back through the door only to hit the lockless door as though it were a solid wall. It won't open. She hits it hard with her hand, splintering the wood. She grasps her hand in pain and tries to kick it open, but the door won't budge. Her mind reels as she realizes she's cornered. She turns back to him. *Shit! He's gonna kill me!* She thinks. He starts walking slowly from the back door, toward her, hands out to his sides and open, to show he doesn't intend to hurt her. She backs into the nook between a wall and the kitchen door. She feels the pantry shelves behind her dig into her back. She thinks about throwing the large can of creamed corn from the shelf to her right at him, but she can't move her hand to grab it.

"*Please*! Don't, *don't* kill me!" She's sure he's intent on silencing her.

He speaks in gentle and measured tones, trying to reassure her, "I told you; I'm not going to hurt you, or kill you. I only want to make you forget what you've seen. It's *best* for both of us." He's in front of her, about two feet away. He takes basic control over her muscles when he notices her reaching for the can of creamed corn. "My secret will be safe, and you won't be burdened with the knowledge this world isn't what you thought." He says, softly, gently, and almost hypnotically.

He takes another step closer. She feels the warmth from him against her now, thinking *Why is he warm if he's some kind of vampire? That doesn't fit.* He gently reaches out and strokes her cheek, calming her while trying to ease her mind, but her unconscious shields protect her from the brunt of his mental manipulation. He realizes the only way to break her shields is to overload her with panic, and to do that; he'll have to do one thing she fears the most.

He cocks his head to one side, hating to frighten her, but knows it's the only way. "Oh, there's one other thing..."

Tess swallows, unable to get the words out, or even defend herself physically, though she thinks, *What now?*

He puts his right hand against her left cheek gently. "You interrupted my chosen meal tonight...." He says, with a dramatic pause. When he speaks again, his fangs are visible. "I figure you owe me dinner." He closes the last of the gap and tips her head back, biting into her throat. She feels a brief, but sharp pain as he pierces her skin and carotid artery. Her shields collapse and he plows into her mind, forcing her to mentally retreat as she loses all control to him and all awareness outside her own mind and his presence. He tries to calm her now that he's through her shields.

70

She retreats deep into some dark corner of her mind. The last thing she's aware of before she escapes into total mental blackness is his mental voice telling her, ***Don't worry about Colton. He's about to forget about you, too. He won't ever hurt you.***

With a sigh, Marc withdraws his fangs from her throat, healing over the wounds deftly. He allows her to sag to the floor against the shelf. He crouches down, and reaches into her mind again, making sure all memory of what happened tonight, and of what he is, is redacted away, her shields not even flinching in reaction to this latest incursion. He gently brushes her hair from her face, looks at her with a mixture of sadness and concern, and whispers, "why did you have to follow me into that alley? The last thing I wanted to do was frighten you." He strokes her cheek, then double checks there's no trace of the bite wounds. The epinephrine in her blood left a bad aftertaste, but fear was the only way to get through to her mind.

He scoops her up as though she's a cotton-filled rag-doll, nearly weightless. He telekinetically pushes the kitchen door open, carrying her to her beat-up recliner in front of the television. He uses his PK to push the chair into the reclining position, and gently puts her in it. He turns the TV on low, as she'd had it on before when he 'visited' her after her interview, and pulls the blanket at the base of the chair up and over her. Stroking her cheek again. He says softly, "If only you'd been compatible, this would have been so much simpler."

He's startled by a purring fur ball rubbing up against his legs. He looks down, and there's a fluffy, black cat with bright yellow eyes, weaving in and out around his legs, meowing.

"*Shh.* I guess I'd better find you some food, kitty, since your mother didn't get a chance, and she doesn't need to be woken by a hungry cat." He talks to Mabel. He walks back into the kitchen, followed by Mabel, checks a couple of cupboards until he finds the cat food, and feeds her, throwing the now empty can into the garbage. He turns off most of the lights and picks up a few things

Tess knocked over while running toward the kitchen. After one last cursory look around, he vanishes.

While Marc was in Tess's mind, he found memories of Colton there. He was careful to steer away from more private memories, but got an overview of his appearance from before the man went to prison, and a rough mental signature for him. He focuses on Tess's memories of Ox to locate him. It isn't easy at first, as a couple of years have passed since Tess has seen or had anything to do with him, but Marc eventually homes in on him, and ports in behind a biker bar and barbeque joint, 'The Leather-Studded Pig', on Tunnel Road. There's a lot of noise both from the people inside and around the building, as well as some bikers showing off their motorcycles gunning their engines in what could only be described as a pitiful contest of manliness. He ports a little farther away where he can hear over the cacophony of revving engines, pulls out his cell and makes a call.

"Liz? It's Marc." He dreads telling Liz what's happened, knowing she may push him to send Tess away because of it.

"Marc? Did Tess find you? She was looking for you earlier. Something was wrong, but you know how she is, I couldn't read what."

"Oh, yeah, she found me, all right. Mid-feed." He realizes Liz could have warned him. "If you knew she was looking for me, why didn't you give me a heads up?"

"*Shit*! I'm sorry. I was still annoyed from our discussion this afternoon, and figured I'd let you deal with it. How'd she react? Were you able to...?" She asks until Marc cuts her off.

Marc's tone has an edge of annoyance. "It's under control *now*, Liz. She freaked and took off, but I headed her off at home, and after some hassle, I redacted her memory. I *might* have avoided this complete fiasco if I'd known she was looking for me. I *told* her to call me. I wonder why she didn't?"

"She told me she tried, but it went straight to voicemail." Liz realizes this is partially her fault.

Marc looks at his incoming calls; there isn't one from Tess, but there is a brief voicemail from her saying, "Please call me as soon as possible." He notes the time, and Liz hears him say "*Merde!*" under his breath. "I was in France, visiting Collette's grave. There's no coverage there, or in the small town nearby, so it went straight to voicemail." He also realizes he'd put it on silent, as he wasn't in the mood to deal with people after his graveside confession. He continues to ramble off a few other curse words in his native French. "*Nom de Dieu*! I need to remember to go in and remove the record of her calling me on her cell phone."

Liz picks up her tablet, unlocks it, and taps a couple of icons signing into an app. "What's her number? I'll fix her call log from here." She sighs, as Marc rattles off Tess's number from memory. "You knew this was a possibility. What if you hadn't been able to get through to her? It's not like you could have transformed her." Liz reminds him.

"I know, I *know*! I'll make myself scarce this week. Check out some of the chaos in the Middle East, and give her mental scabs time to heal over, then we'll see." He reassures her. "I need to go deal with something now. The reason she was looking for me was her ex, Colton, got out on parole today, and apparently, he was coming after her to get revenge. She was worried about it this afternoon, and I told her if he ever gave her any trouble, to call me." He explains.

"Are you sure you aren't in over your head emotionally on this?" She asks.

"I'm just going to pay him a little visit. I'm not going to do anything to him other than encourage him to forget her and move on with life. Can you monitor her this week? Make sure everything's okay?" He asks.

"Of course, but you must figure out what to do with her if something like this happens again. You can't keep fighting her tooth and nail to redact her memory every time she stumbles on to your, or *our* little secret." Liz reminds him. "I want you to come by the office as soon as you're done. We need to talk about this face-to-face."

"I know. I also realize with every subsequent memory wipe, the risk of it not holding will increase." There's frustration in his voice. He thinks, *though with her, I just hope the first one holds.* He remembers chasing her consciousness until he could barely sense it anymore, but something didn't feel quite right, like she'd gotten away from him mentally, though he double checked, and her memories are thoroughly redacted.

He hangs up with Liz, ports back to a shadowed area behind the bar, and locates Colton with his mind. He doesn't want to confront him inside and cause a scene, so he waits outside until a man who looks close to the one in Tess's memory, except older, worn and quite drunk stumbles out. He can sense the anger in his mind and touches it briefly, confirming the object of his rage is Tess. He watches him stumble toward a beat-up motorcycle that looks like it's been collecting dust for a while, keys in hand. He's tempted to let him wrap his motorcycle around a tree, or even let his anger get the best of him. Marc hesitates, but takes the better path.

"Excuse me sir, are you sure you're in any state to drive?" Marc pretends to be a good Samaritan.

"What's it to you *assssshole*?" He slurs and staggers toward Marc belligerently.

"It's a lot to me if you're planning to hurt someone I know in your drunken stupor and hate filled little mind." he says quietly but calmly, catching Colton's eye.

The man goes quiet but continues to move into the shadows where Marc has once again retreated. *Thank goodness! He doesn't share Tess's shielding abilities.* Marc thinks as he easily manipulates the man and his mind. Marc dislikes touching his mind, but reaches into it and draws Colton to him mentally. "You're going to forget about Tessa Waterford. She did what she had to, and you should consider she did you a favor by not letting you continue walking that path. You'll also get your life together, move on with it, and *leave* her out of it. I'd also suggest you strongly consider cutting back on the alcohol, and perhaps consider relocating to another town as soon as your parole allows. Should you go after Tess, you'll have to deal with *me.*"

He flashes his fangs at the intoxicated man. "You won't remember any of this except to comply, and if you don't, then I'll have no difficulty finding you. Do you *understand*?" Marc adds.

Now halfway sober, Colton says "Y... yes sir...." while staring at the fangs in Marc's mouth, a cold chill runs down his spine as he knows what he's seeing is real, and there will be consequences for disobeying, that much he'll remember even as the memory of Marc's fangs is erased from his conscious mind.

"I strongly suggest you get a cab home and come back for your motorcycle tomorrow when your head's clear. Tess would still mourn you..." *and feel guilty as hell.* He thinks. "if you wrapped yourself and your bike around a tree." Marc says and disappears.

Colton shakes his head and goes back inside, asking the bartender to call him a cab. He's completely forgotten about his wish for revenge on Tess, and barely even remembers her.

Marc appears in Liz's office where she's waiting for him, feet bare and kicked up on her desk as she leans back in her chair. "So, what's the plan?" Liz's tone softens, thinking, *Dette situasjon er helt Texas!* (Nor: slang–This situation is totally insane) *It's also partly my fault, but we've got to get this under control NOW!*

"I'll come in on Monday morning to see if she has any reaction to me other than the normal one, then I'll head out of town for a week to give her memetic scabs time to heal." He yawns after the trying evening, and sits on the back of Liz's sofa, facing her at her desk.

"Alright." Liz sits up again. "I'll do my best to monitor her, but I can't be sure I'll pick up on everything with that mind of hers. Hopefully, it took. What exactly happened?"

"She was in danger from her ex, Colton. His nickname's Ox, *big* guy. He got out on parole, immediately got drunk, and wanted to get even with her for turning him and the others in. I took care of that. He won't be a problem." He gives her a wide grin. "She must have seen me and followed me into an alley and saw me feeding, and realized what she was seeing. She took off, and I was waiting for her at her home. By the way, she's difficult to use mind-compliance on. I thought I had her under control, but then she nearly put her heel through my left foot. Unfortunately, I ended up having to feed from her to shock her into dropping her focus. Her shields fell, and I could redact her memories."

"Hm... *took care* of the ex? Aren't we protective?" she asks with a slight grin.

"He was planning to break in and beat the hell out of her! I could've done worse than scare the crap out of him and plant the strong suggestion he get a life and forget about Tess." He returns the grin.

"You realize this means we have to make some decisions about Tess soon. Playing it by ear's not going to work long." Liz frowns. "Not if she's already discovered the truth this quickly."

"I still think she'll be a valuable asset to us if she can be turned, and as much as I hate dealing with *Them* directly, if it comes down to it, I'm willing to approach Them personally to ask them to intercede." He ports out before Liz can lecture him again.

After Marc leaves Liz's office, she says out loud "For your sake, I hope They're willing, but I doubt it." She vanishes and the lights go out in her office.

FUGUE

It's early Saturday afternoon, and Tess's living room is still dark because all the curtains are still drawn. The TV flashes light onto the walls nearby, and a sudden, overly loud commercial makes Tess stir. She looks up and her cable box clock says 1:07. Tess closes her eyes again, thinking it's 1:07 a.m., but hears a lawn mower roaring outside her home. She wakes fully, looking for her phone, only to discover it's still in her jeans pocket, and she's been sleeping on it. The battery's nearly dead, but she's able to see it's not the middle of the night, but early afternoon. She stares at the light peeping through the small gaps in the curtains, trying to make sense of it all.

What the Hell? 1 p.m.? She thinks, sitting up, and looking around. *Crap! I'm going to be stiff for days after sleeping in that chair so long. Speaking of crap, I feel like it.* She's light-headed and puts her head back down on the soft back of the recliner. *Maybe I'm coming down with something. Wait, I was in my bed when I fell asleep, I'm certain of that. Have I been sleepwalking? And 1 p.m.? That means I slept nearly 20 hours! I've never slept that long before. Maybe I'm getting sick? Maybe I just needed the sleep. After all, I've been putting in lots of extra hours along with everything else.*

There's a sudden flash of movement and a furry lump of cat settles heavily on Tess's stomach, staring at her and meowing loudly. She moves up her chest and rubs all over her face. "*Holy crap*, Mabel! You scared the *shit* out of me!" Her heart pounds unusually hard. She strokes Mabel for a few minutes, which calms her, then slowly crawls out of the recliner and takes Mabel to the kitchen, more than once feeling light-headed and bracing herself from falling. She starts to open a can of cat food, but the side of her hand hurts when she grips the can opener. She turns her hand to look, and it's badly bruised.

How the hell did I do that? I don't remember... Her thoughts trail off while attempting to recall what happened. Not only is it bruised, but there are also a couple of minor cuts on it with dried blood and a big splinter right below her little finger. She feeds Mabel, and then washes her hands. She notices there's a can in the garbage rather than in the recycle bin. "Okay, either I was a lot more out of it than I thought, or someone else fed you last night." She says, stroking the cat. She turns to go out and looks up, noticing matching spots of dried blood line up to the cuts on her hand on the door, like she'd hit it with her fist and small bits of rough wood caused the cuts.

"Okay, now this is getting bizarre." She says, grabbing a rag and cleaning the blood spots off the door. She heads to the bathroom. She goes in and notices her clothes from the day before hung up on the shower curtain rod. She stops for a moment, pondering, *Okay, I do remember taking those off. I was soaked from running in from the car. What I don't remember is how I got these clothes on. I must be really losing it. Did someone drug my soda yesterday?* She snaps herself out of that momentary distraction and continues with what she was going to do. She sterilizes a sewing needle with rubbing alcohol and carefully picks at the embedded splinter, working it out of her hand. She wracks her brain, but all these things she must have done are a blank in her memory, like she has mild amnesia, but the evidence is there. *Maybe I fell and knocked myself out, and just don't remember? Could I have had some sort of fit or seizure? Weird.* She takes a shower, but has to sit once or twice on the edge of the tub from dizziness. She dries off, puts a proper bandage on her hand, finds some clean clothes and sits on her bed. *Screw it!* She thinks and orders delivery pizza. She drags out her laptop and cell phone, checking her email and phone messages as her phone was on silent. The last number in her call log looks familiar, but she doesn't recognize it. Liz deleted both her call record to Marc, and to the police, eliminating clues that might trigger her memory.

She hits redial. "Hello?" Says a familiar voice on the other end.

"*Alex?* Is that you? How've you been? I see you called yesterday. I must have been sleeping when you called. What's new?"

78

She's oblivious to their conversation from the night before.

"Tess, are you *okay*? We spoke last night, remember? I told you Colton was out and looking for you. I'm guessing he didn't find you or we wouldn't be having this conversation."

"Wait, you say we spoke last night? I honestly don't remember it! Something weird is going on. I must have been sick or out of it. I came home early and napped and didn't wake until 1 p.m. this afternoon feeling like I'd been through the wringer. I must have even fed my cat in my sleep." She says, wondering what else may have happened. "You say Colton is out and looking for me? I can't believe he'd do anything to me, though. He was all talk and no balls!"

"You know, he was pretty sloshed when I saw him. He's probably sleeping it off somewhere. Still, please be careful! Keep your doors locked! Prison can change people, Tess." Alex says.

"I'll keep that in mind...." She trails off. "Hey, stay in touch, okay? I need to do a few things this morning, oh, afternoon. But I want to catch up soon, okay?" Her mind focuses in on the 'keep your door locked' part but she can't remember why.

Tess spends the day feeling unfocused. She's lethargic, and feels rather weak. She ends up spending a lot of the day in her recliner. She flips through the channels on her TV and a Back to the Future marathon is on. She sits, zoned out, dozing off occasionally, and is in bed before 10 pm.

She wakes Sunday morning feeling better but has the feeling she had odd dreams all night. She can't remember any of them. She thinks, *God! I hate that! When I know I've had some vivid dreams, I wake up, and poof! They're completely gone.* She spends the day reading a new sci-fi novel she recently downloaded, and before she knows it, it's time to eat and go to bed. Monday mornings come early these days since she's working again. She crawls into bed; Mabel follows her and curls up beside her. Tess reflects on the weirdness of the weekend, feeling like there's a mystery to unravel, but when she tries to focus and remember the mystery hours, she gets a headache, and an aversion to trying again. She sets her alarm, turns off her bedside light, and sleeps.

Come Monday

Tess oversleeps her alarm, gets up, gets dressed as quickly as she can, and falls back on old habits, grabbing a piece of leftover pizza from the one she'd had delivered Saturday. She couldn't muster the energy to make food Saturday, or even get in the car to go get something. She grabs a huge coffee on her way to work, alternately drinking coffee, and eating her cold pizza while she steers with her left hand. Tess gets to work, and rushes in, cursing herself for being late. She thinks, *Shit! How could I sleep through my alarm? It was practically next to my damn ear, and I still didn't hear it.* She goes in through the front door and sees Kari looking at her with an odd expression.

"Sorry, I'm late, Kari. I set my alarm but somehow slept through it." Tess says apologetically.

"Not to worry! It happens to all of us now and then." She smiles, but Tess can't help but feel like Kari's looking at something besides her face or eyes. Tess feels a hint of that weird tingling on her scalp again, but ignores it, and heads to her cubicle, but Kari stops her. "*Oh!* Tess, Marc wants to see you when you get settled. Don't worry! He's not upset about you being late. He's got to go out of town this week, so wants to make sure you're on target with your projects before he leaves."

"Okay, I'll just get settled in first." Tess scurries down the hallway, feeling bad for being late. She gets to her cubicle, tosses her purse and cell onto her desk, and boots up her computer, doing her best to ignore Jason, who's staring at her from across the room, like she's a dessert to a man on a diet. *I wish he'd go away. Find another, fucking job. He makes my skin crawl.* She thinks while waiting for her computer to boot all the way up. The stress of him leering at her when she's already starting off the week by being late makes her temper shorter than usual.

Once she's checked for any internal messages and synced her tablet, Tess gathers her project folders and heads to Marc's office. His door's open; he's already sitting in a chair by the meeting table when she knocks politely on the frame.

Marc looks up and smiles. "Good morning! I guess you got my message? Come, sit." He motions for her to sit in the adjacent chair. He subtly scans for any signs of anxiety or memory 'leakage' but is careful not to set off her natural shields, as that could trigger the thing he hopes to avoid, a resurgence of memory. He senses some anxiety, but there's enough in her public mind to indicate it's mostly because she overslept, and not about him.

Tess sits in the proffered chair, saying, "Yeah, is everything okay? Isn't this rather sudden?" Tess is nervous about Marc not being there, especially with Jason leering at her again this morning.

"Yes, more or less. We have a foreign branch with some issues. Let's just say I need to go over and do some clean-up work." He answers vaguely, but truthfully. "Anyway, I wanted to pick up where we left off Friday with your projects and make sure you have enough to work on while I'm away. Did you get to do anything over the weekend, or did you take a break?"

Tess smiles nervously. "I kinda took a break. I must have been completely brain-dead Friday night, 'cause I went home, napped and can't remember squat until Saturday afternoon when I woke up. I felt really out of it, so I guess maybe my body forced some downtime on me."

"You've been working hard lately. You needed it. Anyway, I may not be reachable for a few days depending on the local phone service." He smiles, again carefully scanning her mind for any cracks in her memory. "But Liz can reach me if you can't."

Tess sits, putting the folders out where they can both see them, and continues where she left off Friday, going through each project, one-by-one, including her ideas and plans for each. Marc's mind wanders from both the individual projects, and from his attempts at reading Tess, to thinking about how much he admires her. *She's brilliant,*

82

creative, and talented in so many ways. Such a shame she isn't compatible. He thinks, forcing himself to turn his attention back to Tess's work.

"So, it sounds like you've got plenty to keep you busy while I'm away. If you need anything, help with a project or anything around here, talk to Kari or Liz, okay?" He says, giving her a friendly pat on the arm as he stands.

"Thanks, I really appreciate that. When will you be back?" She asks.

"In about a week. If there's anything urgent, let Liz know; she'll be able to reach me." He walks Tess to the door and closes it as she goes out.

Marc leans against his closed door and reaches out to Liz telepathically. *As far as I can tell, she's fine. No memory leakage. I'm going to head over to Gaza now. Got a path from Theo from the Athens office. His team was out on a mission when there was an Israeli missile attack, and he lost contact with them. I'm assuming it will be more a search and recover mission than rescue, and a long recovery in Medical for them. Hopefully, any weak spots in Tess's memory redaction will settle before I come back from Gaza. She was anxious about something, but it was mostly connected to being late this morning, and... possibly Jason? Please keep an eye on him. There's something about him that worries me, especially when I'm not there to watch him.*

Okay, I'll keep an eye on him as well as her. Hopefully, her memories will settle. You lucked out this time, but we're going to have to talk about some sort of contingency plan in case this happens again. We don't need the risk of exposure, nor do we want her psychologically damaged by all this. Liz paths.

I know! Not sure what's gotten into me. I rarely let my emotions get the best of me like this. He paths.

Liz doesn't reply, but thinks, *for an empath, Marc can be pretty clueless about his own feelings. Unfortunately, he may be heading for an emotional crash.*

FLOOD STAGE

Tess heads back to her desk, puts her Bluetooth headphones on, and works on her projects, immersing herself in music and work. She pushes away the feeling Jason is drilling a hole in her back, leering at her every few minutes now that Marc has left the office for the week. It's creepy, but she swears she can feel him leer at her, like it's somehow tangible. Lunchtime comes, and she and Amy go down to a local deli for lunch, coming back about 12:45 p.m.

Mid-afternoon, Tess realizes she's out of paper layouts for making rough mockups before doing her HTML coding and graphics. She goes to the copy room to make some copies of the last blank one, so she can continue working. The copy room is down a side hallway from the main room where all the cubicles are, away from the lobby and other offices. The room is small, about the size of one of the smaller offices. The copy machine and a large, color laser printer are in the room. Shelves lined with paper, toner, and other supplies line one wall. A couple of older, nonfunctional desktop computers lie on the floor in front of the shelves waiting for service or to be wiped and taken to the dump. While she's in there, Jason comes in, and closes the door behind him, surprising Tess. She glares at him briefly, turning back to her copying. Anxiety makes her heart rate skyrocket, and while she isn't aware of it, her shields go up.

He leans against the door, like a human barricade to keep her from getting out. "So, I hear the boss's gonna be out of town for a week?" His tone makes her skin crawl and part of her knows she's in danger, but plays it cool. She thinks, *People like him get off on women being afraid. Maybe if I don't act afraid, he'll tire of this and go away?* She knows that's unlikely. Once Jason sets his mind on a target, he's the kind that will obsess over it, and she's just confirmed she's his chosen target.

85

"Yes, he's away on business, but he should be back in a week." She tries to sound matter of fact and hid her fear. "Can you please open that door back up? It gets hot in here from all the machines." She knows if she demands it, he won't do it. *Shit! I SO do NOT need this!* She thinks.

The copier jams and gives her a loud error beep, distracting her, and the next thing she knows, he's right behind her, way too close for comfort. "Well, you know the old expression? When the cat's away...." He has a slimy, lopsided grin, puts one hand on her behind, and attempts to grope her breast with the other.

"BACK! OFF! NOW! JASON! GET! THE! FUCK! AWAY! FROM! ME!" She raises her voice, saying each word clearly and with a slight pause between words, anger and fear making her bold.

"Or what? You'll call for help? Don't think your patron saint will come running this time. And I doubt big, bad soldier Amy will even hear us way down here, with the door closed, and her headphones on." He doesn't back off an inch.

"I MEAN IT! BACK THE FUCK OFF!" She raises her voice another level. She fights to squeeze away from him enough to elbow him in the gut as Amy taught her, but he has her pinned between himself and the copy machine, certain he can convince her to see things his way, as has happened with other women he's wanted.

"*Come on!* You need a guy to give it to you." He pushes against her from behind and sleazily whispers in her ear. "If you think Marc is ever going to be there for you, you're crazy. I've heard he doesn't get involved with anyone. Probably as *gay* as Liz and Kari."

"IF YOU DON'T GET THE *FUCK* AWAY FROM ME RIGHT NOW, I'LL PRESS HARRASSMENT CHARGES YOU *FUCKING ASSHOLE!*" She says as loudly as she can. Her head is throbbing painfully from the stress. She'd scream, but he has her pinned with her diaphragm against the edge of the copier.

"*No*, you won't." He sneers confidently.

Tess's mind reels, screaming inside, wishing someone, *anyone*, would come stop this insanity. The door to the copy room swings open with a thud against the wall, and Liz asks, "Everything alright in here?"

Thank God! Tess thinks and breathes a sigh of relief as he backs off hurriedly. She unpins herself and pushes past Liz without looking back. She runs to her desk, puts her face down into her folded arms, feeling like her heart is pounding its way through her ribs. Her head's throbbing and she's shaking like a leaf.

"Are you okay, Tess?" Amy asks.

"Yeah, just that *bastard*, Jason!" Her voice wavers, and she lifts her head and wipes tears away with her hand, trying to focus on Amy, but the light makes her head split with renewed pain, so she puts her face back down into the darkness between her crossed arms on the desk. Tess sobs between words. "He had me pinned in the copy room, and now I'm getting a *hell* of a migraine." She whimpers as a new wave of pain and nausea hit her.

"You've got to report him. He should be fired for that crap, even arrested." Amy urges.

"Yeah, I know, but he's the kind that will retaliate, even if he has to stalk me. I've been through that before. I had to get a restraining order on my ex." Her mind wanders to Colton and what Alex said about him coming after her. *How could I forget that?* She thinks. "Besides, Liz already knows something happened. She was the one who interrupted him." She randomly thinks back to Friday night, and has an odd experience, she gets an aversion to remembering that evening. Her nausea and headache increase and she wants to wretch. She feels a gentle touch on her shoulder, startles, but realizes it's not Jason.

Liz asks, "Tess, are you okay? Did something happen back there I should know about?"

Tess looks up at Liz; her eyes a sliver as she squints in pain from the well-lit room. "He's an ass, that's all." She's barely able to keep her eyes open from the pain and light sensitivity. "I... I don't want to make a big deal about it, but I don't want to deal with him, period!"

"I'll see about transferring him out of here, but right now, my concern is you. You look like you're in pain, did he hurt you?" Liz crouches down to eye level with Tess. She tries to touch her mind, and notices her visibly flinch from the feather light incursion. "Headache?" She asks.

Tess nods carefully. "He didn't physically hurt me, no. But I was sure he was going to if you hadn't come in. Yes, I'm getting a killer migraine, so, if you have some migraine meds around here, I can try that, but I left my prescription meds at home. Haven't had one in ages, and this one feels like my head's gonna explode!" Tears of pain and stress flow.

"I don't think we have any here, but even if someone does, you should go home." She says aloud, but thinks, *This is not good. Such a psychological trauma so close to everything this weekend. Will have to ask Kari to watch for signs of PTSD.*

Tess is shaking violently. "Can't drive like this, not even sure I can walk straight. It might help if I can lie down in a dark room for a while." She whispers.

"You can use the sofa in Marc's office. I'll check on you soon. I need to do a few things, and if you're still not feeling well, I'll get our staff doctor to check on you." She says.

"No. Don't need a doctor, it's just a migraine." Tess whimpers.

Liz turns to Amy. "Can you help her get to Marc's office? I need to go deal with something." She gives Amy a knowing look implying Jason is about to get his ass handed to him.

"Sure thing. Come on, Tess, lean on me." Amy stands and reaches out a hand to her.

"Thanks." Tess whispers weakly, cringing as she takes Amy's hand and leans against her. Amy moves her arm around her to support her, and Tess goes down the hall, eyes closed against the bright light, and lets Amy be her eyes. They go into Marc's office, and she lies down, lights off, door closed. The office is blissfully quiet. Tess tries to relax and still the pain in her throbbing head. She nearly falls asleep, but starts at the feeling of warm, gentle fingers massaging her temples.

"What the?" Tess says, opening her eyes a crack.

"*Shh*! It's okay, Tess. My name's Sara, I'm the... doctor on staff here. I know you told Liz you didn't need a doctor, but she's

88

worried about you." Sara speaks gently, and soothingly.

It's okay, (groans) I can't remember having a migraine like this before, might be best to get it checked." She closes her eyes again, still trembling from pain and adrenalin.

"I'm going to try some techniques to help you relax, okay?" Sara explains.

"Hm, uh-huh." Tess mumbles, closing her eyes and wincing as the pain level spikes.

Sara massages Tess's temples, head and neck; working to relax her, while subtly sensing and scanning her carefully, so as not to increase the pain. It doesn't take her long to notice the buildup of psychic energy trapped in Tess's mind. She reaches out to Liz telepathically.

Liz, I see the problem. Why didn't you tell me she's a high-level potential? Sara paths.

Because she isn't. Technically, she's not compatible. Liz admits.

You've got to be joking, with her latent psychic levels? Sara paths, skeptically.

Yeah, I know. That's why she's here, an unexpected anomaly. She's not in the database but has a lot of the qualities and latent abilities one would expect to find in a potential. Marc convinced me to give her a chance and we've been observing her. He thinks maybe They might make an exception and make her compatible now. She explains.

What a shame! Had she been a potential, I'd have said the easiest solution would be to turn her. Have you spoken to our Benefactors about her at all? She asks.

No, you know how they are. They want to stick with tried-and-true methods. Though, it would be nice if they would. Marc may be developing some strong feelings for her. Anyway, what's causing her headache? Stress? Liz asks.

Yes, and no. She has what one would call the psychic equivalent of a hematoma. It's a swelling of psychic energy in her mind, with no place to go. What happened prior to onset? Sara asks.

She had a run in with one of the new potentials. He cornered her in the copy room and made advances. I'm going to transfer him to the Hendersonville office for now, pending a final evaluation. She says.

Ah! Fight or flight. She must have some latent telekinesis from the feel of the energy. My guess is, had she been able, that energy would have manifested and knocked him on his ass, or even across the room, but she has some sort of natural barrier that trapped the energy, creating the backlash. Sara explains.

Yeah, we've had run-ins with her natural barriers. They also keep us out telepathically. Didn't even think about them being two-way. This one's full of surprises. You know, she pushed Marc and Peder out of her mind during her job interview. What do you suggest we do? Liz asks.

That certainly would raise a few flags, wouldn't it? The energy swell needs drained. It will eventually diminish on its own, but it may take days, and I'm assuming you don't want her impaired for that long? Sara asks.

I'd rather she not be impaired at all, or in pain. Can you do anything for her? Liz sounds concerned.

Yes, I think so. Are you going to take her home? Sara lays a cold compress on Tess's forehead while pathing Liz.

Liz makes an executive decision, and says, *Yes, she's in no shape to drive.*

Good. I'll give you a little gadget that will slowly siphon off psychic energy, a little at a time, so it doesn't trigger her shields. You'll need to put it close to her; for example, her bedroom-within a few feet of her. Such a shame she isn't compatible! Been a while since I've seen this much psychic potential. She continues to evaluate Tess's psychic energy profile.

I know. When Marc comes back from Gaza, we'll have to make some decisions about her. If I didn't have a soft spot for him, I probably wouldn't have given her a job, even with her apparent skills. Just too risky, but he felt it was important. Liz thinks, *Best I not tell Sara Tess has already stumbled on what Marc is and he redacted her memory. That would complicate things.*

Sara can sense a mixture of sadness and regret from Liz. *Okay, Liz,*

I've temporarily reduced her pain level, but that won't last unless the energy gets drained, so you should probably come get her. Sara says seriously.

Is she in any danger? Liz asks.

Mostly pain, but there could be some risk if she has any blood pressure issues, but right now, while elevated, her blood pressure is good considering the pain and stress she's dealing with. Sara paths.

Liz enters the room quietly, sitting in an adjacent armchair near the sofa.

"Tess, Liz is here to take you home. Do you think you can walk on your own or do you need help?" Sara whispers.

Tess's eyes flutter open, and she tries to sit up, slowly. She sits up with effort, motioning for the nearest trash can with one hand while covering her mouth with her other, as a wave of undeniable nausea hits. Liz hands it to her, and she throws up.

"Ugh, this is *not* my day, is it?" Tess groans.

"Listen, Tess, I want you to go home, go straight to bed and no TV, Internet, reading, or any distractions; just sleep, okay?" Sara orders, sending subconscious signals for her to obey her medical orders.

"I don't think I can do much else." She allows Liz and Sara to help her up.

Sara places a small object in Liz's other hand. *Place it somewhere near her bed, the closer to her head, the better. It will cloak itself once activated.* Sara paths.

Liz and Sara help Tess up and into a rolling office chair and roll her to the lobby. Amy tags along to help, taking over for Sara. Liz and Amy help Tess stand and walk out of the building, while Kari and Sara hold the doors. Amy has Tess's purse, phone, and tablet, and fishes out her car keys, handing them to Liz. Liz gets Tess's car, they ease Tess into the passenger seat, and put her seatbelt on. Sara comes up and hands Tess a clean, plastic wastebasket, which Tess grasps to her chest like it might try to escape. She keeps her eyes closed as much as possible on the trip home; opening them here and there, long enough to tell Liz where to turn to get her home.

They pull into Tess's parking spot in front of her townhome, and Liz helps her into the apartment, gets her settled into bed, places the psychic siphon under the edge of her nightstand, and the plastic wastebasket next to her bed. The siphon blends in completely with the wood within a couple of seconds after activation.

Liz puts a card with a handwritten phone number on it. "Tess, here's my cell number. If you feel worse, call me, and I'll get Sara out here ASAP."

"Okay, thanks, Liz." She says groggily, then adds, "Hey, how're you gonna get back? You drove my car here?"

"Don't worry, Kari will come get me. Rest now. We'll see how you feel in the morning. Don't rush back if you aren't feeling well, okay?" She paths to Sara. *She's settled in at home. The siphon is in place.*

"Okay, I hate to lose the hours and fall behind on projects. I don't want to disappoint Marc, either." Tess knows she's got some extra expenses on her car coming due, so she worries lost hours will make her come up short.

Sensing Tess's worries about losing not only time, but income, she reassures her: "Don't worry about it, being from Scandinavia, I've set up a Scandinavian style sick leave policy. You'll still get paid. after all, we've already got a doctor's note for you. So, relax! I trust you to get your work done as soon as you're able, and I'm sure if something's urgent, Amy can pick up the slack." Liz pats her on the arm and sends a mental suggestion to sleep. Once Tess's breathing changes to a sleep pattern, she turns off the lights, and leaves Tess's room. She goes down the hall to the living room, feeds Mabel as Tess asked her to, and vanishes.

DISTANT DIVERSIONS

After his meeting with Tess, Marc ports home to change into proper garb, and then ports to a small, temporary shelter in Gaza. A dark-haired man with olive skin, angular features, and a stubbly beard is pacing anxiously, but stops when Marc ports in.

"Theo, sorry for the delay. There was an issue in Asheville that demanded my immediate attention. Have you heard from anyone on your team?" Marc asks as he walks over to the obviously stressed man, hand extended in greeting.

"Unfortunately, not. Nothing verbal or even telepathic, my friend." The man extends his hand to Marc, his worried expression never changing. "Come, sit, and I will tell you what I know." Theo Diamandis, from the Athens center, motions Marc over to a folding table with two chairs. There are maps spread out on the table.

Marc follows him over and sits, asking, "Any idea where they were when the missiles hit?"

"One of our strongest precogs, perhaps you know her? Ariadne?" Theo asks and Marc nods. "She foresaw a collapsed building and many children's bodies. She took a team of five with her to the various schools in the region to see if she could recognize anything. She felt she'd found the place but did not tell me which school it was before the first missile struck near a hospital, and they had to rush into action. In her vision, the children were all in a common room, such as a gymnasium, she believed." He pauses briefly to gather his thoughts, then continues. "I tried to see what she was seeing, and the team ran through the hallways after the missile hit, some distance away, until they found the gym, around 25 to 30 children huddled there, with no teacher. Most were crying. I saw she looked up at the ceiling and knew this was the place. They told the children to go to a classroom, that this room was not safe. As they were scurrying out of the room, a second missile hit near the school. The gym shook, and the ceiling cracked. As usual, her team was composed of strong telekinetics, who could help move rubble in rescue efforts. They kept the roof aloft until the children were out of the room. Then another missile shook the ground hard enough to cave in the roof despite their efforts. That is when all went silent, and I could no longer sense their minds."

Marc has difficulty focusing during Theo's recounting. He keeps worrying about Tess, and whether or not the memory block is holding. He reaches out to touch her mind, but pulls back, knowing touching her mind could cause her memetic sores to reopen. He forces himself to focus on what Theo is saying and makes a conscious effort to barricade his mind against anything coming from Tess. After being in her mind Friday night, he felt glimmers of her emotions during the weekend, and he can't afford to be distracted by them now, or act upon them and risk a resurgence of memory.

"Perhaps we should look at where the bombs fell? Do you have an overview of which schools were near missile hits?" Marc inquires.

"There were over thirty missiles. They were not large, but they did a lot of damage. They were intentionally targeting schools and hospitals because they believed Hamas were hiding weapons in them, believing these places would not be targeted." Theo shakes his head and lets out a sigh. "It is times like this, my friend, I question if our mission on our planet has any hope of success. These people intentionally targeted schools and hospitals! It is sadistic madness! Sometimes, it feels like humanity is becoming more and more cruel rather than more civilized."

"I know, but we have a duty to perform, and we must continue to do so. Our Benefactors believe humanity will eventually mature and become a truly civilized species. It's our duty to keep them from self-destructing before they can achieve that." Marc reassures him.

The two men compare a list of bomb strikes on a map, marking each of them, and eventually narrowing it down to one school. They check a live satellite and confirm much of the roof has collapsed.

"I'd say we start there." Marc suggests. The two men port out and reappear outside a heap of rubble surrounded by partially standing walls. They can see the remains of bleachers along one inner wall as they climb over a low spot in the remaining, outer walls. "My guess is, they're likely under this mess." Marc looks up and sees there are twisted ceiling beams where the roof partially caved in, and what remains above looks close to collapsing the rest of the way.

"I agree, but we must check to see if the children are still here and safe first. Rescue teams are spread thin, and it doesn't look like they've gotten here yet. The children may still be here, somewhere." Theo suggests.

"Agreed." Marc says as they walk over an enormous pile of rubble. "I can't sense any minds below us, so my guess is they are in stasis. Can you confirm?"

Theo closes his eyes and reaches out to his team's familiar minds, but gets nothing. "There is nothing here, but I do sense there are human minds nearby."

They walk across the pile, knowing their people will eventually be extricated, and would most likely recover in Medical, if the damage to their brains isn't too severe.

Marc says, "I feel them, too. I feel fear and sorrow coming from both directions. You go that way, and I'll go down this hall and track them. Our people will wait, but we must get the children out before the rest of the building collapses."

Marc moves down the hallway, navigating around rubble and fallen lockers. He follows the fear until he nears a classroom where it's strongest. Knowing the children are terrified, he reaches out and sends calming thoughts, while also linking with their minds' speech centers, tapping into their language. When he opens the door, the children are huddled together on the far side of the room. He must shove the door hard to get through, as something is blocking it. When he looks behind it, there are chunks of concrete, as well as the body of an adult woman, no doubt a teacher, who'd taken in the children to shelter them. Part of the ceiling must have collapsed and hit her in the head, likely killing her instantly, if the wound was any indication. He turns to the children and speaks to them in fluent Arabic, using the dialect they are all familiar with, so they might be more at ease with him, as a stranger. Had he come in speaking Hebrew, or even English, it would be harder to gain their trust.

He says, "I'm here to rescue you, but we must find a safe way out. Much of the building is unstable and might fall, and some of it already has." He reaches out with his mind and scans the room. He can smell fresh air coming from one wall where a large, free-standing closet is and makes his way to it. When he gets there, he feels a draft. The closet weighs several hundred pounds as it is made of solid wood, but he leans into it and pushes it out of the way. Behind it, there is a damaged window. They must have covered it with the closet until it could be repaired. Marc, who's wearing leather gloves, breaks out the remaining, jagged glass, then turns back to the children. "I will lift you out the window, but you must wait for me outside. *Do not* run off. I will take you to a shelter where they can help you find your parents."

He lifts each child effortlessly, mentally scanning them for any major injuries, and puts them through the opening, making sure they don't touch any of the glass splinters still lying on the sill. They wait, and when everyone is out, he reaches out his mind and cannot sense any others in his part of the building. He crawls through the window, which is a lot snugger fit for him than for the children and counts them all to make sure they are all still there, and none have run off. "Come, there is a shelter about a kilometer away."

He takes them there and hands them off to a female rescue worker, willing her not to ask him who he is, and hazing the woman's memory so she cannot describe him to authorities. A few minutes later, Theo comes in with another seventeen children, including one he is pulling on a makeshift stretcher made from plasterboard. Once the children are handed off, the two men move into the shadows, port out and reappear in the collapsed gym. "We need to get in one of our teams to move this rubble and get our people out. Have them dressed as rescue workers so we can avoid a human team finding our people. I'll let Sara know to expect casualties needing reconstruction." Marc says with a grimace.

The operation takes a couple of days and is starting to wrap up when he gets an incoming call on his tablet. He peeks at the lock screen notification and sees it's Liz. "*Merde...*" He mutters under his breath, knowing the only reason Liz would be calling him is if there's a problem with Tess. He wanders off to find a place to take the call.

WHEN THE DAM BREAKS

Tess can't help but drop off into sleep. The pain subsides as the si-phon drains the excess psychic energy and grounds it out. As she set-tles deeper into sleep, and eventually REM sleep, she dreams. She's back in the copy room; Jason's pinning her there. A feeling of help-lessness and fear triggers something deep inside her, welling up as panic. The scene shakes and shifts, and instead of the copy room, she's in her own living room, facing the inside of her front door, and feels someone behind her, pinning her there, but the feeling is differ-ent, not malevolent and overpowering, but she's still terrified.

Her dream swirls and mists away like a fog rolling through, and she's in her kitchen, cornered, back against her pantry shelf with a door that won't open, and she's unable to move. At first, it's Jason, leering, about to come at her, but his face blurs, changes, and comes back into focus, and it's Marc approaching her, speaking softly, but she can't quite hear what he's saying. She still can't move and feels trapped. She sees him open his mouth, canines expanding into over-sized fangs. Her heart pounds as he moves closer and sinks them into her neck, pain breaking her focus, and her mind spirals down into darkness, fading to black. The dream shifts again; this time, she's in an alley, watching Marc with some woman, discovering what he is; a *vampire*. On some level, she realizes time is out of order, and all of this was what led to him biting her in her own kitchen. Her heart is pounding, and her body and blanket are sweat soaked. She sits bolt upright in bed knowing this is not just a dream.

She sits there, breathing rapidly, heart still pounding, thudding in her ears, making her head throb even though the migraine has gone. She's rocking and shaking. "No! It's *not* possible! He can't be! It must have been a dream!" She says out loud, trying to convince herself, but she knows, in her gut, that it's true. She hadn't slept Friday night away. These were the lost memories from Friday night. Everything falls into place: *Oh, God! The forgotten conversation with Alex, my hand injury and damage to the door. Even how I woke up in my recliner instead of my bed. I was in town, discovered what Marc is, and he was HERE, in my home!* She cringes as the rest hits her. *He really bit me, drank my blood! And somehow, made me forget it all!*

She lies back down, but throws off the damp blanket, kicking it off the bed. She stares at the ceiling, attempting to reconcile the insanity of her newly recovered memories with the physical evidence this all explains. *Damn! How can I go back to work there? Knowing... oh, Hell! What if he can tell I know again? He said he'd recognize my mind anywhere. Telepathic? Fuck!* She thinks, covering her face, as tears flow. She's shaky, but gets up and goes to the bathroom, inspecting her neck for any signs of bite marks, but there's nothing. She splashes cold water on her face, noting the puffiness around her eyes. *Am I going mad? I feel like it, but it all makes too damn much sense!* She grabs a spare blanket and a beach towel from her closet, laying the towel on her bed where the dampness from sweat has soaked into her mattress. Quickly, she takes a shower and dresses in pjs before she crawls back into bed, curling up on her side with the blanket pulled over her, halfway covering her head as symbolic protection. She lies there, in the dark, reviewing the dream memory repeatedly. Little details come back with each once over, including things he said. *He could have killed me, done anything to me. Why didn't he? If he's a vampire, a monster, why didn't he act like one? Why has he been so nice to me since the start? Maybe I should warn the others? They'd never believe me.* She thinks. Eventually, she falls asleep again, her face is puffy and wet; her mind beyond exhausted.

The next morning, she's woken by flickering light coming in from the window. Mabel's there, watching birds, and making chittering sounds from the windowsill. Her tail twitches wildly and moves the curtains enough for light to flit here and there in the room. Tess rolls over away from the window, mind blissfully blank for the moment. She slowly stirs, the fog lifting from her mind, and the memories flood back in, this time, less of a dam bursting and more like an ocean wave crashing over her, complete with the sting of a few jellyfish and sharp shells. Her eyes are still stinging, puffy, crusted, and her nose is clogged. *Something tells me I should call out this morning.* She thinks back to her reflection in the mirror during the night, *How could he have bitten me Friday and there not be any wounds or scabs?* She throws off the blanket and heads to the bathroom to run a warm bath and soak, unknotting the tension in every muscle in her body. Afterwards, she gets dressed in something comfortable and sits with her cell phone in hand. Still feeling shell-shocked. She pulls out Liz's cell number and dials it.

"Hello?" Liz says.

"Hi, Liz. It's Tess." Her voice sounds unusually gravelly and muffled from her clogged nose.

Liz listens to her voice, already knowing Tess is not at her best. "Tess, how are you feeling? Is the migraine gone?"

"Yeah, the pain's gone, but I'm out of it, so I'm going to stay home today, if it's okay with you?" Tess feels torn between taking off when she isn't really sick, and knowing she needs time to wrap her head around everything before she goes near Inspiration Inc, with or without Marc being there.

"Of course! Get some rest. It takes time to recover from migraines that bad. Are you sure you don't want me to have Sara come by?" She asks, and Tess hears voices in the background that sound like Kari and Peder.

"No, I don't think she needs to come by. I just need some time for my head to clear completely." She thinks, *and figure out how I'm going to deal with having a vampire for a boss without letting on that I know.*

"Alright, I've got to get back to a meeting here, but I expect to hear from you later. Call me if you need anything, okay?" She hangs up.

Tess grabs some food from the fridge; more stale delivery pizza from Saturday, but it will do. She adds some extra cheese, canned mushrooms, and microwaves it, sitting with it and a double-sized mug of coffee at her computer. *Thank goodness the migraine and nausea gave up. Now, I only have this dull ache making it hard to even think.* She goes to Google and searches for "real vampires", but mostly finds information about the underground Goth culture, a history of Vlad Tepes, a few websites on psychic vampires, and multiple sites selling prosthetic vampire teeth for wannabes. She spends most of the day searching, bookmarking, reading and even copying and pasting info into a Word document when relevant. She stops occasionally to scarf down some leftovers or grab some snack food from the cupboard, but leaves the TV off, and doesn't even touch her book from Sunday, even though she left off as it was starting to get good. Her mind has become hyper-focused on one thing: the mystery of Marc Girard.

About 10 p.m., her brain refuses to absorb any more information from her hours of searching. *Those were not dental prosthetics or crowns. I know what I saw and felt! They came down into place and were functional. But how did he make the wounds heal up? Must be some sort of survival mechanism. If you hide the wounds, and make someone forget, then no one would know it ever happened.* She thinks. Finding little she didn't otherwise know, she changes her tactic for one last search, searching for anything she can find about Marc himself. There's very little online about him beyond a basic profile on Inspiration Inc.'s website. She can't find an address for him, nothing on LinkedIn, classmates.com, MyLife, or even a personal profile on Facebook, or any of the other multitude of social media sites. She even searches public records and criminal background checks, but it doesn't even spit out so much as a birth date. "Odd, considering you supervise a website development department." She says out loud, in frustration. In the end, she finds nothing of any consequence.

Tess formulates some basic conclusions. *He said he'd know my mind anywhere, and could go into my mind, which means it's going to be damn hard to keep it from him. I doubt anyone would believe me if I tried to warn them.* She leans back in thought. *My only option is to quit, and before he comes back. I* suppose I can get my projects done if I work hard the next three days and through the weekend. I'll tell Liz I don't feel safe since the incident with Jason. I hate to do it. I really like working there, but what choice do I have? I really don't know what he'll do to me if he finds out I still know." Her eyes tear up. *It's not like I can go up to him, tell him I know, won't tell anyone, and expect him to say 'well, okay then! I'll trust you!'* Her fear and uncertainty shift to resolve and sadness; *I don't want to leave Inspiration Inc. I've been happy working there. Hell! Even working with Marc, but if I stay, I'm probably putting my life in danger. Okay, I'll go in early and get working, try to finish my projects, and let Liz know on Friday I can't stay. I hope she'll accept I can't give two weeks' notice.*

She pulls up Marc's company profile, attempting to reconcile his photograph with what she saw Friday night with the man she's gotten to know, and enjoys working with, even has felt a connection to. *Now I know that's a dead end. Or an UN-dead end?* She laughs, half giddy. She shuts down her computer, feeds Mabel, and gives her some cuddles, grabs a snack, and gets ready for bed. *I'll go in early and get caught up. I'll figure something out to tell Liz. Once Marc's back he's bound to realize I know what he is.* She thinks, crawling into bed, so exhausted she's asleep in less than five minutes.

Again, she dreams about Marc. At first, it's a repeat of what happened, but then it takes on a more surreal tone: Marc's in his office, wearing the stereotypical black Dracula cloak with high collar, on top of his casual work clothes. Tess is wearing a long, slinky, 'Morticia' style dress with a low-cut collar, and blood red, long, press-on nails. She goes into his office, bringing in stacks of folders, and putting them down on his desk. He looks up at her and gives her a hungry grin, followed by his feeding on her as though it's part of her job description, and oddly enough, it feels good, not painful. Otherwise, she dreams of waking up in a stereotypical coffin, like him, with fangs, and a lust for blood.

Her alarm goes off at 5:30 a.m. and she wakes thinking *coffee, tea, or my neck? Ugh!* She reaches up and feels her neck for bite marks, just in case. She lets herself have five minutes to review what she can remember of her dreams, and then types in a synopsis in her iPhone Notes app.

She dresses quickly, and pulls her hair back into a messy bun, skips makeup, feeds Mabel, and heads to work early. Her stomach is in knots and she can't bring herself to have anything for breakfast, fearing she might lose anything she eats. She stops and gets a large coffee, hoping the caffeine will keep her awake and help her focus.

She's there even before Kari and Liz. She lets herself in, not turning on the lobby lights, but finding her way to her space, where she turns on her own lamp. She puts on her headphones and works on her projects, going into hyper-focus mode.

About 8:45 a.m., the lights turn on in the main room and she flinches, not knowing who it is. She turns around and peers out the opening of her cubicle. When she sees it's Amy, she relaxes a little, waves at her, and goes back to work.

Amy puts her stuff down in her space, then stands, leaning over the short wall and into Tess's space, tapping one earpiece on Tess's headphones. Tess startles and pulls her headphones halfway off. "Hi, Amy. Sorry! I'm not trying to be antisocial. I really need to catch up on lost time." She smiles at her, but even Amy senses something's off.

"Okay, Tess. Maybe we can go out to lunch today? Grab something at the deli?" Amy asks, concerned for her friend.

"Maybe, but I've been here since before 7, so I'll probably eat early and get back on the clock. I really want to get this done before Marc comes back, so he'll be surprised." Tess says, making it sound as reasonable as possible.

"I don't think you need to go out of your way to impress him. He's already impressed with you, if you ask me." Amy laughs, giving Tess a knowing grin.

Tess blushes, frowning at Amy. "Stop that! He's our boss! I can't afford to let myself end up in the same situation I was in at Digital Danger." Tess brushes it off casually.

"Somehow, I doubt Marc's anything like Colton, from what you've told me. And just think! If things develop between you two, then we could double date, or at least, have enough people to play D&D." She grins.

102

Tess laughs it off. "Please don't get me distracted. I can't afford to go off daydreaming about Mr. Unattainable, or I won't get anything done. It would have been nice... if I could have ended up with... with someone as... as nice as him, but I don't think it's in the cards. Let me get back to work, okay?" Tess puts her headphones back on before Amy can say anything.

A couple of other co-workers come in and settle into work. Tess keeps looking back at Jason's station, not really wanting to deal with him. Around 10 a.m., she peers over the wall and waves at Amy, who takes off her headphones.

"What's up?" Amy asks.

"Any idea where Jason is? I keep expecting him to show up, leer at me, and creep me out." Tess whispers.

"*OOOOH*! Liz didn't tell you? He's been exiled to the Hendersonville office and told to leave you alone or the next move will be out; possibly with a police report if he tries anything again. I told Charlie about what he did, and he told me to tell you if it happens again, he'll help you file a report, even though he's working at a high school. He's buds with some guys that deal with assaults and will make sure it's taken seriously."

Tess visibly relaxes, but not fully. "Thank, *God*! I was so afraid he'd be here today. He's the kind that would be angry with me for him getting caught. I'm pretty sure he came after me because Marc is gone. *God*! I can't stand that guy! I'm glad he's gone." *I sure hope he doesn't know where I live.* She adds to herself, getting flashes of him breaking in to her place. Then, she wonders: *who should I be more afraid of, Marc, a vampire, or Jason, a psychotic asshole? Jury's still out, but part of me is leaning toward Jason. After all, Marc could have done anything to me Friday. Yes, he bit me, but he could have done much worse, and Jason probably would have.*

"You're not alone there. I'm thankful they moved him. If he were still here, I might be the one up on assault charges for beating the shit out of his worthless hide! Of course, I do have Charlie at APD, but not even sure he could protect me after that." She laughs and feigns innocence.

"Hey, my stomach's rumbling, didn't eat this morning, so I'm gonna go take a quick break and eat something, but maybe we can go out later and grab something more? Sorry, if I was a bit off this morning. I was anxious *someone* might be a problem." Tess stands, phone, purse, and tablet in hand.

"You got it, girl! I was kinda worried about you this morning. You did get rid of your migraine, didn't you?" Amy absentmindedly takes off her glasses and wipes them clean.

"Yeah, migraine's gone, but let's just say I wasn't looking forward to having any confrontations today." Tess thinks, *from either man.*

Tess heads to the break room. No one's there since it's so early, so she looks in the fridge. She's learned there are always some odds and ends in there that are free to grab if someone gets hungry. Liz and Kari usually bring in a tray or two of these Norwegian style, open-faced rolls with salami, ham, scrambled eggs, or other stuff. She recently got up the nerve to try the *gravlaks* sandwiches they make; salmon cured in salt, sugar, and dill, and really likes it and is tempted to ask them for the recipe. She grabs a paper plate, and snags a *gravlaks* sandwich, one with salami and cucumber, and one with some sort of liver mousse. *Well, liver has lots of iron, and after Marc drank my blood, I probably need it.* Her thought oozes with sarcasm, but it's the only way she can deal with the reality of knowing her boss literally drank her blood.

She eats, initially checking her Facebook, email, and other social media. When done, she puts down her phone, rocks back in her chair, eating her *gravlaks.* She reviews her memories about Friday, intense emotions leak through her shields as she remembers his cornering her, biting, and feeding on her. She thinks back to the woman in the alley, wondering if she's okay. *I wonder what happened to her? Maybe it was consensual? Maybe she let him do it? Nah, if that were the case, she wouldn't have been staring off into space like a mannequin.* She dwells on what it felt like. She strokes her neck where he bit her. *It did hurt, but that went away. I wonder if there are any long-term effects? Am I going to sprout fangs or... or will I be like Renfield or something?*

***

Liz checks the overview of signed in employees, and notices Tess signed in at 6:48 a.m. *So early? That's odd.* She reaches out mentally to locate Tess and realizes she's in the lunchroom. *Hmm..., good time to check on her and make sure all's okay.* She heads over to the lunchroom, and is about to enter when she senses very odd, emotional energy from Tess. She stays right outside the room, and mentally eavesdrops on any stray thoughts coming from Tess, careful not to actively scan her, and potentially set off her shields. It doesn't take long before she realizes Tess remembers everything.

She closes her eyes and feels the pit of her stomach sink. *Time's up, Marc!* She thinks, then turns around and walks back to her office, shutting the door. She picks up her tablet and taps in a code. Marc appears in a Zoom-like video chat window; broken and burnt ruins of buildings around him. It's evening there and what little light there is, shows through the dust and smoke in the background. Liz hears distant gunshots and screams in between the rumble of heavy equipment.

"Liz? What's up? I'm wrapping up the main recovery here. Is something wrong?" He asks, concerned by her call.

Liz is reluctant to end Marc's little experiment, but clearly, the whole situation is crashing and burning. She hesitates, then says, "You need to come back ASAP. Tess remembers everything. She doesn't know about anyone but you so far, but she plans to quit before you come back."

"What? How? Are you sure?" He tries to find somewhere out of public view and away from some of the noise. He goes inside the shell of a building and turns on a light on his tablet so his face is lit up.

"There's no doubt about it. Her public mind and stray public thoughts were full of not only memories of Friday night, but worry about you finding out she knows, and how to break it to me she 'has to quit'. You should probably know there was an incident here on Monday after you left. I didn't tell you because I know how protective you are and didn't want you to rush back and potentially open her memetic wounds." Liz hesitates, waiting for some loud noises in the background on Marc's end to subside.

"What happened?" Marc shouts over the din.

"You were right about Jason. He waited mere hours after you left and went after her. He had her cornered and was making advances in the copy room. I got there in time, so nothing more than her being frightened happened, and we've transferred him down to Steve's department in Hendersonville for now, with a warning not to pull such things again, and to stay away from Tess." Liz hears him cursing up a storm in French. "Afterwards, she got a severe headache Sara says was a psychic energy build up, likely kinetic, trapped behind her mental barriers. Tess wrote it off to a stress-triggered migraine. From what little I could glean from her projected thoughts, Jason may have been the trigger for her memory resurgence." Liz's expression slips from an 'I told you so' mentality to one of sympathy. "I'm sorry, but you're going to have to try again or we're going to be forced to find some way to deal with her knowing. I can't risk one of us intervening and exposing more than you to her unnecessarily."

She sighs, then continues, "As it is, *They* won't be pleased we've put ourselves in an exposure situation." She leans over and types something into her laptop. "It's a good thing she synced her tablet with her home computer; the remote access software it installed is active, so I just ran a history scan on her home computer. She spent most of yesterday searching for information on 'real vampires', as well as about you. This means she's known for a day or longer. You're going to have trouble redacting that. You need to get back as soon as you can. I'll see if Peder can head over and wrap up for you." Liz's face looks worn as she thinks about what Tess will have to go through now. *I hope for her sake, he can make her forget everything, because the rest of today is going to be hard on her.*

"Thanks for letting me know. I'll wait for Peder, then get cleaned up, and head back. He'll need to coordinate with Sara to deal with our wounded." He pauses. "When I get there, we'll find some excuse to send her into my office. I'll take care of it." He ends the call, leaving Liz to think up an excuse to send Tess to his office.

DAMAGE CONTROL

Liz keeps half a mental eye and ear on Tess while she waits for Marc to return. After eating, Tess returns to her desk and works on her projects. Liz can sense her obsession with getting them done before she quits, so she doesn't leave anyone in a lurch. *Too bad she isn't compatible. That sense of responsibility is becoming less common these days.* She thinks.

About an hour after contacting Marc, Liz senses his return to the building, and gets a path shortly thereafter. *I'm back. Ask her to find some files in my office? Something she's not working on, say, The Biltmore Children's Foundation?*

She can sense Marc's internal turmoil about what to do with Tess. *What are you going to do?* Liz asks.

Not really sure. Wing it. he paths, waves of exasperation coloring his thoughts. *I guess I'll try to get her to cooperate; to let me redact her memory. With her shields, I'm betting that's the root of the problem. I must have missed something that let her memories break through under stress.*

I believe it was more than that. I'm pretty sure Jason played a part. What if you can't get her to cooperate, or she does, and it still doesn't work? She asks.

I'll let you know when I know. And please, no I told you so! He adds.

Okay, the ball is in your court for now. I'll touch base with Sara and see if she knows anything that can help with redacting larger portions of memory or dealing with her shields, in case this goes badly. Liz paths. *Expect her in about five minutes.*

Liz regrets what Tess is about to go through but goes over to her cubicle and puts on her best façade. "Hi, Tess, glad you're feeling better. Was surprised to see you'd signed in so early this morning." She gently puts her hand on Tess's shoulder.

Tess startles, but turns and smiles at Liz. "Yeah, feeling a lot better but wanted to get caught up so I'm back on track before Marc comes back. Wouldn't want to disappoint him." She flashes Liz a nervous smile. *Hell, I don't want to face him. If he finds out I remember, I don't know what to expect, so best to be long gone before he can figure it out.*

"Speaking of Marc," Liz notices Tess tense up at the mention of his name. "I need some files from his office. Would you mind seeing if you can find them for me? They're the files for the Biltmore Children's Foundation. I'm sure they're somewhere in his office, but I need to rush across town for an important meeting, and I'm running late. Will you please see if you can find them for me?"

As Tess heads for Marc's office, her heart speeds up and pounds, anxiety kick-starting it far more than her four coffees so far today have. "Yeah, sure, Liz, glad to. When's Marc coming back?" she asks anxiously.

"He's scheduled to come back Monday." Liz thinks, *I really hate having to put her through this, but what choice is there?*

"Okay. I'll put them on your desk if I find them." She says, getting up to go into Marc's office.

"Good luck... finding them." Liz watches her walk toward Marc's office, knowing this is going to be another rough afternoon for Tess. She, too, has grown fond of the young human and doesn't want to see her in distress.

Tess pauses briefly before going into Marc's office, thinking about the last time she met with him here. He certainly didn't act like a monster. *What if I'm wrong, and it was only a dream? A realistic and painful one at that.* She thinks, as she enters his office. She closes the door behind her. It's mostly dark even though it's nearly noon outside. *He must have closed his curtains before he left.* She tries to turn on the main light, but it doesn't come on, so she turns on his desk lamp, assuming the main light is burnt out and sorts through the stack of folders on the corner of his desk. His high-backed office chair is swiveled toward the window away from her. There's a click behind her, she looks back and sees the door's been locked.

Before she can walk over to unlock it, she hears, "Oh, *Tess*! What *am* I going to do about you?" Marc swivels his chair around to face her, leaning back in his chair, hands clasped together loosely in his lap.

She closes her eyes and breathes more rapidly. "Marc?" She swallows nervously.

"Obviously." He has a look of pity in his eyes as her fear, anxiety, and desperation wash over his empathic mind.

"I... I thought you were going to be out of the country until Monday?" She sounds calmer than she is, her mind is racing with thoughts of how to get out of there as fast as she can. *I've got to get out of here and out to the others. He wouldn't dare do anything with an office full of witnesses, would he? Can I even outrun him that far?*

"It would appear I left a little unfinished business here I had to rush back to deal with." He gives her a slight, non-threatening smile attempting to keep her from completely freaking out.

"Funny, Liz said you'd be out until Monday." She's unconsciously edging toward the locked office door.

"I believe her exact words were I am '*scheduled* to return on Monday'?" He grins, showing an unintentional hint of fangs.

Tess's heart rate and breathing double and her heart feels like it is pounding right through her chest, like the creature from Alien. She starts to turn and run for the door, but runs directly into Marc, who has somehow made it from his desk across the room to block her access to the door. He gently, but firmly, grasps her by her upper arms, and holds her still long enough to start a conversation with her.

He speaks as calmly as he can. "Tess, I thought by now you'd realize you can't outrun me. It's hard to outrun someone who can *teleport*."

A sudden understanding of how he got into her home and cut her off in the kitchen dawns on her. She realizes there's no way she can outrun him, or hide from him, and panic sets in. "*Please*! Don't kill me! I promise! I won't tell anyone!" She pleads.

He gives her a gentle shake to make her stop pleading with

him. "Look at me, Tess!" He gives her a mental push, so she makes eye contact with him. "As I told you Friday night, I'm *not* going to hurt you or *kill* you, but I need to make sure my secret's safe, and I really need your cooperation." He speaks slowly and calmly, maintaining eye contact with her the whole time.

"M... my cooperation?" She stammers out, confused, but it also takes her panic down a notch.

Now that she's finally listening to what he's saying, he slowly loosens his grip on her shoulders, and takes his hands off her arms all together. "Yes, I want..., I need to try again to make you forget all of this, but your mind is special. You have a natural barrier that makes it more difficult to suppress your memories. With most people, it's like they have an open window I can reach through and make them forget what I am, but not you. It's more like all your doors and windows are locked and the curtains are closed. I didn't intend to hurt you that night, only make you forget what you'd discovered." He says as calmly and non-threateningly as possible.

She lets go of her panic, but still has her guard up. "But if I forget what you are, what guarantee do I have you won't hurt or kill me later? I mean, if I don't know, I can't protect myself."

"I guess you'll have to accept my word I won't. I know that's difficult under the circumstances, but it's the best I can offer." Marc steps back and to the side, motioning toward the meeting area with one hand. "Sit, I really won't hurt you, but we need to find a solution to this." Accepting she can't get away from him, she plays along for now, and edges past him, never taking her eyes off of him, and sits on the sofa, pulling herself into the corner. She pulls her knees up to her chest and wraps her arms around them in an unconscious, defensive posture. "Relax. Did I hurt you Saturday? I promise, you *can* trust me."

She gives him an incredulous and angry look. "*Trust* you? You *bit* me and it *did* hurt!" She blurts out, sounding more confident than she is.

He sits on the other end of the sofa and takes a deep breath. "My intentions have always been good toward you. I didn't want to cause you pain of *any* kind, but I was desperate to get through your shield, for lack of a better term, and when I couldn't push through it telepathically, I hoped the brief pain and panic biting you would create would allow me to get through; and it seemed to work." He continues to speak in a soft, reassuring tone, attempting to regain her trust.

She sits quietly for a few seconds, her eyes shine with hints of tears. "But I remembered anyway."

He leans forward, but not enough to invade her rather expansive space, giving her a nod. "Yes, you did; and now we have a problem. I can't risk you exposing my secret. If others find out about me, especially the *wrong* people, then I'll have to go into hiding from people hunting me down. Some will want to kill me or study me in a lab like an animal, not a person. Let me ask you something, you obviously kept your role in the Digital Danger case as quiet as you could, am I right?"

"Yeah, at first, I kept it a total secret. Unfortunately, Colton figured it out and told others." Tess sighs, never taking her eyes off Marc.

"And why did you keep it secret?" Marc cocks his head to one side.

Tess doesn't respond right away, but eventually admits with a sigh of comprehension, "Because I didn't want the people involved, including Colton, to come after me. I guess you're saying it's the same with you then. You worry if people know, you'll be hunted and never get any peace."

"*Exactly!* While I have to go out and feed on people, 99.99% of those I've fed on were never aware of it even happening. I don't take more than they can safely lose, and I don't hurt them. In fact, there's a healing compound that's released when I bite someone that not only instantly stops the bleeding when I'm done, but promotes red blood cell regeneration and general healing. Tess, I *can't change* what I am, but I do my best to be a good person. Do I really deserve to have my secret made public and be subjected to an endless barrage of people wanting to hurt or even kill me?" Marc leans back against his end of the sofa and waits for an answer.

Tess's face softens, uncertainty taking the edge off of her fear and anger. "No, I guess you don't." She lets out a brief laugh under her breath. "Let me guess, I'm the 0.01%?"

"That, you are! But if we work together, I hope we can put you over in the other category, and you can go on with life, oblivious to what I am. The simplest solution is if I can finish what I started Friday night, and remove those memories from your conscious mind, but I can't be sure it will hold, unless you cooperate this time." He explains patiently.

She's been looking down, studying the pattern in the sofa fabric while listening, avoiding eye contact. She slowly looks up at his face. "Are you going to *bite* me again?"

Half joking, a slight twinkle in his eye, he says, "Not unless you want me to."

"Why would I want that? It hurt like *hell*!" She spits out.

"I *am* sorry about that. Normally, it wouldn't have. As I tried to explain, I needed the shock of the brief pain to break through; to make you drop your guard. Normally, there wouldn't be any pain, or memory of me biting someone." He gives her a slight, one-sided grin.

She gives him a look with an implied *'Screw that!'* "Uh, I'll pass. What... what if you can't make me forget this time either?" She asks, nervously thinking about what his alternative solutions could be.

"I'll have to figure out some way to ensure you keep my secret." He says, catching her thoughts of him draining her dry and dumping her body in the French Broad River or of one of her dreams where she wakes in a coffin, like him. Since she's thinking directly about him and in close proximity, he picks up on her thoughts and fears.

He rolls his eyes and sighs. "Tess, first, it goes against everything I am to kill you. I'll figure something out. As to making you like me, put it out of your mind. It's not possible."

"Did you *read* my mind? I thought you said you couldn't." She tenses up.

"Sorry, I can't easily go into your mind and read your thoughts and memories, but when you're thinking about what I might do and you're four feet away from me, it's hard to miss. I can sometimes read your public mind, the part where you sub-vocalize thoughts; especially when it's about me. But back to the subject, I can't make you like me." He leans a little closer to her.

"You can't? Isn't it like in the stories? Or were you born this way?" Her curiosity makes her feel a little braver.

"No, I was turned, ah, *transformed*, but..." He makes a deep, impatient sigh and a pause. "We really should be getting on with this, but if it will make you trust me more, it's a genetic thing. You must be genetically compatible to become like me, and you're not."

"How do you know?" She looks at him skeptically.

He briefly loses patience, knowing the longer they drag this out, the less chance it will be successful, so his tone comes out a tad snappy. "You just aren't. If you don't carry a certain set of genes, then the virus that changed me won't do anything to you even if I try to change you."

She really doesn't want to forget what he is, even though she understands why he needs to keep his secret safe. "Are you sure we can't just agree I'll keep your secret?"

"Yes. Even if I could accept that and trust you to keep it between us, there's another reason to make you forget. I don't want to scare you any more than I already have, but there are others, others like me, who will take issue with any human knowing of my kind's existence." He looks her directly in the eye, gauging her reaction.

Anxiety pervades her voice, making it crack as she speaks. "Others? Like you? More vamp...?" She's unable to bring herself to put the name to what he is.

"It's okay, you can think of me, well, my kind, as vampires. It's more or less accurate, though we don't think of ourselves as such mythological monsters. Most of the mythology and Hollywood invented lore is *BS*. *Yes*, I do have fangs and drink blood. I'm old enough to be your *distant* ancestor, but the rest of it is pretty much *merde*. No *coffins*, I go out in *daylight*, eat regular food, including *garlic*; holy relics are only relics, and have no effect. Here, *take* my hand." He reaches out. Hesitantly, she takes his hand, and he uses his other to grasp hers between his, moving her fingertips over the pulse in his wrist. "See? My heart *beats*, I *have* a pulse, I'm *warm* to the touch. I'm as *alive* as you are. I'm just different." He tries to reassure her. "Tess, my people are the proverbial *grain* of truth behind Vampires, but not the bad guys. No matter what I *appear* to be, I'm the same person you've worked with since you got here, not a *thing* out of a *horror* movie."

Tess is quiet, her hand still between his, feeling his warmth, it reassures her he isn't a monster out of folklore or Hollywood. She makes eye contact, and he can sense a shift in her emotions. "What do you need me to do?" She relents, asking quietly and nervously, deciding this is her only reasonable recourse. She must trust him.

Feeling her acceptance, he breathes a sigh of relief. "Please trust me. I'm hoping *if* you trust me, and relax, I can redact your memories without your barriers snapping into place and blocking my efforts. Besides, now you don't have to find an excuse to quit." He says, with a knowing, lopsided grin.

"You know about that, too?" She asks.

He gives her a sideways look, and raises one eyebrow, silently implying 'Of course I do'.

"I *want* to trust you, but part of me is still afraid." She confides. "All I can do is try." Her hand is still sandwiched between his and he squeezes it gently.

"That's all I can ask of you. Turn around and come over here. I want you to lean against me. The physical proximity may help. Don't worry. I promise, I won't bite this time." He pats the sofa near him.

She hesitates, thinking if he'd been a normal human and her boss, she'd worry he was coming on to her, but follows his lead and turns around to lean against him on the sofa. She sits up briefly and twists around to look at his face. "What if Liz comes looking for me here? She did send me for those papers. Shouldn't I take them to her and let her know I'll be busy for a while? Or away?"

"No, no one will come looking for you right now. I suggested

114

Liz send you on this errand, but she won't be expecting you to bring her the files." He attempts to put her mind at ease.

"Yeah, but Amy might! We were talking about grabbing some food at the deli later. She'll wonder what happened to me." Tess doesn't want to get Amy in trouble, but she worries she may come looking for her when she doesn't come back.

He holds out his hand and his tablet flies from his desk into his hand, and he sends a message. "There, I've fixed that. She won't think of coming to look for you today. I don't want to push you, but we need to get on with this. The longer we put this off, the less likely it'll work."

"*WHOA!* How'd you do that?" She points at his tablet, wide-eyed.

"*Tess!* We need to get on with this! Just accept I have various psychic abilities, including telekinesis, and let's get started. *Please!*" Hints of exasperation punctuate his words.

Tess assumes he must have used his abilities to plant suggestions into Liz's mind, and maybe even Amy's, not realizing Liz is one of the 'others'. "Try to relax as much as you can. Imagine leaving a door open for me to come through." He suggests.

She nods her head and turns back around. She tries to relax, closes her eyes, and leans with her back against his chest. He enfolds her gently in his arms, protectively, but not invasive, the fringes of her mind straying to other thoughts about being held, but she quickly reels in her thoughts from such distractions. She feels that tingling she'd felt her first day during the interview. She startles. "It was *you!* All along? That *sensation*, in my head?" She stammers out, unable to articulate it well.

"If you mean a tingling or pressure in your head, then yes, it was likely me. I tried to read you during the interview, but you blocked me. Not something the average human can do, by the way. Now, let's focus on this, okay?" He says to wrangle in yet another tangent.

She leans back again; relieved to know she hadn't been going crazy when she felt his mental incursions. He starts to sift through her memories, but as soon as he tries to redact them, *BOOM!* Up goes a shield, blocking his efforts. After several attempts, he knows for sure she has no significant, conscious ability to control them. And sits up, pushing her to sit up as well. He pinches the bridge of his nose, closes his eyes, and groans in frustration.

"What is it? You look worried." She inquires.

He leans back again, thinking of how to explain it to her. "First, the amount of memory affected is... *substantial*, but under normal circumstances, not insurmountable. But this is not a normal circumstance. Every time I tried to redact, change, or hide a memory, you blocked me, unconsciously, so your cooperation alone is not enough."

"So, you're saying you can't make me forget?" She asks nervously.

"I'm not ready to give up yet, but I need to think. I need to improve the connection between us, preferably without biting you again," He grins at her. "and somehow bypass your natural defenses." He looks pensive.

"I'm doing the best I can, *really*." She says honestly.

"I know you are." He gently pats her on the arm. He gets up and goes over to his desk with his tablet and taps something on it. After a couple of minutes, Tess hears a faint 'ding' as he gets a reply to his message. He opens a desk drawer and takes out a bottle of silvery-blue, swirly liquid.

"What's that?" She's worried he may drug or poison her. She knows that's unlikely, but her mind keeps going to worst-case scenarios.

"Nothing that will hurt you, but something that could help. Think of it as a psychic enhancement drug. We sometimes use it to help open psychic pathways in people we turn, if there are difficulties." He explains.

"But you said you can't turn me, right?" Her earlier anxiety rises again.

"I can't, but a diluted dose of this could allow us to link telepathically, bypassing your barriers, so I can get the job done. It's also sometimes given to two of my kind to encourage shared dreaming. We sometimes teach that way, as days of learning can be compressed into an hour or two of dreaming and ideas can be easily shared." He explains.

"Is it safe? For me, that is." She asks.

"It should be fine in a dilute dose. At worst, it won't work at all." He explains. "But if it does, it may bypass your barriers and allow us to share a dream space. Hopefully, that will give me the access I need."

"I don't know... that sounds too intimate for my liking." She worries what he might find in her mind.

"Tess, I've been in your mind before, this will just make it easier. I promise I'll do my best to steer clear of anything private that doesn't relate to your knowing about me." He reassures her. "I'm only going to put a couple of drops in some water for you, then we'll wait and see whether you react at all. If you do, then I'll take a normal dose for shared dreaming." He drips 2 drops into a small glass of water, and hands it to her.

"If you're sure it's not gonna kill me, then I guess it's worth a try." Tess takes it, feigns a toast and drinks it down. After a minute, she asks him something that's been nagging her since he told her she couldn't be turned. "Tell me something," She pauses for a couple of seconds searching for the words, "if I *had* been compatible...?" She trails off, finding it hard to finish the thought.

He gives her a sympathetic look and gently puts his hand on hers. "Then I would probably be turning you right now, assuming I hadn't already done so. It would have been much simpler, but it's not an option."

"Wouldn't I have any choice? I mean, I don't want...." She stops midsentence, her mind finishing the thought *to become a blood-sucking monster.* She's self-conscious he might hear her thoughts, and hopes he doesn't.

He hears her, but knows it's a natural reaction, and not personal. "You're exactly the kind of person my people look for to join us: Intelligent, kind, and compassionate; you're creative, with a good sense of right and wrong, highly adaptable, with high psychic potential. If you'd been compatible, I would have tried to convince you, but I'm not sure I, or the others, could have let you slip through our fingers, especially now that you know about me. If you were compatible, you'd also know that, neither I, nor becoming like me, is anything to fear. In fact, you'd likely have wanted me to turn you." He explains.

117

She sits, uncomfortable, letting that sink in. Somewhere, in the back of her mind, his last sentence puts her oddly at ease, yet disturbs simultaneously. Part of her knows there's nothing to fear, as if that knowledge is ingrained in her soul. "I'm probably better off human, anyway. I'm not sure I could get used to biting people or drinking blood." She twists her face into an exaggerated expression of distaste attempting to lighten the mood. "How long before we know if this is working. I don't feel any different yet." She changes the topic, as the idea of drinking someone's blood makes her nauseous.

"If it's going to work, it should be soon. Tell me if you feel at all odd." He says.

She lets out a brief bark of sarcastic laughter. "I've been feeling odd ever since I remembered. Are you sure you used enough?" She asks.

"I consulted with one of my people who deals with such things. She suggested the dosage but said if it didn't work after about fifteen minutes, to try two more drops." He explains.

"Potent stuff, I gue... guess." She shakes her head. Her vision rapidly becomes distorted by colored halos, and everything sounds strange.

"Are you okay?" He asks, one hand resting on her leg.

"I guess so, but I see odd colors; light around things, and when you speak, there's a weird echo, but not when I speak." She describes.

"Are the colors around everything?" He inquires.

She looks around the room at what has a halo. "No, around you, and I can see them when I look at my hands, and your plant over there."

"Sounds like auras. Bioelectric energy fields around living things." He says.

"I've heard of those. *God*! That echo is getting *really* annoying. Hard to focus or hear clearly. It's like I can hear what you're going to say *before* you say it." She closes her eyes and focuses.

Is this better? She hears him say.

"Yes! *Much* better!" she exclaims.

Open your eyes and look at me. Which she does, but his lips are not moving. *I'm speaking to you telepathically. You were hearing my thoughts before I spoke the words.* He explains.

"Oh, that's weird. And I'm doing this?" She asks.

Yes. Humans have latent psychic abilities, you more than most. The drug allows you to access some of those abilities, seeing auras and telepathy. You may have other latent skills as well, but telepathy is the most common, and what I was hoping for.

"This is only temporary, right? If I start hearing everyone around me thinking, I'll go *nuts*." She inquires.

Marc paths, *I don't think it'll be permanent. Since you're not being turned, this should only be a temporary opening of your psychic pathways, and besides, I'm telepathic and actively broadcasting. You might not pick up on other humans around you at all.*

"So, that's why I can't hear anyone else in the building right now? Only you?" She wonders if she could read or even send a message to someone like Amy.

That's part of it. Humans are not usually strong broadcasters unless they have latent or active telepathic abilities. However, I've also psychically 'soundproofed' my office, for lack of a better term, so I don't get overwhelmed by everyone around me.

She contemplates that, then says, "I can understand that; I'm only picking up on you, and it's bizarre."

He grins at her. *We should get on with this. The longer you stay aware, the higher the risk this won't work.* He paths, drinking his dose, but wondering if they aren't already too late. He motions for her to lean back against him as before.

"What will happen if you can't make me forget?" She asks.

We'll deal with that if it happens, but no harm will come to you, even if you still remember. I hope, for all concerned, we can make this work. It will be a lot simpler if you forget it all. He paths.

This time, her mind is more open. A thought flitters around the edges of her consciousness; somehow, she knows he won't be able to make her forget, and her life has irrevocably taken a detour down this strange new path. Yet somehow, it feels right, as though it's meant to be. The thought fades as she feels like she's falling backwards, slipping rapidly into REM sleep. He slips into a dream world with her, back in the alley that night. She's watching him feeding on the woman when she senses someone next to her. She turns, and he's beside her. She's confused, but not afraid like she was before. She feels like an objective observer, detached. "How? But you're there! How can you also be here?"

He puts a hand gently on her arm. "Think, Tess. Neither of us are here. This happened last Friday night. We're still in my office. This is a dream. Remember?"

She gets an odd look and says, "Oh, yeah. This is when I found out about you. Still hard to believe it all." She turns back and watches him pull away from the woman, and sees the bite and his fangs, more curious than afraid seeing it for the second time.

"I need you to relax now that I'm in your dream mind. I'm going to make your memories disappear like a bad dream. If this works, you'll wake with no memories of vampires or any of this. I'll try to substitute some innocuous filler memories from your mind, so you're less likely to get caught up in inconsistencies this time." He says, looking into her eyes. She feels odd, like she can't think. As though she dozes off to sleep even though part of her is still aware. She feels him working, redacting her memories, but no matter what he does to hide it and shore up the memory block, it unravels like a poorly knitted sweater.

She can sense his frustration as he tries repeatedly. She's got no concept of time passing and feels like a detached observer, like being out-of-body, watching a psychic surgeon work on her mind. After a while, even this awareness shifts, and slowly, becomes aware she's leaning against Marc's warm chest. Her eyes are still closed. She feels his chest rising and falling, and his heart beating. She halfway thinks "Ironic, a warm vampire..." She wonders what else is different. He stirs and then she's fully awake, opening her eyes. The room is darker than it was when they began. Even with the curtains closed, she can tell it's no longer daytime, but darkest night. He takes a deep breath. She senses his frustration and a bit of anger at himself, but not her.

"It didn't work, did it?" she asks, rhetorically, since she knows the answer, as she still knows exactly what he is.

"If you can ask that question, I suspect you know the answer already. But no, it didn't work. Every time I tried to redact a memory, and thought I had it securely tucked in your unconscious mind, forgotten, it resurfaced like a wound that wouldn't heal. I tried everything I could think of. I'm so sorry. We'll have to figure out something; some way to deal with you knowing." He says, his expression is one of genuine remorse for putting her in this situation.

"Well, the echoing has stopped. And honestly, now that I know I don't need to be afraid of you, it's not such a bad thing knowing what you are." She says.

He looks above and to the side of her head, squinting. "Hm, you're probably just adapting. From what I can see of your aura, it's still showing active psychic tendencies." He says, nodding to the other part of what she said.

"Oh, joy." Tess gives her head a slight shake. After a pause, she quietly asks, "I'm guessing this means my life will never quite be the same."

"I'd say that's a safe bet, under the circumstances. I'll need to figure out what's the best option, and as I said, it's not only me and you involved now." He says, absentmindedly playing with the ends of her long brown hair, as she still leans against his chest.

"Are you sure the others need to know? I promise, I won't tell anyone. Really! Who would believe me, anyway?" She pleads.

"Tess, I don't want to alarm you, but others already know about you, but this is my mess, so I need to fix it." He admits.

"They do? What if they... I mean, can you be sure they won't want to do something more drastic?" Her heart rate rises as her anxiety does.

"Tess, *no one* is going to hurt you! *That* I can promise you. It's going to make your, and my, and others' lives more complicated, but we'll figure it out. I promise." He sends her calming thoughts, trying to curtail the panic he senses rising.

Tess yawns, rubbing her eyes. "What time is it, anyway?"

Marc looks at his tablet sitting nearby and gives half a laugh. "Would you believe it's a little after 2 a.m.? We've been at this over 14 hours!"

"What? That's *insane!* Someone surely must have missed me when I never came back." She sits up and faces him, looking worried.

"It's alright, but you should go home and rest, and you're in no shape to drive between all of this and, well, you've got to be exhausted. Why don't you go get your things and come back here? I'll take you home." He gives her a small mental push to calm down and go get her things. She goes out and grabs her purse, keys, cell, and tablet and comes back.

"I guess you'll want these?" She hands him her car keys.

"No, come here." He reaches out a hand to her. She takes it and he pulls her close. They both vanish from the office, lights turning off after them.

REALITY CHECK

Marc and Tess reappear in her living room near her recliner. Tess drops her purse, disoriented, and mildly nauseous. Mabel, surprised by their sudden appearance, jumps out of the recliner and runs up the floor-to-ceiling cat tree and hisses at both of them.

"What the...? Did... did we... just... teleport?" She asks, finding it difficult to get her bearings.

Marc gives her a tired laugh. "More or less; that's about the closest term for it. It's an explanation for another time, now that it doesn't look like you're going to forget. You've got enough on your plate to digest already. I figured it would be a lot faster than driving you home. Besides, I didn't think you'd want me to carry you inside if you fell asleep in the car?" He lets out a chuckle.

"Hmmm, yeah, but what about my car? Won't people wonder why it's still in the parking lot?" She plops down in her recliner to keep herself from falling over.

"If anyone asks, I'll tell them it wouldn't start, so you got an Uber. I'll drive it over later. Now, do you have anything to eat around here?" He raises one eyebrow, waiting for an answer.

"If you're hungry, there's a little leftover pizza and Chinese food in the fridge."

She heads toward the kitchen, loses her balance, staggers, and nearly falls, but he catches her. "No, I was thinking more for you. You haven't eaten since this morning, and you need to eat something before you sleep." He pats her on the arm reassuringly and helps her into her recliner.

"Oh, yeah, I can just nuke something." She says, but he continues toward the kitchen.

"I'll fix it, you *stay* put, you're wiped out, and disoriented. You might even pass out, and your condition is my responsibility. Once I get you settled, I need to go tend to my own needs; the sustained psychic effort took it out of me." He yawns and walks into her kitchen.

Tess realizes he's not talking about grabbing a burger at Cook Out or McDonalds, the only two places nearby open this time of night, but his *other* nutritional 'needs'. Her stomach turns, thinking about it. She settles in the chair, thinking about everything this last week, and how it's still so surreal. After a couple of minutes, she smells something warm and enticing, and it isn't reheated leftovers. She's half asleep in her chair, when Marc comes out of the kitchen with a plate and glass for her. He pulls up a nearby TV tray, puts it in front of her, and sets the food down on it. There's a freshly made omelet oozing with cheese, mushrooms, and some warm vanilla milk on the side to help her sleep.

"You didn't need to fix all this. I'd have been fine with leftovers." She's touched and confused he'd go to the trouble.

"I'd say that pizza is several days old, and I'd rather you eat something healthy than all that sodium and MSG in the Chinese food right now. Besides, the warm milk, eggs and cheese all contain tryptophan, which will help you sleep." He sits on the sofa nearby.

"Well, thanks. Who'd have thought someone like you would be a good cook." She jokes.

"Why wouldn't I be? I still eat regular food, besides *blood*. I've had hundreds of years to learn a thing or two about cooking, and I am originally *French*." He gives her a normal, human-looking smile.

"*Hundreds* of years?" Tess laughs nervously, followed by an awkward silence. An idea forms in her mind she knows she shouldn't pursue, but curiosity sparks her courage. "Speaking of your...other dietary needs. You mentioned it doesn't usually hurt when you...." She trails off as she thinks about him feeding on someone, and a spark of curiosity makes her think about what it felt like when he bit her before, and what it might feel like without the pain. She pushes away a recurring thought, or feeling, she wants to know. Some masochistic part of her wants him to *bite* her again. She thinks, *I must be crazy! Don't even consider it!*

"The term we prefer is 'when we feed', and no, pain is not usually involved. In fact, usually, the one I feed from is oblivious to anything going on and won't remember it at all. They may feel weak for a day or so, but there's a compound released when I bite that not only seals the wound, but promotes general healing and speeds up regeneration of red blood cells." He explains.

"So, there's no pain because you have them in some kind of trancelike state? Like the woman in the alley?" She asks.

He pauses briefly, finding a means to explain it to her. "I wouldn't call it a trance exactly. It's like they sleep through it, but it's deeper than sleep. In sleep you're still aware of things, creating memories, even processing information on a subconscious level. It's more like suspending the mind for a time. All awareness is shut down. In fact, I'm not even sure memories are imprinted in that state, and if they are aware, normally, I can bury the memories, except with you, of course." He gives her a lopsided grin, but then continues, seriously. "You really are quite unique. I've certainly never stumbled across a human like you, even one of those who can be turned."

"So, if someone's *awake* when you feed, does it hurt?" She asks, curiously.

Marc suspects there's more to her questions than normal curiosity. "Not if I numb the pain for the person. Though it is extremely uncommon for one of us to feed on a conscious human, we do sometimes feed on others of our kind. With humans, it's always a risk of exposure and most would be terrified." He says.

"Oh, I don't know, I bet you there are lots of women out there who are fans of supernatural romance who would be thrilled to 'feel the fang'." She says half-jokingly.

Another awkward silence as Marc thinks about her comment. "I get the feeling this is more than passing curiosity." He says directly.

She looks down at her hands, avoiding eye contact, while she speaks. "*Busted!* This all still feels unreal, nearly surreal to me. I remember, but there's still this dream-like quality to it. Intellectually, I know you're what you appear to be." She pauses and then forces herself to make eye contact. "I was thinking, if you can do it without the pain this time, I'd offer, unless you prefer to go out and find someone else, that is?" She goes quiet, feeling like she's babbling.

He gives a brief smile, and a pause. "Tess, I appreciate the offer. It shows me you're starting to trust me. And to be honest, I *am* extremely tired right now, and yes, hungry. Finish your food first though. But I'm not going to let you stay up all night asking a million questions. You should sleep, and I don't want you to come to work tomorrow at all. I don't know how long the effects of the drug will keep your psychic senses heightened, plus, I need to figure some things out." He says.

"Okay. I'm pretty sure I'm gonna be pretty wiped out, anyway." She finishes her omelet. "Thanks for the food. It was great, and a nice change from fast food." She puts the tray table aside, and looks straight at him. "So, what now. Should I stand, or what?"

"Come over here to the sofa, so we're both comfortable. I won't take a lot, just enough to hold me for now. You've been through enough." He says.

"Honestly, part of me is curious to know what it feels like when I'm not blindly *terrified*, and, like I said, to know it's all real." She admits.

He reaches up and lightly massages her shoulder on the left side. "First thing you need to do is relax. If you clench up like this," He grips the tight tendon between her neck and shoulder. "Even with me numbing it, it may hurt." He walks behind her and massages both shoulders until she relaxes enough, then sits in front of her. "Are you *sure* you're okay with this?"

She nods curtly. "If I'm not gonna forget, then consider this a step toward accepting what you are and extending a little trust." She tips her head back a little to allow him easier access. He reaches back and supports the back of her head before sinking his fangs into her neck. His fangs pierce her flesh painlessly, like warm needles in wax, her flesh yielding to their path. In her mind, she hears: *Thank you, for this, and for trusting me.*

Then, she's taken by surprise as she feels an unexpected and over-whelming need of her own. Not for food, or blood, but for an intimacy she lacks in her life, and has sworn off after Colton. Marc, being em-pathic, feels her need and is nearly overwhelmed by the wave of emo-tion coming from her. He draws deeper on her throat, but then with-draws, finding himself kissing the wounds to seal them, then wandering up her neck, her breaths getting shorter in anticipation. Without think-ing, he kisses her deeply for a couple of minutes, then she loosens her shirt and tries to loosen his, caught up in her long-ignored need.

Marc realizes what's going on, and using all his willpower, re-gains his self-control and stops kissing her. "*TESS*! Listen to me! This can't happen! You're reacting... we're reacting to the tempo-rary bond we shared tonight, to the intimacy of me being in your mind, and then feeding from you. *Believe* me, your body may want this, but you won't, not in the morning when you'll feel like I took advantage of you." He says, looking in her glazed eyes.

She tries to kiss him again, but he stops her. "*No*! I'm still tech-nically your boss, and I'm responsible for you, so I'm telling you now, *this* is *not* going to happen tonight."

"*Please*, I want to get lost in this feeling." Tess pleads.

"I know, and I'm going to help you, but not like this." He stands away from her grasp. He leans over and places one more kiss on her forehead, and she promptly loses all tension in her body, becoming slack with sleep. He lifts her up, and carries her to her bedroom, carefully removing her jeans after he places her in her bed. He pulls the covers up over her body and sits on the edge of the bed for a mo-ment, looking at her now slack face; he can still feel her need. He touches her forehead gently, wiping the hair away from her face. *Dream, Tess, dream of some fairytale prince sweeping you off your feet and satisfying all your needs, not a vampire old enough to be a long-lost ancestor. Dream until you're sated. We'll talk more tomorrow.* He paths, scribbling a quick note and leaving it by her bed, then gets up and turns off lights around the house.

He starts to reach down and heal the bite marks out of habit, but thinks twice, realizing she may need that evidence in the morning. He once again feeds Mabel after she nearly trips him rubbing against his legs.

"Has everyone been ignoring you, Mabel?" He leans over and scratches the cat behind her ears as she devours her food.

Once all is in place as it was the Friday before, he ports out, knowing this time, she'll remember in the morning, and they'll have to find some solution that will work for all of them.

REALITY HANGOVER

Exhausted on several levels, Tess sleeps deeply and long. She gets lost in her dreams, as Marc suggested, slowly waking around noon, still halfway immersed in a dream about the main character in the sci-fi book she's been reading taking her off to some fantasy planet, and satisfying every need she has. Slowly, the dream shifts from fantasy to waking memory of the night before.

Tess groans and rolls over. "Ugh, from fanciful dreams to what *should be fantasy*." She puts her pillow over her head and tries to go back to the dream. She remembers her need making her act like some wild thing, and is thankful Marc stopped her from doing something she really wasn't ready for. Her head aches dully, like she had too much to drink. She takes the pillow off her head and rolls onto her back, stuffing it under her skull, but closes her eyes as the bright light seeps through the part in the curtains in bursts that makes her head pound.

It's going to be one of those days. She thinks, once again rolling over on her side, away from the window. She sees a folded piece of paper, standing upright with her name on it. She grabs it, squinting, and reads,

Call me when you get up; we need to figure this out.–Marc.

"Not sure I'm up to seeing you right now!" She shouts out loud, and buries herself back under the pillow. Her cell phone rings, and she reluctantly answers it, recognizing Marc's ringtone and number.

"Yeah." She says grumpily.

"Hey, you may not be 'up to seeing me', but we need to sort this out." He says, hints of amusement in his voice.

"Wait, how did you know what I said?" She's ready to be pissed at him for bugging her place.

He chuckles lightly. "You not only shouted it out loud, you shouted it *telepathically*, and since you were thinking of me, I heard it loud and clear. Obviously, you're awake, so I called *you* instead." He explains.

"Why do you have to be so *damn* chipper? I feel like I've got a really funky hangover this morning." She complains.

"This *afternoon*. It's a little before 1 p.m." He gives a slight chuckle, but becomes concerned; Marc asks, "Can you describe how you're feeling to me?"

"I'm light sensitive, have a headache, and feel really weird. I've also got a major case of embarrassment!" She groans.

"Hm, and I did hear you this morning, quite clearly. I'll be over shortly. I need to bring your car by anyway. Get out of bed, get yourself presentable, and I'll bring food. You surely need to eat, and I saw the contents of your fridge." He says. "No arguments. I'll be over in about 40 minutes. I need to take care of a few things first."

"Okay, I'm achy today, probably from sitting too long in one position yesterday, so make it an hour and a half so I can take a hot bath." She knows she can't avoid him but gains a little extra time to cope with it all before facing him.

"Sounds good. See you soon." He hangs up the phone and rocks back in his office chair, as Liz appears in his doorway.

"So, how are you going to explain things to her? She may have accepted what you are, but the rest could get dicey." Liz asks.

"I'll do some creative editing of our 'situation'. I doubt if she's ready to deal with our *creation* story, but I'll tell her the basic truth. We look out for the planet. We've got a vested interest in humanity's survival and do our best to mitigate dangerous situations in the world." He rattles it off as though Tess will have to accept it all.

Liz walks over and leans on the back of a chair, facing him, saying, "She's smart, she'll have questions. She's going to need to know about the rest of us. It'll be hard to hide the fact you're not the only 'vampire' here."

130

She rolls her eyes at the term 'vampire' and sits in the chair.

"Yes, I know, but I'm sure she can handle it. Did I tell you she offered to let me feed from her last night? That has to be a good sign of adaptation." He sighs.

"Yes, but you also said you two ended up in an awkward situation." She gives him a knowing grin as she sips a mug of sassafras tea.

"Liz, I handled it. I stopped it before it went too far." He insists.

"Yes, *this* time. But you're dealing with a human being, a person, and even if you can control your emotions, you've got a potentially bad situation considering your own history." She glares at him, hoping he'll realize the dilemma he's in.

"Liz, I don't see any other option. I'll make it clear to her I can be her boss, and her friend, but nothing more. I can't let myself emotionally invest in someone and then watch her grow old and die! If she could be turned, it might be different." Liz feels his frustration.

"Because the two of you would have been a good fit if she could have been turned?" Liz asks.

He gives her an annoyed stare. "Yes, I'll admit that, but unless you think They'll make an exception and make her compatible...?"

She gives him a look implying their creators are unlikely to make an exception. "You're an empath; you know this isn't only about you. If you don't handle this properly, then she's going to have a hell of a time coping."

"I'll do my best, but this is unfamiliar territory, and there will be trial and error." He packs up a few things from his desk to take with him.

"Remember, her feelings and needs are real. She's not some child you have to keep out of trouble, and she's not a 'pet' human, or curiosity, you can put aside when she gets difficult! She's just left her own reality, and knowing about us is going to make her even more different from other humans than she already is. She'll feel more isolated than ever. You're the one who commented on her depressive tendencies when we hired her." Liz reminds him.

"I know, believe me, I know; and I feel horrible for putting her in this situation. I didn't think she'd find out, but she was too much of a curiosity and mystery to ignore." He says in a huff of frustration.

"You're not alone. She's not an average human. Hard to believe she's *not* in the database, but she isn't. Anyway, keep me in the loop. I need to meet with the others and do some brainstorming." She says and leaves his office.

Marc grabs Tess's car keys he picked up last night, and heads outside to get her car. He runs some errands, gets some proper food for lunch, and extra for dinner, as he assumes there will be a lot of ground to cover.

REALITY SINKS IN, A LOT LIKE A PUNCTURE WOUND

Tess drags herself out of bed, noticing her jeans are hanging neatly, as in folded along the creases, over a nearby chair, and realizes Marc must have removed them. *Well, at least he's a gentleman.* She thinks. She goes into her bathroom and runs the water for a hot bath, tossing in a bath bomb with various herbs to help relax her muscles. She pauses, stands in front of the mirror, and inspects herself. *Hm, am I pale or is it my imagination?* She wonders, then tips her head back, fingering the half-healed puncture wounds. It's only then reality sinks in, as his fangs had the night before.

She closes her eyes and feels the reality of it all wash over her, like a riptide's sucked her out to some strange sea full of mythical creatures. She settles on the closed toilet seat, two fingers still massaging the raised welts on her skin. *It's all real. It really happened. A VAMPIRE!* Her whole concept of reality takes a sickeningly sudden twist. *My life, as I know it, is over. It can never go back to the way it was, how could it? Knowing my concept of reality was so wrong.* She thinks. *I wonder what other mythical creatures are out there I didn't know about? Werewolves? Aliens? Gnomes?* She laughs, feeling giddy.

She undresses the rest of the way, slips into the hot water, flinches back from the heat at first, and then slowly eases herself in all the way. The bath water smells of coconut, mint, and spices. She washes quickly and then allows herself to sink in and soak. She barely catches herself before falling asleep and sinking all the way into the water. She gets out, stretching the muscles in her arms, back, and neck. She brushes and blow-dries her hair. Somehow, doing these very normal things is a strange contrast as she looks at her neck again, thinking about the night before, including how it felt physically and emotionally.

How am I going to face him after that? He must think I'm a silly child with a crush, but I couldn't help it. She thinks, throwing on the least sexy thing she has: an old set of discolored, green sweats, and heads out to the living room, checks her email and Facebook, then leans back in her recliner, halfway dozing until she hears knocking on the door. She starts awake and opens the door. It's Marc, carrying her car keys and a large covered basket.

"Since when do *you* knock?" Tess acts more okay than she is.

"I thought it might seem rude if I just popped in." He gives her a fangless smile. "And as promised, I come bearing gifts, or at least nutritious food." He closes and locks the front door behind him and hands her the car keys. "I filled up your gas tank on the way. You really shouldn't let it get so low." He remarks absentmindedly. She's walking back toward her recliner, when he gently takes her by the arm and makes her face him. "How are you doing?" He mentally scans her, getting impressions of anxiety, mixed emotions, and embarrassment. Despite the lingering fragrance from her bath bomb, he can still catch whiffs of adrenalin and cortisol.

She faces him. "Honestly? Overwhelmed. The immensity of your existence, what you are, screws up my whole concept of reality. It really hit me this morning, when I had the visible evidence before me in the mirror." She strokes the welts unconsciously.

"I considered healing those before I left, but figured you might need the evidence to really believe it. How about you let me take care of that, assuming you're done nursing your 'war wounds'?" He grins.

She tips her head back, and he gently puts his fingers over the welts, rubbing them gently, willing them to heal and vanish. His fingers are unusually warm, like they're radiating heat or energy. "There. Good as new!"

She reaches up and can't find a trace of the welts. "Hmph! Where were you when I sprained my ankle? Could have used that kind of healing instead of 3 weeks on crutches." She jokes, but looks awkwardly at him, needing to break an uncomfortable situation with humor. "So, now what?" She asks.

134

"Let me fix you some food, and we'll have that little talk afterwards. Okay? Maybe clear off your coffee table so we can eat there?" He heads off to the kitchen with the food. After a few minutes, he comes out with freshly baked bread and a plate of cheeses, meats, and some of Kari's gravlaks as finger food. "What can I say, you need protein." He sits on the sofa with her, but not too close. Tess picks at her food nervously.

"Not hungry?" He inquires.

"No, it's not that; I'm wondering what's next." There's a slight waver in her voice. The reality of what he is and what he could do to her starts to seep through to Tess's consciousness. He can sense the shift in her energy, as well as the increase in scents associated with stress and fear.

"*Please*, don't be afraid of me or what I am. I promised you yesterday I won't hurt you and I *will* keep that promise." He says, bluntly, and gently guides her chin to force her to make eye contact with him.

"But what about the others you mentioned? What if they think I'm too big a risk or threat to them? Everything was so surreal before, but now, I understand how close I was to death last night!" She's out of breath, her anxiety makes everything seem overly dramatic.

"You were *never* in any danger from *me*. I promise."

"Even so, you had me by the throat, literally! If you'd wanted to, you could've drained me dry or ripped out my throat! I know you *say* you wouldn't, but you physically *could* have! The possibility was there, and I put myself in that situation. Talk about being a masochist!" She's feeling frantic and unhinged about the situation.

"Okay, Tess, *stop*! We don't *kill* innocent humans, period!" He sounds exasperated. "Now, I need you to listen to me with an open mind. Can you *please* try?"

"I, I'll try." She feels mildly sorry for herself. She picks at her food and nibbles on some cheese.

"I need you to understand some basic things about me and my kind. First, harming innocent humans is abhorrent to us. We do what we can to protect humanity from itself." He says.

"Protect *us* from *ourselves*?" She gives him a 'WTF' expression.

135

"Don't know if you're doing a very good job if the daily news is correct." She says annoyed at what she views as a touch of arrogance.

"Those reports would be a lot worse without us, and we don't stand around asking for thanks for our efforts. We can't, because humans would do their best to destroy us if they knew of our existence, even with all we do for them." He blurts out in frustration.

"Give me an example. What do *vampires* do for humanity besides drink our blood?" she asks in a huff.

"Last year, we prevented 34 terrorist attacks in the US and Europe alone." He says.

"And since they didn't happen, I guess I'll have to take your word for it?" She snaps. "And what about the ones that did happen? Like the downing of that plane over Syria? You all let that happen!" She snaps.

"We, well, I can't say we're only human, but what I can tell you is we're not *omniscient*. We do what we can. We have people who not only monitor the world and events like humans would do, but we also have others like me, who have stronger precognitive tendencies, who monitor trends and possibilities, and look for big events, but we don't get them all. The point is, we have a vested interest in humanity's survival, so we do what we can to keep you safe." He explains.

"You mean, if something happens to us, there goes the food supply?" She says, feeling ornery.

He sighs. "Naturally, that's part of it, but it's far more complicated than that. We were all originally human. We were born human. We have distant relatives, who don't even know we exist, who we still feel kinship with. Plus, being so long lived, we see the world differently than humans do. We see the long game of humanity and where humans may be going in the future, *if you survive.*"

"If you're so precognitive, why didn't you see me and this situation coming?" She gesticulates wildly.

"When I met you, something told me you belonged with us, that we *needed* to hire you. Quite frankly, that went against all our rules." He says.

"*WHOA!* So, it's *your fault* I'm in this mess?" She tries to sound pissed off.

"If you choose to see it that way, I guess you could say I'm largely to blame. I convinced the others to hire you. So, yes, if I hadn't, you would not have been able to find out about me. In my defense, I sensed how much you needed the job, and your unusual abilities piqued our curiosity." He explains.

"My *abilities*, huh?" She comments. "The ones I didn't even know I *apparently* have?"

"Yes. That and other things would normally have been indicative you were a potential for transformation, but you aren't in our overview of people who are compatible, and I've never known that to be wrong." He says.

She pauses, quiet for a few seconds as her expression shifts to one of sudden comprehension. "*Wait,* a second! You said, 'you had to convince the *others* to hire me', and it is normally against the rules. That means there are *others like you* at *work!*" Her fear increases as she wonders who else might be fanged and who's human.

"Yes, Tess. There *are* others like me at work." He knows she won't let it go until he admits it, so admits it bluntly.

"Did you turn them into vampires?" Her voice rises with stress.

"No, I've never *personally* turned anyone, though someone from work turned me and some others who work there. We're more like a family than employees." He explains.

"Who?" She asks anxiously.

"We'll get to that later. We're having a meeting with some of the others in a few days, but right now, let's focus on what we need to sort out." He says, desperately wrangling her back on track, but she's stuck in her own rut.

"How many like you are there out there?" she asks, uneasily.

He gives her a sheepish grin. "Are you sure you want to know?" Tess nods quietly, so he continues. "There are maybe 20 to 30,000 of us spread worldwide." He pauses to let it all sink in.

"Thousands of vampires? How is it people don't know about this when there are so many of you?" Her shock and disbelief are apparent.

"First, we refer to ourselves as Apara, it's ancient Sanskrit for 'others.' We're not fond of the term 'vampire' because it's got so many bad connotations and so much foolishness surrounding the mythology. We hide what we are while maintaining human personas. It helps that most of the legends *are* total BS. Obviously, daylight's not an issue, I have a reflection, don't sleep in a coffin, and don't shrink or burn from holy water, crosses and so on. We also don't harm anyone when we feed. It's forbidden." He explains.

"So, you *never* hurt people?" She asks.

"We never hurt people we feed on. Not that things don't happen during what we do to protect the world. Sometimes, the only choice with the 'bad guys' is to take them out, as you humans say. We don't enjoy doing it, but sometimes, it's necessary." He says.

"This is *insane!* Now I'm going to go around wondering if people I see on the street are human or not." She throws her hands up in the air.

He laughs. "Most people out there *are* human. Fewer than 1 in 200,000 people are Apara. Most likely, before you walked in for the interview, you'd never crossed paths with my kind before."

"And now? Come on, Marc! Who at work?" She begs.

He shakes his head and lets out a sigh, knowing she's like a dog with a juicy bone. She won't let go until she gets every drop of marrow out of it. He relents. "Most of your coworkers, at least all the non-entry level staff." He tries to gauge her reaction.

"Liz? Kari? Peder? Who else?" Her voice sounds panicked.

"All administrative staff, as well as medical staff, and some others."

"Please tell me *Jason* isn't one of you!" Her anxiety skyrockets as she thinks of what someone like him might do with the abilities Marc has already shown or told her about, or what he could have done to her in the copy room.

"No, at least, not yet." Thinking, w*ith his recent behavior, I doubt he ever will be.*

"Not yet? I'm suggesting never. He's *fucking* crazy! He'll never follow your rules. He *would* hurt people." She pauses, putting the puzzle pieces together. "Wait, a minute! You're saying he's compatible?" Marc nods. "What about Amy?"

"Amy's human and a potential transformee. Before you get any ideas in your head about warning her or others, that's *not* gonna
138

happen." He holds an admonitory finger up to her face.

"But they deserve to know! It's their lives! Do you even ask them if it's what they want?" She's frustrated, and flashes back to the 'mandatory promotion' clause in the contract, realizing what that was really referring to.

"Tess, this is far more complicated than I can explain to you right now, because there's so much you don't know or understand about the situation. Chances are, neither of them will ever need to be turned. We don't turn someone just because we can. Those we employ are usually all potentials, present company excepted. It gives us a pool from which to choose new transformees with the right skill sets, mentalities, or talents. Most will go on with their lives for a few years here without knowing what we are or what we do, until they reach an age where it's too late to safely turn them, then we arrange for them to leave; plant a suggestion here or there or arrange for someone to head hunt them into a better job." He explains.

"Safe to turn them?" She repeats as a question.

He controls his irritation at her, and calmly explains. "The older someone is, the harder it is for them to adapt psychologically, plus if you turn someone, say, in their forties or fifties, their physical age regresses to about twenty-five to thirty over the first few months. You either relocate them, fake their deaths or figure some way to explain their 'rejuvenation'!"

"So, everyone at Inspiration Inc. is either a vampire, er... Apara, or a potential, except for me? Why the hell did you hire me? If you hadn't hired me, I'd never have known about you and we wouldn't be in this *God-damn* mess!" She grabs and throws a nearby pillow at the floor in frustration, making Mabel fly out of the room when it comes too close to her.

"I know, and I'm taking responsibility for this. I pushed Liz to hire you. So, I'm now responsible for you." He leans forward and puts his hand on her knee to reassure her.

She pulls away and continues to lash out. "*Why*? Why did you have to hire me? I'm clearly not what you want. I can't be turned, and I've obviously caused trouble by finding out about you." She lashes out as though if she argues enough, somehow, things will all go back to normal.

He gently takes her by the upper arms and makes her look him in the eye. "You were a mystery. You answered the ad, citing the logo. The logo has subliminal coding which potentials are supposed to react to, but you're not a potential. Then, when you showed up for the interview and *we* tried to read you, you pushed us out of your mind." Before she can ask, he amends his statement. "Yes, Tess, *we*, as in Liz, Peder, Jayla, and I were all taking turns reading you in the interview, not just me. You blasted Peder with some sort of energy wave and you pushed me out. Even normal potentials aren't able to do *that*! You have more latent talent in you than any potential we've hired in decades, and we can't turn you. It piqued our curiosity, and when I could read you, I sensed the desperate need to get the job, to feel useful, and to move on from Digital Danger." He says, pointedly.

She sits quietly for a couple of minutes, studying her fingers like they've just become the most interesting things on the planet, then she finally speaks in a much calmer tone. "You're saying, in the end, you wanted to help me?"

He releases her and puts his hand on hers. "Yes. Precognition is not my primary ability. I'm an empath. Do you know what that is?"

"Yeah, I've heard of it. Like Councilor Troi in Star Trek, where she feels others' emotions, but not thoughts? Or is it more like in some sci-fi shows where you can heal someone by taking on their wounds or sicknesses?"

"Emotions, not injuries. We're all telepaths, but some of us pick up more strongly on the emotional aspects, while others may pick up more on psychological nuances. For example, I felt your sadness, your depression, your hopelessness, and your need to be complete again; to be useful, to belong some place. I'm sorry that, I may have ruined your life in the process." He admits.

After a half a minute of contemplative silence, she says, grudgingly: "I'm not sure I'd say ruined. I admit, it's a lot more interesting than what my life was before this." She grins awkwardly. "But what happens now?"

He takes a deep breath, and noticeably relaxes now that Tess has calmed down and shown the first real steps of acceptance. "First thing we need to do is find out if we made a mistake using that drug to open your mind. I was sure it's effects would be long gone by now, but I heard you clear as a bell this morning. We may have opened a psychic Pandora's box, if you get my drift. I believe you've met Sara, our doctor?"

"Ah, yeah. She helped me when my migraine hit. She's one of you as well?" She asks.

"Yes, though she tends to be a rather live wire in an otherwise serious crowd. She doesn't talk about her past much, and she's far older than any of us I know. From what I've heard, she worked among her people as a healer after she was changed, and discovered she had a knack for it. She's never been one that follows the crowd, but she's quite adept at what she does. I want her to look you over. She won't hurt you; I promise. *Oh!* By the way, whatever you do, *don't* get her talking about Star Wars. She's *totally* obsessed with it." He grins and goes out to get Sara, who's been quietly sipping some aromatic, Asian-blend tea in the kitchen.

Sara follows Marc back into the living room, a second cup of tea in her left hand. "Marc, you should go update Liz. I'll keep an eye on our young lady here." She winks at Tess.

"Whatever you think is best." Marc says with surprising deference, and vanishes.

"You've got to know how to handle these guys, Tess. So, this is for you." She hands her a mug of tea.

"Oh, I'm not really a tea drinker." Tess says.

"Humor an *old* woman! It will make you feel better. I promise!" She gives her a smile she can't say no to. The tea is surprisingly tasty and Tess feels an urge to drink it all.

"There. Not so bad, was it?" Sara asks.

"No, it was quite good." She pauses, and then awkwardly asks, "So, you're one of them too? You, you look younger than me." Tess looks at Sara in disbelief.

She grins, and says, "Oh, *yes*! But I've been around *longer* than any of the ones you know. So, they listen to me when I tell them to do something. Sometimes *grudgingly*, but they listen." She says,

141

makes a deep sigh, and sits near Tess. "You've gotten yourself into a predicament, haven't you?"

"I guess you could say that. All this wasn't exactly in the job description!" Tess laughs sarcastically.

"Why do you think you ended up here? What brought you to this point in life?" She examines Tess's mind as she thinks and speaks.

"Bad luck? Probably karma for turning my ex in to the police? I don't know!" She says, frustrated.

"I don't think there's such a thing as bad luck. Whatever brought you here, you are meant to be here." Sara emphasizes.

"Meant to be in the middle of a bunch of vampires that feed on people like me? Yeah, right." She resorts to sarcasm again as a way of coping with it all.

"Yet, there was something about you that chose to answer the ad, and something about you made Marc and the others curious and take notice of you. What was that?" Sara asks.

"Marc insists I'm psychic or something." She stares down at the now empty teacup, avoiding Sara's intense gaze.

"That you are, indeed. Do you remember the migraine I treated you for?" Sara asks expectantly.

"As much as I remember anything from that afternoon." Tess puts the teacup on a nearby table.

Sara looks her in the eye and grins. "*Not* a migraine."

"I've had migraines most of my life. Of course, it was." Tess says dismissively.

"No, what you experienced was a buildup of telekinetic, potential-energy that got trapped behind the barrier in your mind." She taps Tess's forehead as she says this. "The feedback or overload caused the 'pain'" She explains, as though it should be obvious.

"A what?" Tess is confused.

"I believe you had a confrontation prior to your migraine??" She asks, and Tess nods. "You have strong, latent, telekinetic abilities. Do you know what that is?

"Yeah, moving stuff by thinking about it, like in Carrie. Marc can do that." She exclaims, remembering how he made his tablet

142

fly across the room and into his hands.

"Maybe more like a Jedi can do. Let's leave the horror movies out of it. My friend, you have that ability in spades! However, it's been buried for some reason. Your psychic shields work *both* ways. Not only did they keep the likes of Marc out of your mind, but it also kept your abilities trapped inside. That may have caused your earlier migraines." She explains.

"Huh? I didn't even know I had these *shields*, or *abilities* before Marc told me about them. And you're saying they've been there for what? Years? All my life?" she asks, incredulously.

Sara stares above and to the side of Tess's head, looking at her aura. "Chances are, they developed early on to keep your own abilities in check in a world that would not accept such things. Perhaps something happened when you were younger that made you block them. It's hard to know. But when you came here, the psychic energy being used around you triggered them, and your abilities expressed themselves increasingly after that."

"But why would that bring me here?" Tess asks.

"Some things are still hidden, but I'm certain you were meant to come here and be involved. You have all the traits we normally see in potentials, yet you're apparently not one. I can't help but think you'll play a role in something coming, something on the horizon. *No!* Even I don't know what, but you'll have a key role somehow." She says.

"Ugh, my headache's coming back." Tess jokes, pinching the bridge of her nose with her thumb and index finger.

"This is for you only to know. The others, they'll find out in due time. Things happen for a reason. Now, about the reason Marc called me in..." She purses her lips and squints in concentration.

Tess lets out a long sigh. "Let me guess, the medicine he gave me hasn't worn off."

Sara gives her a slight, lopsided grin and says, "Correct. In fact, it's not only opened your abilities, but the pathways are stabilizing; meaning you'll be experiencing more psychic events. So, I'd suggest you work with Marc to learn to control what's already manifesting. Once you get to a stable point, then we'll consider giving you another dose."

Tess's eyes go wide. "Wait! You're suggesting I become *more* of a *freak* than I already am?" Tess growls.

"Yes, Tess. You'll need these abilities for many reasons, including working with my people. None of this will be easy, but it's *necessary*." She looks off into the distance, perhaps at the future.

"I hope you're right, because right now, my life feels out of control, like my life as I know it is over." She admits.

"Or perhaps it is just beginning, and what you're feeling are the uncertainties of death and rebirth, figuratively, of course." She smiles. "Are you with me?"

"I guess so. Not like I have much of a choice with any of this." She relents.

Sara puts her hand on Tess's arm and says, "There's always a choice, even when it appears there's none; you choose how to handle what life hands you. You're meant to be here, but in the end, it'll be up to you to make the best of whatever destiny has in store for you."

Tess feels slightly dizzy, and extraordinarily tired. "I feel strange." Tess has trouble keeping her eyes open.

"You need to know these things, but Marc doesn't, not yet. The tea I gave you will make all this information move into your subconscious mind, where Marc won't see it. Unfortunately, it means you won't remember any of this, not consciously, but it will help you adapt and take appropriate steps." Sara explains, while Tess has trouble focusing and keeping her eyes open. "Besides, I need you to see me as more of a friend than an old wise woman vampire." She chuckles, and the last thing Tess thinks before she succumbs to sleep is Sara's laugh reminds her of Yoda. Once Tess is asleep, Sara places subconscious blocks in her mind, which will prevent her from talking to anyone but Apara about what they are.

SANCTUARY

Sunlight flickers through a small slit in the bedroom curtains, waking Tess. She stirs and turns away from the light, opening her eyes in the process. As her eyes focus, she sees Marc sitting in a chair nearby. "*Ugh*, what happened? Last thing I remember, you went to get Sara, and she came over and gave me some tea and *poof*! That's it. I woke up here. How long have I been out?"

Marc smirks. "It's Friday morning, if that tells you anything. Sara said she had to knock you out to examine your mind. Unfortunately, the drug we used the other night wasn't temporary after all. Now, it's my responsibility to teach you how to use and control your abilities, or we'll end up with a poltergeist anytime you lose your temper." He moves from the chair to the side of the bed.

"So much for even pretending to be a normal human." She laughs sarcastically.

"I'm beginning to doubt you were ever really normal, or you wouldn't be in this situation. Sara made it clear to me I'm to train you, and what I'm not proficient in, we'll get help with from the others." He pauses, knowing the next thing he has to tell her she may not take well. He lets out a long sigh, and looks her in the eye, concern showing. "I realize this is turning your life upside down, but please believe we have your best interests at heart."

Tess breaks eye contact and looks sullen. "Best for whom?"

He cocks his head to one side, realizing she's feeling sorry for herself, but says, "For all concerned, but, mostly, for you, Tess. What can I say? I screwed up. It's primarily my fault you're in this situation, but I want us to make the best of it now that there's no going back."

She listens to his words, tempted to snipe at him with some sarcastic, or even hurtful remark, but she can see and *feel*, his sincerity. "So, what *is* going to happen, other than me going through psychic boot-camp?" She inquires, still with a touch of sarcasm, but without the sharp sting she'd originally intended.

He looks at her, trying to gauge how she'll react, but can't. He jumps in with both feet. "Sara suggested I prepare a place for you in my home. Don't get the wrong idea. It will be your own apartment, just at my home. She told me until you can control your abilities, it's going to become increasingly difficult for you to be in an unshielded dwelling with other humans nearby. My home is not only shielded, let's just say it's nowhere near other humans." He reaches over and gently moves some strands of hair out of her face.

She drags herself up into a sitting position, narrowing her eyes as she looks at him. "I don't know, I like my apartment, and moving to your place feels kind of weird and kinda inappropriate. Besides, I thought you said you lived In North Asheville; there are lots of homes there." She remarks.

"I realize, had I been a normal human man, this would have been rather inappropriate, as your boss, to have you move to my place, but you know I don't have any designs on you in that way. As to what I said about my home, there's more to explain, or maybe it's easier to show you?" He extends a hand and helps her up. She's still dressed this time, and only needs to slip on her shoes, which are next to her bed. "You may be a little more disoriented than last time." He says as they disappear, reappearing in a clearing in a wooded area.

Sunlight peaks through the leaves, making the ground nearby look like moving bits of light. She turns around to look at her surroundings. There's a house about 30 feet away. Beyond the house is a creek or small river streaming by with more woods beyond. She hears birds singing, cicadas and other summer critters, as well as the loud sound of a woodpecker pecking away at a tree nearby.

"Where are we? Up near the parkway or something?" She's more disoriented and nauseous this time, but comes short of throwing up.

"No, nowhere close. If you were to place us on a map, I'd say we're somewhere in Virginia."

Tess wobbles and Marc steadies her. "Somewhere in Virginia?

Don't you know where you live? What city are we nearby? Why would you tell people you live in North Asheville? I get that you can pop from one place to another, but Virginia?"

"Tess. *Calm* down! I'm explaining this the best I can. Technically, part of my home *is* in North Asheville and the rest is *here*. I know that doesn't make sense, but it will. Follow me." He leads her into the back door of his home. "Come on." He says and takes her inside. The home is a mixture of different things from different ages: from centuries old artwork to modern conveniences, such as a large, flat screen TV and media center. "I'll give you a full tour later. The important thing right now, is the front door." He says with a grin. Marc opens the front door and pulls Tess through it. Instead of the clearing in the woods, they're in a residential area in North Asheville, with no wooded area or creek in sight.

"What the *hell*?" Her mouth drops open, and he drags her back through the front door and closes it.

"Have a seat." He motions to a sitting area with a comfortable looking, modern sofa, and some matching chairs, as well as a coffee table made from a huge cross-section of a tree, sanded down, and polished. The base is made from a smaller section of natural tree trunk, without the bark, polished and stained like the top, in a deep cherry wood tone. Later, she'll learn Marc made the table himself from a large tree that had fallen in a storm a few years earlier. She sits in one chair, and he sits in the one next to hers. "Are you at all familiar with Multiverse Theory?"

"I think so. The idea multiple realities exist simultaneously?" She inquires.

"Yes, parallel realities with different histories. For every event or decision, there are multiple branches depending on what happens, or decisions made, from insignificant events to major ones. Some are close to our own, while others are drastically different. You just crossed a threshold between two of them: the world you live in from day to day, and a world where humans never evolved. The two are quite similar, except for that, and some variation in plant and animal life, for example, no domesticated animals, though there are animals that went extinct on earth that still exist here, like the Tasmanian

Tiger. It's why you sometimes hear of an animal thought to be extinct showing up again after many years. It's usually one of my kind who brings a few over to reintroduce the species. But back on topic, we call this place Sanctuary, because that is what it is to us; a place where we can get away from all the random thoughts and emotions of human minds. You'll be able to be here without all of your neighbors' thoughts and emotions infringing on your mind at all hours of the night." He notices she's looking overwhelmed.

"So, you're telling me we're in an alternate what? Dimension? Reality? Universe? If so, how can I simply go through that door and be back in Asheville? I don't get it?" She asks.

He pauses, wracking his brain for a simple way to explain it. "We've got some of our own technology humans don't have. We're able to connect our homes in Sanctuary to placeholder or 'dummy' homes on the primary version of Earth. The front door is a type of portal linking the two homes, allowing transit between the worlds. Physical location in Sanctuary doesn't matter. My home could have been in France and still be linked to a portal home in Asheville." He explains.

"But a physical portal isn't how we got here. We ported? Can you hop across from one world to another? And what if you get to the wrong world?" Tess looks confused.

He laughs lightly. "So many questions! We're only able to go between this and our earth. They are closely bound. When we port, we enter a membrane dimension between the worlds that exists outside of linear space. It's navigated through thought. We can enter one place, knowing where we want to go or whom we want to find, and we exit there, nearly instantaneously. It's not true teleportation, but transportation through that membrane dimension. It takes a little work to learn it, but we can also exit into *this* reality, so I can come directly here, or if I need to bring a human, or humans, home with me, we can drive to my portal home in Asheville, and enter through the portal door." He can see Tess is struggling to grasp the concept at first, but slowly, he senses that proverbial light bulb flicker on.

She gets a quizzical look as she looks at a window with closed curtains near the front door. "So, if I were to look out that window, what would I see?"

Marc gives her a slight smile and a nod. "Good question! If there are humans in the house, then the windows interpolate from the portal home. Otherwise, it's up to me. Usually, I prefer the calm and serenity of the Sanctuary view, but if I need to check the weather in Asheville...." He trails off, leaving her to make a conclusion.

She sits there, thinking. "You know, when it comes to porting and that membrane thing, I saw something like that in a TV show called Eureka once. They couldn't travel like that, but a couple of characters ended up in a membrane outside reality, they called it the P-brane. They could see everyone and everything, but no one could see them, and they people could pass through them." She's trying hard to understand.

"Sounds like the same basic concept." He smiles, leaving it at that. "In any case, an apartment for you will be created here, in conjunction with my home. That way, you won't get overwhelmed, and if you lose control of your abilities, you won't freak anyone out or hurt them."

"Hurt them? Could that really happen?" She's appalled at the thought.

"Sara indicated she thinks you have a high telekinesis rating. It can often react to emotional outbursts, so until you can control it, getting angry could end up sending objects flying at the object of your anger." He grins. "I'm hoping to avoid being a target of that anger."

She rolls her eyes at him, but asks, "What about my apartment? And my things?"

"We'll take care of that. If you really want to keep your place, we'll take care of the rent in the meantime, or I can move your stuff here or into storage if you'd prefer. Your apartment here will be set up so you can come and go as you need to through the portal." He explains.

She looks thoughtful, then asks, "So, this isn't just to keep an eye on me and make sure I don't tell anyone about you and yours?"

He chuckles. "That won't happen anyway. Sara's seen to that. She put in a mental block. You won't be able to tell anyone human about us."

"So, if I'm no threat to your secret, why keep me working for you? Why not cut me loose and send me on my way?" She wonders.

"Because I'm responsible for this, at least in part, and now, with your psychic skills coming out, trust me, you don't want to deal with those by yourself, do you? Look at it this way; you've now got true job security. Besides, aside from the last week or so, I got the impression you enjoy working at Inspiration Inc." He raises one eyebrow, waiting for her response.

"I did... do. Except for Jason, but I understand Liz exiled him to Hendersonville." She looks at him for confirmation.

"Yes, he's in our office down there for now. We've warned him to stay away from you, or the next transfer will be out completely." He reassures her.

Tess feels awkward, as Marc is still technically her boss, but her gut tells her it's important to chime in on her perceptions about Jason. "If he's one of your potentials, I'd fire him, and soon. He'd be dangerous with abilities like you've got. He's bad enough as a regular human. But I'm pretty sure he'd abuse them. If he could've paralyzed me and had his way with me in the copy room, I'm pretty sure he'd have done so and had no remorse about *any* of it." She shivers.

"I'll talk to Liz about him. We need to update his psychological evaluation." He says. "Now, about this training. I'll have your apartment ready soon, but in the meantime, wear this." He hands her a necklace with a silver pendant with an odd-looking opal in it.

"What's this for?" She asks.

"It's a portable, psychic filter. We sometimes use them with new transformees who have difficulty controlling their abilities. It'll augment your own natural shields and keep you from losing control of your abilities. It'll keep unwanted mental chatter out from the humans around you and in public, plus keep you from sending objects flying if you get upset. It'll also protect you from projecting too much telepathically. Your ability to broadcast thought is also increasing, and while this isn't a problem for the other humans around you, if you start thinking about something strongly, we may pick up on it without trying." He explains.

After a few seconds, she puts it on. "You say it will keep me from picking up on other human mental chatter, but what about you all? Aren't all of you telepathic? Won't I pick up on you?"

"It's possible, but... how to explain this? Human and Apara frequencies are not the same. Think of it like cell phones. Some phones are single band. These represent humans. Humans won't pick up on anything unless it is on their bandwidth. Think of my kind as being *dual* band. We can use the same frequencies as you when we need to communicate with or read humans, but mostly, we're on our own bandwidth or network; so, you shouldn't pick up on our random thoughts, as our default frequency differs from yours." He explains.

Tess closes her eyes and lets out a long, controlled sigh, then looks Marc in the eye and says, "Okay, I've officially reached information overload for today. It feels like my brain's melting." Her stomach growls.

"Hungry? You should be. Though Sara said the medication she gave you would suppress the need to eat while you slept, I suspect your body is noticing you haven't eaten since lunch yesterday. I filled up your fridge last night, thinking we'd still be talking by dinnertime, but Sara had other plans. Let's eat out this time. We'll give that filter a test. Come, the meal is on me." He extends his hand again. This time, they appear in a shadowed corner of a shopping plaza. The air is warmer and more humid, and the roads busier than in Asheville. Tess feels only mildly nauseous after this port, but it dissipates quickly in deference to her hunger.

"I understand you like pizza?" He grins widely.

"Yeah, but you're the one who keeps telling me I should eat better, so not sure pizza for breakfast fits that bill." She says.

He pulls her out of the shadows, and they walk down a sidewalk. "You slept longer than you realize; it's nearly noon."

"Oh! I guess pizza's fine, then. But where are we? I don't know this shopping center." She inquires.

"We're up in Maryland. Best pizza I know of is at a place called Ledo Pizza. Hasn't made it to Asheville yet, but when one can travel instantaneously from one place to another, it's worth the hop." He grins and tows her behind him toward a restaurant with lots of cars out front.

"I guess there're some perks to hanging out with you! Saves on gas and travel time." She puts a positive spin on what should be making her feel unhinged.

"Let's get you some food." He opens the door to the restaurant, and they wait in line to get a table. After about 10 minutes, they get seated and order a jumbo pizza with sausage, pepperoni, pre-cooked bacon, mushrooms, black olives, and extra cheese, with mozzarella sticks on the side.

Tess, can you hear me? He paths to her, testing the filter to see if he can get through to her while she wears it.

She looks up at him, confused. "Of course, I can hear you. You're only a couple feet away."

He reaches across the table and taps her lightly on her forehead. *Try thinking a response to me. It's a good ability to have if you need to have a private conversation in a public place.* He grins, as he sees her eyes fill with comprehension that he's speaking to her telepathically again.

"How do I do that?" She asks out loud.

Think about what you want to say and imagine it traveling across to my mind. It will take some practice to get good at it, especially over distances, but try it. He nods at her, implying 'your turn'.

She purses her lips, uncertain what to say. *Can you hear me?* She paths, keeping it simple.

Loud, and quite clearly. Not bad for a first try. He smiles. *What do you want to do about your current apartment?*

Encouraged by her initial success, she falls into the mental conversation quite naturally. *I'm not sure. Part of me wants to hang on to it as a link to normality, but I'm not sure there's any point to that. Besides, my neighbors might get suspicious if they never see me and send the fire department or police to knock down my door and check on me.* She pictures an image of a large ax busting up her front door, but no one's inside.

We wouldn't want them to report you as a missing person, would we? He gives her a lopsided smirk. *Maybe it would be better to consider letting it go? We'll help you find a new place if you want one later. I know finding affordable housing isn't easy in Asheville.*

I guess so. I really hate moving, though. All that packing, lifting, unloading, and unpacking. Waves of apprehension about the process, and a mental cringe at the thought of moving again hits him.

Don't worry, you won't have to do it alone. We'll help you. I suggest we bring what you need over to your apartment when it's ready, and the rest into storage until we see what happens. He reaches over and touches her hand to reassure her.

At that point, the waitress brings the pizza in two half-size, rectangular trays to the table, as well as a double order of mozzarella sticks and sauce. The pizzas are loaded with toppings, and Marc serves her a couple of square, gooey pieces from the tray nearest her. Tess cuts into it and takes a bite. *"Oh my god!* I'm never gonna eat Asheville area pizza again!" She exclaims out loud. Then reverts to telepathy as she stuffs a large bit in her mouth. *You're going to be busy porting me up here at least once a week.* She grins at him, a strand of stringy, molten cheese stuck to her chin. He reaches over and pulls it off and puts it on her remaining pizza. Tess blushes in embarrassment.

Tess eats her entire section, or half a large pizza, as she's much hungrier than she realized. Marc gets a box for the leftovers from his half and the two of them find a hidden spot and port back to her place.

"Back home, safe and sound. I'm leaving the leftovers with you." He says. He notices she's a little too quiet. "Tess, what is it? I can sense something's wrong."

She had a good lunch with Marc and it makes her miss having someone to do things with, which makes her think of the moments after he fed from her the other night. It's difficult for her to talk to him about it, but wants to thank him for stopping things before they got out of control. "The other night, when things got *intense*; I wanted to thank you for stopping me. I know you said it was a reaction to everything, but you could have taken advantage of the situation. Many men would have." She avoids eye contact.

"Tess, it's nothing personal, but you're human and I'm not, and I'm still your boss, technically, which makes things complicated. We need to keep level heads and keep this as simple as possible. I didn't want to put you in a situation I was pretty sure you'd regret." He smiles softly and puts his hand on her shoulder.

"Well, thanks. And thanks for how you helped me afterwards. I guess I've been suppressing such things since my ex. I guess you

153

could say I swore off relationships after that, which is probably a good thing, considering it'll probably be hard to have one if I'm picking up on thoughts, and can't exactly tell anyone about my day job." She laughs it off. She sits on the sofa, and he joins her.

"We're going to have to take things a day at a time. There's no certainty you won't be able to move on with your life eventually, but right now, we need to help you with yourself first and know I don't have any such 'designs' on you, though I would like us to consider each other *friends*." He chooses his words carefully.

"I can live with that. I'm guessing it might be a good idea to think twice before 'sticking my neck out for you' in the future?" She laughs nervously. "or I could end up with more than I bargain for?" She focuses on some lint on her pants to avoid looking him in the eye.

"Most likely, that was a onetime reaction, connected with the psychic intimacy created by the drug, and my being in your mind for hours. While it's possible you may find some pleasure in being bitten in the future, should I need to feed on you, it shouldn't be overwhelming like it was then. I don't expect to feed on you. It's totally up to you. I won't ask unless it's some sort of emergency, and I won't expect you to volunteer. You do what feels comfortable." He says.

"Deal!" She says.

Marc stands and grabs his tablet from the coffee table. "I must make some arrangements for your apartment. Decide what you most need with you immediately, and I'll have some boxes sent over. Don't worry about packing large, we'll port everything over, so loading a truck won't be an issue. Now, other than that, take it easy and give your mind a rest, okay?"

"Will do my best." She watches him disappear in front of her eyes. "I'm not sure I'm ever going to get used to that." She says aloud, and hears a distant, mental chuckle, followed by 'eventually, you will.'

LEAVING NORMAL BEHIND

After Marc leaves, Tess looks around the house, figuring out what she wants with her immediately, and what can go to storage, or the trash. *Ugh! I really hate packing and moving! On the bright side, I won't have to hire movers or rent and drive a truck myself, like last time.* She gets in her car and goes to a grocery store that always has tons of banana boxes and gets about twenty flattened boxes and lids to start with. She stops at a hardware store and buys a couple of flat packs of moving boxes, as well as bubble wrap, packing tape, and packing paper. She spends the evening packing a lot of her knickknacks and glassware she won't need immediately, since that's always the most time-consuming to pack, as things need to be wrapped carefully. In the middle of getting some glasses out of a cupboard, Tess accidentally dumps a bag of flour on herself from the shelf above her drinking glasses. *ARG! Great, more mess to clean up, starting with myself.*

She goes upstairs to shower and strips off her flour-laden clothing. She takes off the pendant she got from Marc, rinsing it in the sink and putting it on a shelf across the room from the shower to dry. She turns on the shower, gets it the right temperature, and gets in. While she washes her hair, she gets an odd sensation on her scalp, similar to what she felt when Marc read her, but she gets the strangest thoughts running through the back of her mind, thoughts of conspiracies and feelings of paranoia. She closes her eyes and pushes them away, but they seep through anyway.

She sees images of guns and boxes of ammo stored under a bed, and then flashes from a computer screen with conspiracy theories about reptilian, alien overlords and how *they're* 'among us'. She gets a flash of faces that look familiar, but she can't quite place them, and a freaky mental image of their faces melting into the faces of so-called alien overlords. She still has shampoo dripping from her hair, down her face and across her eyes, but she gets out of the shower and feels her way across the room and snags the necklace, puts it back on, and gets back in the shower. Blissful mental silence envelops her. *Wow! He wasn't kidding. Not sure who I'm picking up on, but I don't want to be anywhere near them.* She thinks, as this incident makes her relieved she's moving, she just hates the physical process.

She finishes up, goes to her bedroom, and grabs a pair of gym shorts and a sports bra since it's warm and she's alone. She goes downstairs and puts all the flour-covered glasses in the dishwasher to run before packing them. She cleans up the flour and goes back to packing knickknacks.

She uses about half the banana boxes on that and fills the rest with books she won't need right away, setting aside those she'd like to have with her. She puts the boxes meant for storage near the front door. She'll get some of the square milk carton boxes for the ones she wants with her, as they're smaller and lighter to carry. She bags clothing in white kitchen garbage bags. She marks them with black sharpies, S for storage, and A for apartment. The S-bags go on the sofa, and A-bags she puts in a corner near the stairs.

She's still packing at about 11:30 p.m. when Marc paths her. *Tess, is it okay if I come by? I've got some containers for you, so it'll be easier to port multiple boxes at once.* He waits for a reply.

Tess focuses on him, even though he's not there with her, and thinks: *Sure, give me 5 minutes though, not dressed.* She doesn't so much hear a response as she gets the impression, he's waiting for her to say when he can come by. *Last thing I need is for Marc to show up with me nearly topless. Don't want to risk a repeat of the other night.* She digs through the clothes she's been packing, finds a usable t-shirt, and throws it over her sports bra. *Okay! All clear!* She paths.

Marc ports in, looking around. "I'll need to move some of these boxes. Do you have them organized in any way?"

"Yeah, all those banana boxes closest to the door go to storage, as do the plastic bags on the sofa. The rest of what's packed so far is stuff I want at the new place, assuming it'll fit." She realizes he hasn't told her how big it will be.

"Okay, I'll be back in a few." He goes over to the stack of banana boxes and pushes them together so they're all touching, and then puts both hands on them. He and the boxes vanish.

Well, that's impressive. Tess thinks, shaking her head.

Two minutes later, Marc ports in back, doing the same with the garbage bags of clothes. He ports in again looking around. "Do you mind if I rearrange things? The containers are large, so I need a place to put them."

"I guess." She sits on the sofa, feeling she's in the way.

Marc moves things around, including much of her furniture, either easily lifting things, and physically moving them, or porting some items across the room so he has enough clear floor space for a couple of 5x5x5 foot containers, one blue, and one red, which he ports in.

"Wow! I wish you'd been around the last time I moved. Had to do it pretty much by myself. I screwed up my back for 3 weeks." Tess can't believe how quickly he rearranged and organized things.

"There are more boxes inside the containers. Fill them and put them inside. Make sure you put things to go to the apartment in the blue one, and red for storage. Once they're full, let me know and I'll arrange for them to be moved, and bring you two more containers if you need them, okay?" He stands there, hands on his hips, looking around. He can sense the mixed emotions Tess has battling within her. He walks over to her and tips her chin up to look at him. "I know this is turning your life upside down, literally, and figuratively, but it really is necessary. I did a little checking, and your neighbor on that side has some serious psychiatric issues; he's on meds for paranoid delusions. Two doors down in the other direction, police have had to break up domestic disputes several times. Both will be problematic if you can't control your abilities."

Tess gets a look of realization. "About that, I may have already picked up on the guy next door."

"What? Weren't you wearing your pendent?" Marc looks at her as if she's a willful child refusing to eat her vegetables.

"I *was*, but I accidentally dumped a bag of flour on my head and took it off while I showered. That's why I wasn't totally *dressed*." She snaps, annoyed by his attitude. "Trust works both ways, you know that, don't you?"

Marc lets out a sigh, reeling in his irritation. "Okay, what did you pick up?"

"Not so much words, as images and feelings. I don't think he's taking his meds. I got these weird, paranoid impressions about alien overlords among us, and what had to have been a hallucination."

"Can you describe it?" Marc pays closer attention this time.

"Sort of. There was a group of people sitting in a row somewhere. They looked familiar, but I couldn't place them. He was seeing them morph from people into giant, lizard aliens with glowing red eyes, go figure." She looks off, vision unfocused, reviewing the images she saw in her mind.

"Anything else?" Marc reaches into his pocket where his cell is but waits to hear what Tess has to say.

"He has a stockpile of guns and ammo under his bed, or he believes he does." Her vision goes from unfocused to making direct eye contact with Marc, who looks worried.

"Tess, I need to look at your memories to see if I can recognize the people. May I?" he asks, remembering to respect her mind's privacy.

"I guess so. Not like you haven't been in there before."

Marc places his hands on either side of her face and closes his eyes. He slips into her mind without the barriers booting him out and reviews all the visions from her neighbor until he gets to the morphing scene. "*Merde!* It's Asheville's City Council! I'll be right back." He ports out, leaving Tess dazed from his reaction. He returns five minutes later, looking rather flustered. He says, "Okay, I'm taking you to my place for a couple of hours. Things are going to get crazy here soon. He's got plans to assassinate the Mayor and City Council members. He has a small, personal arsenal, including semi-automatic rifles with high-capacity magazines under his bed. He believes they're evil, reptilian overlords. The police are being tipped off, and I don't want you here when it all hits the fan, even with your necklace on, in case there ends up being gunfire." Marc takes her arm and ports her to his home again. "Make yourself comfortable. If you want to sleep, you can use my bed. I need to go coordinate with Liz."

Tess is stunned. "*Marc*? Are you saying what I saw was right?"

He nudges Tess to sit on the sofa with him. "Yes. And quite likely, you've prevented a mass casualty/assassination event. He was planning to do it at the next city council meeting, probably taking out not only the mayor and the council, but anyone who gets in the way." He pauses. "You did a good thing. Even if you took off the necklace." He grins. "I need to go, but I'll be back as soon as things are settled." He ports out, leaving her sitting on his sofa, stunned.

Tess takes out her cell phone and is surprised she has coverage, but checks her Facebook and keeps checking the local news station. Eventually, she finds a local police scanner site, and listens in to a series of communications talking about her building, and her neighbor being taken without a fight, as well as references to a weapons cache being found. She falls asleep on the sofa listening to the online emergency channel stream.

Tess stirs awake when part of the sofa she's sleeping on sinks lower as Marc sits on the edge. Him brushes her hair out of her face, so she opens her eyes, looking up at him. "Hmmm, is it safe to go home now?"

"Yes, and you know you were welcome to use my bed. It's a lot more comfortable than the couch." He smiles down at her.

"I fell asleep here, listening to the local police scanner online. Besides, no offence, but after the other night, it feels, well...." She blushes.

Marc smiles. "Got it! Ready to go home?"

Tess sits up, yawning. "Yeah, house still standing?"

"Yes, I made sure he went without a fight, and no, I didn't hurt him. I used my abilities to keep him from fighting back and got him to surrender peacefully, though he did keep calling the officers Nazi reptiles. By the way, his computer and Facebook are full of conspiracy theories, and he has detailed plans on his computer." He takes her hand and they vanish, reappearing back on her sofa in her apartment. "So, it's now about 3:45 a.m., go to bed. Packing will wait until tomorrow. Oh! Forgot to tell you, we got you out of your lease without penalty and you should get your deposit back."

Tess yawns and looks at Marc with half-closed eyes. "Thanks, I had no idea until tonight my neighbor was that big a nut case. I knew he was a bit off, but didn't think he'd be the mass shooter type."

"Night, Tess." He says, as she yawns, drags herself up the stairs, and waves back at him over her shoulder.

She gets up around 11 a.m. and looks out her window. Several police cars and a forensic vehicle are outside the neighbor's townhouse, and crime scene tape is everywhere. *Ugh, guess I'll keep my ass inside and pack. Don't want to get interrogated by the police about Mr. Crazy Alien Overlords. Aliens! Really! Like they'd have anything to do with this screwed-up planet!*

Tess spends the day packing the containers sent over by Marc, and making lists of what furniture she wants to bring, marking keep, storage and trash using blue, yellow, and red stickers. Most would go into storage, but her bed, recliner, stereo, television, some bookshelves, and a few other larger items would go to her new, temporary abode. Marc told her there's only a mini-kitchen set up, but she's welcome to use his full kitchen anytime, so she doesn't need most of her kitchenware except for a couple of pots and pans, and dishes enough for herself, especially microwavable ones. She looks around at the mess of boxes, bags and the two large containers. *At least, I hope it's temporary. Marc said once I get things under control, they'll help me find another place, assuming I ever get things under control.* She's moved before, but this feels different, like she's really leaving what she once thought was mundane reality behind for something verging on science fiction or fantasy, or even the Twilight Zone. Somehow, the two have become switched, and what she thought was reality for so long, is, in fact, fiction. She's sitting on her old, tattered sofa when Marc arrives with a couple of other people.

"Brought moving help? I assume they're also...." She asks.

"Yes, to both. I figured the faster we get things moved, the better. Do you have an overview of what goes to the apartment and what goes into storage ready?" He looks around the room.

"Yes." She says, handing him a list. "I'm guessing stuff like this sofa aren't even worth storing."

"It's up to you, but if you don't like it, leave it, and we'll get rid of it. We can find you whatever you need." He reassures her.

"Does my pay get docked?" She asks, curious.

"Tess, from now on, that won't be an issue. Even though you aren't one of us, you are with us, and our resources are vast. If you want to keep earning a regular paycheck to put away in your savings, that's fine, but as long as you're under my protection, whatever you need, we'll take care of." He explains.

Tess lets out a slight laugh. "What if I need my sanity back?" She blurts out.

He looks back over his shoulder at her, one eyebrow raised at her question. "Sara's offered her services for that." He says seriously, but with a slight chuckle at her sarcasm. "She asks about you frequently." He motions to the others to transport this and that. "We'll port these containers and bring two more back. Pack them, and we'll unload the others and be back for another two." He smiles, patting her reassuringly on her shoulder.

"I'm assuming I can take Mabel?" She asks, as her cat jumps down from a pile of boxes and cuddles her legs, then goes over to Marc and does the same to his.

"Of course! Besides, Mabel's already claimed me in her territory." He picks up the cat and scratches her behind the ears.

"Well, you did feed her a couple of times. Once you feed cats, there's no getting rid of them." She smiles and thinks, *I wonder if that same rule applies to vampires? Once you feed them, you're stuck with them.*

After about four hours, her apartment is almost empty. She looks at it, again feeling like it's more than a move this time, it's a permanent change to her life beyond relocation, like things will never be 'normal' again.

Marc ports back in. "Ready to go?" His voice echoes in the now empty apartment.

"I need to clean up before I leave, vacuum, wash stuff down." She realizes how strange it looks, nearly empty.

"Don't worry about it. I've arranged for a cleaning crew to come by. They need to take the sofa and a few other things to the dump, anyway." He puts his arm around her, and they port from her place to the apartment created as an extension of his home, in Sanctuary.

"Here we are. You're home for now." He opens the outside door.

Tess's mouth drops open, and she stares at a structure that wasn't there three days ago. "What the heck? When you said an apartment for me, I figured I'd be living in your basement or something, but this is a whole extension that wasn't even here three days ago!" She gasps.

He gives her an amused smirk, saying, "I told you we have resources." He laughs.

"Like what? Star Trek replicators?" She can't believe what she's seeing. She goes in and looks around, halfway expecting it to be unfinished and full of boxes to unpack. What she discovers is a nice, little apartment; one bedroom, a mini-living room, bathroom, mini-kitchen, and a 'library' room where her bookshelves and desktop computer are set up. All her things have already been unpacked and put in place or away except for a couple of boxes she'd marked private. They're sitting on her bed. She looks around and there's even a brand-new cat tree for Mabel, as the other was falling apart. She lets Mabel out of her carrier, and after sniffing around briefly, Mabel goes straight up the cat tree and watches Marc from the top, flopping on her side on a platform and staring down from an upside-down angle.

He looks at Mabel and chuckles. "Replicators? Not too far off! For now, get settled in. Tomorrow, it's back to work, including a promotion. Half of the time, you'll work on your web projects, and the rest, you'll work with me, or with others to develop your abilities."

She stands there, still stunned, but turns to him and asks, "What if I want to go out somewhere? Do I have to get permission from you or what? I know my cell works here, but what about TV, radio, and so on? If we're in another reality, will they work too?" She asks.

He leans against the doorframe to the kitchen and says, "Yes, they'll work, though our equivalent of television works differently. I'll show you later. We're not limited to local channels, or what a cable company may offer. We can pretty much pull up any channel on the planet, be they local, broadcast, or satellite; and yes, there's Internet as well." He gets her remote, flips on the TV, and England's BBC1 is on. There's a different kind of box on top of it, similar to a cable box, but the code on it is a mixture of letters and numbers. "I'll teach you how to use it later, but it'll pick up lots of channels." He grins.

She looks relieved, and says, "*Phew*! I was afraid I was going to be cut off from stuff here." She comments, thinking, *though it wouldn't make much difference since there really isn't anyone who'll miss me.* Her poor self-image rears its head, and a hint of that old 'poor me' feeling sneaks in.

"While you're here, you don't need to wear the pendant unless you're about to lose control." He says as he watches her plop down on a new, but comfortable sofa.

She looks up at him, a pensive look. "This all feels unreal, but in another way, normal reality feels nearly as unreal." She lets out a long yawn, as the long day of packing and moving catches up with her.

"It's going to take some adjusting for all of us. It's been a long time since I've had anyone living this close to me, let alone a human, but it's the best option for now. I left you an assortment of food in your fridge you can microwave if you're hungry. Get some rest, Tess. Tomorrow's going to be a busy day."

She looks at the door as he's reaching for the knob. "Why isn't there a lock on my apartment?" She asks, noticing the lack of security.

He turns back toward her and leans against the door. "And why would you need one here? There aren't any other humans who might break in, and, as you found out, if I or any of my kind want to get in, a locked door won't stop us." He says.

Tess looks thoughtful "Hadn't thought about it that way. And if I want to go out? Do I need you to port me or what?" She asks.

"My door is also unlocked. Merely go through my home to get to the portal door I showed you. Though if you go out, you *must* wear your pendant. The door won't let you out without it. That door, however, *has* a lock to keep humans out. Though not a physical key; it's programmed to only allow certain people through, unaccompanied, and you're one of them." He explains. "Oh, your car's parked out front of the portal home." He says, fishing out her keys from his pocket and tossing them to her.

"Kind of like the retina ID thing on my iPhone?" She asks.

"Something like that; now sleep, you're gonna need it." He opens the door and goes out, closing it behind him.

Tess checks the fridge and grabs some cold quiche to eat, then explores her new apartment, trying to determine where everything ended up. After looking around for a few minutes, she crawls into bed, still in her day clothes. She sets her alarm for 7 a.m. Mabel hops up and curls up beside her. Tess drifts off into an exhausted sleep. Her dreams are unusually quiet and mundane considering she's just left the normal world behind.

MEETING EVERYONE AGAIN, FOR THE FIRST TIME

Tess's alarm goes off, and she wakes disoriented, forgetting for a moment she's not in her old apartment. Mabel, however, doesn't care where they are, and promptly jumps on her chest, staring Tess down and meowing for her morning cuddles and food. Tess sits up and looks around. "Oh, yeah, I'm not in my old place. I wonder where the cat food ended up?" She walks to her mini-kitchen, Mabel nearly trips her by weaving in and out between her legs all the way there. It takes a couple of minutes to find which cupboard has the cat food and cat dishes. She feeds and runs water for Mabel, and notes the new, electric litter box in a small alcove. Going back to her room, she finds clean clothes, takes a quick shower, and gets ready. When she comes out, there's a tray of fresh scrambled eggs with cheese, bacon, and some bread with honey waiting for her, which she eats hungrily. After a few minutes, there's a knock on her door.

"Come in." She says.

Marc opens the door. "I thought maybe I should knock, since you are concerned about privacy. Is your breakfast okay? From the contents of your fridge and cupboards, I get the feeling you don't always start the day off well." He says, sitting in a nearby chair.

"No, I guess not, but while I wasn't working for a couple of years, I fell into some bad habits. I ate what I could afford, and comfort food. Thanks, though. It was great. Were those chives in the eggs?" She finishes up the last bites of her breakfast.

"Yes, chives, garlic, and paprika; but seriously, white toast, ramen, instant mac and cheese? From now on, you're going to take better care of yourself." He insists.

"So says the *immortal* vampire?" She jokes.

He shakes his head and gives her a look somewhere between

annoyed and amused. "Call it indefinitely lived. We try not to think about it as immortal, or some may get swollen heads, and forget what we're about." He chuckles.

She takes a last sip of coffee and then asks him, "It must be strange though, watching human history go by over centuries?"

"Strange, yes. In many ways, humanity is only now evolving beyond the more savage beings they've been for millennia. Granted, their outward behavior and knowledge has changed, but underneath, many, if they feel threatened, would revert to a primitive, 'kill or be killed' mentality. Fear is dangerous in large quantities." He explains.

"Yeah, I know. I keep up with politics and stuff. It scares me sometimes. It feels like humanity is dividing into two different species." She remarks.

He looks at her with surprise. "That's quite perceptive. In a way, it is. Humanity's moving from 'survival at all costs' mode into true civilization mode, but not all can make that transition themselves. Hopefully, future generations will move progressively into the civilized mentality." He stands and extends a hand to her; she takes it, and joins; the two of them are nearly instantly standing in his office.

"Well, that should save me a ton on gas!" She jokes, and continues her train of thought, adapting to this unorthodox means of travel now she's been through it a few times. "But, yeah, It feels like we're at a crossroads between some sort of 'Star Trek' like future, where people are equal and civilized, and some variant on 'Idiocracy'. Have you seen that movie?" She asks, and he nods. "It's like we're at some critical tipping point where it could go either way, like the fearful, 'survival' people, will fight to keep the more civilized people from continuing on their path, rather than being left behind." Tess, running out of breath from her nervous rambling, sits on the sofa in Marc's office.

"Very astute! It really is too bad you're not compatible. We *really* could use someone like you among us." He sits next to her.

She tilts her head to one side and lets out a long breath, saying, "One of you or not, I am 'among you', so if I *can* help, then *let* me!" She realizes this may not be such a bad situation after all, especially after what happened with her neighbor.

Marc looks at her thoughtfully, then says, "Relax. We've got a meeting with the others soon."

"Others? As in others like you?" she asks nervously.

"Of course, but don't worry, they won't bite!" He grins, showing slight fangs. "It's just Liz, Peder, Kari, Sara, and I."

She gives him a dirty look and wishes she had something she could throw at him for that joke. "Won't *bite*. *Hilarious*! I'm guessing they all know about everything?" Marc nods in reply. "And they're okay with it?"

Marc leans back on the sofa and stretches. Liz gave me a few 'I told you so' lectures, but they're on board with all this. We'll each be teaching you different aspects of your abilities. Peder is the best of us with telekinesis; I'm more telepathic/empathic, which we often shorten to telempathic. I have secondary precognitive skills, meaning they're strong, but not my primary skill. Liz has more precog ability than most, and Kari's a people reader." He explains.

"People reader?" She asks, wanting more clarification. "You mean like she can read their minds or something else?"

"We can all read minds, but I suspect you and Kari have the people reading specialty in common. Reading people is more than reading thoughts or emotions. It's an instinct about people and what drives them, or what they will do given certain circumstances. That's why Kari's the first person you met when you got here. She sizes people up and gets an impression whether or not they would work out." He explains.

"You mean whether they'll be good Apara?" She asks.

"Yes, primarily whether they're suitable for turning." He confirms.

"*Ha*! She must have been off the day she let me and Jason through." She laughs.

He straightens up and faces her. "Kari had some reservations about him, but his psychic skills are high, so we hired him. Just because we hire someone, doesn't mean they'll be turned. We observe them, their behavior, and psychological state. It also depends on if we *need* new people. We maintain a balance between our population and humans."

"And me?" She asks.

He lets out a long sigh. "You were a sparkly gem in a pile of dull rocks. She knew you weren't compatible, but she couldn't resist exploring that sparkle, so she set you up for an interview to see what we thought."

"And you all decided I was too, *damn* sparkly to let pass?" She asks.

He chuckles. "Pretty much; all of us were curious, but my intuition screamed the loudest. I still don't know why, and at one point, when I could read you, I saw how much you were on the edge from being turned down or rejected repeatedly. I wanted to help." He puts his hand on her arm.

"You know the old saying 'the road to Hell is paved with good intensions', don't you?" She halfway suppresses a grin.

"Yeah, but now we're on that road together, so we'll have to make the best of it. Now, seriously, relax. They're the same people you've worked with every day since you got here, the only thing that's changed is your awareness of what we are." He reminds her.

There's a quick rap on the door. Liz, Kari, Peder, and Sara come in. Tess can't sense any sign of anger or resentment from them, and her anxiety goes down a notch.

"Good morning, Tess. Marc's right you know. We won't bite! We're all going to work together to make the best of this situation." Liz sits in the chair closest to Tess. Kari and Sara sit opposite of Tess on the other side of the table, with Peder sitting on the other side of Marc on the sofa. Sara has a twinkle in her eye as she looks at Tess.

Tess searches for any sign Liz is merely putting on a positive face, but can't detect any deception. "So, you're really okay with all this?" Even though she can't pick up anything negative from Liz, she still needs audible reassurance.

Liz smiles kindly, making eye contact the whole time. "Yes, Tess. Since Marc failed to wipe your memory, we need to adapt, as do you. It appears you're starting to accept this whole situation, *yes*?"

Tess looks thoughtful, realizing she's taking this much more in stride than she'd ever have expected when she first found out about Marc. "I don't really have a choice, either accept this whole thing is real and you all are, well, not monsters, or assume I'm going mad. Or worse, I could choose not to cope with it and spiral back down into depression."

Liz nods her head. "That's a mature and healthy attitude. We can work with that. I'm guessing Marc's filled you in on a few things?"

"Some, but it's going to take me some time to really wrap my head around it all. He says you all work to help protect humanity, to usher us into a more civilized state. And you're gonna help me learn to develop and control my psychic abilities, which I never really knew I had." She glances over at Marc for reassurance she's summed it up correctly. He gives her a curt nod.

"Tess has a surprisingly good grasp of the world situation." Marc says, aloud, but sends more information about his and Tess's earlier conversation telepathically.

A flash of surprise lights Liz's expression as she looks from Marc to Tess. "Indeed? We'll have to discuss that sometime, but right now, we need to get started. Kari and Sara are going to work with you today. They'll work on a series of psychic aptitude tests to gauge your potential and map your abilities. Sara thinks our standard tests won't reflect your true potential; she's convinced it's significantly higher than they can measure."

Tess looks a little insecure. "I wouldn't know about that. I never knew I had these abilities until Marc told me so. I don't know why I would have any hidden talents, not when I haven't seen any evidence before now."

Sara scowls at her. "Tess, you do have significant potential. Please, trust me on that. And trust yourself to find it within." Tess gets a sudden mental image of Yoda, from Star Wars, speaking in Sara's voice: *Gifted You ARE! Help you we CAN!* Tess rolls her eyes in response to Sara's telepathic, Star Wars quip.

"Tess, you'll have to let us know if we overtax you. We're used to working with others of our own, not humans, albeit, an exceptional one." Kari explains, with a reassuring smile.

Tess takes a deep breath and lets it out slowly, in relief, as she looks at the faces of those around her. Even knowing what they are, she knows she's safe with them. "I was afraid you would react worse than this. I kept worrying you'd be mad at me or threaten me to behave or something, but you really *do* want to help me." Tess's defensiveness dissolves as she accepts these are the same people she's been working with the last weeks, no matter what they are.

Liz smiles. "That's our goal, to help, teach, and safeguard humanity. While we never intended for you to find out about us, now that you have, and we can't change that, we're going to consider you one of us, and that includes helping you learn what you need to. Naturally, it would have been easier if Marc could have suppressed your memories, but I suspect even though you can't become like us, we can find some way for you to help us make a difference. Now, why don't you go ahead with Kari and Sara? Get the evaluation over with and then we'll see where we go from there. I need to talk to Marc and Peder."

"Okay." Is all she can think to say and follows Kari and Sara out of Marc's office and down to a room off the lobby.

"So, Tess, how are you feeling after that, overwhelmed?" Sara asks.

"Not as much as I expected to be." Tess has an odd feeling as she looks at Sara, she's supposed to remember something, but can't.

"Good! Ready to find out how psychic you are?" Sara grins and has a twinkle in her eye.

They start by doing some simple Zener card tests. Duke University developed these cards to study parapsychological phenomena, and are comprised of twenty-five cards in a deck, with 5 each of 5 different symbols. The first round is telepathy, where Kari or Sara looks at each card and Tess guesses which one is being looked at. After about 20 trials, she's able to accurately pick up on both Kari and Sara nearly 100% of the time.

Kari collects and shuffles the deck. "You did extremely well."

"Thanks, but it helps you guys are telepathic and project." Tess discounts her results, figuring it's largely Kari and Sara doing the work.

"Tess, we're doing our best *not* to project, but point taken. We can't exactly put you up against someone like your friend Amy without an explanation for why we're testing you for psychic abilities." Kari puts the deck down in front of Tess, and takes out a strip of paper with each of the symbols on it. "In this test, we're not going to look at the cards. You're going to try to sort them without looking at them, into the five symbols. Try to picture what each card is and put it in the corresponding pile."

170

"Okay, I'll try." Tess sorts the cards out. The first couple of rounds, she gets the normal or chance number correct of four to six, but once she relaxes into it, her scores increase until she's getting about half of them correct, twelve or thirteen, which is far above what one should get by guessing.

"Very good! You're getting the hang of this." Kari exclaims, excited to see Tess do so well.

"Yeah, but on the first ones, I got nearly all of them; on these, only half." She throws her hands up in exasperation.

Kari laughs. "A normal result by someone without abilities is an average of five right per deck. In the end, you were doing twelve or thirteen per deck, and this time, you did it all on your own."

Tess is quiet while she considers that. "Well, that's weird. Maybe it's a fluke?"

Sara touches her arm, showing her the screen of a little gadget that could have been straight out of Star Trek as a modified tricorder. "Not a fluke. Not when you averaged 12 right for the last 10 trials. Besides, this gadget measures psychic energy and patterns, and it's clearly picking up strong activity from you."

Tess isn't quite sure how to take this news. "And that test was for clair... clairvoyance?"

"*Yes!* The next test we're going to do uses a random number generator to give you a number between 1 and 10. We want you to tell us which number will come up next. This will test precognitive ability. If you show positive results, we'll widen the number range to 1 to 20 or 1 to 100, okay?" Kari explains as simply as possible. Again, at first, she gets the chance score of about 1 in 10 or 10%. After a few dozen trials, she increases her score to about 1 in 4 right or about 25%. They eventually increase to numbers between 1 and 100, where the average should be 1%, and she averages 15%, though, sometimes she reverses the numbers, such as saying 63 instead of 36, and while these do not officially count as 'hits', there are enough of those incidences to be a clear pattern.

"So, how'd I do?" Tess shifts in her chair, feeling like she's been sitting too long but is hesitant to ask for a break.

"You did well! Not as strong as your telepathic scores, but you've absolutely got some precognitive abilities." Kari makes notes on her tablet.

They go on with other tests, including having Tess describe pictures in sealed envelopes, or pictures one of them is looking at. The last of the practical tests is for telekinesis. They bring out a six-sided die. "Okay, on this one, we want you to make the die roll the number we tell you to. To make sure neither Sara nor I accidentally do it for you, we're going to wear suppressor necklaces, then we know it's you and not us unconsciously doing it." Kari hands her the die, and after a few tries, she starts rolling the right number nearly all the time. They bring out a second die and have her try rolling the same numbers on both, and then specific combinations like a five and a three. By the time she's done, she's rolling about 85% of what she aims for.

Tess thinks: *Wow! Maybe I should go out to the casino in Cherokee and test this out.*

Kari's telepathic voice interrupts her thought. *I wouldn't if I were you. There are a couple of Apara working there and they'd have loads of questions if they came across a human using PK at the craps table.*

Tess responds with *Well, that's no fun!* Along with a mental pout.

Sara's watching her psychic monitor with glee at Tess's results. "*Bravo*, Tess! Knew you had it in you."

The rest of the day, they do more subtle tests of her energy field, neural pathway resilience, and whether she can manipulate energy. They also test her already significant shielding ability. By the time 5 p.m. rolls around, Tess's head is throbbing, her vision is blurring, and she feels like a low-level electric charge is jangling her nerves.

Tess slumps in her chair, sighing. "Can we quit for today? My brain's melting!"

Kari replies, "I'm honestly surprised you lasted this long. You did extremely well, considering you're human. You've given us a lot to analyze."

"So, did I pass?" Tess asks groggily.

"Well, we have to look at everything, but if I didn't know you weren't compatible, I'd have sworn you were a top potential." Kari praises her.

Sara squats in front of Tess and stares up at her head. "Hmm, I think you need this." She holds up a clear rod, stands and holds one end to Tess's upper arm. Tess feels a flush of pressure and warmth where it touches her skin, and her headache starts to abate.

"That should be helping the pain by now. Your psychic pathways are still raw after the drug from last week. The more you use them though, the less mental 'soreness' you'll experience; a lot like physical muscles." Sara explains. "Here's your necklace back. You should go home and rest after all this. If you're up to it tomorrow, your training will begin." She says and gives her an unexpected hug, and Tess sticks her necklace in her pocket without thinking.

This is all crazy. It feels so unreal. Tess thinks, as she leaves the room and walks carefully down the hall, disoriented, and unstable on her feet. More than once, she braces herself with a hand on the wall because vertigo kicks in. She eventually gets to Marc's office, stumbles in and dramatically flops onto the sofa, covering her face with her arm. "Grooooaaannnn!"

Marc looks at her, partly amused and partly concerned. "Are you alright?"

"I feel like I've been run over by a telepathic freight train." She groans.

"How'd it go? Did they give you any feedback?" He puts down his tablet and heads over to her.

"Sara was giddy with glee over my results, so I guess so. But I feel like I'm psychic road-kill!"

He chuckles softly at her expression. "Look at it this way, it's an experience other humans will never have."

"And that's supposed to make me feel better?" He sits on the edge of the sofa beside her. She tries to sit up, gets dizzy, and slides back down.

"Careful. Lie down. Nap if you need to. I have some work to finish, but when I'm done, I'll take you home." He notices her stomach growling, so asks, "Did you eat anything today?"

"Come to think of it, no. It was late afternoon before I realized it." She yawns.

"Hm, I'll make sure they give you a lunch break in the future.

While we do eat regular food, we don't need to eat as often or regularly, and I'm guessing they forgot you might be hungry. I'll be right back." He vanishes. He comes back two minutes later with several of the open-faced sandwiches Kari and Liz always bring in for lunch, and a cold fruit water. "I'm going to guess you may be dehydrated as well." He helps her sit up enough to eat and puts the plate and bottle on the table in front of her.

"Thanks. I somehow think it's a good idea to avoid discussing hunger or thirst with vampires!" She jokes.

Marc laughs. "If you can joke, I suppose they didn't do you any permanent damage. Go on, eat, and then sleep." He strokes her forehead like a parent checking a child for fever. He stands and turns off most of the lights in his office except for one at his desk so she can sleep. Once she begins eating, she devours her meal ravenously, then sleeps nearly as soon as her head hits the sofa.

A little after 8 p.m., Marc finishes his work, but Tess is still sleeping. He quietly walks over to her, gently touches her hand and ports her directly to her bed. As he's pulling the blankets over her, she stirs.

"Is it time to go home?" She rubs her eyes, and squints at him.

"You're already home." He says softly.

"I am?" She yawns and slowly sits up. "Hm, thankfully, my headache's gone." Her stomach growls even though she ate enough for two lunches a couple of hours earlier.

"I was going to let you sleep, but I'd better get you some more to eat. Psychic work uses a lot of energy, like physical exercise. Any cravings?" He asks.

She yawns again, then says, "No, anything'll do." She sounds exhausted and feels drained.

He comes back a few minutes later with a tray with apple slices, cold quiche, slices of cheese, crackers, carrot sticks and a bowl of shelled nuts, as well as another fruit water. "Wasn't sure what you'd want, but psychic work not only burns calories, but it can make your blood sugar drop into the hypoglycemic range; so, I brought you a mixture of sweet, fat, and protein." He puts it down on the bed.

"What time is it, anyway?" She picks up the cold quiche and

takes a bite.

"About 8:30. You slept nearly three hours." He says. "Feeling any better?"

"Well, like I said, my head's stopped throbbing, but I'm exhausted to the core." She yawns again and looks up at Marc. "So, what were you working on? Or should I say, what, besides webstuff, do you actually do?"

He settles in a nearby chair. "It's complicated. Lately, I've been putting together and analyzing various information that suggests something is, for lack of a better word, coming."

She gives him a 'go on' look. "What kind of information?"

"A mixture of real data, 'intelligence' on things going on now in the world, combined with some of our precogs' impressions, visions, and feelings of anxiety about certain places and subjects." He explains.

She gives a slow nod. "So, you're trying to figure out what they're seeing?"

He leans back in the chair, lacing his fingers together in a thoughtful pose. "Trying is the operative term. The problem is, my people are not really 'seeing' what's coming. They're uneasy, and *believe* it's something major, but can't get a good grasp on it. So, I'm working on correlating world events with their impressions."

"Any luck?" She asks.

He lets out a frustrated sigh. "Only that it's localized in the Middle East somewhere, which doesn't mean much these days. So much is going on there, but whatever it is, it's big."

"Maybe a war? Some sort of terrorist thing?" She finishes her slice of cold ham and aged cheddar quiche.

"Could be either, but it's not anything you need to worry about right now. You've got training tomorrow, and I want you to relax, eat, and get whatever rest you can." He stands to leave.

Tess stops him from leaving. "Marc..."

"Yes?" He turns around to face her.

"Thanks." She smiles.

"For what? Getting you into all this?" He chuckles.

"In a way, but for seeing me through it all, and being

amazingly nice, considering..." Her words trail off.

"You mean, considering I'm a blood-sucking monster?" He says with a grin.

"Well, there's that. But it's the whole thing. You could have been angry, and threatened me or done just about anything, but you've been nothing but nice and tried to help me. It's still over-whelming, but I know I'm in no danger, even being surrounded by blood-sucking monsters." She lets out a sarcastic snort.

He sits on the edge of her bed and takes her hand in his. "It's the way my people are. We aren't the bad guys at all, though I dare say, humanity in their current state wouldn't accept that if they found out about us, hence why it's so important our existence is kept secret."

"I get it, really, I do. I'm still adjusting to everything, and this whole psychic stuff on top of it. I'm not sure which end is up, but I do know I can trust you." She puts the tray with leftovers up on a shelf above her bed, hoping Mabel can't get to it, and then turns back toward Marc, smiling.

His face softens, and he leans over and hugs her. "You can always trust me. Now, I've got more research to do. Let me know if you need anything and take it easy. The next couple of weeks are going to be intense training just to give you basic control and minimal skills. Oh, and I'll make sure they give you a break from now on." He walks out and back to his part of the dwelling.

Fully awake now, Tess pulls out her laptop. It connects automatically to Marc's Wi-Fi, and she checks her email and Facebook. She searches for any news about the Middle East. Eventually, she goes back to sleep, and sleeps heavily.

MORE THAN HUMAN

Tess wakes early the next day, anxious about her training. She checks her email and social media, showers, gets dressed, and once again, breakfast's waiting for her in her kitchen when she's done. Marc has left her a plate of pancakes with syrup, bacon and two fried eggs, and a large mug of hot coffee. She paths to him, *are you trying to get me even fatter than I already am?*

You're going to be training today, so you'll burn off all those calories and more. She gets an image of a large mental grin. *Let me know when you're ready to go.*

Tess eats quickly, rinses off the dishes and brings them with her over to his part of the residence, handing them to him. "Thank you. But you're really going to end up spoiling me. Maybe I can go shopping later and get some stuff for my fridge, so you don't always have to make me meals?"

"It's up to you. I enjoy cooking, so I don't mind at all. Ready to start your training?" He extends a hand to her, which she takes and they port into his office.

"Doesn't anyone ever wonder why they never see you come in the front door?" She inquires.

"With most people, even if they do notice, I can redact their memories or perceptions and make them think there's nothing unusual happening. It's only you I can't do that with!" He lets go of her hand and puts his things down on his desk.

"Yeah, about that, I hope no one gets the wrong idea about us. I mean, we came in together yesterday and today, and I came out of your office, not the front door." Tess gives off a worried vibe.

He sits at his desk and gives her a sideways glance. "Worried about rumors?"

"Something like that. Especially when nothing's going on." She sits in a chair by his desk. "I don't want *anyone* to get the wrong idea. Before Digital Danger, I did some data entry at a place that's long gone, but the boss there was dropping hints he and I, as well as he and another woman there, were sleeping together. He had a real inferiority complex and felt that would make other men respect him. I found out when people kept whispering around me, so I cornered someone, and they told me what he'd been saying. I quit the same day."

"You really haven't had the best luck with jobs, have you? Okay, I get what you're saying. In fact, if you want to, you can even drive to work if it makes you more comfortable. Your car's parked out front at home. Please make sure you wear your pendant. The last thing you need, is a psychic episode while driving that causes an accident." He says, realizing he really doesn't want anything to happen to her.

"Okay, it's a deal. Sometimes I'll drive, and sometimes you can drop me off outside so I can walk in. I mean, it would be another matter if we were, well, you know. But we're not, I'm only subletting an apartment, and I really want to avoid the 'slut rumors', cause here, I certainly can't quit, can I?" She says, expectantly.

Marc gives her an amused look and shakes his head, then checks his internal messages, and there's a schedule for Tess's training. "Looks like Peder's going to work with you on PK this morning, and this afternoon, you'll come back here, and we'll work on your web projects. We should get your two projects wrapped up so we can focus on your abilities for the next few weeks. If you can get the layout and content finalized, I can get Amy to do some of the basic work. If you want to achieve even a reasonable level of normalcy, we need to get your abilities under control."

"I know. Too bad I can't wake up tomorrow and have it all down pat." She jokes.

"Once you get some basics down, we can try shared dreaming again, so we can speed up training, but it would mean taking

178

another dose of the 'blue stuff'." He grins.

"*What*? So, I can be even weirder? No *thanks*!" She scowls at Marc. "Damn it! Let me get used to being this weird before making me weirder."

"Weird is a relative term. Compared to the rest of us, you're relatively normal." He chuckles lightly, shaking his head. "You should get over to Peder; he's ready for you."

Tess leaves Marc's office, and Amy stops her. "Hey, girl! Didn't see you come in. Are you feeling any better? They said you were sick this last week. You're looking pretty good now."

"Oh, yeah, I was not feeling great. Things have been totally upside down, but it's getting better. Listen, I've got a meeting with Peder, he's going to teach me some new skills, and he's waiting for me. How about lunch? I hear Asian Palace is having a carryout deal this week. We could zip over and get some stuff off the buffet and come back here with it." Tess tries to be truthful in a roundabout way so Amy doesn't get suspicious. *Damn! Almost slipped and told her I moved, but then she'd want to know where, and that would be hard to explain.* She thinks.

"Sure, grab me when you're done with your meeting."

"Oh *crap*! I don't have my car today. My *neighbor* dropped me off." Tess fumbles to make an excuse for not having her car. *I may have to start driving in myself just to avoid shit like this.* She thinks.

"No biggie, girl. I've got mine. Something going on with yours?" Amy wonders.

"It's getting a little old and eats gas like popcorn, and my neighbor was going this way to work today anyway." Tess bluffs her way through her mistake. "Gotta run!"

Tess continues down the hallway and knocks on Peder's door. She hears *Come in, Tess*, in her mind.

Tess opens the door and goes in. "I'm never going to get used to that."

"Come sit. You'll get used to it eventually, but if it makes you uncomfortable, we'll stick to traditional speech for now." He faces her as she comes in and sits in a chair by his desk. "I've been looking over your tests from yesterday. You've got strong telekinetic potential. Sara also told me your migraine after your confrontation with Jason was likely bottlenecked kinetic energy that got trapped inside your shields."

"Really? *Weird*, somehow, I *know* that, but I can't remember anyone telling me that until now." Tess focuses, trying to remember where she'd heard that before, but can't.

He reaches into a drawer and pulls out a pile of dice, not only six-siders but eight, ten, twelve and twenty-siders like Colton used for playing D&D with his buddies from work. "We'll warm up with the six-siders, and once you get up to speed with those, we'll try dice with more sides. Same concept but takes a little more finesse and focus. Focus on rolling ones. Do this ten times, and then move on to twos and so on."

She picks up a six-sider, and starts rolling the die, eventually getting it most of the time. She switches to the eight-sider, then the ten and the twenty. They work on it for about an hour and a half. She does well but has trouble with the twenty-sider; often, the desired number would not be on the top side, but to one side of the top.

"Now we're going to try something a little different." Peder stacks six, six-sided dice on top of each other like a tower. "I want you to focus on knocking the tower down. It's a brute force exercise. All you have to do is knock it down, or at least, part of it."

Tess tries, but at first, it's like she can't figure out how to make it start moving. "Why could I do the rolling dice, but not these?" Frustration suffuses her voice.

"It's basic physics. It takes less force or energy to nudge an object already in motion than it does to put an object in motion. That being said, the difference in PK energy need is minor, but it's compounded by your psychological, mental block saying you can't move it without physically picking it up and creating a visible cause-and-effect reaction. It's easier psychologically to influence action already in progress than it is psychologically to initiate said action. Make sense? Watch me." Peder doesn't even look at it and the tower falls, and then rebuilds itself with the dice floating up and stacking themselves.

Tess watches, amazed in one way and annoyed at the ease with which he does it. "Show-off!" She mutters under her breath.

Peder laughs lightly. "Here's what I want you to think about: Do you believe PK is possible?"

"Obviously. You just did it, and I've seen Marc do it before." She answers.

Peder nods. "Do you believe you're able to influence how the dice roll?"

That's a harder one for Tess. "Logically, yes. I know what the probability is and I beat the probability, but somewhere, in the back of my mind, I'm still not sure I'm doing it."

"You mean you can write it off as warped probability, or maybe I'm helping you, or some kind of trick, right?" He picks up a loose twenty-sided die and holds it in his open hand. As Tess watches, it rises off his hand; it spins and twists in the air about 3 inches above his palm. "Hold out your hand. The die is in motion. I'm going to pass it to you to take over."

"Huh? But I ca..." The die floats over to her and floats above her hand.

"Feel the energy surrounding it. Imagine what the object feels like in your mind, continue to see it floating there and spinning. I'm going to let it go on the count of three. One, two... three." He says slowly, and for a split second, she's able to hold it, rotating it over her palm, until she realizes he's let go. Moments later, it begins to wobble, and drops with a thunk to the desk.

"Crap! I can't do it!" Tess whines in a defeated tone.

"But you *did* do it." He grins.

"No, as soon as you let it go, I lost control, and it dropped like a rock." She sulks.

"I only told you I let it go on the count of three. I let it go well *before* I started counting. You only believed I was still doing it, but you were." He watches for her reaction.

Slowly, Tess lifts her gaze to his. "Are you serious? Did I *really* do that?"

"Yes, you did it *without* effort, until you believed it was all on you, and you were incapable. You must relax and just *do* it. You aren't working with muscles where you must *push* it, apply a physical force; see what you want it to do in your mind, you can even close your eyes if that helps, and allow it to happen. You *have* the ability; that much is certain! What you *lack* is belief in *yourself*." He stares her down until he's certain she understands what he means, then motions to the tower of dice for her to try again.

Saying nothing, she looks at the tower, then closes her eyes, and pictures them spread out as individual die on the desk. After about forty-five seconds, she hears dice hitting the table and rolling. When she opens her eyes, they're exactly where she'd pictured them. "Oh, *my God!* Did I *do* that?" She looks at Peder for confirmation.

His blue eyes sparkle with amusement. "That you did. Let's try it a few more times." He remakes the tower. With each attempt, the time it takes shortens. After about ten successful attempts, he changes one thing. "*Open* your eyes this time."

Tess stares at the dice, eyes open, and, once again, she mentally pushes the dice. It vibrates, and the top one skews to the side in the stack, but they don't fall. "What the *fuck* did I do wrong now?" In her frustration, she sends all the dice flying across the room, and bouncing off a nearby wall. "Huh?"

Peder bursts out laughing. "Sara would pull out an appropriate Yoda quote for this. Something about 'do not try, only do'." He gives her an ear-to-ear, mischievous grin. "When you pictured it with your eyes closed, you weren't treating your PK like a muscle, physically pushing the tower to make it fall. You pictured what you wanted it to do, and how it should end up, and your ability made it happen without major effort. When you opened your eyes again, your brain saw it as a need to push from this side to make it fall, like you were going to do it with your finger, and it didn't work, did it?"

"No, it only shook a little and the top one slid about 3 millimeters to the left." Tess pouts.

Peder pauses for a second, opening up his hand, and all the dice come flying back and land in his palm. Tess looks on amazed. "And what were you thinking when you turned these into projectiles?"

She pauses, thinking. After a couple of minutes, a look of understanding spreads across her face. "I wasn't, I wasn't thinking. I was frustrated and wanted the *damn* things far away from me."

A broad smile spreads across Peder's face. "*Exactly*! No thinking about putting force behind them and throwing them physically, you wanted them away from you and your ability did it for you. And here ends the lesson for today. Take these home with you and practice." He dumps the pile of dice into her hands. "Go get yourself some lunch. You're going to be hungry after this. You've burned more calories than you realize. Let's meet again Friday morning and see how you do after some practice."

Tess gets up, hands full of dice. "Thanks. I'll keep working on it." Tess heads out the door and goes back to her cubicle, dumping the dice in her bag.

Amy peeks over the wall. "Ready for lunch? I've been craving sweet and sour chicken ever since you suggested Asian Palace this morning."

"Cool, let me check in with Marc before we go." She heads to Marc's door, but stops herself from going straight in. She knocks, then goes in.

Marc looks up from his computer screen, taking a mental inventory of her mood and aura. "Got a good workout, didn't you?"

"You could say that. It was certainly an experience." She says. "I thought I should check in before I go to lunch."

"Want to grab lunch together? I'm at a good stopping place." Marc suggests, on the verge of standing.

"Oh! *Sorry*! Amy and I are going down to Asian Palace. They're doing a half-price, buffet-carryout special. Want me to bring you anything?" Tess raises one eyebrow, waiting for his answer.

"No, that's okay. You go ahead with Amy." He looks at the time. "How about you meet me here at 1:30 with your projects and we'll work on those together."

"Sounds good." She heads for the door.

"Tess! Aren't you forgetting something?" He asks, knowing

she can get forgetful about certain things.

"Not that I can think of, what?" She looks back at him.

"Your necklace works best if it's on, not stuffed in your pocket."

"Oops! *Thanks*. I guess after practice, I really should wear it, so I don't turn a bunch of egg rolls into projectiles." She heads back out, a light bounce in her step.

1:30 p.m. rolls around, Tess knocks on Marc's door, and goes in. "I know you said you didn't want anything, but I got you some stuff anyway." She takes a Styrofoam food box out of a bag and hands it to him. She pulls her folders and tablet out of her bag and gets ready to work.

"Thanks. You really didn't have to bring me anything." He opens it and takes in the multitude of scents from salmon, teriyaki chicken, mushrooms, broccoli and beef, and other odds and ends shoved into the carryout box. He unwraps the plastic ware and eats some while Tess gets her things organized.

"I wasn't sure what you liked, so I got you a bit of this and that. Hope there's something you like in there." She organizes her layouts for the women's shelter out on the main meeting table so they can go over them.

"It's great. You grabbed most of my favorites. Thank you!" He puts it aside, walks over to the sofa and sits with her and they go over her proposals for the website. "How much of this do you have coded?"

"I've got the templates made up and the menus, basic graphics, and standard pages. I'm working the bugs out of the panic button option, so the main framework for the site is about 85% done. They'll add most of the content through the CMS (Content Management System)." She points to the admin user layout sheet.

"Sounds good. How long do you think you need to finish up this project so we can hand over a beta version for them to test out?" He asks, distracted.

"I can probably debug the panic button today and have a sandbox version ready to go for the client by tomorrow afternoon." She looks up at him and smiles.

"Sounds good. Let's wait with the PPH site until you're done with the Women's shelter. Sorry, I'm distracted today." He rubs his eyes and stretches.

"Same thing you told me about yesterday? The 'something's coming' mess?" She makes eye contact and can sense his stress.

"Yes. A new batch of precog reports rolled in this morning while you were with Peder. It's mostly more amorphous anxiety about the Middle East, and no specifics. If it's hitting so many of us, it's got to be a major event, but I can't correlate things without details." Frustration and exhaustion color his tone.

"I wish there were something I could do to help. I guess I'm adding to your load. Sorry about that." Tess tentatively touches his hand, and he smiles.

"To be honest, it's been nice to talk to someone about it. Just let me know if it's too much for you to handle, okay?" He gets back up and heads to his desk, eating more of the now cold, Chinese food.

"Hey, I'm handling being surrounded by a bunch of blood-suckers!" She says with obvious sarcasm. "I'm sure I can handle listening to you blow off steam about precognitive stuff. Who knows. Maybe I'll catch something you've missed." She gathers her papers into the folder again and sits by his desk.

"Thanks. I'd better focus on this. We can work on telepathy and empathy tonight after dinner if you're up to it." He scoops up some salmon and stuffs it in his mouth while reading reports on his tablet.

"I'll probably be up to it, but I don't know about you. And if you're not, Peder gave me PK practice for homework." Tess watches him focus, and he gives her an absentminded wave as he stuffs a dumpling in his mouth. She goes back to her cubicle.

Amy leans over her half wall again. "So, you two spent a lot of time to-gether today. You met with him this morning and now for a couple of hours this afternoon. Got anything you wanna tell me?" She grins at Tess.

"Nope, not a thing. He's been helping me catch up with stuff after being sick last week." Tess says, hoping she'll drop the subject.

"You two would make a nice couple. And you deserve someone

nice after your ex and that idiot Jason bothering you. Marc acts so protective of you." Amy remarks.

"He's just a really nice guy, but that's it. When I told him, well, them, about my mess at Digital Danger, and how it's been hard to get a job, he took it upon himself to help me. That's just the kind of guy he is, seriously." Tess tries to sound normal. *Well, better Amy than others thinking something could be going on. Amy only wants me to be happy. Unfortunately, I can't explain to her why I'm not in any position to find someone right now, including Marc.*

Tess forces herself back to work, but something is nagging the back of her mind. She thinks about how Amy is compatible, while she isn't. She no longer feels the urge to warn her, as she's stopped seeing Marc and the others as something to fear. In fact, she's oddly jealous Amy can become one of them if they choose her, yet Tess will always be on the periphery; with them, but not part of them. Her mind briefly wanders toward thoughts of how being compatible might have changed the situation with Marc, but she rapidly reels in that distraction and focuses on her project once again.

Tess finishes up the Women's Shelter project by Wednesday afternoon, and the Planned Parenthood on the following Monday. She continues to work with Peder on her PK, Liz with her precognitive abilities, Kari with her people-reading skills, and Marc, at home, with her telepathic and empathic skills. Her strongest, active ability is her people-reading skill; something she realizes she's been using all her life to size people up. She's never thought of it as a psychic ability, just as having a good, intuitive, people sense. It's different from Marc's empathy, however, as she can understand a person's thoughts, actions, and even emotions without taking them on herself. She stays more objective, like a psychologist. Her PK has a lot of potential, but she's still having issues moving larger objects, it's more due to continued psychological blocks, but she's working through them. Unfortunately, if she doesn't wear her necklace, and gets upset, it often takes on a poltergeist-like outlet, and things go flying or drop off shelves when she's angry or frustrated.

Marc's means of working with Tess on her telepathy and empathy is to hold telepathic conversations at home, and having her try to read other humans empathically, but not him. He tries his best to keep his emotions hidden to avoid any kind of emotional entanglement with her. After their brief, intimate incident the first night he took her home, Tess also hides any feelings beyond friendship, knowing Marc will only lecture her on keeping things friendly and platonic. Tess can easily converse with Marc telepathically, but occasionally picks up hints of something more behind his telepathic 'words'. She writes those emotional overtones off as her own loneliness and wishful thinking, especially since she still feels like damaged goods after everything with Colton.

TESS-TING THE WATERS

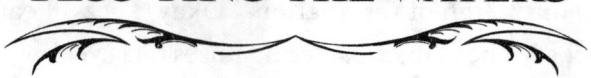

Tess has been working hard on her skills for about two weeks and is feeling more confident. She's sitting in her apartment taking a rare break. She's lying in her recliner; binge watching a Star Trek series to give her mind a break from vampires and psychic training, munching on a bowl of trail mix. It's Saturday afternoon, and Marc knocks on her door. Tess can sense he's excited about something, but can't tell what. "Come in!"

He comes in and she hits pause on her show. "Don't suppose you're hungry at all?"

"Yeah, kind of. Not sure what for." She pops the recliner into the upright position. "Got anything special in mind?" She knows he's up to something, but can't figure him out.

He grins and drops onto her sofa. "Well, get yourself cleaned up. We're going out tonight."

She narrows her eyes and looks at him skeptically, not sure she heard him right. "What? Like a dinner date?"

"No, not a date; a *field* test." He grins.

"Field test?" she asks, uncertainly.

"I was thinking we could go out for the evening, among a room full of undisciplined humans, in a restaurant, without this." He picks up her necklace from a nearby table and stuffs it in his pocket.

She visibly cringes at the thought of dealing with tons of people unprotected. "I don't know. I'm not sure I'm ready for that." She's not in the mood to deal with a lot of people, with or without her necklace.

"Well, we're going to a restaurant, not a full bar or a club. A club's the worst place for an uncontrolled telepath or empath to visit because so many humans are intoxicated, meaning their minds get loud and crazy, a lot like their physical voices." He explains. "Besides, I'll be there if it gets overwhelming. I'll shield your mind until we can get that pendant back on."

Tess lets out a sigh of resignation. "Okay, I *guess* I can *try*."

Marc cocks his head to one side and raises one eyebrow, surprised at her lackluster reaction. "I thought you'd be happier about getting back out among your own kind. Lately, it's been all work or here."

She shrugs. "I *was* planning to take a day off and take it easy. Otherwise, it feels odd now, knowing what I know, being able to do this stuff, and knowing you guys are out there trying to deal with a lot of the crazy shit 'we humans' do. It changed my perspective and priorities." She gets up and looks for something nice to wear from her recently washed and folded laundry. "I was never exactly a social butterfly, and even less so since that mess at my last job. I'm not feeling very sociable with people whose priorities are things like who's going to win a football game or be the next winner on some reality TV show. Such things seem so transient and unimportant anymore."

"Were you even into those things before we met?" Marc asks. "I didn't get the impression you were quite a typical human in many respects, even then."

She rolls her eyes and sighs. "You got me there! I wasn't into those things, but now, they seem even more superfluous. Unimportant, especially if what you all are feeling is as big as you think it is. I'm not sure I'll ever make that kind of difference, but I'll do what I can to help."

"And that's why we have to work on your skills. Who knows what you might sense when you're out and about. Maybe even stuff we miss. I know you've been working hard, and would like a break, but I already made reservations. So, why don't you get ready? I've got to do a couple of things before we leave." Marc returns to his place to get ready and takes a few minutes to check the latest precogs routed his way. *I need a break too.* He thinks.

After 20 minutes, she comes into his part of the dwelling. "Ready as I'll ever be!"

He looks up from his tablet and is surprised how nice she looks. She's wearing black pants and a flowing, flowery top with a square neckline; something she bought at a vintage shop; a style they used to call a handkerchief top, with two lace edged handkerchiefs sewn to the shoulders for sleeves. She's done her makeup and even styled her hair. "You look *very* nice. I believe eating less ramen and mac and cheese has done you some good." He smiles, gets up, and heads for the door, waiting for her to follow him.

"Yeah, the carbs really aren't great for me, but unemployment wasn't either." She notices Marc's hand on the doorknob, car keys in hand. "Aren't we going to 'pop' over to wherever we're going?"

Marc chuckles, his eyes sparkling with amusement. "*My!* Aren't we getting *spoiled*?" He notes a blush of embarrassment on Tess's face. "No, I thought we'd drive tonight; Do things the human way." He says, "But I'm driving." He smiles. "Don't want you getting angry at the other drivers and unconsciously blowing out their tires with your brain." Marc laughs.

"Marc!" She punches him in the shoulder.

"OOOO! Was that a gnat I felt?" His eyes sparkle as he eggs her on.

"No fair picking on the weak human." She pouts.

"Come on, I've made reservations for us at a farm-to-table place downtown." He opens the car door for her.

They get into his car and drive about ten minutes south, through town, to the restaurant. It's busy, and they have to wait in a short line outside for a few minutes until their table opens up. Tess feels uneasy, as she hears both voices and thoughts around her, a blended cacophony of input. Add in splashes of emotions from those around her, and she unconsciously digs for her necklace in her pocket, remembering Marc has it in his. Marc notices her agitation and extends his own shields around her mind.

"Sorry, wasn't expecting quite so many people. From what I can glean from some of those around us, many people are in town for a festival this weekend. So, our table isn't quite ready yet, but we should get in sooner than the walk-in clientele." He nods to the long line of people waiting to get in, while they are in a short line of people with reservations. She relaxes a little, grateful for Marc shielding her for the moment.

Finally, Marc hears his name called, and they're able to go to the front of the line, as their table's ready. Tess is still anxious without her necklace, but she feels Marc helping barricade her mind from the worst of it.

As Tess enters the restaurant, she still gets bits and pieces of thoughts and emotions from people, but not nearly as much. Her focus shifts to the wonderful smells of the food around her. *It's odd, but as I've worked on my psychic skills, my regular senses have gotten stronger too. Hmmm, wonder why?*

Since Marc is shielding her, he can't help but pick up her query and paths back. *It's because your psychic skills are augmenting your physical senses a touch, like increasing the gain on a mic or using binoculars, except with multiple senses. That's my guess. Not like we've had another human to compare you with.*

Didn't realize you were listening. She paths.

I wasn't, not actively, but with me shielding your mind; it's hard to miss your public thoughts. He paths with a mental grin.

A woman brushes against Tess's arm on the way back toward the restroom, flooding Tess briefly with feelings of urgency and a lack of equilibrium. She panics, feeling overwhelmed and off balance.

He takes her hand and squeezes it to remind her he's there. *Relax, Tess. Tensing up is going to make it harder to control.*

Sorry! That caught me off guard. She was drunk, as well as needing to pee. I'm guessing touch can increase telepathic signals? She fights to regain her own equilibrium after feeling the other woman's lack of it.

Yes, that's why I had you lean against me when I tried to redact your memory. Didn't work, but it did improve the connection.

The waitress leads them to a table with a window view of the street, facing Pack Square and the Art Museum. A lot of people are milling around the square, as there are vendors setting up for the annual Pride Festival the next day. The waitress hands them menus and promises to be back shortly.

Now, let's order something good. Whatever you want! He paths.

When their server comes to the table, Tess orders a wild mushroom tortellini with Marsala wine sauce, and garlic marinated chicken. "Is that okay? It's kind of expensive." She feels like she should order something less extravagant.

"I told you, whatever you want. The cost isn't an issue." He orders the same as Tess. "What can I say? It sounds good." He chuckles.

Now, Tess, while we're waiting for our food, take those deep, slow breaths we talked about and imagine your shields protecting you completely while I let go. On the count of three, He paths, *one, two... three.*

Tess pictures herself surrounded by a crystalline bubble where nothing can get through to her, aside from Marc's mental voice. She can see all around her, but she's protected from everyone's thoughts and emotions.

Now, imagine a small part of your shield becomes semi-permeable, allowing air to flow in and out through a small section, except, it's not air, but thoughts, and it's flowing in toward you, but only where you look, and you can control the rate of flow, so if it's too much, you can slow it down or turn it off all together. Choose a person in the room and try to catch what they're thinking. He paths.

Tess focuses on a woman at a nearby table, sitting with a man who is talking non-stop while she just listens. She hears, *"I'm gonna kill Sherry for setting me up with this guy! If he were any more self-obsessed, he'd forget I was even here!"*

Tess giggles at that. *She's not having a good time. Blind date, and the guy won't stop talking about himself.* She says.

Good! I heard her too. You're spot on. He commends her. *Now, try the man at the bar there, third stool from the right.*

Oh, I'm going to be sick, literally. He's so drunk his thoughts are slurred and it's making me nauseous. She paths.

Again, spot on. The woman two seats to his right?

Tess blushes a deep shade of red. *Ahhhhh! She's only out for one thing tonight, any way she can get it.* She blushes from the woman's fantasies.

Marc grins. *So far, so good. Now, I want you to lightly scan the room. Look for minds that stand out in the crowd. Strong emotions, such as anger, are things we often look for when watching for potentially dangerous situations.*

She reaches out to see the people around her mentally and they have different 'colors' around them. Most are slow swirls of mixed colors; some are a duller greenish gray; they're the intoxicated ones. Out of the blue, she senses a red-hot mind, and its anger is directed at her. "What the *hell*?" She says out loud.

What is It? Did you find something? He's concerned by her reaction.

Yeah, someone's extremely angry, and... it's directed at ME! DAMN! Jason's HERE, and he's spotted us sitting together, he... he's ANGRY! Thinks that... well, he's got the wrong idea about us, and thinks I used that to get him reassigned to the other office. She summarizes what she's picking up from him.

Jason's here? Hm. I'll make sure he doesn't bother you. He paths. *Go on; see what else you pick up.*

He, oh God! He's aware someone's reading him! How's that even possible? She panics as telepathic tendrils from Jason's mind reach out, tracing her mental signal to the source. Tess slips into a full-blown panic attack. She loses control of her shields while attempting to disentangle his mental tendrils from her own. There's a mental roar in her head as dozens of mental voices and random emotions flood her mind, uncontrolled. Literally, blinding pain strikes, and she can barely see anything around her. She looks around, but all she can see are colors and energy; everyone's mental chatter and auras overload her senses.

"*Damn!* I can't get it to stop!" She says aloud, hyperventilating.

194

"Tess! *Focus*; imagine the walls protecting you again. Get them up! Protect yourself!" He whispers to her, realizing he can't get a telepathic word in with her mind bombarded and overloaded.

She can barely hear him over the roar in her mind. She tries to stop it, but as soon as she shores it up part way, it floods in and knocks it down again. She picks up on mundane thoughts about restaurant patrons' food, other people they're with, someone's sexual daydreams, Jason's anger at her and something else even more ominous than Jason. Those dark thoughts catch her attention and draw her to them. She hears dark and hateful thoughts, *"Gonna get those fags"*, *"they'll learn not to defy God's law!"* She sees images of an explosion and tinkering with a device-a bomb. Her head's throbbing: she can't hear Marc's voice but feels him pulling her gently out of her seat. She can hear him speaking to someone; she can hear the words but can't grasp their meanings.

Marc, in reaction to Tess's distress, flags down a waiter. "My companion's having a major, migraine attack. I need to get her out of here. This should cover the bill. Please pack the food up for takeout, and I'll come back for it before you close. Anything over the cost is yours as a gratuity." He hands him a business card and the money to cover the meal, willing the man to do as he's told. Marc walks Tess outside, and away from people, wrapping his own mental shields around her again, as well as his arm and ports her home. He sits her on the sofa in his living room, hoping getting her away from the mental cacophony will relieve her distress, but she just sits there shaking and rocking, unfocused, and not speaking. She doesn't realize where she is or react to his presence.

Marc yells out telepathically to Sara. *Sara! I've got an emergency with Tess! I need you!*

Before he can finish the thought, Sara's there, and checks Tess. "What the *hell* happened?" She demands with obvious concern in her voice.

Surprised by Sara's reaction, he says, "We were doing a field test on her telepathy. It was going well until someone she knew was there and was not happy to see her, to put it mildly. He's a potential, and apparently, more aware of his own psychic gifts than we knew."

Sara shakes her head, closes her eyes, and asks, "Not that Jason fellow?"

"Yes, it was." Marc looks on concerned, wishing he could do more for her.

"That explains it. The fear and adrenalin triggered this, same as it did her memories about you after he cornered her in the copy room. But it must have been more than him that did this, she's nearly in shock." Sara examines Tess, checking both her physical vital stats and her energy field and mental pathways.

"When she panicked, her shields collapsed, and everything hit her at once." He looks concerned. "Is she going to be alright?"

"Probably, but it's going to take time. Let me get a proper read on her. Sit and *give* me some space!" Sara snaps, impatiently.

"Tess! Look at me, hear me!" She uses gentle, mental persuasion to get Tess's attention. Slowly, after a few minutes, Tess's eyes focus more and she looks at Sara, memories of the dark thoughts of the unknown man and his plans fly intuitively from Tess's mind to Sara's with a strong sense of urgency.

"Oh *my*." Sara says aloud, sitting on the coffee table in front of Tess.

"What? What's *wrong*? Is she going to be *okay*?" Marc demands, desperate for answers.

"*YES!* Yes. *Eventually.* However, she overheard something at the restaurant; something you need to deal with as soon as possible." Sara transfers those thoughts and the mental signature Tess gave her.

"*Merde!* The Pride Festival in town *tomorrow*? *Damn!* When are these humans going to learn to let people who are different be different? Okay, Sara, I've got to deal with this quickly. Can you please stay with Tess?"

"Do you really think I'd leave her alone in this state? Now *GO* do your job!" Sara commands him in a forceful tone she rarely uses.

"I need to go back to the restaurant to try to track him down, assuming he's still there. Can you get Liz to assemble a crew to watch the event tomorrow in case he's not alone in this attack?" He waits until Sara nods and he vanishes.

Sara turns her attention back to her patient. "Tess, it's me, Sara. Look at me! Can you hear me?" She says aloud. Tess, still shaking, focuses on Sara. "It's alright, Tess; you're safe now, back home. Marc and others are en route to prevent the attack. Tess, you did wonderfully. Tess, you've probably prevented many deaths and injuries." Sara repeatedly uses Tess's name to help hold her attention and draw her back to a more normal mental state.

Pain shows in Tess's face as she cringes at sounds and light in the room, but she snaps out of her fugue. "*Sara*? It was awful! Not only was I hearing his thoughts, but the mentality made me physically ill. How could someone be that small-minded and hateful. Jason was there too! He hates me, and he... he's telepathic! He knew someone was reading him!" She sobs, both from emotional distress and pain.

"It's alright, you're safe now, and you need to rest. I'm going to give you something to calm you and help with the pain. You need to allow those psychic pathways to heal. You're dealing with what we call psychic burn. Your synapses had to deal with more than they could handle, but you'll be fine; now rest." She uses a small tool to infuse a drug into Tess's arm. Tess drifts off to sleep, and Sara ports her to her bed and makes her comfortable. She sets up a small monitor to alert her if Tess's status changes for the worse. She goes back into Marc's living room to wait for him. She contacts Liz about what's happened and the planned attack on the Pride Festival, setting things in motion to prevent it from happening.

Marc ports back in about an hour later, carrying a bag with carry out boxes, and looking more than a little worse for wear, but relieved. "Where's Tess?" is the first thing out of his mouth.

"She's sleeping. She'll need a good bit of rest after this, but what'll help her even more is knowing you, hopefully, can prevent the attack." She gives him an expectant look.

Marc plops down on the sofa, putting the boxes of food on the coffee table. He breathes a deep sigh before saying: "Oh, yeah. He was still there, stuffing his face in premature celebration of all the 'holy vengeance' he planned to reap. Quite a piece of work, and he was not working alone. We have enough to pass on to our contacts in the local police to take down the local network and one that spreads over nearby states. Tess should be proud of this."

"Let her sleep and you can tell her when she wakes. She may sleep a couple of days. That psychic overload took its toll and may have opened more pathways like snaking a drain." She takes out a translucent rod with a green liquid in it. "If she's still in pain when she wakes, give her this. Her synapses are pretty, *damn* fried! You should have had a backup plan in place before going out like this."

"I did. But unfortunately, it didn't take Jason into consideration. Sara, do you mean she'll be even more sensitive after this?" He runs his fingers backwards through his hair, frustrated.

"Let's just say we need to have a talk about your girlfriend." She gives him a knowing grin.

He gives her an annoyed glance. "Sara, you know as well as I do, I don't have 'girlfriends' and certainly not a human one. I'm not going through that emotional hell again! I'm responsible for her, and I'm her friend, that's it!"

"Marc, you need to understand something about *'your friend'*." She says with stinging sarcasm, letting him know he's not fooling her for one second. "She's very special, and will be even more so in the future, but right now, she's doing things no *human* was meant to do, not at this stage in their development. Even though she may see it as 'cool', the overall effect on her psychologically, will be to isolate her progressively from her own, especially if she can't get control over her abilities." She shakes a finger in Marc's face.

"Are you saying we shouldn't be helping her develop her potential?" He looks unsettled.

A look of exasperation washes over Sara's face. "*No!* She needs to develop them if she's going to be among us. The problem is, she *isn't* one of us either. Don't you get it? She's now more than human, but not one of us. She's alone in her predicament, no matter how much we're her *friends* and help her. She has *no one* who she can truly identify with." Sara emphasizes each word in her last sentence like she's hammering a nail through Marc's oh, so thick skull.

Marc sits quietly, thinking, then says, "What do you suggest? She isn't compatible, so I can't turn her, as much as I wish I could. I can't make her forget, nor take away these abilities she's already unlocked." Frustration tinges every word he utters.

"Hmm, I suspect you no longer wish she could forget. You've grown accustomed to her presence in your life and would miss her if she forgot everything and moved on." She gives him a knowing look. "Be there for her. She needs you." She says, but thinks *and you need her, even if you don't know it yet.* She smiles. "I've got to get back to my duties now. But don't disturb her. Let her sleep until she wakes, and then reheat what you have in those boxes and let her eat until she's sated. She'll need it." She stands and vanishes, but leaves a parting *Get some rest. Liz is going to need you early tomorrow. I'll come by and human-sit Tess, though I doubt she'll wake up for at least a couple of days.*

With that, Marc puts the food away in the fridge. He contacts Liz and makes arrangements to meet her and the others on Pridefest duty at 8 a.m. His empathic skills will be critical in picking up anger and hate from any other potential terrorists. He crawls into bed and forces himself to get a few hours of sleep. He wakes off and on, worrying about Tess, and mentally peeks at her clairvoyantly and empathically, to make sure she's still sleeping peacefully. He smiles when he senses Mabel curled up protectively against her, and goes back to sleep.

LIMBOLAND

A day and a half after the restaurant incident, Tess wakes to Mabel head butting her cheek insistently. She's still groggy, and her vision a tad blurry. She reaches up to rub her eyes, rolls on her side, and something slides across her collarbone; she's wearing the pendant again, though she can't remember putting it on. Before she can reach out and call for Marc, there's a knock on her bedroom door.

"Come in." She's surprised how weak her voice sounds.

Marc comes in with a plate full of food from the restaurant on a tray. "It's not exactly breakfast..." He smiles. "... but let's call it 'doctor's' orders." He sits on the edge of her bed and places a tray with legs over her lap as she slowly sits up, still feeling weak and wobbly.

"Mmmm, smells wonderful! Is it from the restaurant? I'm starving like I haven't eaten for a week!" She picks up her fork and eats ravenously.

"You should be. You've been out for about a day and a half." He rests his hand on her leg to reassure her.

"What? How could you let me sleep so long?" Her voice is dripping with annoyance.

"Same thing, Doctor's orders. Sara insisted you sleep until you woke on your own." He explains. "How are you feeling?"

"Okay, but a little hazy about everything. What exactly happened?" She remembers some of it but doesn't trust her own memory.

"Long story short, you were doing really well reading people, but something went wrong, and you lost your shields. You were overwhelmed by the psychic input. I had to get you out of there, but I went back for your dinner." He adds a big grin to the last part.

She looks pensive as she eats her food. She gets an odd look in her eyes. "That wasn't all that happened, was it? Jason was there, wasn't he?" Marc nods, "and someone else..." She trails off, her expression shifts to one of abject horror. "Marc! We've got to do something! A bomb! He's going to attack Pridefest!" She puts her food aside in a rush and tries to get up.

"Take it easy!" He stops her from getting up. "First, Pridefest was yesterday, and it went off without a hitch. Not the bomb, the festival." He speaks as calmly as possible.

"Was I imagining it all? I was sure he was going to set off a bomb?" She leans back against her pillows again, feeling uncertain.

"Oh, he was, several of them, but thanks to you, I went back and found him. He's in jail, his bombs have been disposed of and his mind and computers had enough information about a subversive network to shut it down. We also picked up three others who were planning to do other things at the event. You saved a lot of people." He smiles at her, feeling proud of his human protégé.

"Really? But you found him, not me." She has a hard time accepting his praise.

He knows her self-image issues are kicking in so he reassures her, "But we wouldn't have found him if you hadn't overheard him thinking about his plans."

"Maybe, but I should have kept it under control." Waves of frustration wash over Marc from her. "And what were the others going to do?" Part of her doesn't want to know. What she'd seen in the one man's mind was enough to turn her stomach.

"From what we could glean from their minds, one of them had an AR-15 with a high-capacity magazine, ready to shoot into the crowd, and the other two were planning to throw Molotov cocktails to hem them in so they'd be easier targets. They were working with the bomber, so we had a mental image of two of them, but I would have found them anyway from the hate and adrenaline emanating from them." He observes her emotions and reactions. "As to your control issues, Jason is your Achilles Heel. He was the trigger for you losing control this time, and, it he was the trigger for you remembering the night in the alley as well. He cornered you and made you feel you were in danger, which is how you felt the night you saw me." He pauses. "Tess, I really am sorry for frightening you that badly." He rubs her arm in a gesture of remorse.

Her mood softens once she realizes not only has the danger passed without anything happening, but it wasn't her being incompetent, it was her previous dealings with Jason that made everything crash and burn in the restaurant. "I know now, you never meant to hurt me, and only did what you had to. Maybe, somehow, I was meant to remember. If what you say is true, I helped stop a home-grown terrorist attack; perhaps that's why all this happened. If I hadn't called for the interview, gotten the job, followed you that night, found out, and had you been able to make me forget, then maybe, there'd be a lot of people in pain or dead today, probably including some people I know."

"Don't forget, this'll be the downfall of a major network of these homegrown threats, and who knows how far that will reach. They have connections to some of these militia groups and right-wing religious groups that have sprung up in the last couple of decades. If this guy was going to set off bombs here, who knows what plots the others would have planned and implemented in the future?" He reminds her, staring her down until she accepts her accomplishment.

"I guess I'd better get used to 'being here', huh? Maybe dealing with you all is a small price to pay for making a difference?" She feels better in one way, but in another way, she's still grieving her old life, when she was an ordinary human being.

"I was looking at my Facebook feed the other day, and I'm realizing how little I've got in common with all my friends anymore; how many of the things they post seem inconsequential now, and oh! The politics that get posted. If some of them knew about you guys, they'd completely lose their *shit*! They'd have their stakes and pitchforks and holy water ready to go. I guess, in some ways, I'm wondering if I'll ever be able to live a normal life again. I'm not sure, with all I know now,

I'll ever fit in a world that doesn't know what's really going on." She has difficulty making eye contact.

He feels the pain behind her words, and it echoes in his soul. He remembers what Sara said, but awkwardly consoles her without letting his own emotions get out of control. He says, "It depends on what you mean by *normal*. You'll always know about us, and being aware of things we're doing, your view of the world has changed irrevocably. Once your abilities are under control, you can choose whether to use them or not.

I know telepathy is one of the hardest to cope with. It's tempting to investigate someone's mind and know their intentions, but it's also frustrating, because sometimes you see things you really don't want to see, including unfavorable reflections of yourself in another person's eyes, or not so honorable intensions. Plus, you'll always have our secret, which you can't share with another human." He feels her grief over her old life, even with what she's accomplished.

"So, I'm pretty much *screwed* when it comes to having any kind of relationship with another human." Her face reflects a sort of sad resignation to the situation.

"It really depends on you. You're still human, you could find someone, have children, if you wish, but you'll always have a tie to us, and our secret to keep, and such a burden can be a strain if your partner senses you're keeping things from them. It's not impossible, but it will be more complicated than if you were still as you were before all this." Sara's words echo in his mind about not really wanting her to forget and move on, that he'll miss her no matter what. He realizes the idea of her finding someone else bothers him, but he shoves those feelings back into a mental lockbox to ignore them, reminding himself *she's human-it just can't be.*

The look on her face shifts from sadness to frustration. "Listening in on people at the restaurant is coming back to me, flashes here and there. The kinds of things most people were thinking seem somehow, petty and immature in the big scheme of things as well, and it's really hitting me now. It's like a friend of mine told me once. She went to live in Europe for a couple of years. She said after that, so much of what people were obsessed with here, seemed silly. I guess it's kind of the same thing?" She forces herself to make eye contact.

"Both experiences change your perspective on reality, and change your priorities. Maybe, before this, your priority was getting a job to pay your bills, but that's not an issue now, and it may feel less important to you; while preventing those deaths and injuries, and possibly others in the future, become a priority." He pauses. "I know you feel alone. You're more than human, but not one of us." He channels what Sara told him, realizing Tess really is in a unique and difficult position.

Her eyes get watery. "Yeah, something like that. I don't belong in either world, though in some ways, I belong less in my own than with you all, and yet.... Now don't get me wrong, I feel like a curiosity or a pet human in your world."

He tips her chin up to make her look at him. "You're much more than that. You're my friend. Probably my best friend since Liz, who turned me centuries ago."

"Liz is the one who turned you?" She remembers him mentioning someone at work had turned him, but she hadn't known whom.

"Yes, back then, only some people did the turning, sometimes more than one at a time, if needed. Things were much less organized back then; less businesslike." He explains.

"You say businesslike, but I thought Liz and Kari...?" She trails off.

"Yes, they're a couple." He laughs. "Have been for several centuries. Liz turned both Kari and her own brother, Peder, as well as me... and many others." He says. "By business, I mean we know who's a potential and we're able to plan more, who to turn, who not to turn. I wish I could explain it so you can understand."

Tess takes a slow breath before saying: "You know, I don't even know how old you are. You all talk in centuries, but you've never told me much about yourself. I know you're 'old as dirt'!" She smirks. "French, empathic, and precognitive, but not really much else, other than you're a good person."

He shifts awkwardly on the edge of her bed. "Where to start? I was born in 1562, in Charolais, France, northwest of Lyon. I was a minor son in a large, influential family, but as a minor son of a minor son, I stood little chance of inheriting my grandfather's wealth or power."

"What did you do? Did you have a job or anything?" she asks, her interest piqued.

"That I did. As a child, and later as a young man, I always had an insatiable thirst for knowledge. Being in an upper-class family, I was well educated for the time. I absorbed every lesson like it was food for my soul. So, when I reached my 24th year, my grandfather summoned me and told me I was to become a *repetiteur*: a private teacher or tutor for the family's children. My old teacher was growing old and infirm, so they apprenticed me to him to learn all he could teach me. He had a vast library of books, which was rare for the time, and I must have read nearly all of them. Books on planting, art, science, strategy, medicine. I guess that's part of the reason they chose me to become Apara." He reflects.

"So, how did you become...? I mean, I know you said Liz turned you." She waits attentively for his answer.

He gets a distant look in his eyes as he pulls up centuries old, and painful memories he's pushed aside. He says, "As part of becoming the family tutor, my grandfather granted me a small plot of land, a house, a stable, and enough land to grow some staple foods in lieu of a salary. That suited me fine. I was betrothed to a young woman from a good family, and that would give us a good life." He gets a melancholy look and Tess feels a knot forming in her gut.

"What happened?" She asks.

"Let's say things didn't work out between Collette and me. She broke the betrothal, and I was heartbroken. I turned to drinking, and one night, Liz showed up with her long blonde hair and blue eyes and lured me off from the local tavern. I thought she would ease my pain, but she turned me, and I became Apara." He lets out a long sigh as he remembers.

"I'm sorry. That must have been a difficult time for you. I didn't mean to bring back any painful memories." She reaches over and touches his arm lightly.

"It's alright. It turned out for the best in the long run. It gave me something to focus on besides Collette and my broken heart. I was given three years to put my affairs in order before I would have to leave my family; otherwise, they'd soon see I wasn't ageing. My older sister was as hungry for knowledge as I ever was, and probably smarter. But my grandfather did not see the value in educating women. They had other purposes in his mind." He gives her a sarcastic grin, and he can tell Tess understands. "Anyway, she had three boys, all different ages, so I made sure she would sit in on the lessons I gave them. I also left her a key to the library of books I'd inherited from my mentor when he passed, with the excuse her boys were always welcome to study beyond what I taught them when they were ready. Of course, I knew she would sneak in and read them herself, and she did." He smiles, remembering peeking into the library in the middle of the night and seeing his sister reading by candlelight. "When my three years were up, I rode off in stormy weather on my horse, and had a convenient accident, dying, by human standards. My stubborn old grandfather was forced to let my sister become the new tutor in my stead, and I moved on to my new life with the Apara." He finishes his story and smiles at Tess.

Marc feels Tess's heart clench with a deep sadness, a hopeless feeling of resignation as she asks, "And there's no way to... *turn* me? To make me *compatible*?"

Marc hesitates, a twinge in his own heart as he thinks about it, and he debates telling her that, while possible, it's unlikely he'd be allowed because it's considered too risky at her age. He lets that small hope fade and says, "No, you're either compatible, or you aren't, I'm sorry." He wishes it could be otherwise, but also realizes if she wishes she could become one of them, she really has accepted they're the good guys, and perhaps that will let her feel at home with them.

"Okay." She lets out a long sigh. "I guess I'll have to make do being, well, more-or-less human. Would you mind handing me my laptop? I should check my email and stuff." She changes the subject.

Marc gets her the laptop. "Call for me if you need anything, really." Marc squeezes her arm gently, feeling the sadness she wants to hide from him.

"It's okay, I'll be fine. I've got some thinking and mental adjustments to make. By the way, do I need to wear this now?" She picks the pendant up off her chest.

"Yes, for now. Sara said she thought the psychic overload may have opened more pathways, so until they can test you out and evaluate you, it's best you wear it, even here. You can still call for me mentally. It'll prevent you from turning into the neighborhood poltergeist or getting overloaded again. You can consciously override it if you need to." He says, and walks out the door, closing it behind him.

He leans against her door, feeling her emotional turmoil, and it strikes him deep in his own heart. He thinks *No! Must keep this platonic! I don't think I could stand to watch her age and die if I took her as a human partner.* He thinks, doing his best to keep his emotions guarded, and thankful Tess is wearing her pendant, so she won't feel the pain he feels when he acknowledges they can't be more than friends, as she'll never be like him. He goes off to his home office and continues researching for the ominous 'black cloud' alerts for the Middle East, and stuffs his emotions into that mental lockbox once again.

EMOTIONAL PURGATORY

Tess has to stay home for a couple of days, Sara's orders, to make sure her synapses have sufficiently healed before going back to work. Training is put on hold while they do some new evaluations. Tess's abilities have nearly doubled without using the drug on her again. Once they've got her new baseline, Liz works with her on control, and soon, she has a reasonable handle on her gifts, so long as her emotions stay in check; but if she loses control, her abilities become unstable. Even so, Liz asks her to go without the pendant, in order to learn better control. She's only to wear it if she goes out in public, but otherwise, at work or home, she goes without it. If she loses control at work, any human witnesses can be made to forget, because it's more important for Tess to learn control without the pendant.

One afternoon, after work, Tess is craving Rocky Road ice cream, and doesn't want to bother Marc about it since he's focused on the Black Cloud precogs. *I might as well go out. Car's battery's going to go flat if I don't use it occasionally. Now, where did I put my keys? Marc! I'm going out for a few.* She paths.

Okay! Make sure you have your necklace. Where are you going? He replies from his home office, where he's once again immersed in correlating precog reports.

I'm running to the store. Won't be too long. If I go anywhere else, I'll let you know. She paths as she goes out the door, gets in her car and drives to the grocery store. She takes her time and goes up and down the lanes, browsing. *I'll grab the ice cream last. I just need a break from home and work.* She thinks, as she rounds the end of an aisle and goes down the cereal lane when she sees someone familiar. She backtracks, and goes on to the next aisle, hoping he didn't notice her. *OH Shit! It's Colton. And from the look of things, a new girlfriend.* Even though she has no desire to have anything to do with Colton, something aches within her seeing him with someone else. Not jealousy, but it's like a cosmic magnifying lens on her loneliness. *It's not fair! He's got someone in his life. The bastard that threatened to beat the crap out of me has someone, and I'm stuck in limbo!* She grabs her Rocky Road and gets out of there before he sees her. As she's going out to her car, she gets the oddest feeling she's being watched. She feels a tingling on her scalp, but it feels clumsy or heavy-handed compared to anything she's experienced with Marc or the others. *Oh, hell! What now?* She thinks and looks around, but can't see anyone specifically looking her way, though she gets the impression it's coming from across the street, from the organic grocery store lot. She scurries to her car, hoping whoever it is can't follow her to Sanctuary. Once she puts some distance between herself and the store, the feeling abates.

She drives up the narrow road leading to the public façade of Marc's home and parks. Grabbing her ice cream, she crosses the portal to Sanctuary. She heads into her apartment, sending Marc a quick *I'm back.* She can tell he heard her, but also that he's focused on his work. She fixes an oversized bowl of Rocky Road and settles in on her sofa to check her social media accounts.

There's no email but spam in her inbox. The only instant message is from Amy, wondering if Tess has seen a folder she's misplaced. There aren't more than three likes on a couple of posts she made earlier. *What's the point? No one from my old life misses me. I haven't seen any of my old friends since way before I moved. I only had that call from Alex. Only friend requests are obvious romance scammers looking for gullible, lonely women to prey on.* She briefly laughs out loud. *Ironic, I'm surrounded by real vampires, but the true bloodsuckers are people like those scam artists.* She closes her laptop and pulls out a book to read Amy lent her. *What's this thing about?* She flips over the book to read the synopsis. *Great, it's a paranormal romance about werewolves and shifters?*

210

UGH! I don't even want to think about whether such things exist! Got enough on my plate with supernatural creatures in real life without reading paranormal romance books. She tosses the book onto the coffee table, then sits there thinking about seeing Colton and whomever he was with at the store. *He actually looked happy. Karma is out to get me for sure. I must have royally fucked up in my last life to get this one! Orphaned, adopted, oddball in school, first job after college and my dick boss tries to tell people I'm sleeping with him, then Digital Danger, and when I finally find a place that feels right, I'm surrounded by vampires! I know! They're the 'good guys'. It's not fair. I don't fit in with humans anymore and I can't join them either! It's like being in purgatory, and I'm the only one there.* She finishes her ice cream, lies down, rolls over on the sofa and falls asleep.

About 11 p.m., Marc realizes he hasn't had anything to eat since breakfast, so takes a break from his work, and makes food for himself and Tess. He goes over to her apartment and knocks. There's no answer. He can't quite remember if she ever came home after going to the store. He thinks she did, but he was so engrossed in his work, he's not sure if she said she was home, or if he only thinks she did. He worries she may not have come home, so he quietly opens her door, and is relieved to see her curled up on her sofa, asleep. He sits on the arm of the sofa, putting a plate of food on the coffee table in front of her. When she doesn't stir, he gently touches the upper middle of her back, and she starts awake, withdrawing from his touch.

"Oh, *Hell!* You scared the *crap* out of me!" She rolls over and sits up to face him, taking in the smell of homemade chicken Alfredo on the plate in front of her. "Mmm, smells good." She pauses. "Sorry I snapped; I get uneasy when anyone touches me there unexpectedly." She picks up her fork and starts shoveling in the chicken and pasta.

"I didn't mean to startle you. I was uncertain if you'd come home or not, and when you didn't answer, I got worried." He can sense her mood is off. "Is everything okay?"

She looks up at him and gives him a smile, but he can sense

some sadness hidden behind it. "Same old, same old! I'm struggling to keep up and adjust to things way beyond my pay grade!" She gives a small bark of ironic laughter.

"Still feeling caught between worlds?" He senses something more is bothering her.

"Yeah, I don't think that's going to resolve itself anytime soon. You'll probably pick up on it anyway when we practice, but I saw Colton at the store today." She admits.

"Did he behave himself? Did he threaten you?" Marc remembers the night he confronted him.

"No, he never saw me. He was too busy with his new girlfriend to notice me. It's ironic, you know; maybe karma is still after me for turning him in?" She wants to cry but doesn't want Marc to see her crying.

"Karma brought you to us, so it can't be all bad." He nudges her knee in a joking manner, smiling.

"Yeah, it brought me here, and while I may have made a difference a couple of times, it feels... *oh*! I can't put it in words! It's not fair that asshole is with someone, and happy, and I'm stuck in limbo between 'human land' and the Twilight Zone! *Oops! No* pun intended. You definitely don't *sparkle*." She sticks a large load of pasta in her mouth, so she has an excuse to shut up.

He realizes she wants to get off the subject. "If you don't mind me asking, why don't you like anyone touching you on your upper back? I've worked on your shoulders before to relax you when we practice, but you didn't have a problem with that." He waits for her to answer.

"If I know it's coming, I can deal with it, but if I don't, it throws me for a loop. When I was little, I was in a terrifically bad car accident, and there were injuries there. Still have scars. For a long time, it was painful if anyone touched me there, like the nerves were hypersensitive. It's okay now, but I still react sometimes, part of me still expects pain." She sits there, twisting her fork in the pasta, but not eating.

"I didn't realize. I'll keep that in mind in the future. Talk to Sara about the scars. She may be able to heal them for you." He suggests.

"I've lived with them close to 25 years. It's no big deal." She takes a huge bite out of the garlic bread that came with the Alfredo.

Marc notices the paperback book lying face down on the coffee table and picks it up. He looks at the dark cover, showing a woman, some wolves, a deer, and a full moon on the cover. He flips it over and reads the blurb on the back, then gives Tess an incredulous look. "Really? Werewolves and shifters?"

"It's *Amy's*. She lent it to me. Swore it would be something I'd like and could help my moodiness. I don't even want to think about whether other supernatural creatures besides you guys exist." She laughs and pauses for a few seconds. "They don't, do they?" She looks uneasy and worried.

He laughs. "Nope! Only us. No werewolves, shifters, fairies, trolls, and so on. And we don't consider ourselves supernatural either, just different. There are biological and genetic foundations to what we are, all caused by a gene-altering virus. You should know by now we're not undead, or part demon, angel, or whatever the latest stories theorize we are."

Tess breathes an exaggerated sigh of relief. "*Thank God!* I've got enough on my plate with *you guys*."

He laughs at her relieved reaction. "Sorry I was so late with dinner, I got caught up in work, and suddenly realized how late it was. I've been preparing for a meeting tomorrow, but not here in Asheville. I have to pop over to our offices outside London to coordinate with some of our people there, and that's going to be 5 a.m. our time. So, unless you want me to drop you off at the office that early, I could ask Liz or Kari to pop in and get you around 8:30." He cocks his head to one side.

She pauses, and then sighs. "No, I don't think I want to go in that early. But don't worry about having someone come get me. I'll drive myself in. My car battery was nearly dead from not driving lately. Besides, I hear the trees on the Parkway are starting to turn a little early this year, and I could take the long way home up the parkway through Weaverville. I miss the scenery by popping back and forth all the time."

"That works, but if you change your mind, you can reach out to either Liz or Kari and they'll come get you." He yawns. I need to get at least a couple of hours' sleep before I pop across the Pond. I'll see you after my meeting but suspect it will be early afternoon or even later before we get done."

"Sounds like you're in for a hell of a long day." Tess remarks.

"Unfortunately. Some new precog impressions have come in we need to go through. Some are getting the impression it may involve other areas in Europe too, but I need to talk to them firsthand to be sure they're related." She notices the exhaustion in his eyes.

"Goodnight, Marc. Get some rest. You clearly need it." She goes back to her Alfredo. Marc ports out and straight to bed.

OVER THE HILL

Tess drives to work the next morning, traveling from North Asheville to the office off of Sweeten Creek Road, South of Asheville. She forgot how heavy traffic could be in the mornings. *God! This drive is taking forever! Was easier when I lived in East Asheville, only about a ten-minute drive.* She can hear Marc's remark from the night they went to the restaurant in town: *"My! Aren't we getting spoiled!"* *I guess maybe I have gotten a little spoiled, or at least, impatient, when it comes to getting places quickly.*

She gets to work and practices with Kari all morning. Around lunchtime, she knocks on Liz's door. "Hey, any idea when Marc's getting back?"

"I heard from him about 30 minutes ago. They're bringing in some others from Paris, Hong Kong, and L.A., so he probably won't get back until sometime tonight. Do you need to be dropped off at home after work?" Liz asks, knowing Marc usually ports them back and forth.

"No, but thanks. I drove in today. Thought I'd take the parkway home and see the early fall colors." Tess goes back to work.

About 4:30 p.m., Tess gathers up her stuff and heads for her car. As she goes outside, she looks up; the sun is bright and there's a light breeze. No clouds in the sky. *Perfect day to look at fall colors.* She thinks, as she walks to her car. While she's unlocking it, she feels that odd, clumsy tingling again, like she felt when she finished shopping, and she thinks, *Shit! I should have mentioned that to Marc last night. It's probably nothing. Just my oversensitive brain cells picking up stuff.* She takes out her necklace from her bag and puts it on; remembering she's supposed to wear it in public, and especially while driving. With the help of that, she's able to mostly quash the tingling, and heads for the entrance to the Blue Ridge Parkway on Hendersonville Road. Shortly after getting on the Parkway, she notices a couple of cars behind her. A blue Honda soon goes around her and heads on up the road, and an older, dark SUV. It keeps its distance for a while, matching her speed. She drives past Tunnel Road, where she used to get off to go home if she took the Parkway.

She passes the Folk Arts Center, a local craft-guild gallery and shop. She continues up the road, and it winds its way higher and higher up the mountain where most of the leaf watchers like to pull off into an overlook. She plans on stopping at the one looking east, but it's completely full. *Oh well. Guess I'll settle for looking from the road. My turn off's coming up anyway.* She sees much of her rear-view mirror go dark in her peripheral vision and glances up to see the dark SUV is now tailgating her. *Oh great, just what I don't need. An asshole on my tail!* She peers at the driver in the mirror and sees he's wearing a hoodie with the hood up and dark glasses. She gets a very bad feeling. Seconds later, there's a thud and a lurch as the SUV bumps her from behind.

"What the *fuck*?" She exclaims out loud. The car backs off for the moment. *No way in hell I'm stopping, even if his bumping me was an accident.* It doesn't take long before she knows it was not accidental, as he speeds up, ramming the left part of her rear bumper hard enough to send her into an uncontrolled, partial spin, jumping the side of the narrow road, going up a slight incline and over the hill. She screams, both out loud and mentally, seeing it's a long way down the mountain. As she's careening toward the edge of the mountain, a mental dam breaks and her PK kicks in. At the last second, she's able to alter the angle of her car just enough to head toward some trees instead of off the edge and into the valley below. This still leads to a nasty crash into some trees, crumpling the front of her car and pinning her below her knees. Her airbag doesn't work, and she smacks her forehead on the top of the steering wheel, cutting a gash across her forehead, blood streaming everywhere.

She's floating on the edge of consciousness when she hears a voice. At first, she doesn't recognize who it is or why it would be strange to hear someone outside her car. She hears metal being torn apart, her car door being torn from its hinges, and fresh air blows across her face.

"*TESS*! Are you okay?" She hears a male voice say, and feels a warm hand on her forehead, the pain lessoning dramatically, at least where she hit her head.

Recognition trickles into her rattled brain cells. "Marc? Marc! Is that you?" The side of her head is resting on the steering wheel, her face toward him, but her vision's blurry.

"Yes! I heard your telepathic shout and tracked you here. I'm going to do what I can for you here, and then get you some help." He reassures her.

Tess groans in pain as her head throbs, and every muscle screams at her brain in agony. Marc can hear her sobbing in between ragged breaths. He can sense her fear she's dying and must take a mental step back as her physical pain nearly overwhelms him. Part of him is frantic; he's terrified he may lose her, so works quickly and checks her over systematically, healing small, surface wounds as he goes. He notices a pool of blood on the floor under her pinned legs. *Merde! This looks bad!* He thinks, and paths to Sara: *Tess has been in an accident on the Parkway! She's pinned. I can port her out, but I'm not sure how safe it is to move her.*

What? Is she conscious? Breathing? Sara paths, porting to an examination room to prepare for Tess's imminent arrival.

Semi-conscious. Floating in and out. Breathing, yes, but her breathing is raspy. She hit a crop of trees, which crushed the front of her car. Airbag didn't deploy. I've healed what surface wounds I can reach, but there's a fair amount of blood on the floor by her feet.

I need you to stay calm. The first thing you need to do is bite her and force Trinaline into her system. This will help stop any remaining bleeding, including internally. It sounds like she may have some bleeding in her lungs or chest. That will also help her body replace the lost blood, but we may have to give her a transfusion when you get her here. After you bite her, if she's conscious, I need you to find out if she has any back injuries. See if she can feel or move her toes. I assume she's in a seated position? Sara paths efficiently in a few seconds.

Yes, seated.

Show me so I can see what angle her back is relative to her legs. Sara says.

Marc focuses on Tess again, letting Sara see through his eyes, and he hears a telepathic *Got it!* From Sara

"Tess, I need your left arm." Marc says.

She tries to lift her arm, but it hurts and feels so heavy, she drops it after a couple of seconds, groaning in pain. He gently picks up her arm, brings it to his mouth, and carefully bites into it. The adrenaline rush from his bite brings things into focus. "What the *Fuck*? You're feeding on me now?" She gasps out.

His mouth full, he paths to her: *Not feeding. Infusing your body with Trinaline. The healing compound released when I feed, but I'm not taking any blood. You've lost plenty as it is. It will help stop any bleeding, including internally, and speed healing. Just another minute.*

Tess loses focus again, floating in and out on the edge of consciousness.

Marc withdraws his fangs from her wrist, healing over the wounds. "Tess. *TESS!*"

Her speech is slurred. "Whaaa?"

"Tess, stay with me! Can you feel your toes? Try to move them."

She opens her eyes and halfway focuses on his face. "Think they're moving. Legs cold, back hurts." She closes her eyes part way. "Call 911."

"No, we can take care of you better than the hospital can. Sara's waiting for us. You're pinned. I'm going to port you out, but it may hurt when the pressure is off your legs. Porting you to Sara in three, two... one..." his voice fades out as the world around her blinks out, pain surges through her legs as blood flow is unblocked, and she lets out a muffled scream as her face is turned into his shoulder. Marc ports her into a waiting examination chair set to the same angle as she was sitting in her car seat, to limit additional harm to her back until Sara can scan her for spinal damage.

Sara immediately infuses her arm with painkiller and a mild sedative. She's conscious, but out of pain and relaxed, unable to panic.

"Tess, I'm going to take care of you now. You're safe." Sara looks at her legs, hints of bone showing through the skin under her knees. She focuses, and puts her hands over the wounds, willing the surface wounds to heal up, to prevent any more major blood loss. She paths to Marc. *Both legs are extensively broken. I'll do what I can to heal them, but I need to wait until she's knocked out for that. You were right. She has some bleeding in her lungs, and possibly around her heart.* She puts her hands on Tess's head. *Mild hematoma, but the Trinaline stopped any bleeding in her skull in time to avoid any brain damage. She's lost a fair amount of blood, but she's not dangerously low, so we'll see how her levels are tomorrow after more Trinaline.*

Is she going to be alright? Mark's voice is heavily laden with concern, but Sara can sense underlying panic he may lose her due to her injuries.

"Yes, I believe so. I need you to gently hold her in this position while I lower the back of the exam table and check her spine." Sara makes sure he understands the importance of keeping her absolutely still.

Marc stands in front of Tess, slipping his arms under hers, holding her still and upright while Sara lowers the back on the table. She lays her hands on Tess's lower back. *Not broken, but out of alignment. Will adjust and then we can lay her down.* She uses a combination of pressure from her fingers and PK to realign the vertebrae, and then the two of them gently lay her down, her legs still hanging down off the end in the same position as in the car. Sara checks her neck and puts a light brace on it until she can knock her out and deal with the whiplash injuries.

Marc pulls up a chair and sits alongside the examination table, opposite Sara, holding Tess's hand. Tess is weak but conscious. "Tess, can you open your eyes, look at me?"

Her eyes flutter open and she focuses on his face. "Am I, am I gonna die?" she asks, and Marc can see a tear meander down through the dried blood on her cheek.

"No, Sara's going to take care of you, I *promise*! Can you tell me what happened? Did you lose control, or did you have to swerve for a car or a deer?" Marc feels her clench his hand briefly.

"Hit... ran off road. Inten... intentional..." She stammers out.

"*What*? Someone *intentionally* ran you off the road? Marc's anger boils up from deep inside. "Who? Did you see who it was? Was it anyone you knew? Can you describe the car?"

"W... words n... not working well. Look... read mind?" Tess struggles to string clear sentences together.

He looks in her mind and sees the dark SUV, and the driver, unrecognizable thanks to the hoodie and glasses, and what happened. "*Damn!* Can't even tell if the driver was male or female."

"Male. Felt male... can't explain, but know..." She struggles to keep her eyes open.

"If you have what you need from her, I need to knock her out and deal with her legs and other injuries. You can stay, but she needs to be totally out." Sara comes over to Tess holding an infuser. "Tess, it's okay. Marc has the info now. I'm going to give you something to help you sleep. You may be out for a few days, but you'll be fine."

Tess nods, nearly imperceptibly, as the neck brace holds her mostly still. Sara gives her the sedative/anesthesia mixture, and within three seconds, she's totally out.

"I want to stay, but I need to track this *bastard* down!" Marc's torn.

"Pass the info to Liz. She can get it to the right people. I'll get started on her injuries. Come back when you're done. I won't be moving her for at least a couple of hours." Sara says, clairvoyantly examining the bones in her legs.

There are hairline fractures in both femurs, but her tibias in both legs are shattered below the knee where the car folded in on her legs. Marc ports out. Sara settles in front of Tess's legs and uses a combination of physical and telekinetic manipulation of the bones until the jigsaw puzzle of splintered bones is pieced together in her right tibia. She holds the pieces together telekinetically and grabs an infuser with an actual needle on it. She gently slips it into Tess's leg, into a fracture between the bone fragments, injects a mixture of Trinaline and a temporary bone adhesive that will hold the pieces together, trapping the Trinaline where needed, and dissolving as the bones knit. She wraps an ace-like bandage around Tess's leg, and sprays it with clear liquid, creating a lightweight but nearly unbreakable cast.

Marc ports in again and returns to his chair, holding Tess's hand even though she's out. "How's it going?" he asks, clearly distraught over Tess's condition.

"She'll be fine, but the bones in her lower legs might as well be one of those 3D puzzles Peder likes. I have to focus and rebuild them telekinetically. So, if you're going to stay here, you need to stay quiet so I can concentrate." Sara gives him a look that makes Marc go still.

Sara moves on to the left leg, and the fibula is also broken, but only a simple fracture. Again, she pieces both bones together, injects them with the same compound, and adds a lightweight cast. She repeats the procedures for the broken femurs, which are simple fractures. Sara then starts literally from Tess's head, mentally scanning her for damage, and doing what she can to speed up the healing the initial dose of Trinaline has already set in motion. She removes the neck brace and realigns the bones in her patient's neck to reduce the whiplash damage. She moves down to Tess's chest and gets a pensive look. "There's some blood around her heart and in her lungs. Not so worried about what's in her lungs. Her body's reabsorbing it thanks to the Trinaline, but I'm going to have to drain the hemorrhage from near her heart. It's putting pressure on her heart and aorta." She says as she positions a small sphere like object with two tubes with needles on each end on Tess's chest, then puts the one needle into Tess's arm like she would an IV, taping it into place. The other, she gently pushes into the pooling blood near her heart. Blood comes up the tube, passing through the ball, and back down into her arm. "This…" She points to the ball. "filters out and destroys any clotted and nonviable blood and returns anything viable to her system."

Marc looks relieved as he notices Tess's pulse becomes less labored and more regular. Sara continues her methodical examination and healing session until she makes it to her feet.

"Okay, she's out of danger now. You need to go home and rest." Sara has her hands on her hips, knowing Marc will be reluctant to leave Tess.

"I'd like to stay with her." He says, worrying something might go wrong if he leaves her.

Sara lets out an impatient breath. "Let me put it this way, I need to clean her up now, which means stripping off her damaged and bloody clothes and cleaning her skin. How do you think she'll react if she finds out you were here, watching?"

Marc nods curtly. "Call me if anything changes." He ports out, but not home; He checks on whether Liz has any news about the hit-and-run driver and asks Peder to return to the meeting in Europe for him and let them know he won't be returning, but will contact everyone tomorrow.

Sara keeps Tess under for eight days until the bones have cemented themselves back together. She receives additional infusions of Trinaline, and by the fourth day, her blood count is back to normal.

Marc is sitting by the bed when she comes to on the eighth day. "*Tess?* How are you? You're safe; everything's okay now." He says, reassuring her awkwardly as he moves strands of hair out of her face.

"Where am I?" She asks in a quiet voice, rough from disuse and dryness.

"At our Medical center, under Sara's care. Are you in any discomfort?" He can see her trying to sit up and helps her by moving the backrest of her hospital bed into a partially upright position.

Tess doesn't answer right away, but tries to remember something. "I was in an accident, right?" She notices an IV in her right arm.

"Yes. You were injured, but you're fine now. Sara says she'll remove the casts and IV as soon as she checks you over." Marc reaches over and holds her hand.

"Casts? How long have I been here?" Tess thinks, *doesn't it take at least six weeks for bones to heal?*

Marc hears her thoughts and chuckles. "Not when you've got Sara to fix you up. You've been out for only eight days. Your bones are essentially healed, but she says you may have soreness and nerve pain for a while."

"*Eight days*? That's insane! How did she...?" Tess asks in disbelief.

"We all have some healing skills, but Sara's are the best. She reconstructed your broken bones and used a mixture of Trinaline and a 'bone adhesive', and her own healing abilities, and you're almost as good as new." He smiles.

Her face gets a distressed look on it. "You found me. I remember that. I steered away from the edge, last second, and into the trees. I assume my car is scrap?"

"To put it mildly." He squeezes her hand briefly.

"Some asshole ran me off the road on purpose." She says, not sure if she remembered correctly or if she'd conveyed that to him before or not.

"Yeah, I know. They found the car, burnt out. It was stolen, and whoever it was burnt it with a high temperature accelerant, destroying any evidence we could use to trace him. Our people did get an energy residue—a mental signature, but it was oddly generic, and untraceable." He explains.

She sits there, thinking: *Who could have done this? Could it have been Colton? He seemed happy with his new girlfriend. I don't think he'd risk going back to prison under the circumstances.*

"Our people think you may have been a random target. Some psychopath who wanted to kill someone and randomly picked you; wrong time and place. The important thing is you're going to be fine. Sara says another couple of days' rest at home and you can go back to work if you're up to it." He watches her for a reaction to the whole thing, not knowing if she'll have a meltdown from her near deadly accident.

"I guess you'll have to port me around until the insurance pays out." Something about the attacker was familiar, but whatever it was has evaporated from her memory.

"About that, there's no police report since you didn't go to Mission. My people retrieved the remains of your car, and salvaged your stuff out of it, but it's totally trashed. I've taken home one of our company cars you can use if you need it. When you're ready, we'll find you a car to replace yours." He gets a path from Sara telling him she needs to do a pre-release exam. "Sara's going to boot me out, but I'll be waiting for you when she's done." He stands, his hand lingering around hers for a second as he walks toward the door and leaves.

Sara comes in. "How're you feeling? Any pain?"

"No, not really. I can't believe you fixed me up so quickly. Thank you!" Tears flow, as well as a slight tremor in her body as she realizes how easily she could have died.

"You'll likely have some symptoms of PTSD. Not only was it a traumatic accident, but it was also an assault on you. And that's not something I can heal. You'll have to deal with the psychological fallout, but if you need to talk, we're all willing and able to take on that role for you. Now, let me check you over and get those casts off. Let's start with the IV." She carefully removes the needle and heals over the track, then uses what looks like a blue LED or mini laser to slice off the casts. "Let's see if you can put any weight on those." Sara helps her up, and while unsteady, Tess can stand with only some minor nerve pain. "Those will go away in a few days, but you can use regular human, over-the-counter painkillers unless they get too bad, then have Marc let me know."

"I really can't thank you enough for fixing me up. I was sure I was gonna die. I was heading toward the ledge, but somehow, I could turn the wheel and aim for the trees at the last second. I figured I had a better chance of surviving that than going off the mountain." Tess remembers that strange feeling of power she had right before redirecting the car.

"Oh! About that." She walks over to a work area and grabs a small box. "Here's a new suppressor pendant."

"Oh, did I lose the other one? Or did it get damaged in the accident?" Tess can't remember what happened to it.

"Damaged, yes, but the wreck didn't do it, you did." Sara sits on a stool and grins.

"Me? How did I damage it?" Tess tries to remember, but all she can remember was a sudden feeling like a dam breaking, and she knew she could steer the car away from the ledge.

"What you're thinking about? That feeling you had... the dam bursting? That was your telekinetic ability overloading and fracturing the stone into several pieces. Like when you had your confrontation with Jason, your PK activated, and this time, pushed through the suppressor and allowed you to turn the car. Yes, you steered, but your PK assisted." Sara explains, waiting for it to sink in.

"My PK? But I've barely been able to do anything working with Peder. Only small stuff!" Disbelief shows in her expression.

"Your PK potential is quite strong, but it's also subject to your confidence level and your emotions. Your lack of confidence keeps you limited, but your fear and panic brought your PK out, just like it tried to do when Jason cornered you, but your barriers blocked it."

"*Wow!* I had no idea." Tess looks pensive.

"Anyway, I assume you don't want to go home in a hospital gown. Marc brought some of your clothes from home. The ones you were wearing weren't salvageable." She points to the pile of clothes on the work counter. "So, get dressed, and when you're ready, go out, turn right and follow the hall out until you see Marc and he'll take you home." She smiles, and leaves Tess to change.

Tess changes, tests her legs, and is amazed how quickly she's healed. She finds Marc in a small waiting alcove. "I'm ready to go home."

He stands and impulsively gives her a hug, then pulls away, "I'm so glad you're okay." He takes her hand and ports her to their home in Sanctuary. "Are you hungry? You should be after eight days. I'll fix you something." He runs off to the kitchen and starts throwing something together. *I've got to get control of myself! Just because she nearly died doesn't change the fact she's human and I'm not. In fact, it only reinforces why I can't let my emotions get away from me. She really could die anytime! She could have died eight days ago! Must get my emotions back under control. I can't go through that again. Not after Collette.*

Marc fixes chicken with mushrooms and rice and brings two plates out to the dining room. "Here you go. There's more in the kitchen, if that's not enough." He smiles. *Why the hell did she have to be incompatible?* He thinks with a mixture of anger and frustration at what he perceives as a cruel twist of fate.

He makes an excuse to take his food and work in his home office. His choice to run off to his office and leave her alone confuses her. She feels a barrier between herself and Marc, but it's not hers. Whatever glimpse she saw of his true emotions has been neatly stuffed back under a psychological rock. She takes her food and heads back to her apartment, eats, cuddles with Mabel, reads and watches more TV. Tess spends about three more days on sick leave, before going back to work. She continues to have some nerve pain in her legs but takes normal NSAIDS to keep it under control. Marc continues reining in his emotions, remaining friendly, and mentoring Tess, but avoids her aside from meals, and working with her on her psychic skills. He makes excuses to bury himself in his work. He redoubles his efforts on the black cloud precog alerts, channeling his emotional energy into finding an answer before it's too late.

TICK TOCK

She's been back at work for about a week when Liz notices Tess is becoming more subdued and withdrawn. It's late afternoon, and all the other 'humans' have left for the day, but Tess is waiting on Marc to take her home. "Hey, Tess. Are you okay? You seem distracted?" Liz inquires.

"I'm okay, I guess. I've been feeling out of it the last few days, the rainy weather brought on a new round of nerve pains, and I forgot my painkillers at home." Tess looks up at Liz and smiles out of habit. The smile turns into a yawn.

"Would you like me to take you home? That way, you can take your medication. Besides, Marc's probably going to pull an all-nighter. The situation our precogs have been sensing is becoming imminent, and we still haven't figured out what it is." Liz says.

"Yeah, he's been hyper-focused on it since I got home from the Med Center. That's his entire focus, these days. If you wouldn't mind taking me home, I should get some rest. I'm tired and I need a little me time." Tess grabs her purse and shuts down her computer. Since there're no other humans around to witness them, Liz ports them back to Tess's apartment.

"Do you have anything to eat? I know Marc can get forgetful when he goes into hyper-focus mode." She asks.

Tess nods. "Yeah, there're plenty of leftovers in the fridge. The last few days, he's been all work, or he's in the kitchen cooking. He's so focused, I don't think he's fed in at least 2 or 3 days. Don't worry, I'll be fine with the leftovers."

Liz thinks, *Uh oh! Marc on a cooking binge often means he's avoiding something.* Liz reminds her, "You know, Tess, if you need someone besides Marc to talk to, you can call me, whether it's about your recent accident, or anything else you might have on your mind."

"Thanks, I've got your number in my cell." She smiles as she sees Mabel come skittering around a corner to greet her. She bends down and scoops the cat up, scratching her head and belly, distracted.

"If I don't answer, you know how to otherwise reach me, right?" Liz scans Tess's aura and sees slow swirls of depressive colors in it. *Oh, Hell! Tess is heading for a psychological tailspin, and Marc is ignoring his emotions again, and no doubt hers. When this crisis is over, I'm going to confront him. This isn't healthy for either of them.*

"Yeah, I know. I need some me time, that's all." She puts Mabel up onto the top level of the cat tree Marc bought for her. Mabel bats at Tess as she goes into the kitchen to reheat some leftovers for herself. Tess also opens a can of cat food for *her little fur-demon.*

Liz leaves and heads back to the office, stopping in to see Marc. "Any progress?"

He looks up, he's got dark, worry circles under his eyes, which is unusual for someone like him. "Not a hell of a lot. The answer's eluding me."

She sits on the edge of his desk. "Why don't you take a break?"

"I can't! Whatever's going on, we're running out of time! The latest impressions are we're talking an enormous loss of life! Possibly tens of millions or more. And not only in the Middle East." He says, fingers gripping his hair like he's going to pull it out.

Liz knows the well-being of millions outweighs the well-being of two, but she still worries about Marc and Tess, wondering how both situations can be salvaged without sacrificing one or the other. "By the way, I took Tess home."

He puts his hand on his forehead, acknowledging his forgetfulness. "*Damn!* I completely forgot she was waiting for me."

Liz sits across from him and squeezes her concerns about the two of them in. She remarks, "She's waiting for you in more than one way."

"What?" He says, confused. But he shakes his head as he understands, saying, "Liz, you know I can't do that. She's human. I... I can't let myself get close to her, only to watch her... die some day!" His eyes look haunted as he remembers how Collette's death affected him.

228

"Marc, you're already that close to her, but you won't let yourself admit it. I'm pretty sure almost losing her recently made you open your eyes a tad, only to become like an ostrich and stick your head in the sand." Liz says, impatience coloring her words. "Anyway, she's home, safe and sound. I already told her you'd probably pull an all-nighter. As for me, I need to spend a little time with Kari tonight." She vanishes before she loses her restraint and tells Marc even more, he doesn't want to hear.

He pushes Liz's comments out of his mind and focuses again on his work. Becoming more and more frustrated, he finds it harder and harder to focus on his work. A little before midnight, he leans back in his chair, closing his eyes to rest for a few minutes. He's thinking about Tess and how he wishes he could turn her and make her his. He pushes this out of his mind as too distracting, and not something he should allow himself to think about. Even so, his mind keeps wandering back to Tess, imagining how her body would feel against his. He breaks the mood by forcing himself to focus on the situation at hand, telling himself he must find the answer *before* it's too late. After that, he can figure out how to deal with the situation with Tess.

A DREAM IS A WISH

Tess eats her dinner and mopes around the apartment. She spends some time looking up old friends and acquaintances on Facebook. *So many of my friends are moving on with their lives, having families. I'll never have that.* She thinks. *The more I change, the less I have in common with any of them. As nice as everyone's been, I'll never belong with Marc's people either. It's not fair!* She thinks, hitting her hand on the desk, causing a book to telekinetically hop off a nearby shelf. "And that's one reason I can't go back to the way things were!" She shouts at the ceiling.

Tess browses the web, looking at the news and seeing all the unrest in different places. She reminds herself: *Well, at least I've made a minor difference so far, though only because I failed to keep my abilities in check.* She sighs, closes her laptop, and reads for a little while. She gets to a point in the plot where the woman in it meets the mysterious stranger who sweeps her off her feet on some faraway planet. *Well, that's depressing. Maybe I should find something else to do.* She goes through her shelf of Blu-rays and takes out "Life of Brian". She sticks it into her player, thinking *some good ol' Monty Python is always tonic for the soul.* She's enjoying it until she gets a feeling of anxiety when Michael Palin, as the Roman Emperor gives an address to the people of Jerusalem. She shuts it off and goes to bed early.

Shortly after she dozes off, she starts to dream, finding herself back in her old apartment on the night she first found out about Marc. She's back by the door, with him pinning her to the front door, the warmth of his body feels so real, she forgets she's dreaming.

"Marc! What are you doing here?" He moves closer, pressing her against the door.

His mouth is right by her right ear, and he whispers, "I'm here to make sure you don't tell anyone what I am." He puts his arms around her waist and pulls her tightly against him. She feels his face buried in her hair near her neck. She can even smell him and feel his warm breath caressing her ear. "I know what you want, I know you want to belong somewhere."

"Please, don't hurt me!" She says.

"Believe me, hurting you is the last thing I plan to do, though you may be tender afterwards...." He trails off with a sultry chuckle.

"Wh-what?" She starts to shake and feels like she might faint. He licks her ear and then her cheek, moving slowly down to her neck. She flinches, thinking he's going to bite her.

"Not yet; first, I'm going to give you what you've been longing for, what I should have given you the night all this happened." He turns her around carefully, pulling her close, his blue eyes reaching into her soul, and she feels his soul in return, giving her dream Marc a dimensionality her dream people rarely have, like he's really there.

After a couple of seconds, he leans down and kisses her. At first, she pulls away, but then, a small part of her realizes she's dreaming, and allows herself to indulge. The room melts and shifts scenes. The next thing she knows, she is in her old bedroom with Marc, and they're making love. She holds on to every second of the dream, savoring it, as she practically never has sexual dreams. The dream shifts again; she feels his fangs slide into her neck, and she climaxes, back arching, and then relaxing as he caresses her. He keeps drinking and then, withdraws, kissing her neck and her jaw, moving up to her mouth. She can smell her own blood on his breath. He whispers in her ear, "You want to belong? To be one of us?"

"Yes." She gasps from the depth of her soul. "More than *anything!*"

Marc leans down for one last deep kiss. He skewers his tongue on his fangs, his blood flows into her mouth, unusually sweet, and she has the urge to drink deeply of it. Like this is what she's supposed to do, and something she'd been waiting for her whole life.

Slowly, the scene dissolves, she can still feel his weight, and taste his blood as she slowly wakes in her own bed, alone, and realizes she's been chewing on her lip. The sheets and blanket are in serious disarray. Mabel is looking at her from the top of her dresser like she's had her sleep interrupted, is annoyed, and her tail is twitching wildly. She lingers in the feelings from her dream, until her rational mind takes over and realizes fantasizing about someone you can't have, who can read your mind, is probably not a good idea.

Crap! Marc's going to be pissed about this. I'm going to get a lecture about keeping things platonic, how it's better that way. She thinks, wondering if she can find any way to make herself forget the dream, even though it's one she'd like to relive repeatedly. Her heart is pounding in her chest, both because of the dream itself and the stress of thinking how Marc will react. *Maybe Liz could make me forget? Or help me hide it from Marc, somehow.* She picks up her cell phone and calls Liz even though it's 3 a.m. Luckily, Liz is awake.

Liz picks up her ringing cell and recognizes the number. "Hello, Tess. Is everything okay?" She's concerned Tess would be calling in the middle of the night.

"Liz, I need your help with something, preferably, before I have to see Marc again." She says, and before she can say more, Liz is tapping her on the shoulder, making her jump.

"I'm here, what is it? It must be important if you're calling me at 3 a.m." She sits on the edge of Tess's mattress.

Tess blushes and looks embarrassed. "Yeah, about that, maybe I'm being silly, but I had a dream...." She tells Liz, uneasy talking about it.

"A dream?" Liz raises one eyebrow.

"Yeah, one I'd rather not have Marc pick up on telepathically or *empathically*." She says, sheepishly, her blush deepening to crimson.

"Ah!" Liz understands what Tess is worried about. "One of *those* dreams?" She has a slight grin. "I'm rather surprised you haven't had any before now with as close as you two work together, you know, with telepathy and all."

"I never dream like that, and well, when I do, it, it rarely gets very far; but this one... well, it was intense, to put it nicely." Tess blushes and has a lopsided grin.

"In other words, the dream was a full-blown, X-rated, feature film?" Liz asks with a sparkle in her eye.

Tess leans forward, looking Liz directly in the eye. "Yeah, and, well, you know how Marc is, he wants to keep everything platonic. I thought, briefly, that might have changed after my crash, but whatever I saw in him emotionally, crawled back under its rock and everything went back to good ol' Platonicville! Knowing how he feels about us, I don't want this to complicate things." She tells Liz.

"And how do you think I could help with this?" She can sense the warring emotions in Tess. *She wants that connection to Marc but is afraid it will push him even farther away. She'd rather have platonic than rejection. Marc is a hardheaded ass sometimes!* Liz reflects.

"Maybe you could make me forget the dream? If it's not in my conscious mind, he might not notice it? Though, I hate to forget it, it was the closest thing I've had to sex since before the mess at my last job." She says, blushing.

"Hm, could be tricky. Your mind is resistant to redacting." She gives her a sad but knowing look.

"Even if I want it done?" She asks.

Liz is quiet for a few seconds, debating how to handle this. "Ah, but there's the twist, Tess. You don't really want it done. You just told me you really want to wallow in it, savor it, replay it, right?"

"In some ways, yeah. It was... the best one of those dreams I've ever had. Hell, it was the 'best' sex I ever...didn't have." She laughs, giddily, feeling like her heart is ripping in two, and she could lose it at any moment.

"Let me tell you something about Marc. Something that will probably help you understand why he resists becoming close with you, or anyone else." She pulls herself all the way on the bed and sits cross-legged, facing Tess.

Tess gives a slight nod, and says, "Okay."

"When I'm done, you can decide if you want me to try to redact your memory or not, okay?" She says, and Tess nods. "I don't know if Marc has told you or not, but I was the one who turned him." Tess nods. "When I first came across him, he was a young man, quite intelligent, well-educated for the time, and betrothed to a young woman from a good family. Shortly before they were to marry, his fiancée fell in love with another, and left him. He was devastated. At which point, I entered the picture and, shall we say, distracted him from his problems by turning him. Unfortunately, he couldn't let go of his love. She married the other man, had children with him, and eventually died of TB. Marc watched over her through what there was of her life, and even kept an eye on her children, from a distance, after she passed, making sure she survived in some form through them. He visited her grave every week for many years, and still does, from time to time. That's why he's resisting his own needs and desires when it comes to you, Tess." She explains. "He's afraid of your mortality, and the loss he will, eventually, have to endure."

"What? Are you saying the feelings are mutual?" Tess asks, unsure if she's hearing her right.

"Is that so hard to believe? Yes, he cares about you very much. In fact, part of him connected to you from the start, but he resists allowing himself to bond deeply with anyone, let alone a 'short-lived human', who he will have to mourn eventually. Though I dare say, he will mourn you even if you never 'fulfill' your dream. Your close call with death may have been what made his emotions crawl back under a rock. Your mortality and the pain it will eventually bring him hit him hard." She notices tears glistening in Tess's eyes, either from her own sadness and frustration, or perhaps, in sympathy for Marc's story. Liz telekinetically grabs a box of tissues from across the room, handing it to her.

Tess sits quietly for a few minutes, wiping an occasional tear and blowing her nose. "Liz, as much as I want him, I don't want to cause him any pain, either. Maybe you should try to make me forget the dream. Can you put in some sort of posthypnotic suggestion to not have another one?" She ignores her heart dropping into her stomach as she acknowledges the impossible situation, she's in. "It's probably better not to hope than to get rejected or disappointed, especially now I know he cares, but won't act on it." Tess's tears are flowing more freely from her deep, emotional pain.

"Tess, I so wish we could have found a way to turn you, or your bond with Marc would break down this insane emotional restriction he's put on himself. I've watched him for centuries keep his liaisons casual; never letting his emotions go. However, if you really want me to do this, I will." Liz says. "At least, I'll try."

"There's one more thing, at the end of the dream, he asked me if this is what I want, to belong, and he turned me. I wanted it so badly but know he can't do that. It felt so right! It was like I was supposed to be one of you. I don't want to remember that either, because it can't happen." Tess's nose is running, and tears are streaming down her cheeks uncontrollably. Liz reaches over and gives her a hug, and holds her there until she settles down, and her crying subsides.

"Tess, look at me." Liz cups her face with gentle hands, massaging her temples. "I'm going to try, but there's a good chance it won't hold. Your emotional connection to it all is very strong, and with your history...."

"If it doesn't hold, I'll just have to deal with it." She tries to sound logical and brave. Liz slips into her mind and sifts around her memories. She lets her do what she must until her mind is at peace and is without thought for a time, like her mind is suspended in the ether. Liz leaves her in a dreamless sleep.

Liz looks down at the young, human woman she's come to consider a friend, and in some ways, family. She thinks, *Good luck, Tess. You're going to need it.* She ports back to Kari, who immediately picks up on what happened, and Liz's turbulent emotions regarding Marc and his eternal, self-imposed isolation. Kari hugs her partner; they hold each other close and go to sleep.

WHEN THE LEVEE BREAKS

Tess's alarm goes off, and Mabel immediately pounces on her chest, purring and meowing for breakfast. Tess has no memory of her dream, or Liz's nocturnal visit. She feeds Mabel, fixes a couple of fried eggs, and gets ready to go to work. She goes into Marc's part of the dwelling but doesn't see or hear any sign of him. She goes upstairs and knocks on his bedroom door but doesn't get an answer. She carefully opens it and peeks in. He's not there, and his bed hasn't been slept in. *I guess she wasn't kidding when she said he was going to pull an all-nighter.* She thinks.

It's odd not seeing him this morning or having him there to port her to work. She returns to her room and grabs the car keys for the Honda he borrowed and heads out to drive herself to work. She arrives at work, saying her usual good mornings to everyone and stops by Marc's office to see if he's there. He is, looking like *Hell* warmed over, tossed in a dumpster. and warmed over again.

"Wow, I didn't think people like you could look that much like crap. Rough night?" She leans against his doorframe, concerned by his appearance.

He looks up and gives her an exhausted, half-smile. "Come in, close the door. Yes, very frustrated. We've got it narrowed down to certain groups, which appear to be coordinating toward some terrorist goal, something big, but we can't see what, and we can't figure out how they're communicating and coordinating. There's no sign of couriers, no sign of cell phone usage, short wave, Internet or even the use of gaming system networks, as some have used before, but they are on the move and some-how coordinated." He crumples up a piece of paper he's been making notes on and throws it at the wall in frustration.

"Anything I can do?" She's never seen him in this state and worries he may be on the verge of some sort of collapse, psychological or maybe physical.

"Right now, maybe just be here for me to vent to?" He yawns.

Tess stands behind his chair and massages his neck and shoulders, as he often does for her. She sees hints of red tension in his aura where his muscles are knotted. "Hmmm, that's nice, but I *need* to focus, and that's *not* helping my focus at all." He gives her a slight smile as he takes one of her hands in his. "*Sorry*, I didn't come home last night. I trust you found some food and made do?" He feels guilty for forgetting about her the evening before.

"Yeah, but how about you? Did you go out and eat or feed at all?" She notices his paler than usual complexion, dark circles under his eyes, and a mental feeling she can only describe as 'frazzled'. She's more than a little concerned, and sits on the corner of his desk, staring him down to get an answer out of him.

Marc sighs, knowing Tess's stubborn streak, and answers honestly. "No, I've been focusing on this all night. I'll take a break later and go out and feed, though if you wouldn't mind, would you go to the Chinese carryout on Airport Road, and get me some food? He holds out his wallet to her.

She takes it, sticking it in her tote bag. "I guess so, but Chinese food for breakfast? Are they even open this early?"

"Not exactly, but they know me, and my weird hours." He smiles, but Tess sees exhaustion and worry in his eyes.

"Anything in particular?" She opens the notes app on her iPhone to write his order down.

"Ask for Li and tell him I sent you. He'll know what I want. By the way, he's one of us." His tablet beeps, and he looks down at it, distracted, as new data comes in.

"One of you guys? A vam... Apara? *Sorry*, one of these days I'll get used to using that term. *God*! I've been there several times and had no idea!" She shakes her head at her *faux pas*.

"Yeah. I keep forgetting you aren't one of us." He says, distracted. "And get yourself something too, have lunch with me?"

"It's 9 am! You're the one who's always after me about eating a proper breakfast."

"Well, brunch, then." He says, the usual sparkle lacking in his tired eyes.

Tess heads out of his office, shaking her head. She drives down to the restaurant, knocks on the door, as it's locked. An Asian man who looks like he's around 25 answers the door. She says she's looking for Li, and Marc sent her. He smiles, and opens the door, bowing, and swinging his arm in a 'come in gesture'.

Forty-five minutes later, Tess brings in several bags of Chinese food and puts them on the meeting table by the sofa. "Here you go. As you said, Li knew what you'd want." She unpacks the food on the table, taking out paper plates Li included, as well as chopsticks, and plastic ware. "He was confused about me." She laughs lightly and sits on the sofa.

"Oh?" Marc gets up and comes over to the table. His stomach growls as the sweet and pungent odors of the Chinese food reach his nose.

"Yeah, he knew I was human, but he said he could sense something more. He said my 'mental vibration' is closer to one of your kind." She smiles.

He looks at her thoughtfully and shrugs. "Hm, he probably meant you were too psychic to be human." He takes a bite of sweet and sour shrimp.

"I guess so. He was pretty damn surprised a human knew about you all but took it in stride. Anyway, he said to give you his regards and said he's still waiting for you to make your next chess move?" She opens up several boxes, scooping out a little of each onto her plate, realizing she's hungrier than she thought.

Marc gives a wistful laugh. "We've been playing a very long game of chess. But it's been a long time since I've had time for it. He keeps the board at his place."

"You mean between me and this precog stuff, you've been pretty busy?" She raises an eyebrow and stares at him.

"That too, but it goes in cycles. We'll play fairly often for a while, and then take a break and then get active again." He practically inhales a shrimp egg roll.

"So, you do have a life outside work?" Tess snorts.

He gives a half-hearted chuckle, then says, "Yes, but lately, it's been too crazy for much else." He's distracted as he wracks his brain about the Middle Eastern problem even as he eats.

"Yeah, including keeping me out of trouble." She laughs, then notices he somehow looks worse; paler, and in pain. "You're really worried about all this, aren't you?"

"Yes! It's got a lot of our people agitated. Now, it's not only the precogs, but a lot of us feel this unease, like an itch at the back of the mind. Something's going to happen, and soon, and feels like we're talking a catastrophic event. If the trends are right, millions may die!" Worry shows in his blue eyes, making them look shadowed and darker. "Thanks for the food run and company. I really appreciate it. I should get back to it, though."

"Marc, unless you've budged from this office since last night, I know you haven't fed in at least four days. You told me once you needed to feed every two to three days?" Her voice is heavy with concern. "You're obviously not going to solve this if you can't focus, and if there's one thing I've noticed about you, if you don't feed, your focus sucks."

"You're probably right, but it feels like the answer's right on the edge of my consciousness. I'll be fine. I'll feed tonight; I promise." He stands and goes back to stare at his screens, tablet, and scratch pad.

Tess hesitates, mulling things over, but decides his health is more important than her blood count. She thinks, *oh, crap, I'm probably going to regret this, but...* She walks over to his desk and stands next to him, then sits on the edge of the desk, moves her long brown hair away from her neck, and says: "Well, if you won't go out and feed, then I guess I'll deliver that too." She puts her hand on his arm, and nearly withdraws it, as his skin feels much cooler than usual.

"Tess, you really don't need..." He says but can't finish his sentence as he looks up at her and can not only see but feel the blood

240

throbbing through her carotid.

"See, can't even finish a sentence when you're hungry. It's okay, I know you won't hurt me, and you *need* to feed." She makes direct eye contact with him, and then tips her head back, and waits.

"Alright, but I don't want to make a habit of it. I don't want you to feel you need to do this or that I expect it of you." He stands and draws her up as well. "I appreciate this, and yes, I'm hungry."

He holds her chin with his fingertips, gently moves one arm behind her to support her back, then leans in, blocks any pain, carefully sinks his fangs into her neck, and feeds. He must focus to control how hard he draws and how much he takes, knowing he's waited too long. He takes slow, controlled draws on her throat. About half a minute in, Tess's mind reels. She's lightheaded and dizzy, but not from blood loss. She flashes back to the intimate part of her dream from the night before. She's disoriented, as the suppressed memories flood her conscious mind, and overflow into Marc's as well. Marc stiffens, not only seeing her memories, but feeling the emotions connected to them. He stops feeding and instinctively heals her wounds. He struggles for control and holds himself very still. "*Tesssss!*" He says, in a hiss. "You know that can't be, either thing! As much as I care about you, we must *remain only friends.*" He gasps, grappling with his own need to fulfill part of her dream.

Tears of horror and embarrassment run down her cheeks. She looks at him, and says, "Marc, sometimes you can sure be an insensitive asshole, for all you claim to be an empath!" Several knickknacks fall off the shelf on a nearby wall. "You *may* have *superhuman* ability to control *your* emotions, but as you keep pointing out, I'm *only human!* I can't turn my feelings off with the flip of a switch!" She storms out of his office, telekinetically slamming the door behind her. Marc drops into his chair to deal with the residual waves of memory and emotions, feeling dumbfounded at Tess's words and reaction.

A minute later, Liz comes in without knocking. "Kari just informed me Tess blew out of here like an angry bull. What the *hell* happened?" Her tone is as it might be with an errant offspring.

"It's nothing. She'll get over it." He mumbles, not wanting to rehash the same old discussion with Liz.

Liz, sensing from Marc's reaction her redacted memory dam has broken, drops in a nearby chair with a sigh. "You really are *clueless*! And *stubborn*, if not outright *pigheaded*!"

He looks at her, mouth gaping in surprise and irritation. "What? Now you're angry with me too?"

"Not angry, no, at least, not entirely at you." She sighs. "Let me guess. You saw her dream, didn't you?"

"Wait, you *know* about that dream?" He stands, confusion and a touch of anger in his eyes.

"Yes, she had it last night, and was afraid of how you'd react if you thought she was having romantic thoughts and feelings about you. She asked me to help her suppress the memory." She looks at him, hands on her hips, patience with him run out.

He sits back down on the side of his desk. "Last night, you say?" He remembers his distracted moments where he let himself indulge in similar thoughts. "It may be partially my fault she had the dream. I was distracted and my mind wandered last night."

Liz's eyes open wide in surprise, sarcasm putting a sting in her words. "You mean you *actually let* yourself entertain forming a bond with her?"

"Not seriously! How can I? She'll be dead in a few decades, and I've been there before. I can't go through that again! She can't be turned. Not unless you plan to plead on my behalf to our Benefactors to make her compatible." A sigh of frustration escapes from his mouth. "From the look on your face, I'm guessing you aren't willing to take that option?"

She shakes her head slowly. "You know what they'll say. It's too risky. They may even opt to work on her memory and repress her abilities. That would not be a pleasant experience for her. That, I'm certain of. It was hard enough on her to realize people like us exist, or backstory will certainly freak her out!"

"Well, what the *hell* do you suggest? I give in to her desires? Is that fair to her? She can't have children with me. She won't have a regular life." He barks out at her.

Frustration makes Liz speak her mind. "Listen to yourself! She won't have a regular life *now*! That ended the day she walked in the door. She's stuck in limbo! She may be human and short-lived, but she's not completely human anymore either! She'll *never* find another *human* she can share any of this with. She'll always be *alone*, and you should understand *how* that feels!" Her voice softens. "Not to mention, to work so closely with her, especially with telepathy, you had to know that level of psychic intimacy would lead to a bond forming between the two of you!"

"Liz, I did my best to avoid that when working with her. I worked on telepathy between the two of us, and had her work on reading other humans, not me, empathically." He says, his forehead resting in his hands, only to look up at Liz at the end.

She can sense the frustration and pain he's hiding. She sits on the edge of his desk. "You, of all people, know you can't completely separate telepathy and empathy. The two of you have been doing this dance of avoidance around each other for weeks. You not wanting to get hurt, and her not wanting to upset you by being an 'emotional human'. You know, her asking me to hide her dream speaks volumes!"

"Liz...." He says, knowing she's had it with his years of keeping himself above emotional entanglement.

"It shows she cares about you so much; she'd rather suppress her own desires and needs than risk pushing you away because you know how she feels." Liz reaches over and lightly touches his arm, while maintaining eye contact the whole time.

Marc sighs. "I know how she feels! *Believe* me. But I... I can't go through that again. I might *mess* things up." He exclaims, pain visible in his eyes.

An 'A-ha!' moment hits Liz, finally finding the last puzzle piece to Marc's self-isolation. "Oh, Marc." Liz puts her hand up to her face and massages her temples, then looks him in the eye. "You think you drove your betrothed away, don't you? You feel *responsible*? All these years, I thought it was just her loss, but you feel guilty for her leaving you! I'll bet you think if she'd stayed with you, she might not have died from TB."

Marc bangs his desk once with his fist in frustration. "*Yes! Okay!* I've wondered for centuries what I did wrong."

"Marc," She takes a long, slow, deep breath before continuing, finally resolved to come clean with her own, long held secret. "You didn't do anything wrong, or anything to drive her away. It was all my doing." She spaces out the words in her last sentence and waits for those words to register, and braces for his reaction.

"What? What are you talking about?" He's confused by her confession, and more than a little shocked.

Liz calmly tells him the truth, "They'd chosen you to become one of us. I was doing my job. They felt once you were married, it would be psychologically too difficult for you to make the transition. I was told to fix things. I planted the suggestion in her mind to fall in love with Luc. It wasn't your fault." Liz braces herself for a backlash.

Marc's expression is a mixture of anger, sorrow, and betrayal. "What? All these years, and you never told me this? *Merde!* What the actual *fuck*, Liz? You let me go for hundreds of years thinking she'd chosen to leave me, and now you tell me you *made* her leave?"

For the first time in years, Liz feels like crying herself, but holds it in. "I felt horrible when I saw the pain I'd caused, but I believed it was necessary. *They* felt it was necessary. I've wanted to tell you but couldn't bring myself to. I didn't realize until now you blamed yourself for her leaving and even her untimely death. I'm *so* sorry! But the fact remains you shouldn't let this prevent you and Tess from being there for each other for however long it's possible. She needs you, but *you* need her just as much, and while a 'few decades' may be a drop in the bucket for you to resist that intimacy, for her, it's her *entire lifetime*. Think about that, please, for both your sakes."

Marc calms down, taking control of his anger, and sits silently, lost in thought, exploring the waves of emotions that hit him from Tess's dream, her anger, and embarrassment at his discovery, as well as Liz's confession and rebuke.

"I do care about her a lot. But right now, I've *got* to solve *this!*"

He waves his hand at all the information on his desk in one last attempt to put off what he knows he must do.

Liz loses patience with his avoidance. "You're not going to solve anything in this state. Transfer your findings to me, and I'll give it a look with fresh eyes, while you go and fix this mess of yours. You know, you, Kari, and Peder are my family. I've turned many over the years, but I only consider you three my family."

Marc cracks a lopsided smile. "*Alright*! Should I start calling you *mom*?"

"Uh, no. Are you going to go after her?" She holds her breath, hoping he'll say yes.

"Yes, she's blocking me telepathically, though; she really must be pissed off. I'll check at home first and then find her somehow." He gets closer to Liz, taking her hand in his. "Here, this is all the information and ideas I've had so far." He sends her the information telepathically, not so much as words but in a huge 'data packet' of information. "My notes are there, and all the data is in my tablet. Call me if you figure anything out."

"If I *need* you, I'll call, but you need to deal with this now. Tess has been, let's just say, Kari and I have been worried about her mental state since before her accident. She's truly trapped between worlds. She can never go back to her own, not fully, but you can make her a part of ours, a real part. I may not have or be able to turn her, but she's become family." Liz admits. "Wait! Doesn't she have the blue, Honda sedan?"

"Yes, why?" He asks.

Liz grabs her tablet and opens an app. "All our vehicles are GPS lojacked. She punches in a code, and a blue, blinking dot pops up on a regional map." She hands it to him since she'll be using his. "Wait, a bit until she stops somewhere and has time to cool down before you go to her. I'd suggest getting yourself cleaned up before then. You not only look like Hell, you kinda smell like it too!"

Marc nods and vanishes.

NEED

Tess flies out of Marc's office in a huff, speaking to no one. She grabs her purse and reaches for her keys, only to have them fly into her hand from three feet away. She stomps out, doing her best to keep more things from flying around the office unbidden as there are other humans nearby. She blows past Kari, who attempts to ask her what's wrong, and gets to her car. She's so flustered, she has trouble using her keys to unlock the door, so channels her energy into the lock, telekinetically unlocking it. She gets in, closes the door, puts the key in the ignition, and pauses. She's out of breath, so wills herself calmer, knowing if she drives in this state, she could have another accident. She calmly gets her pendant from a small metal case in her bag and puts it on. *I don't need to cause anyone else to have an accident, either.* She thinks after struggling not to turn the office into a scene from Poltergeist.

I can't go home, if he even bothers to come looking for me, that's the first place he'll go. I need to block him so he can't track me. She focuses, doing her best to change her 'shield' to camouflage her mental signature. *Now, where to go? Some place public, some place where I can hide for a while, figure everything out. Hell, some place I can distract myself from feeling like shit.* She picks up her cell phone and opens her movie app. *Perfect! They're doing a Marvel Marathon at Asheville Pizza all week before the new Marvel movie comes out. I'll buy the all shows pass and sit there until I, and he calms down.* She turns the ignition and drives to the pizza and movie house on Merrimon Avenue, north of town. The walls are covered with old movie posters, and they have "in-theater" ordering. She goes in, waits in line, and orders a double order of 'Homer's Garlic 'Doh Knots' as comfort food, and a large soda. She hides in an innermost seat in a row, against a half wall. She settles in to watch the movie. The room dims, and the second Captain America film begins. She stuffs her face with the garlic knots. *Ugh! I shouldn't be eating all this junk, but screw it! I deserve a little comfort food today.* She thinks.

About halfway through the first movie, those sitting in her row abruptly get up and move further down in the theater. She thinks *that was odd, didn't even hear them say anything about moving; maybe it was the garlic?*

Someone comes in and sits next to her. Without looking, she knows the aura and mind of the man sitting next to her, and she lets out a long sigh. Marc's found her. *Oh crap! I thought it would take longer for him to find me. Maybe my shields aren't so good after all?* She carefully scans his mood empathically. She expects him to be angry and lecture her about how they must keep things professional and platonic and she's being an emotional human; but as she sits there, she can't sense any of that, his mood isn't at all what she expects. More like he's figuring out what to say to her.

I'm not sure how you found me, but I really need some me time. I'll be home later. She paths.

All company cars are lojacked. I waited until you settled and hopefully calmed down. I promise, I didn't know about the lojack until Liz told me after you ran off, but she gave me the app to find you. She feels a mental, uneasy grin. *Tess, I'm not here to lecture you, I'm here to apologize.* He paths.

Taken aback, she paths: *Apologize?*

We need to talk, and it's hard to talk when you're distracted by Capt. America's ass on the screen. I promise, you'll want to hear me out. He paths.

Tess senses a need in Marc she's never felt before, one he's never let her or even himself feel. *What is it?*

Please, come home with me. He paths.

I thought you had so much work to do. She knows the work is beyond important, but part of her resents his using it to avoid her, or it feels that way.

He takes her left hand in his. *Liz took over for now. Right now, we need to talk.* She senses sincerity, no anger, and a need to explain himself.

248

Curious, she consolidates the left-over 'Doh Knots in one box, grabs her purse and phone, and nods to him. They get up and quietly leave the theater.

She senses amusement from him. He paths, *Garlic? You know that doesn't bother me, right?*

Hmph! I'll admit the thought crossed my mind, but I really needed some comfort food, and they're my favorite carb on the menu. He lets her pass him as they head out the door, putting one hand on her back as she goes by. She digs out the keys and they head for the car. A light drizzle is falling, and she thinks, *the weather is mirroring my mood today.*

Once in the car, she says out loud. "Okay, what is so damn important you had to GPS me and drag me out of the theater?" She feigns annoyance, but part of her hopes he's come after her to show her she really matters to him.

The rain goes from a light drizzle to a downpour, giving Tess even more reason to stay there and hear him out. "I'm not sure where to start." He pauses. "After you stormed out, Liz made me see things differently. There are some things you need to know about me. But please, let's go home and talk?" He still needs time to put his feelings into words without sounding like an ass or an imbecile.

Tess turns the ignition, headlights, and wipers on, and drives out of the parking lot and onto Merrimon Avenue, covering the short distance to the human world façade to their home in Sanctuary. She parks and sits for a second outside their home. "If this is gonna be another lecture about keeping things platonic, I swear! I'll go back to the marathon and stay until I get sick of Marvel movies!" She lets anger and annoyance seep into her words and prepares herself in case he rejects her as she fears.

Marc, unexpectedly, reaches behind her head, draws her closer, and leans in and kisses her. She resists briefly thinking *What the fuck?* But then, a wave of emotion and need from him, matching her own washes over her. She gasps at the flood of emotions and gives in to the kiss. After a couple of minutes, he pulls away, leaning his forehead against hers. "Hmmm, shall we go inside?"

Breathlessly, Tess says "Uh-huh." And undoes her seatbelt, gets out of the car, and skitters wildly for the house through the pouring rain. The door unlocks at her touch, and they rush inside, closing the door behind them, breaking into laughter, as they're both breathless and drenched. He comes up behind her, and puts his arms around her, nuzzling her soaked hair.

"I have to ask, why the sudden change of heart?" She turns around, his arms still around her, holding her close.

He leans down, resting his cheek on her head. "Truth is, part of me connected to you the first day you came in. It was like meeting an old friend, or more, but, as I told you, when I was turned, I'd just lost my betrothed to another man, and it left some deep scars. I've been avoiding being hurt again, and in the process, I've ignored how much I've been hurting you."

"Liz mentioned Collette left you for someone else." She's still a little skeptical about Marc's change in attitude, afraid he might pull back again after giving her a taste of his affection.

"She told you, huh? Did she tell you *she* was the one who pushed my intended to leave me?" His voice contains overtones of pain and betrayal. "Because she only told me today."

"No, she didn't. She kinda left that part out." She's shaking nervously, hoping this isn't only a temporary bit of vulnerability from what Liz told him.

"Yeah, she left that part out for me too. All these years! *Centuries*! I kept myself above making a bond with someone. I never allowed myself to get close for fear of..." He trails off.

"Liz said you had trouble getting close to anyone because you're afraid of losing them. She said your ex-fiancée died young. Tuberculosis?" Tess relaxes into his arms, sensing the pain, frustration, and need pouring out from Marc, like water finally eroding a dam.

"Yes. Back then, we called it the White Plague or Phthisis. Collette died when she was 32. The truth is, I thought I'd done something to make her leave me." He pulls her close, into a long hug. He lets her go but takes her hand and guides her to the sofa in his living room. "All these years, I couldn't get over the feeling if I hadn't driven her away,
250

she might not have died so young; that somehow, I could have saved her. I figured, if I hadn't done something wrong, she never would've left me." He admits. "So, I avoided driving anyone else away by keeping things casual or platonic, never making any commitments or strong emotional ties. I chose never to turn anyone or find a partner among my own because I thought something was *wrong with me*, and I'd hurt whoever I'm with, and make them leave. Yes, there were times I was with others of my kind to satisfy needs, but it was never my emotional ones." He reaches out and holds both of her hands in his, slowly looking up to make eye contact after his soul wrenching confession.

Tess feels his emotions flowing from him, and through her. It takes all her effort to stay even a little objective and patient. "And now that you know Liz made her leave?"

"Hmmm, it puts things into a different perspective, and I know it's rather late to ask, after baring my soul to you, but do you? Is your dream how you really feel?" He gazes into her eyes.

"Yes, why wouldn't it be?" She asks.

"Because, last night, I briefly indulged in some of the same thoughts, and I'm afraid I may have influenced your dream telempathically." He holds eye contact, studying her reactions.

She sits, quietly, thinking about what to say next. "Even if you did somehow influence the dream, my feelings for you are real, I just didn't dare let myself show them, because I knew you wouldn't approve."

Marc lets out a long sigh and grins, "I guess I'll just have to cope with your mortality, because if we take this step, you'll be stuck with me for the rest of your life." He holds her hands, waiting for her to respond; hoping she'll say yes, but he fears he's already ruined things by being too distant.

Her face and mood soften as she lets herself accept his sincerity. She takes a chance on him not changing his mind. She gives him a sultry smirk. "*Hey!* Where else am I gonna go?" She says and leans in to kiss him. He responds in kind, enthusiastically, passionately, leaning her back on the sofa. After a few minutes, he scoops her up like she weighs nothing.

"So, your place or mine?" He grins.

"I think you mean *our* place now, don't you?" She says, motioning up the stairs to his bedroom.

He carries her to his bed, an old style, heavy wooden canopy bed like you might have seen in old France, with heavy, thick, carved posts and wooden frame, and deep, royal blue velvet curtains tied to the posts, gold threads running through them. He puts her down on the bed and joins her, kissing her, and undressing her, watching her for any signs of hesitation or regret. When she reaches over and helps him undress, he relaxes and knows he's not pushing her too fast; she wants this as much as he wants her. As they make love, it's not just their bodies entangled, but their minds; the deepest form of intimacy two people can have.

Afterward, they lay silently on their sides, with Tess's back curled into Marc's front, Marc strokes her back, feeling the irregular skin across her shoulders.

"Tess? Are these the scars you told me about?" He traces the larger areas of scar tissue.

"Yes, but I'd rather not think about that right now, if you don't mind. I don't want to ruin the mood with bad memories." She says.

"Okay. I was just curious. You'd told me about them, but I've never seen them before. Your clothes always hide them. They're a lot worse than I'd imagined." He slides his arm back around her, hugging her close. Marc senses unexpected emotions from her, like something's wrong, almost like he's done something amiss.

"Tess, are you okay? Something doesn't feel right. Did I upset you? Or hurt you? Was I too rough?" He strokes her hair.

"No. It's nothing, really." She reassures him.

Marc edges back and nudges her shoulder, so she turns around and faces him. "No, there's something. Anger? No... disappointment?"

Her expression softens, and she cups his cheek with her hand. "It was beyond my hopes and dreams, but, well, it's stupid, because I know the other part of the dream was wishful thinking." She explains.

"You mean the part where I turned you?" He brushes the hair from her eyes.

"Yeah. It's crazy, but part of me was anticipating it.

Anticipating you, well, biting me, and part of me feels like... like..." She's frustrated because she can't put things into words.

"Like I didn't finish what I started?" He says, with a gentle grin.

"Not exactly. I mean, this is embarrassing, but I wanted you to bite me, even if the rest couldn't happen. I wanted that rush like the night in my apartment. It was like a part of me was waiting for it, needing it, and I know it's crazy. I shouldn't want someone to bite me." She admits.

"Under other circumstances, I may well have bitten you, but I already fed from you today. To do so again, when our emotions are all tied up in it could have led to me taking more than I should. As to it being crazy to want that, let me give you a little perspective. I've fed from you three times now, four if you count me pumping you full of Trinaline, but that was a special case. The first one was by force, I didn't block the pain completely, and you obviously didn't enjoy that one. But the other two times, you had a different reaction. What do you think the difference was?" He asks.

Tess is quiet, but then her expression changes to one of com-prehension. "I *offered* to let you feed from me?"

"Yes, you were willing, and you shared yourself with me. In some ways, that can be even more intimate than sex itself. Think about it. My fangs entered you, but I also took part of you into myself. You became part of me, temporarily. Add to that, I numbed any pain in those two cases, and it takes on a very differ-ent feeling." He strokes her arm gently.

"Is that why I reacted the way I did? Wanting you that night?" Part of her wonders how much of her reaction was real.

"No, it's more than that. We share a connection and have for a long time. And yes, I know you were having feelings for me even before you found out what I am. If we didn't have that bond, that connection, then no, you likely wouldn't have reacted that way. With partners among my kind, it's common to feed from each other during sex, not out of need, but because it is a form of intimacy. Let's say it can *add* to the experience." He grins. "Next time, I'll show you what it can be like, I promise." He leans in for a playful kiss.

Tess lies there, silently, head on his chest, her mind going in so many directions at once. She remembers something he told her that day in his office, when he tried to make her forget: "When someone is turned, you basically feed from them and then give blood back?" She asks.

"Yes, that's how it works, assuming someone's compatible. The virus that transforms us normally resides, inert, in our bone marrow, and isn't detectable in our blood. If someone's compatible, then the compatible genetic sequence activates the latent virus, and releases a flood of viral particles into our bloodstream, keyed to the DNA of the person who was fed on. They stay in the system for up to an hour, so if, in that time, we feed the person our blood, it binds rapidly to their DNA, multiplying and spreading; it rewrites their genes, eventually transforming the person. Usually, I'd drink a lot more than in a normal feed; enough, they'd die without the virus or an immediate, major transfusion. Taking so much weakens the body, allowing the virus to run its course more easily. The body has to give in to the virus to survive." He explains.

"But any amount will do, won't it? I mean, you could feed a little and give the person your blood and they'd turn?" She asks.

Marc wonders where she's going with her questions. "Well, yes, if that person's compatible, it only takes a few drops for the initial infection to take hold, but any transformation would likely be prolonged and painful, as the body's immune system would fight it tooth and nail."

She pauses thoughtfully. "I, I want you to do something for me."

"*Anything!*" He continues stroking her hair unconsciously.

"There's an expression. 'If it quacks like a duck, walks like a duck, swims like a duck, and looks like a duck, then it must be a duck.' Everyone keeps saying how I would have been the perfect potential, my psychic skills, my personality, my ethics. Isn't it possible I'm compatible and somehow overlooked?" She asks.

He gives her a sympathetic look, knowing how much she wants to belong. "I wish it were that simple, but our database is very thorough."

"I want you to try to turn me. You told me once if you tried to and I wasn't compatible, nothing would happen, but if I am, I'll turn. It *is* that simple! Please, Marc, *try!*" She begs him, pleading with both her eyes and voice.

"I can't. Not now." Before he can explain further, she

254

interrupts him, anger flaring.

"Why the *hell* not! I just want you to try! Feed from me! Then give me your blood, like in my dream! Something deep inside me tells me it'll work! I know I'm *supposed* to be one of you." She pleads, tears welling up in her eyes, her cheeks flaming with anger and frustration.

He takes her by her shoulders, sitting her up so they're facing each other. He speaks slowly, and calmly, trying to diffuse her anger. "I'm not unwilling and I want to try, but I *don't* have the time right now. I feel guilty enough having come here when time is running out with millions of lives in the balance! But I couldn't focus until I made my peace with you. If I try to *turn* you, and by some *miracle*, you're compatible, it'll take time for you to change. Possibly up to two days. I'd want to be here to see you through it, and I don't have that luxury right now. Whatever's going to happen *is imminent*! I want to stay with you, bask in these feelings, but I need to go back and solve this problem!" He pulls her closer and holds her tightly, his explanation successfully diffusing her mood. "I promise, I'll exhaust whatever options there are, but after the crisis is over, because if you start to turn, I won't leave your side until it's over!" He lies down and pulls her down with him, her head again on his chest, his heart pounds against her ear. "I can stay a few more minutes, love, then I *have* to go back to work."

Tess grasps his hand tightly. "I'm gonna hold you to that!"

They lie together in comfortable silence; just being together before he has to go back to work on the pressing, black-cloud alerts. He gently strokes her hair, while she runs through all the thoughts and feelings that went through her mind while they were together; not only the emotional mélange of two minds embraced, but also things he had on his mind about the black-cloud alerts. She lies there, pondering the things which stump him the most. After a few minutes, an idea takes form in her mind, and she must break the silence. "You know how you said a lot of you had a feeling like an *itch* in the back of your minds?"

He murmurs, "Mm-hmm."

Tess continues. "And you know how I could feel you all

reading me telepathically from the start? It was also like that—a crawling of my skin on my head, like an itch."

He yawns, then says, "Yes, quite a surprise to all of us." He leans over and kisses the top of her head.

"You also told me human and Apara telepathic bands are different, and how you can communicate on my band with me, but your band isn't accessible by humans?" Tess feels like puzzle pieces are falling into place.

"Where are you going with this?" He wishes he didn't have to think in the last few minutes they have together; he just wants to be with her.

She twists her body so she can prop herself up and look him in the eye. "When Li was talking about me being more like your kind, he wasn't talking about me being psychic, I heard some of *his* thoughts. He reacted because my public thoughts were close to Apara frequencies."

"Hm, with being exposed to us so much and working with me, you may have adapted to our frequencies. Honestly, I've nothing to compare you to. There's never been someone like you; a human that's worked with my people so closely." He cups her face in his hand, one corner of his mouth turning up in a smile. "Liz told me tonight she considers you part of her family."

"She does? Wow! I'm flattered." She pauses for a second, and then pulls herself back on track and continues. "But my point is, that feeling you and the others are feeling—I felt it in your mind tonight, and it's nearly identical to what I felt when I first came to Inspiration Inc. What if the mental itching your people are feeling is people, somehow communicating on a frequency close to yours? A frequency you *wouldn't* be monitoring because you don't expect humans to use it."

As the idea sinks in, he recalls something from decades earlier, and gently nudges Tess so he can get up. He stands and grabs his clothes. "Tess, I *must* go! You *may* be on to something." He leans down for one lingering kiss, and then vanishes while putting one leg into his pants.

BOOM

Tess lies there for a few minutes, savoring every detail she can muster, but her mind keeps wandering back to what they talked about. She can sense the agitation in his mind from there. She takes a quick shower, and then goes to her apartment for clean clothes. She's accosted by Mabel, meowing angrily because she's hungry and feeling ignored. Tess feeds her, gets dressed, and heads back into work. It's after 7 p.m., and the place is unusually busy. The parking lot is mostly empty, as all the humans who work there have gone home for the day, but the office is full of people, including many she doesn't know. As she comes in the door, Kari looks up and gives her a knowing smile, to which Tess rolls her eyes.

"*Ugh*! Working with a bunch of telempaths sucks! Kari, is Marc in his office?" She asks.

"Yes, but there're several others in there at the moment." There's an underlying 'you may not want to go in there right now' vibe present.

"It's okay. I just want to check on his progress, nothing else." She misunderstands the vibe as 'not the time for romance'.

Tess walks down the hall at a good clip, sensing Marc's agitation and an urgency in his mind. She bursts into his office, where there are several people now staring at her, most of whom she doesn't recognize. Those who don't know her are looking at her strangely. She can hear random half thoughts from them, which surprises her. They're uncertain what to do with a human in the room.

"It's okay, everyone, this is Tess. She's the one who suggested they might be communicating close to our frequency. You don't need to hide anything from her." Marc approaches Tess and quietly says, "You didn't need to come in, believe me, you've *done your* part." He ushers her out of his office and into an empty one nearby.

"I couldn't help it. I could sense your agitation even from home. Does this mean I was right?" She asks.

He reaches for her and pulls her into a tight embrace, then lets her go before saying, "*Yes!* What you suggested helped me solve it. And if I'm right, just in time. We believe it's going to happen in the next week because of some visual clues in some precogs. We think it may be associated with an upcoming, Jewish holiday.

"Well, what is it?" She asks, eager to know.

"We haven't figured out the details yet, but we know it's going to be some type of attack, but the details have been evading us; however, you were right about them using a close frequency. The Russians developed an implant that created artificial telepathy back in the Soviet, Cold War Era. The implants work on a frequency marginally off our own telepathic range, and transmit through the membrane we port through, Limbo. The terrorists acquired and are using modernized versions of those implants to communicate; that's why we couldn't see how they're communicating. We were picking up on their 'chatter' like interference overlapping with our frequency. Now, we've got to pick up enough of their chatter and interpret it to know what they're planning." He explains quickly and simply. "I've got to get back in there. We're working out exactly what they're planning. It's big, and it could happen anytime. But if we can do it, you may have helped save a lot more than you did when you overheard the Pride Fest plot." He gives her another quick kiss and heads back into the fray in his office.

Tess feels a familiar mind behind her. "Liz?" She turns, knowing she's there.

Liz sighs and looks haggard. "Tess, you need to go home. There are *too* many here who don't know about you, and things could get complicated quickly." She anticipates her next question: "No. They won't do anything to hurt you, but right now, every second we lose explaining to them about you, we lose precious time. Take my hand." She extends her hand and Tess takes it. The next thing she knows, she's back in Marc's living room in Sanctuary. "I owe you a major debt of gratitude. Not only did you help us solve this, hopefully in time, but you also helped undo what I did to Marc. This is the first time I've not felt lingering pain in him since I turned him. If there's ever anything I can do for you, tell me."

Tess thinks, *find a way to make the rest of my dream come true.*

Liz looks at her with a sad expression, having picked up her thought. "I'm afraid that may be the one thing I can't do for you, but if there's a way, then after this crisis, I'll find it." She hugs Tess. "Stay here, this could be a long couple of days, and I know Marc wants you to stay safe."

"Is there any danger here?" Tess looks upset.

"We don't know yet. Not in Sanctuary, but perhaps in the US and other places, so best to stay here. Our precogs have mostly seen Jerusalem as a focal point, but there have been a few who've seen other cities in their visions, including here in the States. Stay here!" She vanishes.

Well, the car is still at work! She mentally shouts at Liz.

Good! STAY THERE! Liz replies so strongly it's nearly audible.

Tess, blown away by it all, grabs her laptop and checks the news. She punches in the code on Marc's media center to get CNN on TV. She's amazed at the technology he has; his media center can receive any broadcast, cable, or satellite channel from around the world. Marc explained to her it's not just for entertainment. Having access to 'local' news and information in potential danger zones is critical when localizing precogs. She finds the entertainment part fun, and she's taken to watching BBC, and other international English-speaking stations.

A couple of hours later, her cell phone rings with Marc's ringtone. He starts speaking before she can even say hello, "*Tess, listen* carefully. I need you to stay where you are. We're closing all the portals just in case."

"What? What's going on? What are they going to do?" Her heart skips a beat, and her stomach feels queasy.

He pauses, and then says, "I can't get into details right now, other than an international terrorist group is behind it. They're assembling nukes; they've been bringing in what appear to be harmless parts by seemingly unconnected couriers and assembling them. We've already stopped several couriers around the world, but we think they may have completed one, in Jerusalem, as they've been pilfering uranium from uranium refineries in the Middle East, including Israel, making that the easiest bomb to complete. I've got a huge team heading there now to search for it. We think we disrupted the process in most countries, including the U.S. enough to prevent any detonations here, but in case we're wrong, *stay* where you are!"

Tess gets a sinking feeling. "Are you going over there?"

"Yes, they need as many of us over there as possible. Some of us will look for the bomb, and others will help with the massive evacuation, we can use our abilities to make people leave when some would normally resist. We think they're all supposed to be on a world timer, to go off in several cities at once, but we believe only one has been completed and armed. There's no way any of them except the Jerusalem one would be ready for the Jewish holiday, so we're not sure what the overall motive is. Some saw that, and others saw things suggesting late October or early November like pumpkins on lawns and no leaves on trees. We need to find the completed one and disarm it." He sounds extremely stressed and exhausted.

"Please be careful! I don't know what I'll do if..." She tears up.

"I'll be fine. I promise. Must go!" He hangs up, and a 'black cloud' descends on Tess's mood.

She paces the house anxiously, even opens the door, and goes out against Marc's orders, but it only opens to the clearing in the woods in Sanctuary, not Asheville. She's stranded, and feels helpless, trapped as an observer who knows what the stakes are, while most of the world is oblivious. She flips between several news channels, settling for a while on BBC World News. Her stomach growls. She gets up, goes to the kitchen, and digs through Marc's fridge to find something to eat. He'd thoughtfully ported the leftover Chinese food home for her, leaving a note:

If anything happens and you need more or need anything, contact Liz. She'll be remaining here to coordinate everything.

She reads the note and feels an ominous chill. The TV in the living room blares a 'breaking news' alert. She grabs a box of cold Moo Shu Pork and a fork and runs back to watch.

The reporter on TV announces:

This is a BBC World Service News alert! Several nations have just raised their alert status to high after a tip of imminent nuclear terrorism. Jerusalem is specified in the tip as particularly high risk, and people are being evacuated as we speak. Other cities around the world are also mentioned, but the tip suggests, in most cases, the threat is believed to have been neutralized. We have classified the source of the tip as highly reliable.

Tess watches for the next couple of hours as they show video clips of people leaving Jerusalem in droves, carrying what they can, in case there's no home to return to.

Tentatively, Tess reaches out to find Marc. She senses his mind, but he doesn't notice. *Marc? Are you okay?* She paths.

Fine...Tess...busy! Sorry! Can't talk! He paths.

Tess lies back on the living room sofa, telepathically eavesdropping on Marc's mind. She mostly picks up on his emotions: Stress, worry, anxiety and even some outright fear. She gets flashes of images from wherever he is, people around him, coming out of their homes, and walking or driving out of the city; children crying as many of them make a long march out of Jerusalem, or are packed into overcrowded buses. Tess's anxiety shifts into high gear, and she sobs, fearing the worst. She cries herself to sleep with the TV on in the background but is startled awake by the sound of screams on television and a sense of urgent panic from Marc. She reaches out to him instinctively, as the feed from Jerusalem goes bright white, and then to dark static, and she knows the bomb has detonated. She screams for Marc in her mind, panic and desperation working like an amplifier. She can still feel him in her mind; his thoughts are of her, and of dread he'll never see her again, as he waits for the blast wave to reach him. She knows the blast is approaching him rapidly, and feels the first searing pain when there's a flash of blinding light, and a deafening roar; debris flies out of the light. Her mind burns with excruciating pain, far worse than her psychic burn from the restaurant. Blinding light making it impossible to see anything. The last thing before she loses consciousness is a weak voice in her mind saying her name, and she knows somehow, Marc has made it home.

She isn't unconscious long, her subconscious mind fights to the surface again, driving her to get up and get to Marc, to reassure herself he's still alive. Her eyes flutter open, the bright light is gone, but she still has ghost images in her vision, making it hard to see. The light panels on the walls are either burnt out or flickering, giving the room a surreal, twilight feeling. The TV has gone black and there's a hot electric odor. Her vision's blurred with a blue afterimage from the flash; her ears are ringing loudly, and her head aches horribly, but she lets herself drop to the carpet and crawls in the direction she thinks Marc's path came from. She cuts her hand on something sharp as she crosses the floor; pain rips up the nerves in her arm. She pauses, closes her eyes, and calms herself. She reaches out with her mind, clairvoyantly, and moves in the direction she believes Marc is in. After a minute, she hears a groan near her, just to her right, and adjusts her course, finding him. She feels Marc's burnt arm, and moves up to his face, skin burnt and flaking off. He moans again, and whispers, "Tessss?"

"Yes, Marc. It's me! You got out! You made it home!"

"*Get back! Radiation....*" He says weakly.

"I don't give a *shit*! *Please* don't die...." She rambles frantically, as he loses consciousness. "Marc? Marc!" There's no reply. She moves her hands across his chest, and can feel a weak, irregular heartbeat. "Oh, *God*! There's got to be something I can do." She tries to reach out to Liz, but her mind feels like a raw sore doused with rubbing alcohol, and blinding pain shoots through her head anew. Her eyes have finally begun to clear, and she reaches for her cell phone, but it won't dial out.

Now that she can see again, she notices a pool of blood by his leg. He's bleeding profusely. She carefully gets up, looks around for something she can use to make a makeshift tourniquet, as she'd once learned to do in a first aid class. She spots a basket of laundry on the kitchen table and dashes for it, digging through it until she finds an old sheet and rips it into strips, binding his leg with it. Most of the wound is healing rapidly, except for a spot where a piece of metal shrapnel is lodged. She examines it carefully and grabs a towel from the bathroom. She readies the towel, and pulls the shrapnel out quickly, and presses on the wound with the towel until his body can seal it. After a couple of minutes, she checks it and it's no longer bleeding, but it hasn't healed up properly; but has left a gnarled scar.

"*Damn* it! What was it he said? If he doesn't feed often enough, he won't heal as quickly. Maybe if I feed him my blood? *Marc. Please*, I'm right here. Here's my wrist, drink. I can't reach anyone for help, but I can't lose you!" Marc is unresponsive and breathing shallowly.

She looks at the wound on her hand, but it's dried to a trickle, so she gets up, runs to the kitchen, and grabs a small, sharp knife. She comes back, and braces herself, cutting a slit in her wrist, not enough to bleed out, she hopes, and presses her wrist to his mouth, forcing the burnt and blistered lips open. After a few drops drip into his mouth, still unconscious, instinct takes over and he suckles her wrist, too weak to bring his fangs down. After a few minutes, she feels dizzy and knows she must take her wrist away from him. Still dripping, she grabs one of the remaining strips, and binds her wrist with it, tying it tightly to put pressure on the wound.

She returns to Marc, who's still unconscious, though the burns around his face have faded a tad. He's breathing a little easier, but then coughs, gasps, and his breathing stops. Tess, in a panic, tries again to reach out telepathically, only to nearly pass out again. She grabs the phone and tries again. She gets a slight signal and moves around the house to see if location helps. The further away she goes from Marc, the stronger the signal gets. Finally, she's able to call out when she gets to the bedroom upstairs and gets through to Liz.

"Tess, yes, I *know* what happened. Can't talk now! Searching for missing, including Marc." Liz is about to hang up, but Tess gets in two words that stop her in her tracks.

"*HE'S HERE!*" She shouts loudly into the phone, over Liz's words.

"What? Why didn't you say so sooner?" She asks, distracted, as she gives orders to others around her. "Is he alright?"

"*No!* He's badly burnt, and he was breathing, but he's stopped, and I'm afraid he's *dead*." Liz can hear her sobbing.

"*Calm down!* He isn't dead. He may appear so, but if he was still breathing when he got to you, he'll *recover*. It'll take time, but he will revive. He fed from you this morning, didn't he?"

"Yes, and I fed him now, too." She says.

"Was he conscious?" Liz knows Marc would never let her feed him twice in one day, maybe not even to save himself.

"Briefly, but not when I fed him. I had to use a knife on my wrist." Feeling weak and exhausted, she sits on the bed to avoid dropping to the floor.

Liz is silent for a second as she realizes the extent Tess must care about Marc. "Okay, listen to me. Marc *will* be fine. We'll get to you as soon as we can. Others are missing. Oh, *God!* So many others! And some we've found and triaged are in very bad shape. Sara and her team will be there as soon as possible, but they're deep in the middle of it all. Don't move him from where he is but do what you can to make him comfortable in case he revives and comes to; if he does, contact me. He may know where we can find some of the others."

"How many are missing?" Tess asks.

"I don't *know*. We had over 5000 out there, searching or helping with the evacuation. Marc was doing evacuations. So far, only a few hundred have made it back on their own, including Marc, though I don't know how; the blast disrupted our ability to port. Sit tight! Help will be there as soon as possible." She hangs up.

Tess's eyes are swollen with tears, mixed happy and distraught. She's relieved to know Marc will live, but the shock of the event itself has her reeling. A wave of nausea hits her. She stumbles to the bathroom and vomits. She sits there afterwards, completely spent, tears flowing, but she wills herself to get up, grabs a bucket, and some rags on the shelf in Marc's bathroom. She fills the bucket with warm, but not hot, water, and goes back downstairs to Marc. As she approaches him, she has to keep reminding herself he isn't really dead, or she knows she'll completely lose it. She carefully lifts his head, puts a throw pillow under it, and gently dabs the blood and flaked off skin from his face and bare spots. She finds a few sores weeping blood and bandages them up, soaking up the excess blood with the rags. His clothing is fused to his skin in places. It isn't long before she has to dip the rag back in the bucket and wring the blood out. She keeps working on him, talking to him, telling him it'll be okay, and she's right here with him in case he can hear her.

She feels weak as exhaustion and blood loss take their toll, and she wants to curl up and sob. She's nearly asleep beside Marc, when several people appear in the room with her, led by Sara.

"*Tess!* We'll take it from here now." She helps Tess up off the floor and onto the nearby sofa. In front of her, she notices Marc's handmade, tree-trunk, coffee table is scorched and smoldering. Sara notices how pale she is, and the makeshift bandage around her wrist, a few lacerations, and a bleeding bump on her forehead. "Were you injured?" She points to her bandage.

I cut my wrist to feed him." She says weakly.

"And these?" She points to several bruises and small wounds she hadn't even noticed in her state, including the deeper one on her right palm.

"I put my hand on something sharp when I crawled over to Marc.

The others, I'm not sure. There was a flash, and debris and then Marc was here, and that was all that mattered." She says, exhausted.

"A flash, you say?" Sara turns to her team. "Do a rad scan on this place! I'm afraid we have radiation contamination! And *this* one's human!" Sara shouts, "so time matters!"

"He told me to get back because of radiation." Tess can barely see through her torrent of tears.

"But you didn't listen, did you? Well, good for you, but it wouldn't have made a difference if you had." One of her team hands her a tablet with readings. "This whole place is practically glowing." She tells Tess, and then turns to a female med team member. "*You!* Go get the shower ready and grab some number 13 cleanser. We need to decontaminate this young woman as quickly as possible. And we'll decontaminate out here while you're in there. Strip your clothes off. All of them! They'll have to be destroyed." Sara commands.

Tess is too tired to argue. She follows the female team member to the shower, strips and gets in. She stands, but nearly falls a couple of times out of weakness. Once she's been thoroughly scrubbed down, the woman rinses out all the dead skin and blood from the tub and fills it, putting a different medication in it. While the tub fills, she tends to Tess's wounds, healing simple ones, and re-wrapping the deeper wound on her wrist with a proper, waterproof bandage. She puts a bandage on the larger knot on her head where debris hit her.

"There, the water's medicated to reduce any residual radiation to a safe level. Sara says you should soak here for another half an hour." She instructs Tess and leaves her to soak.

Tess props herself up in the tub but can't stay awake. After about 40 minutes, she's startled by a loud knock on the door. She sits up and absentmindedly says, "Come in."

"It's only me." Sara reassures her. "It's time to check you over." She holds up a clean, generic bathrobe for Tess to step into. She stands slowly, bracing herself against dizziness, and gradually lifts her legs over the tub edge with Sara's help. "It's all right, here you go." She puts the robe on her and ties it off. "Lean on me if you need to. I'm stronger than I look." She winks at Tess, who uses the small woman to stabilize her gait.

They pass through the living room. The sofa's gone, as well as the table. The carpet and room have been decontaminated, but still has scorch marks here and there. "Relax, he's in good hands. I've sent him to the Med Center. He's getting the best care possible." She takes Tess upstairs to the bedroom and gently sits her on Marc's bed. She takes out her tablet and a small extension device and scans Tess for radiation. Tess is silent, too tired, weak, and nearly in shock to make the effort. "Looks like you're clean of radiation, and this" She holds up a clear tube with purple liquid in it. "This should undo any damage done by the radiation." She injects a second medication, saying "This, you've had before, it's more Trinaline. It'll help you regenerate your blood count faster. *Unfortunately*, I can't give you a transfusion. We need all the blood we have stashed for our wounded. You're anemic, but not dangerously so. Are you in pain?"

"My head hurts like *hell*. It's like after the restaurant, but about a million times worse." She says slowly and with much effort.

Sara scans her again, frowning. "Very odd, you appear to have yet another psychic burn, but it's more like you've had a surge overload, like when lightning strikes. Were you doing anything psychically strenuous?"

"I felt Marc panic and reached out to him, and the next thing I knew, he was here, and there was a flash, and it felt like a bolt of power shot through me." Tess explains, having trouble keeping her eyes open.

"Hm, it's possible the energy from the blast could have piggybacked on your telepathic link. Not sure." She suggests.

"It felt like Marc latched on to me for dear life." Tess rambles.

"He probably used you as a beacon so he could port to you and rode the blast home." Sara thinks out loud.

"Yeah, maybe, that would fit with the flash and debris. It was like he was ejected from porting with everything else." Tess lets out a long yawn.

"We'll worry about exactly what happened later. I'm going to give you the same thing I gave you after the restaurant, and I want you to sleep as long as you need to. Liz will check on you tomorrow morning." Sara tucks Tess into bed. "And we'll talk again soon." She says, and then vanishes as she turns off the bedroom lights.

CHRYSALIS

At first, Tess sleeps heavily, as she's exhausted beyond anything she's ever experienced. As the night progresses, she feels increasingly worse. She wakes several times, feeling achy and cold. Toward morning, she wakes and runs back to the bathroom and dry heaves. She assumes it's probably stress, so crawls back to bed, grabbing a plastic wastebasket on the way, just in case, and forces herself to sleep. She wakes a few more times, feeling awful, but too weak to go to her apartment to find medication for a fever.

About noon, her cell phone rings a familiar ABBA tune. She groggily picks it up as it's Liz. She hits accept. "Liz?" She says weakly.

"Tess? You don't sound well. Are you okay?" Liz's voice is heavily laden with exhaustion and concern.

"I don't know, I don't think so. Maybe it's a reaction to whatever Sara gave me, or maybe they missed some radiation, but I feel awful." She sounds weak, and unconsciously moans.

The next thing Tess knows, Liz is standing there with a hand on her forehead. "You're running a high fever. Didn't Sara give you a once over before leaving?" She sits next to her on the bed, concerned.

"Yeah, she did, but I woke up a few hours later, puking." Fever chills make her shake and her teeth chatter.

Liz's nose twitches, and she gets an odd expression. "Tess, what *exactly* are your symptoms?"

"Nausea, vomiting, achy, fever type stuff, and a headache from Hell, but I've had that since the nuke went off." She squints, rubbing her temples to ease the pain.

"By any chance, do you have any facial, sinus, or dental pain?" Liz asks.

"Yeah, I thought maybe that was a sinus infection, or an abscess." Tess tries to sit up, unsuccessfully, falling back, and having to roll over on her side and grab the wastebasket again, heaving.

"Tess, is this where you cut your wrist?" She unwraps the bandage as Tess nods. Liz gasps as she finishes unwrapping her wrist and there's no wound. She removes the bandage on Tess's head as well, with the same result. "Tess, with your permission, I need a small taste of your blood."

"My blood? Not sure I have much left after Marc, but here." She offers her "good" wrist, not realizing the other has already healed.

Liz gently takes a small taste, and then sits up and back. "*Herre Gud!*"

"What? Am I dying or something?" Tess looks worried after Liz's reaction."

A look of disbelief and surprise brings Liz's face to life, and she smiles despite everything that's happened in the last twenty-four hours. She shakes her head and says, "No, you're definitely *not* dying. I'm not sure how to explain this; you're not even sick, you're transforming!"

It takes about half a minute for Liz's words to register. "*What?* You mean, into one of *you?* You told me that's not possible."

"It isn't. Well, shouldn't be! But it's clear that you are." She sends out a mental summons for Sara, who appears out of nowhere, looking grumpy and exhausted; her white doctor's coat covered with smudges of blood.

"What's the deal, Liz? I was in the middle of getting survivors into re-gen tanks." She stands there, hands on her hips, waiting for an explanation.

Liz's eyes glisten through her exhaustion. "Well, you tell me. Our friend here has nausea, aches, fever, and pain in her sinus area, among other things."

Sara looks at Liz, squinting her eyes as though she's trying to figure out if Liz is joking. "*Really?*" She whips out her diagnostic tools and comes over to the bed. "Tess, I'm going to draw a small sample of your blood with this. It won't hurt." She runs a series of tests. She looks at Liz with a question in her eyes, pathing: **What the Hell? Liz, this says she's in transition? I thought you said...**

I know. She's not in the database. Yet we can't deny the evidence. Could the stress or radiation have done something? And how did

270

she? I mean Marc was in NO shape to turn anyone. Liz asks.

"Hey, you two, I'm right here! And I *can hear* you. Talking, thinking, pathing? About me." Tess grasps her wastebasket again, dry heaving.

Liz looks at her thoughtfully, rubbing her back to sooth her while she throws up air and bile. When she finally stops, Liz asks, "Tess, I know last night was a painful experience, but I need you to tell me exactly what happened. Tell me everything you can remember *after* you fed Marc."

Tess recounts everything she can; tears fall again as she remembers Marc's burnt body, and his breathing stopping.

Sara's consternation shows as a deeply furrowed brow, as she tries to figure out what happened. "So, is there any chance you could have ingested his blood at any point?"

Tess gives her a dismissive look. "No, I would've remembered that."

Sara looks at the analysis that pops up on her tablet. "It's Marc's blood that's infected her, though. I can see the DNA markers here. Is there anything you can think of, any way his blood could have gotten into your system?"

Tess considers the question, then says, "Could it have entered through an open wound?"

Liz's face lights up with sudden comprehension. "Yes! It must have been your wrist?"

"Yeah, and I had a cut on my right palm too, but they healed that. I tried to wash some of the blood off him. He was still bleeding, and I guess I wasn't thinking, I wrung out the blood in a bucket of water, and...." Tess recounts.

"The blood in the water entered through your cuts. That would explain the slow progression of the transformation. You're still in a relatively early stage. If this had been an ordinary turning, you'd have most likely been near the end stages. This explains the prolonged fever and nausea." Sara explains as she makes notes on her tablet.

"Is there any danger?" Tess's voice is weak and gravelly from all the stomach acid and bile that's burned her throat.

"No danger at all, though I'd like to speed up the process for your own sake; shorten the discomfort." Sara suggests.

Tess looks thoughtful. Liz tries to read her but can't. "What is it? I thought you wanted to become one of us?"

"I did! Do! I just wish Marc were here while I'm going through it all." She says wistfully. "I begged him to try to turn me before all *Hell* broke loose, but he told me he couldn't because he didn't have the time to be here for me if I did start to turn. He promised he'd try after the crisis passed, but then...." She cringes as she thinks about all that's happened.

"Well, think what a wonderful surprise he'll have when he recovers." Sara gives her a tired, but wide grin. "Now, pack a few things to take with you. I want to supervise the rest of your transition, so we don't get *additional* surprises."

Tess slowly and carefully gets up, unsteady on her feet. "*Shit!* Everything's in my apartment."

Liz lets her lean on her, and ports her to her apartment. Tess sits on her bed and points out what she wants with her and Liz soon has a small duffle bag packed with some clothes, books, and her laptop. "I can't believe this is really happening!" She laughs weakly. "If you'd asked me 6 months ago if I'd want this to happen, I'd have thought you were insane. But now, I don't know, it feels like it's the thing I've been waiting for all my life. It goes with the feeling I've had here since the start; this is where I belong." Tess, once again overwhelmed by emotion, cries. Mabel sneaks out from under the bed, and stares at Tess, then runs back under the bed. "Mabel! You silly thing."

Liz finds cat food for Mabel, but the cat doesn't come out.

"She'll probably come out eventually. She gets weird sometimes around other people." Tess reaches her hand up to Liz to help her back up, her duffle bag slung over one shoulder.

"She's probably confused by the changes in your body. Pets can sense medical changes. As to your feeling like you belong with us, apparently you were compatible all along, and often, that's how people feel when turned; like they've finally become what they were meant to be. It also explains why you adapted to our existence more easily than I expected." Liz gives her a tired smile.

Sara and Liz port her to Medical, and then take her to a room and get her settled in.

"Is this where Marc is? Can I see him?" Tess looks at Sara pleadingly.

"When this is over. Right now, he's in a healing tank. His radiation and blast burns run deep. The good news is since you fed him before he went into stasis, it should shave weeks off his recovery time." Sara says.

"Weeks? How long will it take?" Tess dreads the thought of being alone, without him for God knows how long.

"It'll still take him at least three weeks, and possibly longer. The radiation messes up the regenerative abilities. Most that survived may take months to recover, some over a year. Marc was apparently further from the blast; though I'm still amazed he made it out. There were others further away that didn't. So, your connection must have been the key. The EM pulse apparently scrambles our guidance. Some got out but ended up in random places, such as the middle of the ocean; one even ended up partially embedded in a mountain, so Marc was lucky." Sara says.

Tess's eyes look haunted as she remembers that moment of panic when the bomb went off. "I felt his panic and reached out for him and the next thing I knew, he was here."

"He must have been able to use you as a beacon. You saved his life." Liz puts one hand on her shoulder.

Tess takes that in and after a minute asks, "How many died in the explosion?"

"Humans or us?" Liz asks.

"Both?" Tess realizes she's now in the 'us' category, and a brief feeling of relief fills her soul.

"The count is still not settled, estimates suggest maybe 250,000 humans died in the blast itself, though many are dealing with radiation poisoning and injuries. Over 3,900 of us are unaccounted for. It may not sound like that many compared to the human toll, but that's about 15% of our entire population. However, if you and Marc hadn't solved this, then I fear many millions would have died. Appropriately enough, you're the first new one of many to come. We'll have to build up our numbers as quickly as possible just to get back to our pre-Jerusalem levels." Liz yawns, exhaustion setting in as her hours of running on adrenaline reach a crashing point.

Sara interrupts them both. "Enough, you two! You'll have plenty of time, literally, to discuss all this *after* Tess completes her changeover. Liz! You've got responsibilities." She hands Liz a tablet.

Liz looks at the information, nods, and vanishes.

"Well, let's get on with this, shall we?" Sara motions for her to hop up into the hospital bed while she prepares some ampoules of medication for Tess.

"What are you going to do?" Tess asks.

"Normally, when someone's turned, we drain a significant amount of blood and replace it with our own. In your case, Marc drank some, but you only got traces of his in your system; enough to infect you and start the transformation, but not enough to overwhelm your immune system, hence the fever, and the nausea. Had he been able to do so, I'd have had him take more and give you more in return, but he's not. Your immune system has been attacking the virus like it would a cold or flu. It won't work, but the slower the infection spreads, the longer and harder your body will fight, and the harder it'll be on you." Sara comes over and stands beside Tess's bed with three infusers.

"What if my immune system wins?" A new wave of nausea hits her. Sara hands her a basin to throw up in, but only bile comes up. "*Ugh!*" Tess groans.

"It won't win. The virus is too strong, but you'll have more of this until you complete." She takes the basin and puts it aside. "Now, lie down. This works as an immunosuppressant. It shuts down your immune system so the virus can run its course unimpeded. This, you've had once before. It'll help with the psychic channels. And finally, this one, is going to make you sleep through it. You need the rest." She injects her before she can object. Tess starts to complain, but her eyes flutter closed, and she sleeps.

WAKING UP WITH NEW EYES

Tess wakes to a cool breeze through an open window and all the scents of the nearby forest. She opens her eyes, and it's like she's seeing the world for the first time. Colors are brighter and crisper. She can smell and discern a dozen unique odors at once, from the pine trees outside to the moisture from a nearby river, and mushrooms growing in the forest. She can even hear the river, the wind, and voices down the hallway clearly, as though each is the only thing she hears. Her mind processes them all at once. She stretches, and feels the texture of the sheets and blanket around her, and she smells, "Marc?" She says aloud. She turns on her side, and he's there, in the next bed, still battered, but better, and breathing again.

"I promised you'd see him once you transitioned completely. See? He's breathing again." Sara reassures her, as she walks into the room.

"Am I?" Tess is afraid something has gone wrong. "Every sense feels heightened, but aside from that, I don't feel much different."

"What did you expect? To wake up and desire to go around attacking stray humans and suck them dry? You watch too much television!" Sara winks at her.

Tess gives her a surprised look at her sarcasm. "*No*! I thought, I don't know, I'd feel different."

Sara laughs, "Disappointed you're still yourself, perhaps?"

"Honestly, I'm relieved. I only hope he'll be happy about it." Tess glances over at Marc.

"I'm sure Marc will be more than happy." Tess hears from the doorway, as Liz and Kari come in. Liz puts on her best face, but Tess can sense something's wrong, like a spark has been extinguished in her.

Tess feels a knot in her stomach forming as she looks at Liz,

275

thinking, *Something's very wrong.* "Liz, what's wrong?"

It surprises Liz that Tess can see through her well-rehearsed façade so easily, "Don't worry about it. You need to get back on your feet and help Marc do the same as he improves. We need you both now." She avoids answering the question, but Tess can sense what's wrong, along with an increasing pessimism in Liz's mind.

"*Oh no!*" She exclaims. "Peder, he didn't make it out?" Tess sobs as the loss hits her, too. She got to know Peder through her time working with him on her PK.

Liz looks at her, stunned she's picked up on that so easily. She thinks, *Even Marc has trouble reading me that clearly.* "No, he's still unaccounted for." She sits next to the bed. "The last I heard from him, he'd just found the bomb, so was literally at ground zero. The terrorists added a proximity trigger; so, no one could get close enough to disarm it without their remote to turn it off. He sent out a general path for everyone to evacuate, as it started counting down from 15 seconds, and then mental silence. Very few of our people had time to react to his warning."

"Liz, I'm so sorry." She reaches over for Liz's hand.

Liz stares off in thought. "It's always a risk, isn't it? Though most of the time we forget that. We think nothing can hurt us permanently. We do our jobs, sometimes getting hurt or put in stasis, but we always recover. But now we know one big thing can be fatal to us." Tess senses the overwhelming weight pressing on Liz; the pain of loss, not only of Peder, but so many others, and guilt, considering she'd sent many of those people out on this mission.

Kari, sensing the direction Liz's emotions are going, interrupts, "*Anyway!* Sara says they need your bed space for recovering wounded, so she *summoned us* to take you home and give you a crash course in... everything." Kari's interruption breaks the nearly overwhelming emotional link between Tess and Liz. Tess snaps out of the connection and shakes her head, a sad expression still visible, she refocuses on Kari.

"Well, Marc already explained the whole saving the world from itself thing. And I've certainly witnessed that firsthand." Tess blinks, refocusing. "Is there more?"

Liz looks her in the eye, knowing it's not going to be easy explaining their origin and purpose, something other potential transformees get subconsciously implanted at around seven years old. "It's a bit more complicated than that. Try to be open-minded because this is going to take some explanation and adjustment. But then again, now, we all have to adjust." She stands, extends a hand to Tess, Kari picks up her never-opened duffle-bag, and they port back to Marc's home. Mabel comes out of hiding from under a replacement sofa in the living room, and cuddles Tess frantically, only to stop and sniff her. She looks at her, then sniffs her again, but goes back to cuddling her legs furiously. Tess leans down, picks her up, and strokes the cat lovingly.

Liz motions for them all to have a seat in the living room. "By the way, Kari came by and fed Mabel for you every day, as well as moved her and some of your things over to this part of the dwelling, so you don't have to run back and forth."

Tess looks at Liz, confused. "Every day? How long was I out?"

"Sara kept you out for ten days. Fed you intravenously. There were a few unusual issues with your transformation. Your telekinesis went amok, and you still had a bad case of psychic burn from the energy blast, so she kept you under to heal." Kari explains.

Liz motions for Tess to come over and sit next to her. "Before we get too settled, there's something important you need to do, and that's feed."

"But I'm not *hungry*." Tess says.

"No, but you will be soon. Sara had you IV fed, so you may not feel the hunger as strongly as most newly turned; but I need to make sure you know how to feed yourself. For now, you'll mostly feed from bagged blood, but you should know how to feed from a live donor. Face me. Put your left hand behind my neck, use your right to tip my chin back, and then lean in closer. As you do, your fangs should slip out, and into place instinctively. Picture the area where you're going to bite going numb, then gently bite me; let your intuition guide you. Your body knows how to do it even if your mind doesn't." Liz guides her through the process carefully.

Tess reluctantly follows her instructions, and before she knows it, her intuition kicks in and she feeds from Liz. She's amazed at how it feels to feed—the warm liquid, a mixture of sweet, salty, and metallic actually tastes good. After a minute, Kari gently eases her back from Liz. Kari explains, "Tess, take your fingers and put them over the wounds, picture them closing up, growing smaller, fading into normal, healthy skin."

Tess follows Kari's instructions and is surprised how easily it works. "This is going to take some getting used to."

Liz pulls some tissue from her pocket and hands it to Tess. "Your feeding will get less messy with practice."

Tess takes the tissue and dabs her mouth and chin. She looks at it, and it's clear a fair amount of blood had dribbled down her chin. She grins. "*Oops!*"

"Tess, what I need to explain to you, is going to make the whole idea of 'vampires' look like child's play, and that's the origin and purpose of our kind. Have you ever wondered about the virus that changes us? Where it came from, and why it's so selective?" Liz raises an eyebrow, waiting for Tess to answer.

"*Origin*? Don't viruses evolve like everything else?" Tess asks.

"Most do, but not this one. It's been a stable, non-mutating virus for a few thousand years." Liz waits for that fact to sink in.

"You mean like measles or chicken pox, as opposed to the flu or Covid?" Tess is confused as to where this is going.

"No, this is *not* a natural virus, even though it's been around for *thousands* of years. It's a *created* virus, *genetically engineered* to rewrite our DNA and make us what we are." Liz speaks slowly and clearly, so there can be no misunderstanding.

"Wait, a minute! You're saying it was manmade? That's *not* possible! There was no such thing as genetic engineering that long ago unless you're implying Atlantis or some mythical advanced ancient technology." Tess is incredulous to Liz's claim.

"No, Tess. No one on *Earth* had that technology back then, and even now, it's only becoming a real science." She pauses, waiting for Tess to connect the dots.

Tess looks perplexed for a couple of minutes, and then the proverbial 'light bulb' turns on in her mind. "*No*! You're not saying it's extra-terrestrial in origin?"

"*Yes*, that's exactly what I'm saying." Liz pats her on the leg for figuring it out.

"Wait, a minute! Why the *hell* would aliens make *vampires*? That makes *no* sense." Her mind feels overwhelmed by the concept. She looks at Kari, who nods at her, confirming what Liz told her.

"If you can be patient, I'll start from the beginning. It'll make much more sense if you know the whole story." Liz speaks patiently, like she's explaining why the sky is blue to a child.

"Okay, I'll do my best, but it sounds like a bad movie on SYFY." Tess leans back and makes herself comfortable.

Kari leans over and quietly says, "If it were on SYFY, we'd be the bad guys, and crossbred with sharks." Kari interjects with a wry smile, to which Liz gives her a sidelong glance of sarcastic thanks for lightening the mood.

"Are you familiar with the theories about ancient astronauts?" Liz says as she taps on her tablet.

"Yeah, like Von Daniken and so on?" She asks.

"More or less. There are pictographs and other drawings, found worldwide, that imply visitations by beings from elsewhere." Liz hands her the tablet, which shows many images of cave paintings and other things that indicate alien visitations in ancient times. "There really were such visitations. An alien race came here millennia ago. They were very long-lived humanoids, and they explored the galaxy. Throughout the galaxy, however, while they did find other intelligent life forms, they felt a unique kinship with primitive humans. Something about our creative spark, our emotions, and similar physiology reminded them of themselves. Unlike Star Trek, they intervened in humanity's development, at first observing humans, and eventually, they taught them various skills, and gave them useful knowledge. They set up in different parts of the world where early tribal civilizations had formed, and taught them some basic mathematics, astronomy, agriculture, masonry, and other skills to make their lives better. They stayed for several earth years, but then left, promising to return."

"Because they were so long lived, their space faring technology was not focused on getting from one place to another quickly. So, by the time they returned, nearly 200 years had passed on Earth. Much they'd taught the humans was lost due to wars, natural disasters, or plagues, and what memories of them had been passed down had been changed so much the primitive cultures often elevated them to gods, or even *demons*. They did, however, have the technology to manipulate genetics. They chose representatives from each culture that showed superior intelligence and altered them." She pauses.

"Is *this* where they created vampires?" Tess jumps in.

"Not *yet*. At first, they altered these human representatives, our first diplomats, by extending their lives by giving them their own infinite regenerative ability. They gave them perfect and rapid cell and tissue regeneration, resistance to illness, as well as enhanced psychic abilities and intellectual capacity. Our *Benefactors*, as we call them now, are highly telepathic, and being able to communicate ideas and concepts telepathically was much more efficient than adapting to the primitive human languages of the time. Even now, they often prefer telepathy over verbal communication. These select few were called Apara, or 'the others'." Again, Liz waits to see how Tess reacts to this information, and whether she makes the correct conclusions or not. "However, when they increased human psychic aptitude, it manifested in other forms as well, including precognitive, clairvoyant, and telekinetic abilities far greater than in our Benefactors. They also gave us our porting ability to allow us to travel to distant cultures and lands and spread the knowledge they gave us. It's somewhat different than most of the abilities we have. The virus rebuilds neurons on a molecular level in a dormant area in the brain into a type of bio-technology that lets us slip from here to Sanctuary, and Limbo, the non-linear dimension between the two worlds."

"So that's where the name came in? *Huh*! Okay, so they gave a few humans immortality and power. Hm, doesn't sound like the brightest idea, if you ask me." Tess shakes her head.

"*Bingo*! While it was a practical move, they didn't fully understand primitive human psychology. When they left the planet again, and returned a couple hundred years later, they found many of their 'diplomats and teachers' had anointed themselves demigods, gods, wizards, kings, and so on. Knowledge and immortality are power. They collected their chosen few, and spent years studying human psychology and what went wrong. *This* is where 'vampires' come in.

They looked at human mythology and fears. Based on that, they changed our predecessors to deter them from exposing their true natures They took DNA from various alien samples, and created a genetically altering virus, which would rewrite the DNA to give humans abilities and longevity, but would also create a dependence on humanity, hence our need for blood. They also seeded humankind telepathically, with nightmares and fear of us. These early Apara were told there were ways normal humans could kill us to try to keep the Apara in line. They would need to feed but had to keep their differentness secret."

Actually, there isn't a lot that can kill us, but our ancient ancestors didn't know that. This time, when our Benefactors left, most of their representatives behaved themselves. They stuck to the rules they must feed but not kill, and secrecy was of utmost importance, or humans *could* kill them. They were also told to move to other tribes or villages when their lack of aging became suspicious. They would travel around, learning and teaching, and working as healers. Once they had passed on their knowledge to a village or tribe, they would move on to another before anyone could become suspicious that they weren't normal humans."

Tess follows along, and then asks, "Okay, so you said they were the early versions?"

"Yes, there were still a few who strayed and let the power go to their heads. Some of these cultures practiced blood rituals and sacrifices, and discovered their own blood, with the active virus, could change other humans whom our Benefactors had not vetted and approved. Unfortunately, some of them were not as willing to follow the no killing and stay hidden rules. This is where a lot of the vampire mythology became strongest. They were told to hunt at night, to stay hidden, so humans thought we only came out at night because during the day, we blended in like any human. They thought we slept in graves or coffins, because sometimes, our kind can be temporarily *killed*, as Marc, and *many other* survivors *appeared* to die. Our bodies shut down outwardly and appear dead while major cellular and structural repairs take place. This 'stasis' state allows energy to be focused on healing. Sometimes, those who were in stasis were taken for dead and interred. It was much worse in cultures that burned their dead. When they were seen leaving their graves, or appearing after they were known to be dead, I'm sure you can understand how the mythology was born." Liz says. Tess nods, feeling stunned. "Much of the modern mythology came from the fertile minds of Bram Stoker, other authors like Anne Rice, and Hollywood."

"Our Benefactors have made more changes since, refining the virus, and making it less transmittable by creating a genetic key sequence that must be present in a human for the virus to work. Once the virus transforms someone, it becomes dormant and resides in our bone marrow, so one of us must feed on a compatible person, activating the virus, and releasing it into the bloodstream. If the compatible person, then ingests or otherwise gets activated blood into their system within about an hour or so of being fed upon, their DNA will be rewritten by the virus and they will become one of us, but if they aren't compatible, then they won't change." Liz explains.

"Marc told me about that part, how the virus works." Tess frowns. "But you told me I'm not compatible?"

"True. We didn't think you were compatible, because we couldn't find you in our database of genetic carriers, which we get from our Benefactors. Over the centuries and millennia of trial and error, they refined their system. They used to pick young adults they deemed appropriate, and introduced one virus that would inject the sequence, and then one of us would turn them. Unfortunately, there was a psychological rejection rate of up to 25%. Adults sometimes couldn't cope with the transition, with becoming a 'monster', so to speak. Some went mad, others became difficult, or chronically depressed, while others fell into place and did their jobs. Eventually, they could scan human DNA at a distance, as well as detect young children with high psychic potential. They would pick them up, evaluate them, and if they felt they had good potential, intelligence, and a likelihood of psychological stability, they'd be 'asked' on a basic level if they are willing to help humanity. If they agreed, the genetic key sequence was inserted into a junk segment of their DNA, and they were given subconscious training in their early years, which could be triggered should they one day be tapped to serve, in other words, turned. It made the rate of adaptation increase to over 98%."

Tess's mouth drops open, but nothing comes out at first, then says, "*Damn*! Are you saying I was abducted by *aliens* as a kid?"

"You must've been, because you wouldn't have turned if you didn't carry the genetic key, and the only way to have that key is through them, as it doesn't occur naturally, and can't be passed on to offspring. The mystery is, why weren't you in our system? We thought you fit the profile of a potential, but we couldn't find you, and you aren't tagged." Liz explains.

"Tagged?"

"Yes, when selected, a child's implanted with a form of organic implant that functions on a base telepathic level, giving off a low-level beacon they can trace and find you when they need to." She explains.

"So, if you thought I might be compatible, then why didn't you do a DNA test for this 'sequence'?" Tess asks, as if it should have been an obvious option.

"Because we don't know the sequence. Only they do. We've always relied on their word on who is or isn't compatible, so it's never been needed. We're given the information on who is compatible and their early evaluations. At some point, certain subliminal triggers are planted in the unconscious minds of potentials, such as elements of our logo. Remember how you said you reacted to it?" Kari asks.

"Yeah, it stood out, I felt like I was driven to call." She recalls.

"That brings potentials to us, or other similar recruitment centers. We do the adult evaluations, and hire those potentials which are still good prospects, in case, like now, we need to increase our population to do our job; to protect, teach and shepherd humanity into an age of maturity, when our Benefactors can make themselves known. In the meantime, we're working to keep it from going to *Hell!*" Liz gripes, as stress has frayed her nerves.

Tess sits on the sofa, thinking. Liz and Kari can sense the emotions shifting as she comes to grips with it all. "*Huh!* So, when it comes down to it, I really *am* supposed to be here. I was *meant* to become one of you?" Tess's sudden epiphany makes her mentally step back and re-evaluate everything that has happened these last months. "I'm meant to be here. Oh, *God!* I've always felt I was supposed to do something, but the last couple of years, since Digital Danger and everything, I felt like my life had derailed. Now, I know why working with you all has felt so right." Happy tears, and tears of relief, flow.

"I can see why we felt the need to hire you and understand why you had all the traits of a potential, but weren't one. Now, we need to figure out why you aren't in our system and why you aren't tagged." Kari interjects.

Tess's eyes light up as she thinks about her situation. "Does your database have any DNA on file?"

"Yes, there's a basic gene print of each potential, highlighting certain sequences which suggest potential psychic strengths and so on." Kari answers.

"Can you search for a match?" She asks. "I mean, if you take a sample from me, could you use that to search? Maybe I got misfiled somehow?"

"I'll have to investigate that. I'll see if Sara has a pre-transformation sample in her system for you, as now, your DNA has been significantly altered." Kari nods and vanishes, going to see Sara.

"Normally, these long explanations aren't necessary, because of the subliminal information they implant. We can only assume whatever happened, it happened before you were 7 years old. That's when the mind is mature enough to cope with certain information, and still flexible enough to accept all of this." Liz explains.

"Liz, how are we gonna break this to Marc? Oh, by the way, while you were out, your errant human joined our ranks! *Congrats*! You finally turned someone! *Yay!*" Tess jokes.

"Tess, he *wanted* to turn you. He was extremely frustrated you weren't a potential. None of us, however, ever really thought much of the idea the database could be wrong. We even discussed approaching our Benefactors about making you compatible but didn't think they'd do it because of the risks involved. Trust me, Marc will be relieved you're not only alive and well but will be with him for a very long time. Now, I hate to do this to you. I'm sure you still have a million questions, but I need to check on the latest updates on the missing and recovering and look into who can be tapped to join us. We'll need to replace several thousand people and probably add more to compensate for the world's instability after Jerusalem, and I'm not sure where we'll find so many suitable potentials. We'll talk tomorrow about what happens next. In the meantime, stay here! You're not to go out among humans until I know you can control yourself and your needs. If you need anything, let us know, and we'll bring it to you." She leans in and gives Tess a hug, and then wearily vanishes.

POINT OF NO RETURN

As soon as Liz and Kari port out, Tess heads straight for the bathroom and looks at herself in the mirror, making notes of any changes. *Hm, acne and acne scars are gone, and I'm pretty sure I lost some weight.* She thinks, happy for small favors. She pauses for a moment, focusing, and tries to force her newly formed fangs to come down. When they lock into place, she opens her mouth and stares at them and shivers. *Those look so weird on me. I got used to Marc being all fangy, but myself?* She fingers them like she needs to prove to herself they won't pop out like bad Halloween prosthetics. She sits on the closed toilet, coping with it all, and wishes Marc was there with her, both to explain everything and comfort her. Even though she didn't die, she still grieves her old life. *There's definitely no turning back now.* She thinks.

Her stomach grumbles, and knows she's already 'fed', so assumes it's real food she needs. Since it's been over a week, she throws out all the leftovers, and looks in the freezer. After a couple of minor issues, she cooks some chicken with garlic, paprika, salt, pepper, and a little curry. She notices every odor and taste is subtly different, like she can taste *each* spice, flavor, and texture exploding on her taste buds. She experiments with various foods, taking out cheese, lunchmeat, fruit, some nuts, and crackers from a cupboard; a mixture of sweet and savory, so she can experience what each thing tastes like with her new senses.

Tess hears Sara's voice from behind her, making her jump. "Good thing you're not human anymore, or I'd have to put you on a diet."

Tess turns around. "*Sara!* You startled me!"

"I have to do it now before you get your senses in gear.

Eventually, you'll learn to sense when someone's porting in, and then there won't be any fun in trying to catch you off guard." She gives her a mischievous grin. "Come over here and sit with me." She pats the chair next to her at the kitchen table.

"If you're here to give me the whole alien origin story, Liz and Kari beat you to it." She motions for Sara to help herself to the finger food on the tray.

"No, I made some adjustments to this." She holds up a new necklace. It's larger and the opal-like gem is black with multi-color, holographic, swirling fire. "I'm afraid I needed to up the settings. If I'm right, you're going to need it until things settle down, and someone has time to teach you a thing or two."

"I guess so. I'm not sure what happens next. It sounds like things are chaotic, with Peder missing, and Marc and others incapacitated." Tess says in between nibbling on something sweet and savory.

"I told you some time ago you would be important to us." She holds up her hand. "You don't remember because I masked the information. Marc needed to come to certain conclusions himself, you both did."

"You mean?" Tess asks, but feels awkward.

"That you care about each other and need each other. If he'd known I'd told you certain things, he'd have focused more on that than on you as a person. Now that you two have found each other, you'll share an important destiny. You'll draw on each other's strengths and compensate for each other's weaknesses." She stands and puts the necklace on Tess.

"This is really getting crazy. If you're right, I'm not sure I'm up to the challenge. I mean, what makes me so special I've got some huge destiny?" She's insecure, and once again, finds it hard to make eye contact.

"Someone has to play that role, why not you?" She snickers, then continues. "For whatever reason, your preparation to become one of us was incomplete. The foundation was barely laid, giving you a unique perspective. Most of those turned in the last three centuries were all pre-conditioned with the way things work; the rules, how to

288

do things and so on. You have ten times the talent most potentials have and are not cookie cutter conditioned. You'll be the wild card. You bring something new and unusual to the table. Something, I don't quite know what, but it'll make a big difference in how we move forward now. You've already made a big impact. Many more would have died had you not seen the connections we all missed." She explains.

"But the bomb still went off! I'd say I was too late." She sighs.

Sara pauses, taking a slice of Pecorino Tartufello cheese, an Italian cheese with truffles, stuffs it in her mouth, and then speaks. "Precognition is a tricky thing. Not only is it often unclear, but it's often filled with symbolic interpretations of people and events. Sometimes there's more than one outcome seen. I was speaking to someone Marc worked with on the precog reports, and in the end, there were two separate sets of precogs. One vision foresaw something primarily in Jerusalem in early October. Some people, however, saw it as happening in late October or early November, and in other cities as well, including in the U.S. In either case, the bomb was going to go off in Jerusalem. What we didn't see was it would be our intervention setting it off early, while the others were prevented. Since we didn't know about the proximity trigger, there was no way we could have stopped that one bomb. We did prevent the alternative scenario, and even reduced the death toll among humans in Jerusalem by intervening. However, had you not given Marc the idea that eventually led to cracking the terrorists' communications, then the second scenario likely would have come to pass. Ironically, it was an international group of anti-technology terrorists. They targeted major cities around the world to force depopulation, de-centralization of governments, and a return to pre-industrial living. You made a major difference and will continue to do so." Sara forces eye contact with Tess the whole time.

"It's a nice thought, if you're right—that I'll really make a difference in the future. I guess I'll have to play it by ear." She pauses thoughtfully. "I really wish Marc was here. This is all so fantastic but also a little scary and frustrating at the same time. I was going to bread some chicken, and went to crack an egg, and didn't know my own strength, and crushed the egg just picking it up. I'm worried I could hurt someone without intending to."

"Yes, it's a possibility. You're now much stronger than any human. It'll take time for you to compensate for that strength." Sara explains patiently. "If you'd been properly prepared, it would come naturally. Therefore, Liz said for you to stay here for now. Speaking of which. I'll send over parcels of blood for you. Keep them in the fridge. Until Marc is better, you'd best not try to feed on any humans alone."

"That suits me just *fine*! That still creeps me out!" Tess admits, laughing awkwardly.

"You'll need to feed more often in the first months, as your body continues to adapt and change. If you get hungry, *do not* put it off! That's the fastest way to lose control for someone like you. Now, you're also likely to tire more quickly. Your body has been through hell, as has your mind. And yes, it's normal to mourn your humanity. You were born human, and even though you never died to become what you are now, it's still a figurative death. I'll stop in once a day to check on you. Liz and Kari will stop in as well, but they have their hands full." She sneaks more cheese and some grapes.

"Don't you? I mean, with all the injured?" Tess keeps feeling she doesn't deserve such special attention.

"The main wave of survivors has been processed, and I have plenty of staff to see to their needs until they wake up. Frankly, they're not much trouble when they're in stasis or unconscious and regenerating. Awake and grumpy is another matter." Sara snickers. "Right now, we change the IV blood bags once a day and watch their progress. Speaking of which, I did an evaluation on Marc this afternoon, and confirmed it should be about 3 more weeks until he regains consciousness and hopefully, comes home. Do you want me to break the news to him when he wakes?"

Tess smiles, happy to know it won't be so long before Marc's better. "No. I want to be there when he comes to. I want to see his face when he realizes I'm like him."

Sara gives her a big grin. "*Excellent!* I knew you'd have the strength to face all of this. Now, eat, sleep, rest, relax, and feed when the need hits you. I'll forward you more of our written history and information we have about our Benefactors, so you can familiarize yourself. I'm so glad you've joined us! You *are and will be* needed. Never forget that!"

"I realize I've been grieving my humanity for months now. I haven't really felt fully human since I found out about all this and started with all the psychic stuff. What's that saying? When one door closes, another door or window opens up. My physical humanity is a thing of the past, but my true humanity is still a part of who I am. I feel that." She smiles softly.

"*Never* let that go! *Always* keep a link to that core inside you. It will guide you, and us, in the future. Must get back and make sure my staff hasn't been freaking out at having so many patients. I'll let you know when Marc's ready to come out of it. I can keep him under until you get there. Though I'm thinking by then, you might want to find something nice to wear. I so rarely see you in anything but those dumpy clothes." Sara snickers and vanishes.

Tess sits there, alone, except for Mabel, who's crawled up into her lap and is pawing at some meaty tidbits on her tray. She absentmindedly strokes her cat, realizing Mabel reflects what Sara said. She realizes her owner is different, and yet still recognizes her. Who she was has carried over to who she's become, and she'll do her best to stay herself for however long this new life lasts.

Tess finishes up her snacks, washes and puts away the plates, and feeds Mabel. As she walks up the stairs to Marc's bedroom, she notes how eerily quiet it is without him. She enters the room, and it feels like a smack in the face, as she can smell him everywhere. She misses him, and crawls into bed, hugging his pillow from the night they were together, and cries. The room feels so empty, so wrong without him there. She hears Mabel scratching at the blanket hanging over the side of the bed. "Come on, silly girl." Mabel hops up and comes over to Tess, and flops down as close to her as she can, purring loudly, her belly exposed for a tummy rub. Tess falls asleep to Mabel's loud purr.

ANOTHER KIND OF TRANSFOR-MATION.

A couple of weeks pass, with daily visits from Sara; while Liz and Kari take turns, making sure Tess is coping and feeding as she should. Unfortunately, there's no time to deal with training her with all the literal and figurative fallout after the Jerusalem disaster, so Tess is told to stay home, where she can't get into any trouble with her newfound abilities or needs. The front door portal remains closed, so she resigns herself to being *stuck* there until she can get her bearings. She thinks, *I need the rest and recovery time*, as Sara told her, but gets restless with the daily world news reports, countries blaming each other for harboring the terrorists, and several groups attempting to claim or deny involvement. She ends up turning off the TV, digging out a banana box of books from her apartment, and starts reading a humorous Piers Anthony series of books she hasn't read in years.

One evening, she gets a path from Sara. She senses overtones of excitement. ***Tess! I'm coming by!***

Tess closes up her book, the 10th one in a series she's read since she's been stuck at home, and waits for Sara to pop in. Sara appears in front of her, carrying a pot of hot, wild mushroom soup. "Thought you might enjoy a change in diet. Took a couple of hours this morning and went out foraging." She puts it down on the coffee table and heads to the kitchen for bowls and spoons.

Tess inhales deeply, taking in the aroma of the steaming soup. "Smells wonderful! Thank you!"

Sara comes wandering back in, carrying two bowls, a ladle, and spoons. "Been a long time since I've made this, but I remember from the night of your restaurant incident you like wild mushrooms, so

thought I'd share, and let you know I'm bringing Marc out of his in-
duced coma tomorrow evening. I assume you want to be there?" She
puts a bowl of hot soup on the table in front of Tess.

"*Yes*! Of course! I guess, come get me? I'm not allowed to port
yet, and I'm not even sure how to get there from here." She says,
smiling excitedly. Relief suffuses her now she knows he's really
getting well enough to come home.

Sara gets a mischievous grin and says, "You're in for a treat. Liz and
Kari are going to pick you up early and take you out on a few errands.
Three weeks stuck in this house, and you've, well, come on, the soup will
wait." She drags Tess to the bathroom and places her in front of a full-
length mirror. "Look at yourself. *Really*! You've barely brushed out your
hair, but your complexion has changed, and you're still wearing those
dumpy sweats. Have you really looked at yourself since you were turned?"

"Well, right afterwards, but..." Sara interrupts Tess before she
can finish her sentence.

"You've been moping around here, bored. Take off that sweatshirt!" She says.

Tess's eyes go wide at Sara's order. "But I don't have a bra on
underneath." Tess objects.

Sara gives her an exasperated look. "I'm the closest thing to a
doctor around here, do you really think that matters to me?"

Tess hesitantly pulls off her oversized sweatshirt and really
looks at herself in the mirror. "*Whoa*! I, what happened?" She sees
the new, slender her, and notices all the stretch marks from her
weight gain are also gone, and her musculature is more toned.

"The virus perfects the human form." Sara explains. "It eventually makes one's body become an ideal, healthy weight, musculature, and so on. Blemishes fade, scars disappear. Even your hair. It
may be knotted, but it's healthier looking than I've ever seen it."

Tess looks at her make-up-less face and realizes she's attractive with no makeup. "Marc's not going to recognize me."

"Tomorrow morning, you'll go with Liz and Kari. They'll take you shopping, and find you some new, better fitting clothing. I'd suggest you discard the old stuff, unless it has some sort of sentimental value, as you'll never need such large sizes again." She says with an ear-to-ear grin. She watches Tess, as a look of sadness and uncertainty shows in Tess's eyes.

"What is it, *child*? What worries you so?" Sara asks.

"It's just, Marc and I ended up together before the bomb. I'm worried he may have regrets." She looks down at her hands, avoiding Sara's eyes.

"Regrets? What regrets?" Sara prompts.

"Partly because he gave in to his, I guess, hormones, and if he hadn't wasted time with me, maybe more people might have been saved." She suggests.

"*Tess*. You, my dear, are letting your insecurities cloud your vision again. We've been over this *before*." She comes up and stands next to Tess. "Marc's had feelings for you as a person since you came here. You two connected on some unconscious level from the start, and that helped heal something deep inside him that has been in pain since he was turned. I can vouch for that, as I've known him all this time. Secondly, was it not you that came up with the missing puzzle piece? If he hadn't been with you, and you hadn't seen the problem in his mind, you wouldn't have been able to give him your unique perspective." She hopes that will finally settle Tess's self-doubt.

"Sara, what if, like many trauma victims, he doesn't remember we slept together? What if he goes back to wanting to keep things platonic because he doesn't remember them otherwise? Surely, that kind of trauma could have caused memory damage." She worries aloud.

"No, our brains and bodies don't work that way, a human, *yes*. Neurological damage is done that does not repair itself, but that would not be the case with one of us."

"Even so, I worry he may feel differently. He was stressed, and so was I. You know, heat of the moment crap." Tess says.

Sara interrupts her. "*Tessa Waterford!* What you are doing now is called *catastrophizing*! Imagining things so much worse than they are and always seeing the worst-case scenario. *Stop* it! You needn't worry about that. I don't think you could get rid of him now if you tried. Trust me. I'm a doctor!" She grins broadly as she paraphrases one of Tess's favorite T-shirts, making Tess roll her eyes.

"Sara, next time they do a female Doctor Who, you should go for the role." She suggests.

"Oh! I plan to. Did I ever tell you I was an extra in every single Star Wars film?" She laughs, and Tess feels herself relaxing.

"Yes, Sara, *several* times." She pauses, reflecting. "Maybe I *am* worrying too much." She admits.

"Yes, you are. The main thing that kept you and Marc apart was your mortality, and that's no longer an issue. He won't reject you now. So, I need to get going, but make sure you feed either tonight or in the morning. You're going out in public, and the last thing you want is to be distracted by need. And wear your pendant!" Sara says, as she dishes out more soup for Tess and puts the leftovers into the fridge for later.

"Will do, Sara, and thank you." She says.

"For what? The soup?" She says with a twinkle in her eye. "That's what I'm here for, healing of all sorts. Goodnight." She disappears.

Tess does as told and makes sure she finishes a pack of blood from the fridge before she goes to bed, taking a long, hot bath, and again, looks over her body. *Wow! I hardly recognize myself.* She thinks, having had a history of being chubby for years. She turns her torso so she can look at her shoulders in the mirror, noticing the years old scars from her childhood accident have faded to slight discolorations. She pulls on an oversized t-shirt, crawls into Marc's enormous canopy bed, and Mabel joins her. Even though it's been over three weeks since he's been there, she can still catch whiffs of Marc's scent as she falls asleep. She dreams of her night with Marc, and how her prior dream may have been prophetic after all; he did end up turning her.

In the morning, Tess gets woken up by the persistent ABBA ringtone belonging to Liz.

"Hello?" She answers groggily.

"Hey, Tess, it's Liz, ready to go?" She asks.

Tess sits up, using her other hand to rub the sleep out of her eyes. "Oh, yeah, soon. I fell asleep without setting my alarm. Give me 15 minutes."

"Sure, I know you don't have much dressy, but maybe if you wear what you did to the interview? We're going to be shopping where they don't see many customers in sweats." Tess hears an amused snort from Kari in the background.

"Sure. I think it's here and not in storage." She thinks, *maybe it's time to get things out of storage and get rid of stuff, and unpack the rest. It's not like I'll be moving out on my own.* She gets ready and waits. Liz and Kari knock on the door, and when Tess answers it, she sees they have reopened the portal as well, as the door opens to North Asheville again.

Liz, sensing her reaction, says, "Yeah, we thought it time to let you out in more ways than one. You've shown you know when you need to feed. But I still want you to only go out when you've recently fed, wear your necklace, and preferably, with Marc or one of us, for the next month. I don't want you getting overwhelmed by your new senses, skills, and needs." They enter the living room. "Ready?"

"I guess so, where are we going? The Mall? The Outlets? I used to do most of my shopping at Goodwill and Walmart, but I'm guessing that's not what you had in mind." Tess says.

Kari looks at Liz with a knowing smile, they each slip one arm under one of Tess's and vanish, reappearing in an alley somewhere. The air is moist, like they're near water, and the sun is lower than it should be in Asheville.

"Where are we?" Tess asks.

"Los Angeles. You, my dear, are going to get a proper makeover. One of my earlier transformees does makeup in the movies. He's agreed to do a little Hollywood magic on you." Liz grins mischievously.

"I don't think you need to go that far. I mean, Marc's seen me at my literal worst." Tess looks from Liz to Kari and knows they're not going to take 'no' for an answer.

"Tess, it's the least I can do for you, considering you helped him heal in more ways than one, and you're absolutely one of the family now. Come on! First, a little shopping. We get to pretend to be normal gals on a shopping spree. And before you protest, money's not an issue! You like something, you get it!" She insists.

They walk out of the alley and onto a busy street lined with high-end shops: Clothing, jewelry, shoes, an Apple Store, and other places where money can disappear quickly. They enter an upper scale boutique, and Liz has a word with the saleswoman, who promptly comes over and walks around Tess, sizing her up. "Yes! I know exactly what she needs. Some new designer pieces came in this week, and I believe the colors and styles will suit her perfectly." The woman is giddy over the commission she'll make on this transaction.

They spend a couple of hours there, though Kari slips out and goes to the shoe store across the street to find some shoes to match some clothes Tess has already picked out. In the end, there are several new outfits lined up and packed, paid for and most are ordered to be sent to an office in L.A., Liz paths to Tess: *Our main west coast center. They'll port it back to us in Asheville, but THIS one, you're going to take with you and change into after you meet Andrei. Then lunch and then Marc!*"

Tess feels overwhelmed and guilty by the way she's being pampered but follows the two women along as they hail a cab and ride to a small, private stylist, near some of the major studios. They get out and before they can get all the way to the door, a tall, broad-shouldered, dark-haired, bearded man, clearly of eastern European stock comes out, arms stretched wide.

"Lissa! It's been so long!" He has a slight Russian accent. "Come in! Everything's ready." He speaks and gestures in a flamboyant and gregarious style. "Is this the one, huh? Hm, good bone structure. The hair will have to be cut, but the color is a lovely shade of brown with blonde highlights. *Wonderful!* I feel like a sculptor again! Starting with raw clay and working on a masterpiece." He says, as they go into his salon.

Tess paths to Kari *I'm not sure if I was just complimented or insulted? Raw clay?* Kari grins and squeezes Tess's arm subtly, getting her to notice her host has stopped talking and is looking at her expectantly.

He turns to Liz and says, "Ah! Newbie? Still needs to learn how to path privately." He has a glint of humor and understanding in his eyes. He turns toward Tess laughing gregariously. "It was a compliment, as I only work with *quality* clay. Come! Let's see what beauty lies there waiting to be released."

The salon is empty. It has tall ceilings, and bright white walls with gold candelabra lights decorating the walls. The floors are a multi-tone, interlaced wood pattern that looks like an elaborate mandala. Tess and the others walk in and their footsteps echo in the large space. "My crew has today off. I told them I had a special client coming in. Very 'hush-hush', if you know what I mean?" He grins and lets out a baritone laugh. "Lissa, Kari, wait here. You know me. When I 'sculpt', I do it without others watching." He walks off with Tess, carrying the dress bag with her clothes in it. He hangs the bag in a changing room and goes on to the hair and makeup area. He washes her hair and then moves her to a comfortable swivel chair to work on her.

They spend about an hour there. First, her hair; cutting and styling it in the first real haircut that isn't from herself or a discount, walk in hair place she'd had in years. She looks at her hair in the mirror as it dries, and notices for the first time, hints of her childhood blonde are showing through the mousy brown it had become as an adult. Then he gives her a quick manicure. "What are those? Tooth marks on your nails? Not chewing them with your fangs, I hope."

"No! My cat, Mabel, likes to chew on my fingers." Tess giggles.

"Now!" Says Andrei, "As to makeup. You need only a little here and there to accentuate the lines of your face and bring out the blue in your eyes."

"*Wow*, I hadn't realized how much I've changed these last weeks." She stares at herself in the mirror.

He swivels her chair away from the lighted mirror, leans down and whispers in her ear as though he's telling a secret, "It's one perk of becoming one of us. But it never hurts to accentuate the natural with a little tweaking here and there." He winks at her. He does a light job of makeup on her, subtle blush, a little eye shadow, liner, and a little light lip color. He leads her over to the changing room, where her new clothes are waiting. She changes into a lovely blue and green pastel dress with a flowing skirt, and a new pair of shoes and hose to match. When she comes out, Andrei exclaims:

"Now! That is a *masterpiece!*" He leads her over to a full length, three angle mirror, her eyes covered by his large hands, uncovering them when she's properly positioned in front of the mirrors:

"*Oh my!* I look like a...." She stammers out.

"Like a movie star?" He asks.

"Something like that. I'm... I'm in shock! You sure know how to turn clay into art." She says, using his metaphor. She spins around a couple of times, looking at all angles.

"My dear, it's like sculpting. The secret is the beauty was always there, one only needs to know how to bring it out. The makeup is quite subtle; most of what you see is purely YOU!" He says, as she turns around to see all angles in the mirror.

"Thank you, Andrei! This is amazing!" She smiles, and her eyes glisten.

"Now, no crying. You'll ruin the makeup, and I'll have to start all over." He admonishes her jokingly. "Marc will get a proper welcome home. The two of you thwarted the worst of the bombings, and this is but a *small* thank you."

"But one bomb still went off. So many killed!" She turns to face him.

"Did Lissa not tell you? Because of you and Marc, several additional bombs were thwarted. One in London, another in Oslo, Paris, Munich, Berlin, Moscow, Hong Kong, New York City, Dallas, and here, in L.A.! Had it not been for you, I would not be here to give you this makeover! And for that, I am *eternally* grateful!" He bows formally, in thanks and respect.

"I didn't realize. Sara told me they stopped other bombs, but not the details. So many people." She realizes she really made an enormous difference in the world, and no one, outside of others like herself, may ever know. *Not exactly something I can brag about on Facebook.* She thinks, and he laughs.

"You must really get your training in telepathy. Your mind leaks quite badly." He motions for her to follow him and takes her out to Liz and Kari. "Ladies, may I present: 'Tessa, the unknown savior of Los Angeles!'" He says, again with flare and a bow.

"Very nice, Andrei. You've outdone yourself once again!" Liz says.

"Anytime, Lissa. All three of you are welcome anytime. As I told her, had it not been for her and Marc, I would not be here now to do this. By the way, Mira sends her regards. She was caught on the edge of Jerusalem but is recovering at home. She also sends her thanks, in fact, she sent you a gift." He gives Tess a small box with a bow.

Tess opens it and the velvet-lined box contains a gold charm bracelet with an iconic symbol from every city she helped save, along with a charm with a symbol of thanks.

"Wear that and remember what you've accomplished. And the many who owe their lives to you." He emphasizes.

Liz, Kari, and Andrei talk for a while, catching up on the latest news in their lives, while Tess sits on a nearby sofa, feeling stunned and overwhelmed at the immensity of what she thought might have been a silly idea, and the consequences it led to. *I really had a hand in saving millions of people.* She thinks. *I was feeling guilty because so many still died, thinking had I not distracted Marc, but Sara nailed it. Had he not been there, I wouldn't have come up with the idea, and he wouldn't have acted upon it. Tens of millions would likely have died, and the world would be in even greater chaos than it already is.*

She hears Sara telepathically. *As you now see, as I have seen all along, you belong with us, and you're key to the future. The latest news is this terrorist act by the militants was so extreme, their own nations are seeking them out and putting an end to them behind the scenes. There may finally be peace in the Middle East. Sometimes, even bad things, such as the one bomb inflicting so much death, are needed to shock people into action and bring people together. It'll take time, and it won't be without bumps in the road, but in the bigger picture of this planet, this point in history will be a critical turning point, and it pivoted upon you. Just don't let it give you a big ego. Stay as you are, but never be afraid to contribute. Your insight is unique. By the way, be back here by 6 p.m. Eastern time. I plan to bring Marc out, then."* Tess feels a warm mental hug envelop her. She doesn't realize she'd closed her eyes to focus on Sara, but opens them to find Liz and Kari standing over her with curious expressions.

"Nodding off?" Kari asks.

"No, I've been thinking; absorbing everything that's happened. Didn't you say something about lunch? I'm starving!" She decides it's best to keep what Sara said between the two of them.

"Yes! We have reservations." They say goodbye to Andrei, and snag another taxi, taking her to an Asian fusion restaurant near the famous walk of stars. As she's walking along, she notices people staring at her, and tentatively reaches out to listen in on random thoughts. She's amused by how many people think she must be some famous actress or model.

The women go in and are seated near a koi pond, and eat their lunches, barely speaking aloud, but conversing telepathically, about how much Marc is going to be shocked by both her inner and outer changes. For the first time, Tess truly starts to accept her so-called destiny, thinking, *this is really where and what I'm meant to be, and I'll do my best to see this world into the future.* She smiles at Liz, realizing, for once, Liz didn't catch her random thought; her newfound confidence has allowed her natural shields to function again. *My, and Sara's secret, and I'll stay true to this idea and myself.* She thinks.

WE MEET AGAIN

After lunch, Liz looks at her cell phone, which is on local time, and says, "Okay, we should get back to Medical. It's about 2:30 now, which means it's 5:30 p.m. there. Didn't Sara say to be there by 6 p.m. Eastern, Tess?"

"Yes! Oh, *God*! Now I'm getting nervous." Tess anxiously balls up her napkin and puts it on her plate.

"Why?" Kari wonders.

"I don't know, I just am! I haven't spoken to him since that night." She blushes.

Liz and Kari guide Tess to another dead-end alley where they can't be seen by any random humans. "Relax! Now, do you remember what the medical center looks like?" Liz lays a hand on her arm.

"More or less, at least the parts I was in." She focuses on re-membering all the little details.

"Picture the lobby with the towering glass windows, vines, and indoor pond. Close your eyes, and picture yourself there. Now, open them." Liz says.

She opens her eyes, and she's standing exactly where she'd pic-tured. "Did I do that?" She's excited she's successfully solo-ported.

"Yes. Your first solo port. Now, let's go check in with Sara." She says, and the three women head up the stairs to Sara's office.

Sara comes out of her office, hands on hips. "Well, it's about time! I was getting ready to come collect Tess myself." Sara feigns irritation. She leads them to a private room, where Marc lies, still unconscious. Most of the scars from the burns have faded, but a few of the deeper ones still vaguely show as discolored areas of skin. "I'd suggest only Tess come in with me. He'll still be weak, and the shock of her condi-tion and appearance will be enough for the moment." She winks at

Tess, who follows her into the room, and they close the door behind them, while Kari and Liz wait outside.

Tess goes over and takes his hand in hers. He's breathing regularly, and she can hear his heart thumping out a strong rhythm. Sara makes a few adjustments to a small machine near him, and after a couple of minutes, he begins to stir.

Sara motions Tess to move back at first. "Marc, can you hear me? It's Sara. You've been out for around a month, but you're nearly recovered now, and I need the bed space for others!" She feigns grumpiness.

"Sara? What? How long? A month? What about Tess? Who's taking care of her?" He tries weakly to sit up, his voice raspy.

"*Relax*! You aren't totally healed. Don't make me knock you out again!" Sara chastises him.

"You *wouldn't*." Marc's voice is weak, and he coughs from raising his voice after long disuse.

"No, I'm sending you home soon, but someone wants to see you first." Sara steps aside and motions for Tess to come forward.

"Tess? *Wow*, what a vision to wake up to!" He smiles, reaching out a hand to her. When she takes it, he gets an odd expression. He turns to Sara, who nods, confirming his suspicion. "H... how?" His voice cracks. "Did Liz talk *Them* into it?"

"I'll let Tess fill you in. I've got other, less *troublesome* patients to see!" She leaves the room to talk with Liz and Kari.

"You're one of us? How's this *possible*?" He pulls her closer, and she sits on the edge of his bed.

"Verdict's still out, except somehow, your infallible database was wrong. You probably don't remember much, because you were unconscious for most of it, but you ported home, followed my mental shout, they say." She says. "I did what I could for you. You were bleeding badly when you ported in. I stopped most of it, but the only thing I could think to do was to feed you. You weren't conscious, so, I cut my wrist and fed you that way."

"*Tess*! That was *so* dangerous. I told you I'd already fed from you that day. You could've easily bled out and I wouldn't have been able to heal you." He caresses her hand in his but has an anxious expression after what she did for him.

"And if I hadn't, you might still be in a coma, and I'd still be human! Besides, you're *worth* the risk to me." She says bluntly.

He sighs, "You're right, and I'm grateful. I guess I need to stop thinking of you as a fragile human now, don't I?"

"Sorry to snap. Liz also got after me, but it's a moot point now. I'm one of you. Anyway, after I fed you, some of your blood got in my wounds, and well, I woke up in the middle of the night sick and puking. When Liz came to check on me, she figured it out." She sits silently as Marc takes in her story and what she was willing to do for him. "I guess me being a short-lived human isn't an issue anymore?" She has a sheepish grin running ear to ear.

Marc squeezes her hand, weaker than she expects. "That stopped being an issue before you lost your humanity." He quietly says.

"Sara told me to think about it this way, I may not be human, but my humanity's still there, in the core of who I am. She told me never to let that go." She explains.

"And so, you shouldn't! I let mine go for too many years, but you helped me find it again." He pauses, tired from talking. "Tell me, I know the bomb went off. How bad was it?"

"Bad enough, but only the one bomb went off. A lot of people lost, both humans and your, no, *our* people. But as I found out today, there were 10 others that were never completed, so it could have been much worse. By the way, Andrei sends his regards and thanks. L.A. was one that would have been lost if we hadn't stopped them." She senses the pain he feels at the loss, as well as the relief more were not lost.

"I'm guessing he's responsible for this vision before me?" He smiles; amazed by the change in her appearance from when she was human, as well as the feeling of growth as a person he senses in her. "And you? How are you holding up? Adjusting to everything?" He asks, struggling to stay focused.

"I've missed you, but I know you'd have been with me if you could've. I'm so glad you're *still* with me. I was afraid I'd lost you. I felt your reaction when the bomb exploded." She grips his hand too tightly, not realizing her own strength, and Marc gasps at the pain. When she realizes her error, she relaxes the grip, uttering "Sorry!"

Marc sighs, saying, "It's okay, nothing broken, love. I remember the bomb going off and. I couldn't port out; couldn't get a lock on where I wanted to go. You were all I thought about in the seconds before the shockwave hit. Then I heard your mental shout. I followed your mind home." His voice strains and cracks as he remembers the fringes of the blast hitting him as he ported out, desperate to reach Tess.

"Don't strain yourself. We'll have plenty of time. Sara wants to check you over and Liz needs to talk to you, too." She pauses, debating whether to tell him the bad news, but figures it's best he knows before Liz comes in. "Peder didn't make it back." She says, her expression shifting to sadness.

"I suspected as much. He was on a wide band path he'd found the bomb, and to evacuate ourselves. Then it went off. I had a little time to react but couldn't port... until... I heard... your... mental... shout." He says, each word coming with a pause as exhaustion overwhelms him.

"I was told the EM pulse screwed with porting, especially one's sense of direction. You need to rest. Don't worry about all this now." She reaches over and strokes his face gently.

There's a knock on the door, and Sara comes in with Liz in tow. "Marc, Liz needs a few minutes with you while you have the strength, then we'll get you fed, and if you're up to it, we'll get you home. Tess, Marc won't rest if you're here. Kari's going to help you port home. It may be awhile before he follows. I need to do a thorough exam before I can let him leave." She says. Kari comes in and guides Tess out into the hallway.

"Let's get you home. You'd best let me port you. Your aura's very frazzled." She takes her by the arm and ports her home.

"He's *so* weak. Do you think he'll ever fully recover?" Tess drops onto the sofa, wiped out from the day in LA, and her emotional reunion with Marc.

"I'm sure he will, now he's definitely got something worth fighting for." She smiles. "Do you want me to stay with you for a while?"

"No, I'll be okay. I need to do a few things around here. Clean up. Make the house ready for him." She says, feeling a deluge of emotions now that Marc will be coming home.

Kari leaves. Tess busies herself putting things away, changing the bedsheets, and, of course, feeding Mabel. She sits on the bed with her laptop, catching up with news and a few messages. *Hm, maybe it's time to let Facebook go. I hardly talk to anyone anymore. What would I say? Hi, friends, I'm not human anymore! How are you?* She thinks, but decides not to do anything hasty. She closes her laptop and lies down, thinking *I'll rest briefly, and then get back to making things ready for Marc.* She's so exhausted, she slips into a deep sleep, waking only when she feels warmth against her back, as Marc gently lies behind her on the bed, and puts his arm around her, pulling her close.

"Marc?" She says, half awake.

"I sure hope you weren't expecting anyone else!" Some of his natural energy and humor's been restored after eating and feeding.

Tess rolls around and reaches around him, holding him tightly, as though she might never let him go, tears cascade down her face. "I'm so glad you're okay and back home." She leans in to kiss him.

Marc barely responds, which confuses Tess, who pulls back, wondering if Marc *is* having mixed feelings after all. "No, Tess, no mixed feelings, I'm not up to anything more than being here with you, and knowing you'll be with me for a very long time." He whispers. "Let's sleep, and we'll catch up in the morning. You'd think after being unconscious for over a month, the last thing I'd need is more sleep." He rolls on his back and pulls Tess's head onto his chest, and absentmindedly plays with her hair. "We'll have plenty of time together." He says softly, as he dozes off into a comfortable sleep, his arm protectively wrapped around her.

THE REAL FALLOUT

Marc and Tess spend about a week getting reacquainted at home, while Marc regains some of his strength. He catches up with everything that's happened since the bomb, including the loss of life, and political turmoil of its aftermath, as well as the aftereffects of the bomb, including the track of the radiation worldwide.

One morning, Liz calls. "Marc, I know you're still not 100 percent yet, but could you and Tess come in for a meeting tomorrow morning? We need to make some plans. We're down over 3000 people worldwide and we need to figure out how to not only recoup our losses, but also increase our base population to compensate. We have already turned some of our potentials in the different centers, but we're coming up way short."

"Yes, we can make it. I'm starting to feel more myself again. You say I should bring Tess, too?" He asks.

"Yes. In fact, Kari's got some answers for her about why she wasn't in the database, and that brings up one area to explore regarding potentials." Liz says.

"Really? I'm quite curious about that myself. We'll be there bright and early." He finishes up the conversation and hangs up.

The next morning, Marc and Tess reluctantly get ready to go into work, they've been enjoying their time together since he got home.

"So, how's your porting? Have you soloed yet?" He asks.

Tess laughs. "*Once!* They let me port once on my own when we came to see you."

"Well, let's try an easy one, picture my office." He suggests. The room swirls out and they're in his office, the lights come on when sensors detect their presence. "Not bad. No roughness phasing in." He remarks. "We should get over to Liz's office. The meeting's about to start, and there're several people here from other centers."

"Okay, but didn't Kari want to see us first? Didn't she need to fill us in on something?" She asks.

"Oh, yeah! They think they figured out why you weren't in our database." He grins, knowing Tess has been wondering about that.

"*Really*? Let's go!" She heads out the door and down to see Kari, leaving Marc behind in her excitement. Kari's sitting in a side office, waiting for them. Marc catches up by porting in behind her in the office.

"Well, look at you two! You've obviously been getting to know each other quite well this last week." She comments, knowingly, and watches Tess blush. "Have a seat. I assume Marc told you we've figured out how we missed you? I did as you suggested, it took some reprogramming, but I did a DNA search with a sample Sara cultured from some hair she found in your brush, and you didn't show up in the main database, so I searched another one we rarely access. Your DNA raised a flag there."

"Really? So, what database *did* I show up in?" Tess asks curiously.

Kari sighs, "Inactive potentials. As in *deceased*."

"*Deceased?* Don't think that can be right." Tess says, her face scrunched up in confusion.

Kari hands Tess a tablet with the file's summary page pulled up. "It also came up with a different name. It lists you as Marie Elizabeth Scott."

A sudden flash of understanding crosses Tess's face. "Oh, my *God*! I didn't even think of that. That **is** my actual *birth* name, not my current legal name. It was changed when I was four years old. Remember me telling you about the car accident I had when I was three? My parents both died in the accident. I was injured, burns and bits of metal and glass along my back and shoulders. I used to have the scars to prove it, but they've all healed up now." She says, "My aunt and her husband adopted me, and changed my name to Tessa Marie, in honor of my mom, and then my last name to Waterford after the adoption was finalized. I don't remember much of it at all, I only know what they've told me, and I rarely even think about it anymore."

"That explains it. Including why you weren't tagged. The tag is usually implanted near the spine, between the shoulders. If your injuries were substantial, it was likely removed or destroyed. Which would also explain why they considered you deceased. No signal from the implant, as it usually 'dies' with the subject, or when it's removed from its host." Kari sits back and looks thoughtful, as the implications sink in. "This could mean there are other people in the inactive files that may still be alive; a small percentage, but something to add to our list. We should get over to Liz now and fill her in." Kari says, as the three of them go over together to join the meeting.

There's a pause as they enter the room, and the others in the meeting stand and clap to welcome Marc back, as well as Tess, who they now know was key in figuring out the terrorists' plans. Tess blushes and feels awkward but sits with Marc on the sofa they've left open for them.

Liz sits in the chair at the head of the table. "Now we can get down to business. I've asked everyone here because of the fallout from Jerusalem; and no, I'm not talking about the radiation, though we have some of our people in key scientific positions contributing to the cleanup through selective release of technology from our Benefactors. I'm talking about the fact we lost roughly 10 to 15% of our people in the explosion, and with the current international instability, we need to not only make up for those losses, but increase our numbers. The problem is, we never prepared for such a massive recruitment. We rarely turn more than a few hundred to a thousand in a century worldwide, let alone over 3000 in order to bring us up to pre-Jerusalem levels. The potentials exist, however, most of them would normally be substandard. Either their ability ratings are lower than we'd usually want, or they're no longer acceptable due to psychological reasons, or life situations such as marriage or having children. As you know, we're strongly encouraged never to turn anyone once a family or strong relationship has been established." She makes fleeting eye contact with Marc.

"So, our problem is this, how can we increase our population quickly without damaging ourselves by turning people who will be less useful or even a problem?" Liz scans the room, inviting suggestions.

Kari speaks up first, telling them about how Tess was in the inactive files, and she would share the new algorithms which would let centers search for DNA matches in both parts of the database in case a similar incidence occurs.

Tess, true to her promise to Sara, speaks up and suggests, "As some of you know, I was human until the night of the bomb, but have known and worked with Marc and others for a while now. When I turned, Liz and Kari explained to me about, what did you call them? Our Benefactors? Anyway, I asked them, if I had all the traits of a potential, and all potentials have this special genetic sequence, why didn't they just test me for that? But apparently, you all don't have the actual sequence as *They*'ve never disclosed it. Perhaps, under the circumstances, it's time to ask for that information." She pauses briefly, and then continues, trying to be confident. "Not only could you confirm if an individual is compatible, but you could search genetic databases worldwide for people with the sequence. For example, all the ancestry sites which test your DNA, and tell you where your ancestors came from, or the Human genome project, or any other medical databases where DNA is collected."

"Hm, that would be quite useful." Liz says thoughtfully. "Kari, could you run that through the right channels?"

"On it!" She replies, tapping enthusiastically on her tablet. "You know, Liz, that may be useful if we want to track down any of those from the Lost Mission. We could combine a general scan for the genetic sequence with a specific search on those who show up as carriers and see if any of their genetic profiles match the Lost Mission gene-prints."

"True!" A spark of excitement glints in Liz's otherwise sad eyes.

"Lost Mission?" Tess asks.

"Yes, there was a period a few years after you were born, where unusually strong potentials showed up and were tagged. Unfortunately, our Benefactors on that screening mission were lost in transit to a base they set up closer to Earth. Their equivalent of the database was eventually recovered, but it was damaged. All the names and location specifics were lost, though the DNA coding remained, completely unmarked. All their tags were also useless as they, being organic, depend on a 'mother' form, which was destroyed in the accident. Think yeast or fungi, where a main organism buds or creates spores, except these maintain a base, telepathic field until the offspring mature after about 75 years. We could run an additional search through to match up any found with key sequences in the world bases. Hmmm, that might work." Liz starts getting enthusiastic about the possibility of tracking some of the Lost potentials.

"Sounds like you could use that as grounds to get the sequence from them. You could also cross reference names with social networking and other online sites, school records, and try to narrow down locations?" Tess suggests.

"Yes, and we could use those pages to get an indication if they might be psychologically suitable or what their life situation is, before ever contacting them, and use our subliminals to attract potentials via social media. You know how quickly memes can go viral! Tess, you're full of ideas!" Kari says, and Tess brushes it off as no big deal.

They go on with various ideas and plans to implement them, taking a break after a few hours. Tess notices Marc's unusually quiet.

She leans over against him and rubs his back with her open hand. "Are you okay?" She whispers.

"Yes, just tired, but very proud of you, *love*. You're jumping in with both feet. Funny, I thought I'd have to help get you up to speed, but I'd say it might be harder for me to keep up. At least for now." He gives her a tired smile. "Can you port me home now? You can come back if you wish, but I've done all I can for today." He says, frustrated with his own weakness.

Tess wraps her arm around his waist and ports him home, as Sara insists, he limit his porting until he's recovered more. He sits on the sofa while she grabs food and a bag of blood from the fridge for him. When she comes back, he's already fallen asleep. Tess grabs a knitted blanket her mom made that she brought with her when she moved, and gently lays it over him and turns out the lights. She puts the food and blood back in the fridge and leaves him a note:

"Marc, left you food in fridge; going back to brainstorm with Kari and Liz. Holler if you need anything." She reads it and realizes the roles have reversed themselves, at least temporarily. She leaves the note on the coffee table and gently kisses him on the cheek, and ports back to work.

BAD APPLE

A couple of weeks have passed since their brainstorming meeting, and hundreds of potentials employed by various centers have been transformed. Worldwide, 615 new transformees have joined their ranks. At the Asheville office, Amy, and three others have been turned since shortly after Jerusalem. Unfortunately, not everything has gone smoothly.

Marc's mostly been recovering at home and doing what he can from there. He still gets tired quicker than usual and needs to feed more often due to continued healing. Tess stays with him most of the time, rather than going in to the Center. While Sara provides bagged blood as necessary, Liz and Kari have been teaching Tess to feed directly on humans, and then letting Marc feed from her.

One morning, Marc gets a call from Liz: "Hey, can you grab Tess and come to my office? We've got a couple of issues to deal with. Some who aren't adjusting well and possibly one or more who may have to be dealt with in other ways."

Marc pauses before replying, not sure he's interpreting Liz correctly. "What? A rogue?"

Liz sighs and speaks with dark, seriousness in her tone. "That's what we need to determine. I'd like Tess in on this as well. Kari keeps telling me her people intuition is unusually acute. Can you two meet me in about half an hour?"

"Of course. Tess is out picking wild mushrooms nearby, but I'll get her, and we'll port in shortly." His voice is heavily laden with concern. He hangs up and gets ready to head into the office.

Tess comes in, sensing Marc's unease from outside. "What is it? You're worried."

"That, I am. Liz needs both of us in a meeting. Potential

problems with some of the new transformees." He gets his shoes on, goes into his home office to grab his tablet to take with him.

Tess follows close behind, asking, "How serious?"

"Not sure, but she implied some may be critical." They take each other's hands and port to his office, and then the two of them walk down the hall to Liz's office.

On the way there, Tess sees Amy, recently turned, working with someone on her telepathy. She looks up and catches Tess's eye. Amy paths, *You, too?*

Tess nods and grins, pathing, ***Talk soon! Hugs!*** With everything that's happened, she hasn't spoken to Amy since before Jerusalem. She's ecstatic knowing Amy is one of them too, so she won't have to hide things from her any longer.

They walk into Liz's office; Liz, Kari, Sara, and a woman in a police uniform with an Atlanta PD emblem on the arm are there. Tess looks at her, wondering why a police officer would be there, until she realizes the woman's one of *them*. An *Apara*.

Liz stands, shuts the door and starts the meeting. "Alright, everyone, we've now turned 615 people worldwide since Jerusalem. 616 including you, Tess; and five total here in our offices. That's almost as many as we turned in the entire Twentieth Century!" She adds. "Most have gone well, though there are always issues when we can't pair people up with a dedicated partner for supervision. Unfortunately, sometimes we've got people supervising between five to ten new transformees, especially in the larger centers, as we just don't have people available who aren't partnered up. Granted, there are, unfortunately, a fair number who were left alone after Jerusalem, but most of them are not ready to take on a new partner. We may not be human anymore, but the grieving process is more complicated for some of our people, as we've had so few actual deaths over the years, at least before Jerusalem".

Liz nods to Kari, who takes over. "Most of the issues are minor, primarily adjustment based; however, we have had reports from three cities of suspicious deaths where puncture wounds were present. Some of our people in law enforcement," Kari nods to the Atlanta policewoman, whose nametag says, 'Officer Holly Jensen'. "However, cleaned up the evidence, so we won't get the 'vampire wannabe killings' headlines we all know and hate, even if they are only in the tabloids." She pushes a button on her tablet, transferring an overview of the data to the others in the room.

Liz continues where Kari left off; the two of them often work in tandem, as they've been together so long. "The problem is, we're not sure if we're dealing with one, two, or three rogues since the killings are spread out."

Tess asks, "Liz, which cities were the bodies found in?"

"Charlotte, Atlanta, and Richmond" She brings up a map on everyone's tablets, showing the three cities with glowing red dots linking to unredacted police reports and crime scene photos.

Tess ponders the possibility of a connection. "So still in the same region, the Southeast?"

"Yes, so far." Liz replies.

"Could be one person then." Tess suggests.

Liz nods to acknowledge Tess's input. "Possibly, but not necessarily. You can't think about it as driving distances, because with the ability to port, it could be three different continents and still be the same person."

"I realize that, but as a newbie myself, I've only ported to places I've been before, though Marc's told me it's possible to use either a photo, clairvoyance, or home in on someone's mental signature as ways to get to new places. I'm thinking most newbies, would still prefer to stick to familiar places, and those places would be more likely in the same region. If you've been somewhere, you have an innate feel for where it is in your mind." Tess is still nervous speaking up but promised Sara to do her best to contribute, even if an idea seems silly at first.

"I see your point. Perhaps you and Kari should work on this for a while. I've got the profiles of all the recent transformees, and all the unredacted crime scene reports. Since you're a people intuitive, I want you and Kari to go through them, see if you can find any red flags, and put them into the 'likely suspect' category, such as former residences, odd behavior reports from their supervisors, and maybe check their social media too. While we've told everyone to be careful what they post publicly after they were turned, you never know what subconscious clues might come up." Liz suggests.

"Alright, I'll give it my best shot." She glances at Marc and tries not to look nervous at her first official duty in her new life.

"I want the rest of you to get in touch with your contacts at the other centers and make them aware of this issue, and check for any similar occurrences in their territories, and keep an eye open for any of the new transformees that might be behaving strangely. They could be accidental deaths. It's all been such a rush to build our numbers up we haven't been able to give them all the proper supervisory period we usually do, however, I'd be much more willing to deal with three accidental deaths, under the circumstances, than one who's gone rogue. We've got enough issues without having an unstable Apara running around risking exposure." Liz explains, looking exhausted.

The meeting winds up, and everyone but Marc and Tess leave. Tess puts her hand on Marc's arm and paths to him, *I'll catch up with you. I need to talk to Liz for a sec.* She gives him a look letting him know she wants to talk privately with Liz. He heads off to their office to contact his share of the other centers.

"Liz, are you okay?" Tess asks.

"Yeah, it's just been a busy few weeks." She downplays her exhaustion and mood.

"If you'll excuse me for saying so, I think it's more than that." Tess gently puts her hand on Liz's arm.

Liz gives Tess a shrug and a sad look. "Should have known your people reading skills would focus on me sooner or later. It's normal. I guess you could say normal grieving. I miss my brother."

318

"That part is obvious, but...," Tess works up the courage to tell a woman around 800 years her elder she senses something more is going on. "I get the feeling there's more to it. You were doing okay, but the last few days it's like you're, I don't know, haunted?"

Liz looks up; her skin is even paler than usual under her blonde hair. "Tess, it's nothing, really."

"No, I felt that. I don't want to overstep, but I get the feeling something new is going on that's, well, haunting you. That's the *right* word. Nothing else fits!" Tess moves closer to Liz and sits on the arm of a chair.

Liz slaps a pile of folders down on the table in front of her, sitting back down in her chair, with a strained expression. "You *really* are a talent and a half!" She says, exasperated by Tess's perceptiveness. "*Dreams!* That's it. *Just* dreams. I've been hearing Peder in my dreams, calling out to me, but it's impossible! He was at ground zero! He *couldn't* have survived!" She wipes away a tear rolling down her cheek.

"Is there any chance he could've gotten away? Maybe even been blown clear somehow? If he went into stasis, maybe he's only now healing and coming to somewhere?" Tess asks.

Liz's voice is filled with sorrow and lacks her usual energy; it's nearly a soft monotone. "I don't see how that's possible. We searched everywhere nearby that wasn't ash."

"Do you only hear him, or do you see him, too?" Tess asks calmly.

Liz closes her eyes, remembering, and as she describes it, Tess can see what she's seeing. "I don't see him. I see flashes, images— trees, scorched glassy sand, bushes burned away, debris everywhere. The images and voices come and go." She says.

"Scorching, debris, sand, some of which has a thin layer of natural glass on top?" Tess asks.

"That's exactly what I see. That, and his voice, pleading with me to help him." Her eyes look hollow as she thinks about it.

"When Marc ported in, there was a flash from the blast, debris, radiation, and some scorching here and there. We recently had the carpet replaced, as some of it had melted, fused together. Is it possible he could have ported out at the last second?" She asks.

"He couldn't have had time, and I doubt he'd have been able to if others, further away, couldn't." She answers.

Tess pauses, thinking. "Are there any buildings or landmarks?"

Liz tries to remember. "No, only nature."

"Just nature? How close are the two realities? How are the portals made?" She asks.

"I'm not sure what you're getting at. It's technology our Benefactors gave us, but as far as I understand, an electromagnetic field is created which makes a stable rift, or portal that bridges the two worlds." She rambles the explanation off like she's reciting something she learned in school, but doesn't really understand.

"When we port, we exist in the membrane between the two universes. It isn't so much teleportation as passing between the realities, or just outside one, taking a 'shortcut' from point A to point B, but we can port directly between them as well. It's not like how we have 3 dimensions here or in Sanctuary. The space between is without dimension and depends on the mind for guidance. The two realities were somehow bound to each other by our Benefactors, as there are many such worlds, but we can only travel between these two. It's technology they've used to deal with overpopulation. Instead of colonizing other planets, they find an alternate version of their world that's uninhabited, and anchor it to their main world, then expand into it." She explains.

"So, what would happen when the initial EM pulse of the bomb hits? Could it create a portal or blast a temporary hole between the realities?" Tess asks.

Liz gives her an odd look. "Are you suggesting he could have gotten blown through a spontaneous portal?"

"Maybe not a proper portal, but if it thinned the veil between realities enough and he was trying to port; you did say it was only nature around him. No signs of civilization? Just scorching and debris, and when Marc ported to me, it was also from this world to the other. Could it be possible?" She asks.

320

Liz looks thoughtful, a renewed spark visible in her eyes. "Maybe. If he began to port right before the bomb went off, but before he was fully in the membrane, it could have knocked him off course, even taken some of the blast in his wake to the other reality. Marc found you by blindly following your mental voice, but I'll have to talk to some of my people in tech."

"Liz, I was getting flashes of your memories when you spoke. I want you to look again and tell me: were you seeing Peder at all in the images? Or could you have been seeing through his eyes?" Tess asks, remembering seeing what looked like a damaged arm, as if the viewer were seeing his own arm.

"*Gud!* (Nor: God!) I missed that! It's from *his* perspective. The flashes are him opening his eyes and looking around, well, maybe. That, or my brain is smarter than I am when making my dreams. You could *really* be on to something! I'm not going to get my hopes up, but if he were pushed into Sanctuary, he could have been lying there in stasis. Tess, thank you! Even if this isn't true, it gives me something to work with. It really feels like Peder's been calling me, which is why it's hit me so, *damn* hard! And if he's alive, others could be too! We assumed everyone was vaporized, but maybe.... Tell the others I'll be out for a while." She vanishes.

Kari comes running into Liz's office. "*Liz*? Tess, where'd she go?"

"It's complicated, but Peder may be alive, and she's gone off to check on a hunch I had." Tess meets Kari's gaze head on.

"What? How?" She asks, urgently.

"I'm not sure I can put it all into words again, but maybe...." She closes her eyes and sends the whole concept to Kari telepathically.

Kari's eyes go wide as the information articulates itself in her mind. "That's downright brilliant! I knew she's been having the nightmares but didn't know the extent. Start looking through all the profiles. See if you get any feelings about anyone. I need to be with Liz either way. If she finds him, I doubt he'll be in good shape, and if she doesn't, I'll need to be there for her." She ports out.

Tess picks up her tablet and a box of folders and heads back to

Marc and their office. For now, they're sharing his office, since it's partially shielded to cut back on stray thoughts and emotions. Sometimes, being a strong telempath isn't so easy, and shielding provides relief without having to constantly block stuff out. She comes in and plops down on the sofa and pours over the unredacted reports of the three deaths. All three were women, all in their late 20s, and Caucasian. All three had light brown hair and blue or gray-blue eyes. In two cases, there were also signs of sexual assault, but whoever it was didn't leave any DNA to trace. Tess gets a sinking feeling.

She turns around and waves at her partner urgently, saying, "Marc, I suspect we're dealing with one person, and his attacks were intentional. If they'd been accidental, he'd have left DNA, but he didn't, and there are similarities between the victims' descriptions. He planned these assaults and murders, whoever he is." Her face blanches at the thought of someone like that having all the powers they have.

After a minute, Tess's expression erupts in horror and dismay, "*NO!* Please tell me they didn't!" She blurts out, and grabs the tablet, skimming through the names of all those turned since Jerusalem. She drops into the chair with a thud. "*FUCK! God Damn it!* They did it! They *turned* him!" She's nearly hyperventilating with panic and anger.

"Who? What are you going on about?" Marc is now beside her, stroking her back to calm her.

"They *fucking* turned Jason! I'd bet my life he's the one! From the first day I met him, something dark and nasty in him told me he was capable of nothing short of pure evil!" She rambles, her PTSD kicks in, giving her the shakes.

"I know he has issues, and Peder was supposed to put a note in his file to follow up with new psych evaluations, but pure evil?" Marc asks.

"I've been in his head, trust me, there's something dark and empty inside him, like a black hole." She hands him the tablet. "Check his file. See if Peder ever got around to making that note. I'll bet you since there was no likelihood he'd need to be turned prior to Jerusalem; Peder didn't rush to make the notation. He was pretty busy, as were you." She tries to calm down, as she's feeling lightheaded from hyperventilating, though it's unlikely one of their kind would ever faint.

Marc takes her tablet and looks up Jason's file. "You're *right*. No such notation. He was one of the first turned after the bomb because his psi-rating was stronger than most."

"*Damn* it! I know I should look through the entire list, but my gut says he did it." She takes back the tablet from Marc and checks his history. "I seem to remember him saying he lived in Atlanta earlier. Look! Prior residences: Atlanta, Charlotte, and Richmond. There's the link! All cities he's familiar with."

"*Merde*! Let me check with our people on a couple of things in those cities. You say there were sexual assaults as well?" He asks.

"Yes, two of the women were sexually assaulted. The other, besides being drained, was strangled." She clicks on a link and an image pops up.

Marc gasps when he sees the photo of the first victim. "Tess, she looks an awful lot like you did when you were human; similar look, build, and hair."

Tess pulls up the other two killings to look at the victims. "Oh, *crap*. I'd call that a damn, clear pattern."

"He's taking his anger out on women who remind him of you." Marc closes his eyes. "Tess, I don't want you to leave my side, do you understand me?"

"You don't have to tell me twice." She pauses, lost in thought, then asks, "Do you think he'll come after me too?" Her anxiety rises, as well as her heart rate.

"He may, especially if he doesn't know you've been turned, though he'll probably assume you have been since you're with me. He'll want to frighten you, hold his power over you. These other incidents, they could have been dress rehearsals."

"But he can't... can't *kill* me. I'm one of you. *Right*?" Her pulse pounds in her head.

"It would take a lot to kill you, pretty much either destroying your brain, or dispersing you into fine bits so you couldn't coalesce and heal, but that doesn't mean he wouldn't try to kill you or hurt you badly, both physically and psychologically. He's likely physically stronger than you, and, unfortunately, more skilled in his abilities. I'd hazard to guess you, by far, have the greater potential, but he was prepped, taught all the skills he would need to use his talents unconsciously, while you're still getting the hang of them. We need to tell the others and get the ball rolling." He exclaims with increasing urgency.

"But what if I'm wrong? I mean, it's just intuition, a gut instinct. I haven't even looked at the others' files."

Marc braces Tess by the upper arms. "I'd trust your intuition any day. I wouldn't be here today if you hadn't intuitively pulled me out of that inferno! Besides the pieces fit. Stay close to me!" He picks up his phone and makes a call, but no one answers. "Do you know where Liz went? I can't get through to her cell, and I can barely sense her telepathically."

"She went to investigate something; a chance Peder might have survived." She says.

"What? Let me guess, another of your intuitions?" He's not angry, merely comprehending Tess has a lot of power for one so inexperienced, and that means a lot of ups and downs in the future.

"Sort of." She worries she's causing more trouble than good.

"Now don't get that way. I didn't mean to imply you did anything wrong. I'm figuring out how we can deal with this. You said he knew you were scanning him when he was still human, didn't you?" His mind making his own connections, as Tess nods. "Okay, we need to do this carefully. If he was that aware as a human, his skills as an Apara are likely to be even more formidable. If we aren't careful, he'll know we're on to him and he'll flee." Marc worries Jason may once again come after Tess. He pulls her up from her seat and into his arms, hugging her gently. "I don't want anything to happen to you, not even temporarily."

"I've been through so much the last weeks, but this scares me more than anything." She admits. "I swear he wouldn't have stopped that day in the copy room if Liz hadn't intervened. Knowing what I know now, I guess she picked up on my panic."

"Yes, she did. She told me so. We should have fired him and purged him from our system, but there were other crises to tackle. Listen, I can't reach Liz or Kari, I'm assuming they're together?" He looks at Tess for confirmation.

"Yeah, Kari felt she should be with her either way." Tess gets a sinking feeling in the pit of her stomach as she realizes Jason has become a bigger problem for her than ever before. The security she's felt since becoming Apara is gone. He might not kill her, but if he got hold of her, he could make her life miserable. She tunes out everything around her, as her mind freezes with dread at the thought of Jason being a murderer, and of his obsession with her. She feels a hand on her shoulder and jumps.

"*Sorry*! Didn't mean to scare you, but you were completely *gone* for a second. Are you okay?" Marc inquires.

"No. *No*, I'm not. I've seen inside his mind. It's a dark and scary place!" She admits, putting her hand on top of his. He sits with her on the sofa, holding her. He feels her shaking. She's shaking uncontrollably. "I haven't been this afraid since Jerusalem! I'm really worried he's going to come after me!"

He pulls her into a protective hug. "It's funny, until recently, it felt like so little could hurt us, but after Jerusalem, and finding you, I think about it more often. I'll protect you as best I can, but right now, I need to get things moving. I can't track down Liz or Kari. I can get a slight sense of them, but can't pin down their location. Do you have any idea where they might have gone?"

"Liz and Kari? I'm not exactly sure. How parallel, geographically, are Sanctuary and this Earth? We were going on the assumption the EM pulse might have pushed Peder through from this one to the other, like you were." She pulls back from Marc; her expression worn.

"*Ah*, no wonder I can't reach her. If you're right, they'd likely be in the region where the bomb went off, but in Sanctuary. Any

I

bleed-through radiation would probably interfere with our psychic senses." He pauses. "I don't want to leave you alone right now, but you're safer here. I'll get Sara to stay with you while I look for Liz and Kari." He says, while simultaneously reaching out for Sara. *Sara, can you stay with Tess for a few?*

Sorry! In the middle of an admission. Liz just got here. She found Peder and said she could sense others nearby. Sara paths.

That's fantastic! I was about to go look for her. Can you ask her to come back to the office as soon as she's able? Pretty sure Tess figured out who our Rogue is, and it's worse than we thought. He paths.

Yes, heard about that. Who's the suspect? She paths in between checking Peder's vitals and wounds.

Jason Templeton. Marc paths.

Marc is chilled by the sudden, total, mental silence. After a minute, he hears *Shit. Is she sure?* from Sara.

She's pretty sure, and she's got a valid argument to back her up. Plus, we think he's symbolically assaulting and killing Tess. All the women resembled her. He paths.

Sara goes off on what can only be a telepathic cursing streak in some ancient language. *I'll pass this on to Liz, but I'm not sure she'll budge from Peder until I give him a once over. Make sure Tess is NOT left alone! Not for one, damn second!* Sara paths, and breaks the link.

After about ten seconds of Marc looking off into space and making strange expressions, he focuses again. "What is it?" Tess asks.

"I won't be leaving you alone after all. Liz and Kari are with Sara. She found Peder, alive, and possibly others as well. Looks like your intuitive track record is batting a thousand. I wish you weren't probably right about Jason too. Sara's passing on the info to them." Marc says.

Before Tess can reply, Kari appears, her face a mixture of anger and stress. "Jason? They turned Jason? I'll *kill* Steve! I told him when we transferred Jason to his office, he was likely *unacceptable!* Tess, are you *sure*?" Kari asks.

"Pretty much. He's lived in all three of the cities where the women were killed, plus all of them looked a lot like me, I mean a *lot*. And it feels like him. The last time I ran into him, at the restaurant, he was so angry at me, and he was aware of his psychic skills even while human." Her voice shakes as her anxiety about Jason builds.

"We're going to need more proof eventually, but first, we need to bring him in and neutralize him." Kari says.

Eyes wide at Kari's comment, she asks, "You're gonna kill him?"

"No, not unless absolutely necessary. Neutralize, in our vernacular, means stripped of all his abilities. Other than a continued need for blood, he'll be reduced to human-level abilities, both physical and psychic. It's a drug we use which blocks all such abilities so the person can be contained." She explains. "It is rarely needed, so I'll have to see if Sara has any in stock."

Tess nods. "Well, you'd better use double strength, because if I'm right, he could use his abilities before he was turned." She pauses. "Oh *God*! I just had a *horrible* thought. You know how we can influence people telepathically?"

Nodding, Kari says, "Of course. What are you thinking?"

"I wonder if Jason could have had a similar ability while human. He kept acting like he thought he should be able to convince me and was frustrated I didn't give in to his 'charms'. I did have some of that tingling thing around him sometimes. I wonder if he used his abilities to get people, specifically women, to give him whatever he wanted." She looks disgusted.

Kari looks pensive, eyebrows furrowed. "That could be. Most of our abilities are founded in the basic human psychic abilities. We don't see too many potentials with any major abilities before they're turned. Most of them may be aware, or peripherally aware, that they have abilities, but if he knew and actively used them while human, I could picture him misusing his abilities very easily, and most people would have no natural defense against him. I'll get Sara to make up a strong batch of the neutralizing agent and prepare it for delivery. I'm betting the hard part will be sneaking up on the weasel."

"If he knows we're on to him, he'll likely run, and if he could hide his ability level and psychological issues from us, he may also have a natural ability to cloak. If he cloaks and goes underground, we'll have a *hell* of a time finding him, and I'm afraid Tess is not safe until he's in custody, and neutralized." Marc says.

"*Agreed*! Tess was not only the unattainable object, but *you*, Marc, beat him to his goal. Tess, didn't you say he was angry you were with Marc at the restaurant?" Kari asks.

"Blood-vessel-popping furious! In his mind, he accused me of sleeping with Marc to get him to transfer Jason out of here. Of course, that was before we became a couple." Tess says.

"Let me go have a few words with Steve and see if they've noticed anything odd from him. Maybe we can get him to use the neutralizer on him. Jason would be less likely to suspect something from him." Kari says and vanishes.

"This means we're going to need some bagged blood on hand. You are *not* going out feeding until this is under control, and I can't leave you alone to go feed 'for you'." He gives her a serious look, knowing Tess can be rather pig-headed, and independent.

Tess's face turns melancholy. "Tess?" He queries.

"It's nothing, it's stupid." She says.

"What?" He asks.

"I hate feeling helpless! It felt so good to make a difference earlier, but now, I feel like a mouse waiting for a cat to pounce! You shouldn't have to protect me from that evil *asshole* like I'm some invalid, because I didn't get my 'training' like I should have."

"And that *wasn't* your fault. I'm just glad you found us, and we found each other. It will take time, but once you work on your skills, I bet you could kick his *ass* literally and psychically! But right now, I need to protect you. I don't know what I'll do if I lose you now. Kari's getting the ball rolling." He strokes her hair, as he sees her eyes start to glisten with budding tears again. "I promise, I won't let anything happen to you." Once again, he pulls her close.

328

After a few minutes, Kari pops back in, agitated and mumbling under her breath. "Okay, I spoke to Steve. Jason's been acting way too guarded and being late to check in with his handler. They also caught him feeding on a co-worker, and he's been reprimanded and warned. However, he was very apologetic Jason was turned. Steve was dealing with the fallout after Jerusalem, and one of his staff made the call. I've arranged for neutralizing injectors to be made up and delivered to Steve, as well as all of us, in case we have a run in. Be extremely careful not to accidentally dose yourself, or you'll be helpless for at least a week. Sara's making it strong. Once we catch him, we'll be able to determine if he's guilty or not, even if we're pretty sure of the answer. Now, while we're waiting for Liz to get back, and the neutralizer, I want you to show me all your actual evidence, not your personal bias, that implicates Jason." Kari tells Tess, sitting with her. The three of them go over the files, Jason's earlier residences, his personality profiles, and so on. "Were there any others in the system that might be suspects?"

"To be honest, I never really got past Jason. I reviewed the crime scene reports and then it hit me. This is something he'd do." She insists.

"I realize that, and you're *probably* right, but we must look at others too, in case your hunch doesn't play out. So, I need you two to go through the other potentials' files and make notes. I'm going to go fill Liz in and see how things are going with Peder. Sara will bring the neutralizer ampoules as soon as they're ready, in the meantime, stay here! And for *goodness'* sake, stay together!" Kari says sternly and vanishes.

BACKFIRE

Tess and Marc pour through the files, one at a time. A few of them rate as borderline psychologically, but none have the overall warning signs Jason gives off. They're about to start a new batch of files when Sara arrives.

"You all can stop sorting. We've got a match!" She exclaims.

"Who?" Marc inquires.

Sara glares at him as if he's a tad daft. "Who do you think? *Jason*! When Kari arrived, with your latest info, I got in touch with our local people who dealt with hiding the evidence pointing to one of us. Standard procedure is to scan the bite wounds with a 3D-holographic scanner. This gives us a bite print. You were right, Tess; the same person killed all three women. And the preliminary match points to Jason." She says. "Now, that being the case, we need to keep you safe. Liz, Kari, and I looked over the victim files and agree they were not chosen randomly."

Tess makes a loud and frustrated sigh. "Oh, *Great*! I kinda hoped I was wrong on this one." Sarcasm dripping from every word. Marc lays his hand on her arm, squeezing it gently as a signal to calm down.

"So, first things first. I only had time to make up a small batch of neutralizer. There are 5 of these ampoules for each of you. They're double strength. So be extremely careful, or you'll end up helpless for a week if you jab yourself by mistake. While you can try to throw and guide them telekinetically, the most likely method of delivery to work is, unfortunately, direct, close contact." She explains.

"Sara, I don't want Tess going anywhere near him!" Marc exclaims.

"Which is why Tess and you are going to stay here. Unfortunately, she can avoid him all she wants, but if he's determined to get to her, he likely will. Now, back to the neutralizer. This" She holds up a small object containing a capsule of blue liquid in it, "is a combination GPS tracker and antidote capsule. I'm going to place this, subcutaneously, along the vertebrae in your necks. If by any chance either of you is ambushed, captured, or hurt, it'll be easier to find you, especially if he does have the ability to cloak. If, by some chance, you jab yourself in a struggle and become neutralized, this is your only hope. You'll need to press on the implant until it breaks, which will release an antidote. Now, this isn't something that'll be easy on you, so it's best not to get jabbed at all. The neutralizer is instantaneous. Unfortunately, the antidote isn't. It's also not going to be painless if you use it, and could even cause seizures." She explains.

"Sara, I notice it's the same color as the drug Marc gave me when he tried to wipe my memory. Is it related?" Tess asks.

"Not only is it related, but it's also a concentrated dose of that drug, Psiamplio, or Psiamp for short. Using it will not only undo the neutralizer but may also open up new pathways and lead to instability in your abilities for some time to come. However, it may be the only thing that saves you from him if you get neutralized, and he gets his hands on you." Sara emphasizes.

"Understood. I'll do my best not to be clumsy and inject myself." Tess says, as Sara walks behind her. Sara moves Tess's hair from her neck and inserts the device under her skin.

Sara gently guides Tess's hand to the lower vertebrae in her neck while Marc looks on. "Now, feel that. *No!* Don't push, feel it so you know where it is. If you get in a bind, put pressure on it until you feel a warmth spreading from that point. That will mean the ampoule has ruptured and the drug will work its way through your system. It's implanted in your neck to be as close as possible to your brain and spine; that way, it'll work quickly." Sara moves on and injects the same type of device under Marc's skin. "Unfortunately, it's not known how quickly the antidote will work, so if one of you accidentally gets neutralized, I want the other of you to retreat somewhere and protect them until they recover.

Understand?" She glares intensely at Marc.

"Got it." Marc says.

Shortly after Sara's finished implanting the antidote capsules, Kari and Liz port in, flustered and emanating frantic waves of worry. "We've got a serious problem. Steve tried to neutralize Jason. I got a brief telepathic cry of warning from him, and then silence. We took some of our security staff with us to the Hendersonville office and found him, neck broken. Jason is in the wind! He knows we're on to him, so he'll likely be more desperate to get to you before we can get him, Tess!" Liz puts a hand up before Tess can interrupt. "Steve will recover, but now Jason has gone underground. We can't track him, so our theory about his ability to cloak is confirmed. You two stay here. We're going to ramp up your office filters. Brought this little add on which should prevent anyone from porting in here. It's programmed to only allow you two, myself, Kari, and Sara to port in here. Anyone else will bounce and be sent to a holding facility."

Tess paces the room, then looks at Liz, saying, "So, Marc and I are cheese in the mousetrap?"

"*Yes*, but stay in here and you should be safe. He may locate you, but if he ports in, he'll be redirected to holding. In the mean-time, Sara, I need you to and attend to Steve and get more neutral-izer made." Liz commands.

"Will do. Tess, watch your back! I don't want you ending up in my center any time soon unless you're visiting someone." Sara vanishes.

"Now *stay here*!" Liz tells Marc and Tess. "We're going to round up more people to search for him. He's officially classified full rogue now, meaning any means necessary are authorized to catch him." She and Kari port out, leaving Marc and Tess alone.

"Marc, I don't *like* this at all! That guy's been trouble for me since day one!" Tess crosses her arms across her chest, visibly up-set and feeling vulnerable.

"Relax! If we're in here, we *should* be fine." He heads over to a small office fridge, and there are several bags of blood. "Good, we've got supplies, at least the kind we need the most." He grins and tilts his head to one side, feeling confident they're both safe in his office. "Just in case we're here for a while." He watches as Tess restlessly paces around the office and gets distressed vibes from her. "Tess, are you okay?" Marc asks, concerned.

She pauses her pacing momentarily to answer, "*Not really!* I feel like a caged animal waiting for a hunter to shoot me!"

Marc gets up and takes her by the shoulders. "Pacing won't accomplish anything other than wearing out the carpet." He pulls her close. "I won't let him get you." He guides her over to the sofa and sits her down, then works on the stress knots in her shoulders, careful to avoid the antidote ampoule along her spine.

"What if they don't catch him? We can't hide in here forever!" Tess asks.

Marc sits with her on the sofa. "That's not going to happen. He's one against the rest of us. He can't take us all on." He tries to calm her down. "Why don't you nap? We could be here for a while." He suggests, and she lies down and attempts to sleep. Marc carefully sends her subtle, telepathic suggestions to doze off, and eventually, she sleeps restlessly, turning frequently, and occasionally making sounds in her sleep. Every time she has a bad dream, Marc gently puts his hand on her arm, sending calming thoughts and energy until she settles.

A few hours pass with no word from anyone. Tess is still sleeping, and Marc is getting anxious. After a while, an instant message pops up on his tablet from Liz. "Marc, got him! All's well. Grab Tess and come to my office ASAP."

"Tess! Wake up! Sounds like they got him. Liz just messaged me and wants us to come to her office!" He exclaims.

Tess stretches. "They got him?" She yawns and sits up, looking relieved at the news.

"Sounds like it. Come on! Liz is waiting!" He extends his hand to her and helps her up.

Still groggy, Tess takes his hand without a second thought; they open the door to his office and start down the hall. They get only a few feet from the door when both feel a burning sensation on their backs. Marc crumples to the ground as the neutralizer takes effect. Several hundred years of his normal strength, suddenly gone, makes it difficult to stay upright. Tess feels disoriented, like she's gone mentally blind, or deaf, and she suffers severe vertigo. She staggers to the wall, bracing herself as she sees someone fly past her and behind Marc. To her horror, she sees Jason put him in a headlock and twist. The sound of crunching bones echoes in her ears. Jason looks up at Tess with a grin that can only be described as pure, sadistic malevolence. Before she can run, he's in front of her, punches her in the jaw and knocks her out.

MOUSE TRAPPED

Drip, drip, drip... clackity, wrrr-wrr-wrr... bzzzzzzzz. Tess rouses, but lies still, her mind becoming oddly focused as the adrenaline from fight-or-flight mode kicks in. She listens to the background noises around her, puzzling them out. She attempts to open her eyes. One opens, but is blurry; the other, she can barely open a slit, and her cheek feels stiff and swollen, as the neutralizer slows down self-healing, active abilities, and physical strength.

She keeps her eyes closed, analyzing the sounds. *Dripping water... a fan? An old one from the roughness of the sound, metal blades... air's stale, recycled... ventilation?* She thinks and takes a slow, deep breath through her nose even though one side is clogged from the swelling where he punched her. *Smells damp: mildew or mold? Basement like.* She tries once more to open her eyes; one opens more fully than the other; a little reddish blob floats around in her swollen eye. Now and then, everything looks pinkish through her left eye.

Damn! He must have hit me really hard. She focuses on other sounds in the room. Tess hears a constant electric buzz and tries to look up without moving her body. *Ugh! Old fluorescent bulbs, flickering; I hate that sound! Hands are numb, wrists hurt, sort of burn. The asshole tied me up, and it's cutting off the circulation in my hands.* Her wrists are raw from the ropes tied tightly around them. Her hands are pulled back behind her, bound by rope, making her shoulders ache. She's lying on an old, military, brownish-green, canvas cot that wouldn't be comfortable even if she weren't tied up, and possibly sporting a broken cheekbone.

Tess tries to ignore the pain and discomfort, and attempts to reach out to Marc, but gets nothing; only a void where she's gotten used to feeling his presence in her mind, even when he wasn't actively in telepathic contact with her. *What the hell? Why can't I reach Marc? Maybe Liz or Kari? NO! I can't reach, or sense anyone!* She thinks, and her panic increases. She tries to break the ropes, but she can't even stretch them enough to ease the circulation-killing bonds. She flashes back on the burning sensation on her back and knows what's going on. *That shithead used the neutralizer on ME!* She thinks.

She looks around the room, but her vision is blurry for anything more than a few feet away, even in her 'good eye', so she has trouble making out the details around her other than there's a lot of gray or beige. She blinks her eyes a few times, trying to clear the haze, and finally sees some details. The room around her is an old, dusky room with metal and concrete walls, no windows, and very stark. There's a door she can see out of her peripheral vision. It almost looks like the inside of a bank vault door, metallic with a heavy locking system and a wheel to turn instead of a doorknob. She strains to get a better look, only to cause the antiquated frame of her cot to creak.

"Decided to rejoin the living?" Jason's voice is dripping with controlled malice. She struggles for a moment, trying to break the ropes, in vain. Her memory's fuzzy. She doesn't remember how she got here but remembers him punching her in her left jaw before everything went black.

"What've you done to me?" She forces the words out.

"Nothing more than you and the others were going to do to me! How's it *feel* to be human again?" He spits out with an audible sneer.

She knows he used the neutralizer on her, but realizes he believes it's a cure, so she plays along. "*Human?* What the?" She thinks *If he believes it made me human, I'm not gonna dissuade him of that misconception. It could give me an advantage once I get the antidote working. Damn! Can't reach it. Here's hoping some of my pre-transformation abilities remain, especially my shields, or I'm up shit creek if he can read my mind.*

"Yeah, couldn't have you popping out on me, could I?" He grabs her by the shoulders and roughly turns her to face him. "You got away from me once, though I don't know how the hell you survived your *accident* on the Parkway!" He glares at her with vehemence.

Tess's breath and heartbeat speed up, shocked at his

confession. "That was *you*? You almost *killed* me!"

"Yes, but unfortunately, you *survived*! Did your savior port you out of your car as you went off the ledge? You certainly *should* be dead." He growls.

Tess goes cold inside, and thinks, *He tried to kill me! He fucking TRIED to kill me! Is he planning to try again now that he thinks I'm human? I guess I'd go into stasis, but still.* She looks up at him. "They're gonna come looking for me. Marc will find me." She says, slowly, weakly.

"Your savior couldn't even save *himself*. He's never going to come looking for you! I dosed him, and *then* broke his neck!" He glares at her, gloating and watching for her reaction. Her mind flashes back on the horrid sound of his vertebrae snapping, and she cringes. "So, as a *human,* I don't think there's any chance he'd survive that, do you? It was too easy! Once I gave him the cure, it was like breaking a dry twig!" He laughs malevolently.

"*No!* I don't believe it!" She exclaims, forcing tears to flow, figuring it's best to act like he expects her to, broken and distraught. She knows Marc will recover eventually. Right now, she's more concerned about what Jason has in store for her. *I'm like a helpless mouse with my tail stuck in a trap, and he's a nasty, sadistic Tomcat.* She worries what he'll do next.

"Well, you *should*. The same can happen to you if you don't do as I say." His voice is full of spite and arrogance.

"Do as you say?" She repeats his words slowly, as a question.

"You treated me like shit from day one! Turned me down, mouthed off to me. No one treats me that way! *No one*! I want something, I get it, and you're no exception!" He blurts out, ranting.

"You acted like I was supposed to fawn over you, but I wasn't interested. You acted like a jerk! That's why I don't like you. Plus, I wasn't interested in any relationships because of how badly my last one ended." She continues to feign sobs, realizing she has to drag the conversation out to give the others a chance to track her GPS implant.

"Yeah, right. You're just another spoiled bitch, and I *know* you convinced Marc to move me to that other office with some little favors." He gives her a nasty grin implying she had traded sex with him for punishing Jason.

"Jason, you cornered me in the copy room. I was afraid you were going to rape me! And no, you know what happened. Marc didn't have you transferred. Liz did! Remember her coming in? She sensed my distress and came to find out what was going on. She asked me later what happened, and I told her the truth. You had me cornered, and I was afraid! Marc wasn't even in the country when any of that happened." She says.

"Doesn't matter! I saw you with him, having dinner in town. I know you were involved with him. What made him acceptable? He wasn't even human." He demands.

"He is, *was* more human than you! He's kind and I, I *love* him. Besides, at that point, *nothing* was going on. We were just out as co-workers, to celebrate finishing a project. That night, at the restaurant, I saw you there, had a panic attack, and freaked out. Marc got me out of *there*." She adjusts the truth accordingly. She thinks: *My pre-transformation shields must be reasonably intact; if the neutralizer only cuts off post transformation abilities, maybe some of my others will come back on their own once I get this headache to clear out. Mustn't let on, though. He needs to think I'm completely helpless, or things could go south fast.*

"Well, your 'love' is dead! Get *over* it! And if you don't stop being such a major *bitch*, I'll knock you out again! Or maybe, I'll *feed* on you until you beg me for forgiveness." He says menacingly.

"What do you want from *me*? What do you plan to do? Kill me like the women in Charlotte, Atlanta, and Richmond? Oh, *wait*, apparently you already tried to *kill* me!" She snaps out, egging him on, but she can't help it; her realization he was the mystery SUV driver fills her with rage.

"Oh, you know about them? Yeah, I was furious you survived. Once they changed me, and let me off my newbie leash, I found a new outlet for my anger at you; *unfortunately* for those women. The epinephrine in their blood was as good as meth! As to what I *want* from you?" A slimy grin spreads from ear to ear, and his fangs extend to their full length. "I'm going to give you another chance. Now that Marc's gone and you're human again, you're going to choose me, and willingly let me turn you again." He leans against a pillar supporting the ceiling, tonguing his fangs like he's preparing to sink them into her neck.

"And if I don't?" She asks, while reeling her own temper in.

"There are ways to *encourage* you to see things my way. And now that you're human, you don't have any defense against them." He leans forward menacingly, fangs exposed. He leans toward her neck, acting like he's going to bite her, then grabs her wrist and licks it, moving up her hand, and sucks on one of her fingers suggestively.

Ewwww! She thinks, her stomach nauseous from his lewd insinuation. "You'd use your abilities to make someone want you?" She asks.

"Until *you*, it always worked on other women. Would you rather I beat the shit out of you every day until you give in?" He grabs her by the hair and gets in her face.

"*No!* But I can't flip a switch and suddenly *like* you." She explains.

"*Nobody* said you had to *like* me, just *choose* me! And now that the competition's gone, what else do you have?" He believes he's twisting the proverbial knife after 'killing' Marc.

Tess knows she's got to play along and make her reactions believable, so she forces more tears to flow, closes her eyes and sobs, then looks up at him, feigning fear in her eyes. "They'll still look for me, even if Marc can't, they know you're the one now. Liz will have people looking for me." She says, sobbing in between words.

"They won't find you. They can't read anything down here. We're in a lead-lined fallout shelter from the 1950s; one that's not on any maps either, as someone built it without a permit. They can't sense you here, and even if you could contact anyone telepathically, it would be hard through these walls." He gloats.

Tess thinks: *Damn it! If the walls are lead-lined, I bet the GPS won't work either. Fuck! There has to be some way I can let them know where I am.*

"How do you get in or out if it's lead-lined? Does it affect porting as well?" She asks, hoping he'd answer without too much thought.

"That's right. So, no one will be porting in to rescue you even if they could locate you. I've got the only key to the main door. It's the only way in or out." He gloats. "And that wheel is so old and hasn't been lubricated, a mere human like you couldn't possibly open it, even if it weren't locked."

Tess squeezes her eyes closed in pain for a second. "Would you be willing to give me something for this headache? You hit me pretty damn hard. My head feels like it's splitting open." She begs.

"Why would I do that? Not like I have any here, since *vampires* don't get headaches." He laughs.

She thinks, *Oh, yes, they do. At least from psychic burn.* But answers him out loud. "Because if I can't get rid of my headache, I'm going to start puking all over the place." She puts on a show of desperation and sorrow.

He looks at her, debating. The idea of her puking in this enclosed space makes him cringe. He never could stand the smell of vomit growing up, as his mother often threw up when she drank, and made him clean it up. "If it'll make you less of a *fucking bitch*, I'll see if I can get some. In the meantime, think about your predicament. You wouldn't want to end up another dead bitch on the street somewhere, would you?" He unlocks the door, turns the ancient, creaky wheel, and slips out.

In the couple of seconds while the door is open, Tess tries to send a telepathic blast to Liz, careful to use private mode so he won't notice. *FALLOUT SHELTER!* is all she has time to send, worsening her headache exponentially, thinking, *I hope enough of my pre-transformation skills are left to get through to her.* Her head throbs from the effort.

Tess looks around the room, searching for anything useful in case she can get loose, especially anything she can use as a weapon, even in her weakened state. She sees a lot of computer equipment on the other side of the room. She recognizes the custom build on the machines from work. *The little rat must have stolen them. Hm, looks like from his supply corner he's in here for the long haul. Must have raided a blood bank.* She thinks, as she notices the remains of an IV blood bag lying on top of a full wastebasket by his computer desk, and a mini fridge under the

342

desk. Tess lies back and clears her head, then attempts to sit up. She keeps falling back on the cot before she can reach an upright position, so tries to use her pre-existent PK to make a pencil roll off his computer desk and onto the floor, while lying down. It takes a while, but it eventually rolls off. *Okay, that settles that. It doesn't cut out all abilities, only those that came with actual transformation. Doesn't give me too much to work with. My native shields must be working, or he'd probably have already beaten the crap out of me or tried to kill me. He clearly doesn't realize I'm not human, and Marc's only in stasis, which he'd know if he could read me. If I can play along with him or get him to think his mental control is working on me, maybe I can buy some time. Damn it! I wish I could activate the antidote. If I could get that going and stall until it runs its course, I could catch him off guard.* She closes her eyes again, hoping it will lessen the incessant throbbing in her skull.

A few minutes later, Jason returns with a bottle of generic migraine medicine. He gets a cup with water and two of the pills for her. "You're gonna have to help me up, I can't take them lying down." She says. He puts the pills and cup down, roughly picks her up, and puts her in a sitting position. "Ouch! when you hit me, you hurt my neck. I'm having trouble holding my head upright." She says.

Exasperated, he puts his hand behind her neck, holding it while she takes, and swallows down the two pills. She goes into a coughing fit, faking coughing spasms, and pushing back against his hand repeatedly until she feels the warmth from the ruptured antidote ampoule. She thinks, *Now, to bide my time until it works.* She says, "Can you help me lie back down again? It may help if I sleep while the medication kicks in. I used to get a lot of these migraines before I was Apara." She says, squinting her eyes and cringing in pain. It isn't fake, unfortunately, after her efforts, her head hurts, and she feels a new pain building as the antidote spreads in her system, including up and down her spine, and into her brain.

He pushes her back down on the cot. "You have an *hour*; then I *want* your answer." He leaves her there like a sack of old laundry.

He goes over to the computer and focuses on the screen. Tess isn't close enough to see exactly what he's reading, but she recognizes the layout on the screen, even from across the room. *Damn! He's got access to the database. Kari's going to personally kill him!* She thinks.

She lies there, feeling the heat spread from the drug, down her spine and out to her limbs, and up into her head. It feels like fire turning to electricity, traveling along her nervous system.

As her telepathy returns, she picks up on a small voice, not her own, rambling on about looking for others who can be turned. *No! He can't!* She thinks in horror, as she telepathically sees the screen through his eyes. He's looking up other compatible women in the region and finding them on social media and dating sites. *Making his own little vampire harem. To Hell with that!*

She feels her abilities strengthening. She thinks, *No, must keep them hidden.* She uses her natural shields to hide the increasing energy levels as her abilities resurface. Twice she fights the feeling of seizures coming on, willing herself to be calm, and forcing the pathways to accept the additional levels of energy. *Sara wasn't kidding! This feels like my brain is on fire! Like my abilities are 'Hulking out'!* She thinks.

She pretends to sleep and hatches a plan to deal with Jason. She clairvoyantly scans the room, looking again for anything she can use as a weapon, and spots a jar with the remaining two neutralizer ampoules. *That's it! I've got to get to that! But first,* she thinks. She focuses on the ropes binding her hands and legs, willing them to weaken with her PK, making them so fragile by fraying the fibers from the inside out, it will take little effort to break them when it's time. She feels the concussion and fractured cheek he gave her healing, the swelling is fading, and her head's no longer throbbing. However, the antidote has made her mind raw with its new power. She thinks *He's probably still physically stronger than I am, but Marc said I have the potential for far more power than him. Plus, so long as he thinks I'm human, I've got the element of surprise on my side.*

She carefully listens in again, so he doesn't sense her. *Luckily, he's too, fucking arrogant to think I can read him now.* She thinks. As she listens, she realizes he plans to turn several others, *'safety in numbers'*. He thinks. '*Turn only women, no competition.*' There's an odd mental shift, and she sees flashbacks in his mind. Memories long suppressed. Abuse as a child. His mother, an alcoholic, whose husband left her, abused him, demanding he obey her every command, including ones no child should have to. He grew up to be like her, abusive and manipulative. Demanding he gets *everything* he asks for. *If he wasn't such an asshole, I might feel sorry for him.* She realizes he may be a victim of his upbringing, but he still chose to be a jackass. Tentatively, she stretches her mind beyond the lead-lined walls. She can nearly reach Liz. She can sense her but can't quite make contact. She sees Sara working on Marc, speeding the healing of his vertebrae. Sara stops and looks around. Tess feels tenuous mental tendrils reaching out to her mind, making brief contact, and withdrawing. She can see Sara speaking curtly to Liz and Kari; the two disappearing from the room. *I guess maybe she got my message. Assuming what I saw wasn't just wishful thinking.* Her awareness shifts again, returning to the room she's in. She senses Jason standing over her. He nudges her roughly.

"Hour's up. *Wake* up!" He says angrily.

"Okay. *Okay!* Give me a second. My headache is still throbbing." She stalls while her mind once again locates the neutralizing ampoules.

"Well, are you gonna choose me, and let me give you back the gift I took away from you? Or do I have to *convince* you?" He balls up his fist in his hand, implying more violence, and bears his fangs.

"Why do you want me so badly? It's not like I was some beauty queen. When I met you, I was a dumpy nerd with unkempt hair and zits. Surely you could have found better?" She lightly scans his mind for any subconscious reactions.

His mind flashes on his mother again, and Tess sees the connection: *She looked like me! Talk about your Freudian screw-ups. So, he wasn't just killing me; he was killing her when he killed those women!*

"I have my reasons! One way or another, I *get* what I *want.* So, what's it gonna be?" He bares his fangs threateningly.

Tess takes a chance and hits him on a psychological level.

"Your mother didn't teach you how to treat a woman, did she?" She gauges his reaction as she sees the anger brewing in his eyes. *Got to get him distracted.* She thinks.

"Leave my *mother* out of this, *bitch!*" His voice elevates in warning, and his aura gets nasty hints of angry red and black.

"Did I hit a sore spot, Jason? Didn't she *like* you either?" She provokes him.

His ire rising by the second, he draws back to punch her again, and then his face drains as Tess telekinetically throws both neutralizers, from the jar across the room, and into his back, hitting her target square on. He loses his balance, staggering. Tess breaks her bonds, jumps up, and kicks him in the stomach, knocking him across the room and into the desk with the computer on it, causing a power surge that blows out the computer, followed by the entire pile of equipment crashing onto the floor, smoke rising, as a burnt electrical smell fills the small room.

"I've really got to remember to thank Amy for those lessons!" Tess says aloud, hands on hips, while staring at Jason, lying in a heap of damaged computer components.

"H... how?" He stammers, growing weaker by the second.

"Simple, I'm nobody's *bitch*, you *asshole!* The neutralizer isn't a cure. There *is* no 'cure'. It didn't turn me human. It only neutralized my abilities and strength. But I got them back." She grabs him by the arm, pulling it painfully behind his back and dragging him across the room, grabbing more of the undamaged rope he used to bind her, that's lying on the floor near the cot. She binds him up, not caring to consider his comfort, since he clearly reveled in causing her pain when he bound her up. "You murdered at least three women, tried to murder me, kidnapped me, attempted to kill two others of our kind! And no, they're not dead! They'll recover. You're so up *Shit Creek* right now! You're *fucking* screwed!" She pulls the last knot tight, making him wince in pain. She uses some duct tape from his tool kit and puts it over his mouth before he can start mouthing off. She fishes the key to the door out of his pocket and unlocks the door to the shelter, turning the corroded wheel easily, opening the door, and allowing fresh air to rush in, as well as Kari, Liz, and several larger, male Apara, who pop in as soon as the door opens.

"Tess. Are you okay?" Liz is surprised by Tess's apparent freedom, the still healing bruises, and black eye Jason gave her when he took her, as well as the bound and gagged Jason trying to squirm out of his bonds on the cot, until the cot collapses, dropping him hard on the floor, and knocking his head against the wall behind him. Liz continues. "I got your fallout shelter message, and Sara got a general location on you, but it wasn't until you opened the door that we could zero in!"

"I'm okay! My nerves are a bit worse for wear, but I *got* him!" She motions toward the now miserable, royally pissed, and neutralized Jason, lying on the floor, unable to get up. "How's Marc? I know Jason broke his neck. I remember the sound of his bones crunching when Jason attacked him." Tess asks, as Liz hugs her.

"He'll be fine. He's semi-conscious now, but temporarily paralyzed while his spine mends. He's been worried sick about you." Liz says.

"Yeah, I was too. He thought the neutralizer was a cure that turned me human. He had me tied up. Long story short, I had to trick him into helping me rupture the *damn*, antidote ampoule, but it worked. I located the last two neutralizers and used my PK to throw them when he was distracted." She grins broadly. "I *royally* pissed him off so he wouldn't see them coming." The adrenalin in Tess's system makes her shake.

Here's a tip, Tess, a lead-lined bunker may make it hard to communicate or sense through, but you're still thinking human when it comes to porting. Liz paths.

But he said no one could port in or out through the lead walls? Tess paths, confused.

That is mostly a way of thinking, as in three dimensional, as in THIS world? When you port, you aren't passing through walls, you're passing between realities and there are no walls. But if you believe you can't, you'll self-limit. Liz paths.

Tess reacts with a sudden understanding. *I hadn't thought about it that way! But why didn't you all port in then?*

Because, while we could have ported in, it did block our ability to sense you, and we needed to sense you to home in on you, but you could have popped home as soon as your abilities returned and avoided a confrontation. Liz suggests, chuckling mentally. *Next time something like this happens, if it happens, get your ass out of there, first opportunity! Don't take on the big bad alone! Marc would be devastated if something happened to you!* She paths, then says aloud, "We'll take over from here. Are you up to porting back to the office? Marc's going to want to see you, and Sara will want to look you over." Liz says, mentally noting the unusual energy spikes in Tess's aura.

"I'll go in a second." Tess turns to Kari and paths. *I need to give you some information I picked up from his mind.* She touches Kari's arm briefly; the information about Jason's childhood abuse, his mother's resemblance to herself, and his plans to turn other women he found in the database he hacked, flashes to Kari's mind with unusual speed. She turns to Liz and paths; *He apparently stole some equipment from the office stores and hacked the database. You might want to get someone to do a history on all his searches. Well, if you can salvage the drive. Sorry about that. He was planning to turn other women he found in the compatible database, but I'm not sure if he has yet or not.* Tess is feeling better by the minute now that her levels of adrenaline are leveling off. "I'm heading back now." She feels like she's climbed a proverbial mountain, no longer feeling helpless, and feels rather euphoric. She ports back to the office, running over to where Marc's lying on the floor.

"*Marc.* I'm okay. I got him. Are you okay? He thought he'd *killed* you." She rambles out, hyper.

Tess hears a weak mental reply. *Antidote working slowly. Body energies focused on healing first. Can't talk. Sara will kill me if I try, as it could undo the realignment of my spine. Proud of you, Love.*

"Sara?" Tess says.

"He'll be fine, child, but I don't want to move him yet. It took me hours to telekinetically piece together the bone fragments in his neck to speed up healing, like I did with your legs after your accident. How about *you*? Did he hurt you?" She asks, looking at the fading bruises on her face, but Tess also senses an additional layer of meaning, wondering if he'd sexually assaulted her as well.

"Worst he did this time was punch me in the jaw, knocking me out. He threatened to do more if I didn't do what he wanted me to." She plops down in a nearby chair, as Sara looks her over. *Ah! Feels good to sit in a comfortable chair.* She thinks and her back muscles unknot and relax.

"*This* time?" Sara asks, sensing there's more to the story Tess isn't telling her.

"Yeah. *This* time. *Last* time, he literally tried to kill me. He was the *one* who *ran* me off the Parkway!" Her anger simmers.

"*Damn*! I may kill that *cur* myself!" Sara's livid about the damage he's done to her. It was one thing to think it was a random incident, quite another to know it was an assassination attempt.

"It gets worse." Tess frowns. "He claimed he killed those women because he wasn't able to *kill* me. Though it wasn't only me he was symbolically killing." Tess paths the information about Jason's abusive mother.

Sara makes a sound of disgust. "No excuses for him, and don't you dare take on his guilt for the other women's deaths! That's his warped way of thinking. Nothing to do with you." Sara stares Tess down until she's sure Tess accepts what she's saying. "Hmmm, he dosed you too, with neutralizer?" She asks, making conversation.

"Yes, but I eventually got the antidote going. He thought it made me human, so never saw it coming when I had his last neutralizers get him in the back. *ZING*! Good thing I got him when I did though, as he was ready to beat the shit out of me by then." She gives Sara a wicked grin.

"Oh? Because you wouldn't do as he demanded?" She asks and uses a small scanning device to assess the effects of the antidote. She puts her hand on Tess's left cheek, speeding up the healing.

"No, because I *egged* him on. Found his *weak* point. I used his mom against him and got him so pissed off he was ready to beat me senseless, and that's when I dosed him and then knocked his ass across the room with a kick Amy taught me back when I was still human." She says, proudly.

"You're not permanently damaged. However, the antidote has expanded your already formidable abilities. I want you to stay home until I can map the changes and see if you can control them. *Sometimes*, I wonder if you have any concrete limits to your abilities. They keep expanding!" She puts her hand on Tess's. "Besides, someone has to take care of Marc until his spine heals completely. A couple more hours on the floor and I'll set a neck brace, but he should lie still as much as possible for the next few days." She explains.

"I'll take good care of him. I promise! Honestly, it's strange, but I feel more in control of my abilities than I did before." She exclaims.

"Perhaps that's some confidence showing through." Sara suggests. "But I still want you to stay put and wear your pendant. Your abilities may still expand for a while and your ability to control them may change."

"I feel pretty good. I handled this myself. *No one* had to rescue me until I'd already taken care of the worst of it, and it felt good to know I could do it." Tess says.

"The drug is also contributing to your current emotional state, like giving you a big dose of adrenalin and dopamine. Go *home*! Get a hot shower or bath and feed. The antidote burns a lot of energy, so you'll need blood shortly. I'll have someone pop over and stock your fridge with more. I don't want you out feeding until you're cleared. Got it?" Sara says insistently.

"Yes, ma'am!" Tess feels shaky as her adrenalin levels continue to drop, and the first hints of need set in.

"I'll make sure Marc makes it home as soon as he can be safely moved." She says. "And *NO* tempting him to be a bad boy. He needs about a week before he can participate in any, hm, extra-curricular activities." Sara says with a knowing grin.

"I'll do my best, but you'll have to convince him, too." She knows Marc's own stubborn streak all too well.

"If he won't behave, I'll have to knock him out and put him in the medical center." She looks over at Marc with a smirk. Marc is not amused. "Now, go home!"

Tess vanishes, and Sara returns to her patient. "You're going to have your hands full with that one. If you thought she was gifted before, you may be in for more than you ever bargained for."

Marc looks at her questioningly *What do you mean?* He paths.

"I mean, the antidote, combined with the stress of the situation, has opened her psychic pathways like a super-sized bottle of mental liquid plumber!" She explains. "I'll have to make a custom suppressor necklace for her until she can control her abilities."

Will it affect me the same way? Marc asks.

"I'm not sure, but I suspect not. Her pathways are still more pliable, as she's only been one of us a short time, not to mention she lacks some of the conditioning and pre-training current potentials receive. Besides, you're probably *too* set in your ways. And the stress of the confrontation added to the effect." She explains

Do you think the increase in abilities will cause her any problems? Or instability? Marc asks, concerned.

"No, our dear Tess is on the right path. She'll be fine. If she could adapt to being with you, she can adapt to *anything*!" Sara jokes, with a wink and a laugh. She looks at him for a second, wondering if he picked up what Tess said about her accident. "There's something you should know because it may add to her PTSD. Her accident, a while back, Jason was the one driving the SUV, and he was attempting to *kill* her. I'll fill you in on the rest she told me after you get some sleep. Jason is neutralized for now, so she's out of danger, but I got the impression his little revelation shook her badly."

I'll kill that bastard! Marc paths, anger building in his gut.

"Calm down, lie still, no more talking or pathing, and give yourself a chance to heal, or I'll knock you out."

Yes, Ma'am! He paths to her sarcastically.

A DOOR ONCE OPENED

Tess ports home, feeling oddly giddy, considering what she's been through. She writes it off to having handled Jason without help, and takes a long, hot bath. Once in the tub, she feels her muscles unknotting now her arms and legs are no longer bound. The raw rings around her wrists have mostly healed, leaving only a slight discoloration where the ropes rubbed her skin raw. Her adrenaline levels continue to drop, and she crashes.

As she relaxes, she drifts halfway off to sleep, and yet, her conscious mind is hyperaware. She feels every small lap and caress of the warm water, as well as the rose-scented bubbles from the bubble bath popping individually on her skin. There's a slight draft coming under the bathroom door from the cooler bedroom air and she hears Mabel sticking her paws under the bathroom door, trying to get in so she can sit on the edge of the tub and stare at her 'mother', making sure she doesn't drown. She tries to move, but she's paralyzed, her body leaden like it weighs a ton, muscles uncooperative. She opens her eyes and sees both darkness and a hazy view of the room around her. She reaches up with her hand to grab a wall grip, and feels her arm move, but it goes right through the grip. At the same time, she also feels her arm beneath the lukewarm water.

What the hell? She thinks. She tries harder to get up. This time, it feels like she's sitting up, but it's strange. Instead of water, it feels like she's pulling herself out of some sort of mire, as if something is clinging to her skin and keeping her sucked down. She can see, but it's not normal, like she can see the entire room at once. She sees her arm lift out of the water but can still see it in the water at the same time.

Something's seriously screwed-up! Maybe he gave me more of a concussion than I thought? She thinks, trying harder to get up. She feels herself rising, as if she's floating. It feels like the mire is letting go of its hold. A little further, and she starts with panic, as she realizes she can no longer feel herself breathing. In a burst of panic, she falls back, but there's no splash of water. She wakes with a start in the bathtub, disoriented by what she's experienced. Mabel meows loudly under the door in that odd way she sometimes does when she's looking around the house for Tess, a strange, loud, but strained 'meooooow' like she's asking a question or calling out to her.

That was one weird-ass dream! She thinks. She washes off the last of the soap and gets out, grabbing her robe. She heads to the bedroom, crawls onto the bed, and grabs her cell phone, calling Sara.

"Hi, Sara, it's Tess. I just wanted to check on Marc." She's hoping for good news.

"Ah, Tess. I've moved him to the medical center for the night. He still needs time for his spine to properly heal, and the only way I can keep him still is to have him where I can keep my eye on him. The good news is, he may come home tomorrow evening." Sara reassures her.

"Okay, whatever you think's best. Can you tell him to get better from me? I'd feel better if he was here, but I get it. Is Jason still under lock and key?" She asks.

"Oh, yes. We have him totally knocked out for now. Kari's going to do a read on him tomorrow; along with some of our psychological experts, to see if there's any hope for redeeming him." Sara explains, as she gives instructions telepathically to the techs getting Marc settled in. "Now, get some rest, *young* woman! And don't forget to *feed!*" She says with added emphasis on the word 'young'. "Liz says to call her if you need anything."

Tess rolls her eyes. "I'll be fine, I had some odd dreams while I dozed off in the tub, that's all."

"That's not surprising, with all you went through. Not to mention the antidote is bound to heighten your brain activity for a while due to elevated levels of various neurotransmitters. You should be okay at home, but I want you to stay there until I can get a special necklace put together for you. You may be oversensitive to telepathic and other stimuli for a while. Now, get some sleep! Or do I have to come over and knock you out with something?" She threatens, and Tess can picture her grinning.

"Goodnight, Sara." She hangs up. She's shaky, so carefully goes down the stairs to the kitchen before going to bed. She opens the fridge and sees it's been stocked with extra blood bags, as well as a 1-quart container of Sara's mushroom soup.

I get the feeling I'll be here for a while, if that's any indication. She thinks, puncturing and indulging in a bag of blood. Mabel has followed her downstairs, so she feeds her on autopilot. She goes back and grabs the soup and heats it, scarfing it down quickly. She feels drowsy afterward and sends out a telepathic shout to Sara: ***Damn it, Sara! You dosed the soup, didn't you?*** In reply, all she gets is the impression of a Cheshire cat like grin superimposed on Yoda's face, making her roll her eyes, carefully get up, and pull herself up the stairs to their bedroom.

Tess crawls into bed, pulls up the covers, and wishes Marc could be there to keep her warm. Mabel follows before Tess can sleep, curling up on Marc's pillow beside her. Tess drifts off to sleep, feeling her body drift into a very relaxed state, and yet, her mind is fully awake. She can see all around her again, as though she's lying with her eyes open in bed. Once again, her body refuses to move.

Crap! Not again! What the hell is going on? She thinks, trying to move and wake herself up. She has that feeling of pulling herself out of a sucking bog again, rising a little, falling back, rising more, and then falling back. There's a burst of energy, a roaring sound, a brief flash of light, and then she's free to move. She can't feel herself breathing again, but it no longer worries her. She looks around and sees Mabel run out of the room, knocking over some knickknacks on the way. The cat turns around and peers back through the doorway, back arched, hair raised, and tail puffy, looking wild-eyed. "Mabel! *Stop* that, it's only me." Tess says and drifts next to Mabel, extending her hand to soothe her. When she does, her hand passes through Mabel, making the cat jump, tear down the hall, and vault the stairs to the living room, hissing all the way.

What the? Is all Tess can think. She looks around and notices someone's still lying in bed. She thinks, *Oh! Did Marc come home after all? Snuck out on Sara. She's going to be pissed.* But as she thinks this, she moves closer to the bed, only to see her own long brown hair with blonde highlights flowing across the pillow.

No! Am I dead? She thinks, worried, but she can see the blanket rise and fall. *I don't get it? How can I be here and there and? Oh! I wish Marc was here.* She thinks. She drifts toward a wall. She gets the oddest sensation, like walking through a similar mire, but more rigid, as she passes through the wall, and outside the house. The next thing she knows, the scene blurs and she's next to Marc in his hospital bed, knocked out as Sara had threatened.

This is one freaky port! She thinks, looking for someone to ask what's going on. An Asian man comes in the room but doesn't notice her. He checks some settings on a device near Marc, and turns to walk back out, walking right through her.

Now I'm back to wondering if I'm dead, and some kind of ghost. But how can I be dead? In her frustration, she's no longer focused on Marc, until she notices him stir.

"*Tess?* Is that you?" He whispers weakly, without opening his eyes. The device beeps and his eyes flutter open. Sara comes running in.

"Why are you awake?" She demands, as though he should know why he's not passed out cold.

Don't know. Thought I heard Tess. But when I opened my eyes, she wasn't here. He paths.

"No doubt a dream." She reassures him. "You two have such a tight bond after all you've been through, you probably touched her mind telepathically, though how you broke through the sleep inducer, I'm not sure." She complains. "*Now! Back* to sleep with you." She leans over to turn up the setting on the inducer. When she's sure he's in a deep state of restorative sleep, she turns to walk out, passing through Tess. However, she pauses, an odd expression on her face. "*Hmph!* Very odd." She says aloud.

Tess grows tired suddenly, as if her energy has run out. She feels like she's falling endlessly backwards. At first, she moves in slow motion, then the world blurs, speeding up with lights flashing by in streaks; like the warp speed effects in Star Wars, only with colors. As she's about to hit the ground, she starts awake in her own bed. "*Damn!* Another wild dream." She says aloud and looks around for Mabel. She's not in the room, but Tess notices the knickknacks strewn on the floor, a couple of them broken, exactly as she'd seen in her dream. Once the initial adrenaline burst subsides, she's exhausted, and thinks, *I'll deal with it in the morning.* She rolls over and is asleep before she can yell for Mabel to join her.

Tess wakes up two days later, with Mabel rubbing furiously against her cheek and pawing at her face. "*Okay!* Mabel! I'll feed you in a second. *Silly* cat! It's not like you're gonna starve after *only* a few hours."

Tess rolls over and Marc is lying in bed, asleep, next to her. *Huh?* She thinks, then grabs her cell phone and unlocks it, looking at the time and date. *Oh shit! Two days! Damn it, Sara!* She telepathically shouts into thin air. *You damn well dosed the blood to make me sleep longer, didn't you?*

A sudden reply from next to the bed startles her. "I didn't think you'd get the rest you needed if I didn't." She says, bluntly. "Besides, I wanted to give that brain of yours time to settle down and stabilize after the antidote." She picks up a small, crystalline device and studies it. "There's clearly been some unusual psychic activity. You mentioned strange dreams."

Tess reels in her annoyance and answers Sara. "Yeah, it was weird. It happened a few times, first in the tub, and then when I went to bed, and maybe off and on after that, but I was so knocked out, I only have vague flashes." Tess slowly, and thoughtfully, tries to remember more.

"*Details* please!" She studies the mental wave patterns recorded by the device.

"It was weird. Like I was *here* and not *here*. It felt like there were two of me at once, and then I would only feel the one, but could see the other. I went somewhere else, with Marc, in the hospital. He called my name, and you walked through me. Mabel got scared when all this happened and ran off."

"You're saying you visited Marc in Medical? *That* could explain how he broke through the sleep inducer." She pauses, getting an amused grin. I don't suppose you've ever heard of astral projection or out-of-body experiences?" Sara asks as she sits on the edge of the bed, next to Tess.

"Yeah, but it's not something I've ever experienced." She admits.

Sara chuckles, amused Tess's abilities have once again caught her off guard. "Well, I'd say you have now. And it's highly unusual for one of us to have that ability. Our condition usually binds the mind or soul to the body quite firmly, so we don't 'wander off' if we're seriously wounded or in bodily stasis."

"Is it dangerous? I mean, if I'm injured and, go into stasis, will I go 'walk about' and not come back?" Tess asks, worried.

"No, I don't think so, but it's something to keep in mind." Sara places a new opal-like necklace around Tess's neck. "This should keep your skills in check until we can see what doors were opened by the antidote. You've always had high potential. Stronger than most. I dare say your potential has few limits. While you've learned to embrace it, and accomplished much with it, you are still quite young, and lack the prep most recent transformees have. Wear the necklace all the time unless we're testing you. I want this done safely, so you don't get overwhelmed."

"And to keep me from doing any damage or hurting someone." Tess realizes the other side of the coin Sara isn't talking about.

"That, too, is always a risk, though you don't have it in your personality to intentionally hurt someone, other than in self-defense. I suspect you could lose control if we aren't careful." Sara gently strokes her upper arm reassuringly. "Now, I suppose I should wake him up?" She says, nodding her head to Tess's sleeping partner with a knowing grin.

"Yeah, that would probably be a good idea! But, what about him? Will his abilities be enhanced too?" Tess asks.

"Perhaps, a little, but his psychic pathways are set fairly firmly after hundreds of years of use. Yours are still pliable because you're new to them. It's like learning a language as a human, the older you get, the harder it becomes to change the mental pathways and learn a new language, but when you're young, you can open up new areas of the brain to multiple languages. Does that make any sense?" Sara turns a dial on a small, metallic sphere near Marc's side of the bed.

"I think I know what you mean." She ponders.

Marc stirs and opens his eyes. "Where?" He inquires, disoriented, but then realizes he's home, in his own bed. His eyes focus, and he looks around him and sees Tess sitting next to him on the bed, smiling.

"Welcome home, stranger!" She gives him a mischievous grin.

Marc sits up slowly, stretching. "How long?" He says, looking from Tess to Sara.

Sara grins. "A little over two days. You both needed a rest, and still do. Liz says for you two to stay here for the next week. We'll be checking in on both of you, so behave!" She chastises them. "Tess needs some re-evaluation, but she can explain that to you." She says with an ear-to-ear smirk and vanishes before Marc can say anything in reply.

"Re-evaluation?" He asks Tess, as he props his head on his hand and lies on his side. Tess lies down to face him.

"The antidote did a 'roto-rooter' on my psychic pathways again. There were some side-effects. I visited you in the hospital without my body, for one. Scared the cat to death in the process." She giggles.

"*Without* your body? Hmmm, I thought I sensed you. It woke me up!" He says. "But honestly, I'm so relieved you're back home and okay! He didn't *hurt* you, did he?" He asks, worried about what Jason may have done to her.

"Physically, yes, but nothing more than a punch to the jaw and a little rough handling. He wanted me to give in to his *charms*. He thought he'd turned me human, wanted me to willingly let him turn me again, and be 'his'. UGH! I was *not* at all tempted." She quips with a wink and a wry smirk.

The tension in Marc's body lessens now that he knows Tess wasn't put through more than a little roughness, considering Jason's earlier behavior. He lets out a sigh of relief. "Well, that's good!" He strokes her arm. "When I first came to again, they hadn't yet administered the antidote, and I couldn't feel you. I worried he'd ...." He trails off.

Tess puts her hand on his, reassuring him. "We're both okay, and he's locked up, *fully* neutralized. Sara said they're going to see if they can re-deem him. I have my doubts on that. When I got my abilities back, I briefly felt... *him; his mind.* It was like watching a black hole that can never be filled up, always craving, desiring; driven by a deep pain of some sort." She tries to put words to what she sensed from him in the bunker.

"Hopefully, they'll sort him out. In the meantime," He leans over and kisses her, making moves toward a proper reunion.

"Hey, not that I don't want to, but Sara says we shouldn't do anything for about a week, until your neck fully heals." She says quietly but wishes she didn't have to restrain herself.

"Tess, I'm fine! A little tender, but Sara doesn't know everything. Besides, touch can be healing!" He grins, and goes back to kissing her, stopping briefly to say, "and if it does cause any problems, I'm sure she'll fix me up good as new, but right now...." He trails off.

Tess and Marc spend some much-needed time reuniting. As their intimacy reaches its peak, a light-panel on the wall flares into life and cracks with a loud, sizzling sound, going black.

Tess gasps and then giggles, covering her face with her hands in embarrassment. "Did I do that?"

"I believe you did!" Marc looks over at the now smoking light-panel. "Sara needs to give you a stronger filter." He shakes his head and laughs.

Tess laughs at first, but then becomes more serious, realizing this could be a real problem. "What happens if I can't get control over this stuff?"

"You will. It may take time, and a little help to do it, but you will." He rubs her back to ease her stress-tempered muscles. "We'll work on it together, and I'm sure the others will help, too."

Tess lies in bed, thoughtfully, as Marc kneads and massages her back. She drifts off to sleep with a little telempathic encouragement.

Once she's asleep, Marc reaches out to Sara. *Sara? You're going to have to up the power on her pendant.* And sends her a mental image of the smoldering light-panel.

After a few seconds of mental silence, he hears. *Oh, dear! That one was made especially for her; stronger than any of the standard ones. Keep her at home until tech can come up with something; don't go out anywhere! We'll have to set up a series of tests and training, but from what I sensed, combined with what you just told me, and her out-of-body travel, she may be well beyond what's normal for us. She's always been gifted, but this may be a whole new ballgame!* Sara paths with a hint of exasperation.

She's worried she may not be able to control it. He admits.

Again, a mental pause, and then she admits: *It's possible she'll never get full control, especially since she lacks the subconscious training. We may have to call in the real experts.*

Marc mentally cringes, having dealt with their Benefactors occasionally, and found them overwhelming psychically. *I hope that's unnecessary. I have enough trouble dealing with them face to face. I'm not sure how she'll handle that.* He flashes back on an encounter with one of their alien Benefactors about 120 years earlier, remembering how exhausting extended communication with them can be, and how vulnerable he felt, as he had the impression they could see into every nook and cranny of his soul.

On the other hand, she may surprise you. With her increased ability, she may handle the experience better than most. However, let's not jump ahead of ourselves. You two take it easy, and I'll set up the tests and training. It will all work out. She pauses, then confides in him, *I've known since before she was turned she would be important to us. I believe the current slang is 'a major player' in our, and Earth's future. And while we lack in numbers, maybe her gifts will make up for some of that? Get some rest. You're still recovering! Besides, if I'm right about why she blew out that light-panel, you're already over-exerting yourself!* She leaves the conversation with a mental chuckle before Marc can reply.

Marc gently strokes Tess's hair as he ponders everything, pulls her back against his stomach, and curls up around her in a protective manner, joining her in slumber.

FOREIGN WORDS LIST

NORWEGIAN:

Elskling	Dearest, lover
Gravlaks	Fish cured with sugar, salt, and Dill
Herre Gud!	Dear God!
Kjæresten min	Dearest one, my love, dear

FRENCH:

Faux pas	Mistake
Merde!	Shit!
Nom de Dieu!	In God's Name!
Repetiteur	A private teacher or tutor

www.ingramcontent.com/pod-product-compliance
Lightning Source LLC
Chambersburg PA
CBHW071510260626
47170CB00002B/331